"A CRACKLING AND BIGHEARTED NOVEL THAT DOESN'T SHY AWAY FROM HARD CONVERSATIONS. . . . GUIDED BY AVIVA'S ECSTATIC, EXUBERANT VOICE, *HUMAN BLUES* IS A POWERHOUSE." —*OPRAH DAILY*

"RIOTOUS, VISCERAL." —*VANITY FAIR*

"FEW CONTEMPORARY WRITERS EMBODY FEMININE SWAGGER LIKE ELISA ALBERT, A NOVELIST WHOSE WORK IS EQUAL PARTS PHILIP ROTH, SARAH SILVERMAN, AND, WELL, *HER*." —*GAWKER*

"FAST AND SWEET, WITH ENOUGH ATTITUDE TO PUT SLEATER-KINNEY OR EVEN LIZZO TO SHAME. . . . [A] LIFE-AFFIRMING HOWL INTO A WILD WORLD." —*BOOKPAGE*

"A HEARTFELT, FUNNY, BRUTAL STORY ABOUT THE THINGS WE CHOOSE TO BE AND THE THINGS WE END UP BECOMING." —*TOWN & COUNTRY*

"THRILLING." —*LITERARY HUB*

"A BELLOW-WORTHY WAVE OF BLISTERING PROSE." —*PUBLISHERS WEEKLY* (STARRED REVIEW)

"PROVOCATIVE, FAST-PACED, AND DARKLY FUNNY. . . . [*HUMAN BLUES* IS] AN ENERGIZING READ FOR ANYONE WHO'S EVER BEEN TOLD, 'OH, YOU'RE JUST ON YOUR PE[R]..." —*GOOD HOUSEKEEPIN[G]*

"REVOLUTIONARY." —NPR

"Poignant, hilarious, and scathing. . . . [A] rollicking journey to self-acceptance in a culture obsessed with motherhood."

—*Booklist*, starred review

"Darkly funny."

—Corinne Sullivan, *Cosmopolitan*

"Albert is in a rarefied group of writers . . . who use their considerable charisma and delight in transgression to draw attention to unsung and unseen parts of life in a female body, or a body outside the norms of conventional masculinity."

—Lily Meyer, *Gawker*

"Hilarious."

—Sophia June, *Nylon*

"[A] thought-provoking and multi-faceted contribution to the discourse on bodily autonomy and reproductive choices. . . . The novel is a potent reminder that the body and the voice are inseparable, and that both demand autonomy."

—Kaitlyn Teer, *Ploughshares*

"*Human Blues* is filled with personality as Albert merges questions of fame and fertility into a thought-provoking exploration of agency and expression."

—Eric Ponce, *BookPage*

"Darkly funny [and] tongue-in-cheek. . . . [*Human Blues*] revolves around Aviva's physical body and fertility, but Albert quietly shines in laying bare topics crucial to many women—societal expectations, the push-pull between ambition and parenthood and the question of what it means to truly want to be a mother."

—Jaime Herndon, *Hadassah Magazine*

"[A] fiercely smart, poignant novel."

—Cheryl McKeon, *Shelf Awareness*

"Elisa Albert . . . brings a wealth of wit, humor, and righteous rage to her latest, *Human Blues*, in which she reckons with expectations imposed on the bodies of anyone with a uterus, the predatory nature of the wellness industry, and the ways in which people so often moralize fertility and conception."

—Jacqueline Alnes, *Electric Literature*

"Engrossing."

—*Town & Country*

"A wild ride!"

—Elizabeth Hardin, *Southern Bookseller Review*

ALSO BY ELISA ALBERT

After Birth
The Book of Dahlia
How This Night Is Different

HUMAN BLUES

A Novel

ELISA ALBERT

AVID READER PRESS

NEW YORK   LONDON   TORONTO   SYDNEY   NEW DELHI

AVID READER PRESS
An Imprint of Simon & Schuster, Inc.
1230 Avenue of the Americas
New York, NY 10020

First Avid Reader Press trade paperback edition July 2023

AVID READER PRESS and colophon are trademarks of Simon & Schuster, Inc.

For information about special discounts for bulk purchases, please contact Simon & Schuster Special Sales at 1-866-506-1949 or business@simonandschuster.com.

The Simon & Schuster Speakers Bureau can bring authors to your live event. For more information or to book an event contact the Simon & Schuster Speakers Bureau at 1-866-248-3049 or visit our website at www.simonspeakers.com.

Interior design by Carly Loman

Manufactured in the United States of America

10 9 8 7 6 5 4 3 2 1

Library of Congress Control Number: 2023931713

ISBN 978-1-9821-6786-8
ISBN 978-1-9821-6787-5 (pbk)
ISBN 978-1-9821-6788-2 (ebook)

For MDS

I don't do nothing I don't want to do.

—JOHN LEE HOOKER

1.

VOICE

She was soon to bleed. *Goddamn* it. Another pregnancy test was negative.

You Are Entering the Real World, read the sign posted on the back fence of the property. It was New Year's Day. Trash was nestled in the weeds along the side of the road. Soda cans, fast-food wrappers, plastic bags, and a Handi Wipe square, still intact, upon which someone had scrawled, *This is not a condom.*

Negative. Again.

She had been so patient. So fucking patient! How many negatives by now? More than a year. *Fuck.* Almost two years of negatives. Almost into year three. And again, again, again, *still*: nothing. God*damn* it. Negative. Again. Again! Again. *Again.*

She'd been easygoing about the whole thing for a long time: Whatever happened, happened. It would happen! Of course it would. It would happen. No need to stress. No need to freak out. The important thing was *not* to freak out—everyone knew that. She was (relatively) happy, she was (relatively) healthy, she was in the green half of her thirties, she was in a lovely relationship, and tiiiii-i-i-iiiime, was on her side, yes, it was. But at some point—a year of negatives? Two? Going on three—she'd gotten real quiet. Confused. Scared. Mad. Sad. She'd gritted her teeth, dug in her heels, and tried to find a way to inhabit the situation with a modicum of dignity. She read all the books, listened to all the podcasts. She changed her diet, her perspective, her expectations. She "made space." She "summoned the spirits." She "gathered the bones."

And still: nothing. Nothing. Nothing! Negative pee stick upon negative pee stick upon negative pee stick. Cycle after cycle after cycle. And by now she was straight-up furious. Incensed. What the actual *fuck*. Now she was outright begging. Come the fuck *on*. *Please!* Seriously. There was no dignity in it now. Now she was foaming at the mouth. Now she was gnashing her teeth and muttering to herself. Now she was half-insane with the injustice of it. Now any pregnancy anywhere near her orbit felt like a low branch to the eye.

Last summer the tarot queen of the Berkshires had informed this tearful, barren supplicant that there were cherubs absolutely everywhere, all around. "Great news, hon: you are positively *surrounded* by angels, which means that maternity is *imminent*."

Yay! Wow! Okay! But . . . nope. And nope. And nope. Every godforsaken period, every cycle, every fractal season: awakening, hope, decay, death, awakening, hope, decay, death, around and around, again and again, to death, death, death.

Still, how many times had she recommitted herself to *not worry*?! This wasn't one of those things that could be accomplished with the mind. The crucial thing was to put it *out* of your mind—everyone knew that. You stopped worrying about it, you "gave up," and BAM. You said fuck it and spent your life savings on a trip around the world, and BAM. You had a one-night stand with a plumber from Australia, and BAM. You adopted, and BAM. This was not one of those things that responded well to *thinking*. This was not one of those things you could tell what to do.

So Aviva had officially *relaxed*. She had recurrently *let go*. She had *surrendered*, over and over again. She had been so fucking resolutely chill. For a year. For two! For going on three. And still: negative. Again. Again. Another. *Again.*

Fuck.

It was unbearable. (Ha!) It was inconceivable. (Oh yes.)

She'd walked a hard, uphill mile by now, on the dirt road out behind the property, and stopped to catch her breath, after which she let out a guttural scream into the indifferent, desolate hillside, the chilly blue sky, the smattering of cotton-ball clouds. Then she turned around and headed back, picking up as much trash as she could carry along the way—the soda cans, the fast-food wrappers, the plastic bags, the Handi Wipe square—all of which she dumped into her studio trash can, on top of the umpteenth negative motherfucking pee stick, from where, no doubt, it would all eventually be transported to a dump by the side of some other country road.

The property was an artists' colony, a hybrid rehab/camp/meditation center for creatives, no counselors or authority figures, no mandatory anything. Three dozen writers and musicians and poets and painters and sculptors and composers got a small stipend to live/work here for a few weeks or months at a time, rehearsing inevitable little reenactments of family amidst good old-fashioned no-excuses creative practice and the occasional fuckfest. You had to feed yourself lunch, but there was a breakfast buffet and a starch/vegetable/protein for dinner. You got your own studio space in the woods and if you wanted to make friends you made friends and if you didn't want to make friends you kept your distance, which aroused the suspicion and curiosity of all the people who very much wanted to make friends. Aviva changed her mind every few days about whether or not she wanted to make friends, which made her very popular indeed.

She was here to mess around and make room for whatever might come next. It had been Jerry's idea. Her manager. Aviva's fourth album was dropping in a matter of weeks, and there was a looming tour, biggest of her career thus far.

"You're on the cusp of huge things," Jerry said. "This album is the turning point."

"Keep your pants on, Jer; it's just some recorded songs for sale."

"Whatever, you little twat, you better get your head on for what's coming. Relax. Lie low. Write some new songs. You gotta be a step beyond whatever you're touring with. Lou Reed used to say that."

"Art and commerce being inarguably oppositional and all, right, Jer?"

Her first album had been a punky little DIY effort recorded at an independent studio (aka the Culver City guesthouse of a washed-up producer) when Aviva was barely out of her teens, bouncing between states, apartments, beds, office jobs. Busking on Venice Beach Boardwalk for tips on the weekend. Limited run of a thousand CDs, but it became a tiny cult hit, with surprisingly friendly press, acquired and reissued by a small but respectable indie label. Who doesn't love a young weird plaintive hippie folk-punk freak with big tits?

The second album had been produced by some slick asshole-for-hire. Said asshole had pushed her into the wrong look/narrative/sound. Heavy on the drums, some ironic synth. She had known it was wrong. An uncomfortable costume. But what had she known about the business back then? She had wanted to get along, be agreeable, and was marketed as a more or less crazy bitch nevertheless. The single off that album was a paean to dating amongst the terminally ill, inspired by her brother Rob's doomed romance whilst dying of a brain tumor. Dumb disaster-girl anthem, every breakup an existential crisis, tear-streaked-fuck-me-face video, same old shit. But it had wound up getting licensed to play over the closing credits of a popular TV high school dramedy's series finale, which had led to a mild flurry of cash and indie radio play.

For the third album, she'd switched to a bigger indie and fought to call more of her own shots. She was about to hit thirty then, getting heavy into yoga and medicinal mushrooms and empowered monogamy and hard-core boundaries. Lyrically it was probably her angriest, most political album, but couched in a woodsy, floral motif. Goth-witch lite, good ol' Trojan horse. She was into linen dresses, worn in absurd layers, her hair grown out down to her ass. Turned out you could get away with a lot of radical shit if you came off as sexually demure.

Now, album number four, whole new ball game. Goodbye, indie label;

hello, massive multinational conglomerate. There was real money involved now. She'd been naïve enough to think that moving on up in the industry would engender more creative control, but it just turned out to mean more executives, fretting. Aviva was too in-your-face, they worried. Too on-the-nose. Too confrontational. Not confrontational enough. Kind of a turnoff. And why did she insist on wearing so many *layers?* Would it kill her to show off her creamy décolletage? Put on some tight pants? Could the stylist maybe bring round some suggestions? Maybe a more au courant cut of denim, and some heels? And how about a makeup artist, needless to say.

Poor Jerry: he'd been Aviva's manager back when she was lucky to be playing Jewish singles events. "Babe, *listen*. They won't put any *marketing* behind it if they're not happy with your look, and you know if they don't put marketing behind it, you got no chance *whatsoever* with the streaming."

"Like you know shit about streaming, Jer. How fucking old are you? Do you even know what streaming is?"

He'd been around forever, worked with a million downtown club legends in the eighties and nineties, but had some sort of opposite Midas touch: no one he bet on ever amounted to shit.

"V, you're not in a *position—*"

"To have a say in how I look?! No, Jer. Fuck them. So don't put any marketing behind it, what do I care? It's their problem if they don't market an album they *paid for*. Why is that *my* fucking problem? They already *paid* me, Jer. And I you."

"Honey. Sweetie. Don't make enemies of friends. We all have the same goal here. We want you to be huge."

"I don't want to be huge, Jer. I want to be *good*. You get the diff, right? Respect for celebrity is a fucking frontal-lobe-development disorder."

Her fourth album, though: it was pretty cool. One album, any asshole could put out one album. Two albums, you could still be a flash in the pan. Three albums, not bad. But four! Four albums! Well, that began to be a real body of work. No one could argue with four albums.

Did Aviva want to be huge? No! And yes. And no. It was what her shrink, the Rabbi, called "an internal conflict." I love you, go away, come back, do you like me, fuck you, I love you, fuck me, I hate you, go away, come back. Round and round, again, again.

What would you say this album is about? a marketing exec had emailed that very morning.

It's about . . . an hour and fifteen minutes long, Aviva replied.

Silly marketing twat, why don't *you* listen to the album and decide for yourself what it's about! Isn't that your job? Does independent thinking *physically hurt* you?

"Honey," Jer kept saying. "Sweetie. Baby. Help them help us. Please."

Fine, fine: What was her fourth album "about"? It was about getting to know her body, welcoming the age of embodied womanhood in its prime, leaving the past behind once and for all, ceasing to be a destructive twat hell-bent on wrecking everything. It was about wanting a fucking baby. There was no valor in destruction, she'd come to understand; valor resided in creation, nurturance, stability, balance. *That* was what the new album was about. It was about readying herself for motherhood, though she'd sooner die than articulate *that* for marketing. She yearned for motherhood, obviously (*obviously*), but if you couldn't hear that between the bars, well, then go fuck yourself: it wasn't for you to hear.

It was about the menstrual cycle, suffice it to say—source of epic power and torment. It was about resigning herself to a constructive, drama-free relationship with Sammy-Sam, her beloved manny-man. It was about making a *home*. Homemaker: Shocking aspiration for a constitutional and historical shit-thrower, but what more powerful, meaningful work could there possibly *be*? The album was about saying no thanks to all the ruinous crap they wanted you to take and do and be and buy, no thank you to assholes and nonsense, no thank you to exhaustion, bullshit, living life online. (This last bit was pure posturing, though, because Aviva was still living life online.)

In the end, a compromise had been reached: the suits had agreed to let her title the album *Womb Service*, and Aviva had agreed to let the stylist "send over a few things."

And lo! The early buzz was solid. Industry people were into it. A few, of course, said it was offensive tripe and Aviva's voice was annoying and she should shut the fuck up because screw that metaphysical human biology nonsense right up its bigoted butthole, but you can't please everybody.

Regardless: according to Jer *and* the tarot queen of the Berkshires *and* the Rabbi, *Womb Service* was about to take her to a whole new level.

"You'd better buckle your seat belt," said the tarot queen.

"We'll get through this," said the Rabbi.

"I'm gonna retire on you, honey," said Jer. "I'm gonna get me a boat and a forwarding address in the Caribbean."

Hanalei, her yoga teacher, had led her through a guided meditation in which Aviva recalled having her tits cut off before being burned at the stake in a previous life.

But it didn't ultimately *matter* what happened with this fourth album; it was time to get situated in preparation for and relation to whatever was coming *next*. And if that wasn't going to be *the fucking baby she desperately wanted*, it would have to be some new songs. Let the chips fall where they may with regard to the old stuff. Any old bitch could force a baby; any ambitious climber could put out an album.

She lit a fat beeswax candle, popped the weed gummy she'd tucked away "just in case" she turned out not to be pregnant (YET AGAIN), and got down on the floor. Aviva was "process oriented," which meant a lot of floor time, a lot of candles, a lot of tunes on shuffle, and regular cannabis edibles.

The "official" cause of her barrenness was maybe polycystic ovarian syndrome, about which some said eat only vegetables and animal protein, others said take an off-label diabetes drug indefinitely, others said chemically force ovulation and inseminate, and still others said go straight to the nearest fertility clinic with a blank check. No one had the faintest idea how or why this syndrome developed, or why up to a quarter of all women were thought to suffer from it, or how it was connected to endocrine disruption or metabolic disorder or post-Pill syndrome or insulin resistance or estrogen dominance or progesterone deficiency or microplastics or liver toxicity or coronary health or cancer, but if it comes as any surprise that medical science knows next to nothing about biologically female bodies in particular, please head to the library and find yourself a *real* comfy seat.

Over the course of the past few years (One? Two? Whee! Going on three!), Aviva had seen several endocrinologists, a midwife, a naturopath, an herbalist, four different acupuncturists, a Maya Abdominal therapist, and a Reiki master, and she'd laid out her pitiful story for each in turn: menses commenced at thirteen, with long, wonky cycles, acne, and a tragic facial hair problem. Some lazy prick doctor had put her on the Pill at fifteen to deal with all of the above, and cue years of weight gain and suicidality and antidepressants, until she finally woke up at twenty, trashed *all* the pills, and started to pay attention. (What had woken her? Who can say.) She learned to eat decent food, live in alliance with her body, blah blah *blah*. Most everyone now agreed that PCOS was maybe caused by or at the very least exacerbated by the Pill, and that teen girls should be given "time" to work through their "irregularity," which usually resolved itself just fine, but did you know it takes, on average, *seventeen years* for scientific knowledge to be incorporated into standard medical practice?

Everyone Aviva saw had a grand plan to get her ovaries blooming. The first endocrinologist urged her to take the off-label diabetes drug and also a particularly neurotoxic male hormone suppressant, for shits and giggles. The Maya Abdominal therapist said Aviva's uterus was tilted, and offered to fix it in a package deal of six sessions. The herbalist prescribed a tincture and told Aviva to get direct sunlight for at least ten minutes a day and avoid caffeine at all costs. "Do you eat meat? You should definitely eat meat," said the naturopath. "Preferably organ meat." Aviva hadn't eaten meat in years, not since a boyfriend had turned her on to *Animal Liberation*. But fine: now she ate monthly cheeseburgers and once-in-a-blue-moon oysters. The first acupuncturist prescribed herbal powders. The second acupuncturist said no dairy. The third acupuncturist said no wheat. Everybody said no sugar. The Reiki master was a hundred percent certain that Aviva was fertile: whilst not touching her, he'd envisioned a white cat wandering a desert. The second endocrinologist had said Aviva's uterus was in fact *not* tilted, and that she should definitely take the off-label drugs and/or maybe this *new* drug everybody was all excited about, which was a combo forced ovulation and antipsychotic, and then get artificially inseminated.

"I'm not taking jack shit," Aviva told the midwife. "I want to understand what's going on. *Why* is it not happening? If I can address it myself, great, but if it turns out to be some sort of big impossible deal, then I guess I'm out of luck."

"Fair enough," the midwife said. "Anything else you want to share with me?"

"What do you think about fertility and . . . cannabis?"

The midwife raised an eyebrow. "There aren't any studies, but I can't imagine it would *help*."

Something about adrenal fatigue and something about liver detoxification and something about the outstandingly complex relationship between hormones and the endocannabinoid system and something about common sense and something about enough was enough: Did Aviva want a baby or didn't she? The implication being *God*, girl, grow *up*.

Coffee she could live without, alcohol she could live without, veganism she could live without, soy she could live without, sunscreen could certainly go fuck itself. White flour and sugar she could *kind* of maybe *try* to live without. All-nighters she could certainly live without, rock-star mythologies be damned. Synthetic fragrances she could absolutely live without. Preservatives she could definitely live without. But *weed*? That hurt. All her urbane, high-achieving acquaintances mainlined their coffee and psychiatric meds and synthetic hormones and wine and air fresheners and liquor; Aviva wanted only organic dank herb. She had been stoned here, she had been stoned there, she had been stoned everywhere. She *did* like weed in a car and on a plane and in the rain and she *did* like it on a boat and in a moat and on a float and with a goat. In South America they called it "little sister" for the way it would gamely go anywhere alongside you, an agreeable sweetheart. The song "Little Sister," off her third album, had become a bit of a stoner-babe anthem.

Anyway, Aviva had practiced the primary series, kept her blood sugar stable, gone to bed before ten. She'd eaten salad, miso, butter, lentils, eggs, kale, anchovies, avocado, flax. She'd done seed cycling. She'd tried that thing where you sleep with the lights on during ovulation. She'd done *literal* headstands. She'd made an honest effort at keeping a temperature chart until the app malfunctioned and sixteen months of data vanished. She'd watched the clock for her lucky numbers and visualized her swollen belly, the ecstatic birth, the slick screaming newborn, ripe with the power of primordial mystery, naked at her breast. ("Visualize" being the currently culturally acceptable way to say "pray.") And she had waited patiently, so patiently, to be rewarded with a baby, delicious flesh of her flesh. The universe worked in mysterious ways, did it not? ("The universe" being the currently culturally acceptable way of saying "God.")

But here we were, (YET) another pregnancy test negative (AGAIN), and so Mx. Aviva Shira Rosner was going to enjoy her stupid weed edible.

She needed the perspective it afforded her, the sense of humor. The feeling that her benevolent dead brother, Rob, was there with her. And all her grandparents, too. She could *feel* them: ancestors *galore*. She'd been missing the awareness of her good breath infiltrating the far reaches of her good body. No worries about her hair, her face, her clothes. She'd *missed* this. Easy-breezy forgiveness for everyone, including herself. Dancing, alone, midday, shaking out her sorrows. Communicating with the trees. Not caring about the kinds of people who would mock that sentiment, or the sentiment before that, or all the sentiments yet to come.

Shit, it was nice to have a break from the relentless tenor of normative consciousness.

But the tunes on shuffle weren't cutting it. She had to skip a live Lucinda growler, then some weird R. Crumb bluegrass, then a mellow, live Ani circa '94, then a Dylan bootleg, then Rickie Lee, PJ, Nina Simone, Throwing Muses. Skip, skip, skip: nothing was right. Why was nothing right? All this shit, all her usual shit: no. What was she in the mood for? She skipped a jumpy, overproduced Police and then she skipped an early Janis, and then she even skipped Nirvana *Unplugged*, which was odd, because it was *never* not the right time for Nirvana *Unplugged*.

Here it came, though, the edible hitting full force, the familiar settling. Exhale, thank you. *Man*, she had been clenching her shoulders. A long, slow, live Bonnie Raitt in exactly Aviva's key. Okay. This she could tolerate. Blues. Yes. Not bad. It would be good *even slower*. She reached for her guitar and she played along. Nah. Old Tori Amos: no. Plaintive Neko Case: nah. Some downcast Gillian Welch: no!

Nothing was deep enough, slow enough, long enough, loose enough, real enough. And then a rip in the fabric of time. Jackpot. Here it was. The singular voice. Just what the doctor ordered. Delivered by algorithm into Aviva's sonic embrace. Thank you, algorithm!

The patron saint of insatiable, implacable Jewish girls. Short-lived, one and only. Demolished angel, dead at twenty-seven, join the club. Rest in peace, baby. Fallen fuckup. A lightning flash. Superstar, caricature, cartoon. Darling! Precious baby girl, floating downriver in a basket. Take the tunes off shuffle. Hold this voice to the breast, safe and sound.

It wasn't just that she had a killer voice, and it wasn't just that she had a killer ear, and it wasn't just that she didn't give a fuck, and it wasn't just about her lyricism or originality. It was this otherworldly all-*knowingness*. This girl was the all-seeing eye. It was everywhere: in her phrasing, her inhabitation of her songs, in the look on her face when she sang (even when she was blotto). How did she speak with such authority? Her connection to herself was undiluted, which, for most of us, isn't true past the age of, say, six. One of the rare few who don't need to be told how things are. She can see very well for herself how things are, and she isn't afraid to speak the truth. No asking permission. The real thing doesn't knock.

When she was alive, taking the airwaves by storm, Aviva had ignored her, because anything on the radio was, by definition, bullshit. Amy was some kind of throwback pop phenom or . . . something? Anorexic costumed punk bitch? Grammys, tabloids, who fucking cared. Aviva was a *sophisticated musician*. She liked depressive, dissonant shit you could think deep thoughts to, songs on which bass and drums did most of the work and the rhythm was the whole story. Clever shit, for intellectuals. She had no use for some British chick in whore drag, that ridiculous wig, aping bygone girl groups, all over the magazines with the lowlife barfly boyfriend. So what if she had that excellent voice? There was too much shtick in the way. Walking disaster playacting—what, gangster's moll? Really? Keen to get all aproned up, stilettoed and pregnant in the kitchen, stirring a pot with a big wooden spoon, waiting for her big man to come home? Ready with her ass cocked for big man to plow her? Sit tight with her mascara and her curlers waiting for big man to return from work so she could suck his big dick? The whole sex-object/little-missus shtick! Such retrogressive crap. No thanks.

Aviva had missed the point. She hadn't understood. But here, now, coming to terms with a(nother) failed cycle and an(other) impending bleed, she understood perfectly. BAM.

Second child born to a Jewish family in North London in the fall of 1983. Daddy the charming philandering life of the party; Mum the rock. Families are like puzzles; each piece laser cut to fit. Take the pieces apart, hold one up by itself, examine its strange shape, try to make sense of it alone: impossible. Amy dressed up for Purim, had Shabbos dinners with her nan. Daddy sold double-glazed windows and later drove a taxi. An aspiring jazz singer, himself. The karaoke Sinatra. *His* mother, the indomitable Nan, had dated a legendary jazz club owner who'd wanted to marry her, but she wouldn't sleep with him, the story went, so he'd dumped her. Nan's brothers were both jazz musicians, too. Amy was born singing. She sang Gloria Gaynor in the bath. Joyful child. Mischievous, mouthy girl. Mum played Dinah Washington, Ella Fitzgerald. Daddy played Tony Bennett, leaving out lines for the wee babe to fill in. Daddy's exuberant girl! Hurricane of a girl. Dark, luscious swirl of a girl, forever singing. Wild savant, force of nature, corrective, sent to earth to remind us what a human being who hasn't been programmed all to shit can *do*. Heard her big bro playing Ray Charles in his room one day and barged in, demanding, Who is that? Messed around on big bro's guitar, figured out a few things. Got her own guitar. Began to write her own songs. Earnest, funny, unapologetic little songs, and when she opened her big mouth to sing, there was that voice.

Bit of a problem with sex and power, but hey: Who doesn't have a bit of a problem with sex and power, one way or another?

Late in her life she asked big bro to get her a Jewish cookbook so she could learn to make chicken soup. Chicken soup, of all things: to cure what ails. Her efforts failed; the soup was inedible. Anyway, she was past cure by then. Nothing for what ailed *her*.

Her voice is her life, boiled down. Tough girl. Knows who she is, what she wants. Sees everything. Not afraid of her body or its desires. Can keep up with anyone, lock in with anyone. She is unafraid. Look into the eyes of almost anyone you meet and see the fear there. The calculation and the hiding and the lies! Lies the human currency in trade.

Once everyone realized what a massive commodity she was they took away her guitar, and she became a "performer," and folks paid good money to see the fake tits, the burlesque hair, the itty-bitty skirts, the hand on hip for a rote shimmy—pause for a swig of whatever. Rockabilly fuck-doll from hell.

But put destruction on hold for a sec: How artfully could one lick one's wounds? How wittily could one transform one's pain? The goal was never to deny the wounds, nor to gloss them; that never worked, anyway.

ELISA ALBERT

There were two albums in total, not counting the collected oddities and remixes and outtakes and demos. And each of the two albums was inhabited by a totally distinct Amy: the first, strumming her own guitar and telling everyone how it was, almost too shy to make eye contact; the other stumbling around the stage sneering, hollow-eyed, having self-administered the equivalent of a lobotomy, waiting for it to be over.

Painter Anne and Sculptor Sue were at the communal table in the barn kitchen, freaking out because apparently the resident horses were gone and the pasture was dead. The colony was struggling financially, and the powers that be at the small liberal arts college across the highway had struck a deal to find the horses new homes, spray the fields with Roundup, and plant a crop to sell for biofuel.

"I just can't *believe* they would do something so stupid," Anne said.

"I wonder if I should leave," said Sue, who had been through cancer twice and never/always wanted to talk about it.

"*Roundup*, for goodness' sake!"

Poet Rochelle had done some internet sleuthing and printed a few pages of press releases from around the time the devastation had occurred.

"'Environmental stewardship,' do you believe that? Selling this as a positive! What kind of native grasses could they be dumb enough to think would grow on that land now?"

"*Roundup!*"

"And they did this for a total of two hundred grand? As though *that's* going to make such a difference in the long run. Destroyed an ecosystem forever."

"There used to be so many stinkbugs here," Anne said. During past residencies, the dorms and studios had been overrun. "All gone now."

Aviva giggled. The ladies looked at her. What was funny about this? Certainly not the poison spray, nor the future world of infertility and autism and machine consciousness and ectogenesis and lab-grown meat, but

14

the genuine shock at mankind's destruction of nature, which was history's original imperative, after all. You had to laugh.

"The whole ecosystem is just *destroyed*," said Sue, her voice high and tight, as though Aviva didn't understand.

Aviva opened her arms to Sue, who accepted a hug.

"I know, honey," Aviva said. "I know it is."

Some songs came in a wild flood, so Aviva could hardly keep up. These songs were preexisting entities in need of a body; Aviva just had to serve as best she could. She hardly had to work; she just let them come. She was their instrument. Songs, like wild fruit, ripened on the vine and dropped into her ready hands. Her only enterprise was transcription.

Other songs came in bits and pieces, little gifts she found if she foraged, if she was attuned, if she was receptive, if she was at ease in her perfect and sustained attention. Her job with these bits and pieces was to assemble and arrange and rearrange, meet the song wherever it asked to be met. Be its friend. This was known as "craft."

Then there were songs that came slow and hard. Excruciating, evasive. She had to wait and wait and wait and wait for these. You had to stop thinking about it. You had to outlast it. No sudden moves. You couldn't coax, but you could prove yourself worthy by admitting that you were not the boss. *Never* startle or demand. Those songs baited her, eluded her, mocked her. They were malpositioned; they took fucking forever. When they finally came, *if* they finally came, they were lumpy, misshapen. Sometimes monstrous, sometimes runty. And damn if they weren't her favorites.

Come to Mama: the trusty black Epiphone she'd found on a Santa Monica sidewalk when she was twenty-two, freshly escaped from music school and working a soul-crushing receptionist job at a huge label in LA. Guitar had been a childish fantasy; music school a waste of time. The industry was for desperate assholes. Enter the Epiphone, bearing a yellow Post-it that read *TAKE ME* in goofy block letters. Wasn't there enough music in the world? Weren't there enough strivers? But there was the Epiphone, offering itself, practically begging her: *TAKE ME.*

Her first cheap-ass beater, purchased with bat mitzvah money, had been collecting dust in a closet at her mother's house. God, how she'd adored that thing. What joy in messing around with rudimentary chords and covers, those earliest attempts at allowing herself use of her voice. Training her fingers had taken years. Her mother would do this whole elaborate put-upon routine whenever Aviva plucked out a tune: *Oh my God, it's like someone is hitting me, I can't take it, Aviva, Jesus, don't quit your day job. Give me a break and go play that thing in your room, where no one can hear you.*

TAKE ME, said the Epiphone on the sidewalk that day in Santa Monica.

Aviva wasn't a straight-up babe like the music school girls who were getting places, and she wasn't a virtuoso like the dudes and dykes who were getting places, and she'd been working her shitty industry job thinking: Okay. Let the babes and the virtuosos and the go-getters have it; she'd slink off and work her shitty industry job until a better shitty industry job came along, and so on and so forth until maybe eventually she'd be in *charge* of who got to play what, or maybe she'd get married and have some babies and concern herself with that racket, or maybe she'd do it *all*, oh hell yeah, *all* of it, sure, okay, maybe *that*.

TAKE ME, said the Epiphone, and Aviva—BAM—was emboldened to oblige. She brought it to a shop for checkup.

"Nice piece," the shop guy said. He eyed Aviva, mistook her for an idiot. "I'll give you two hundred for her. You could spend three or four fixing her up, but she still won't be worth that much."

Aviva was not an idiot. She took the Epiphone to a different shop, where a different guy said, "Great piece, hey, yeah! Where'd you find her? You gotta be kidding me, *really*? She'll be better than new for a couple hundred. Epic score, my friend!" And she had fucked this second guy, because honesty was adorable.

Soon as that Epiphone was fixed up, Aviva started busking on the boardwalk, learning the hard way, the old-school way, not to give a shit about anything but her own good time. Music school nothing but a bad dream. She got the hell out of that industry job and made some friends at a little club in the Marina. She started writing songs again, mostly for the enjoyment of herself and her new friends. And she recorded that first album in the dilapidated home studio of a hilarious club denizen, a darling grizzled old industry burnout known as "The Man." And then word of mouth and touring and three more albums and a thousand club dates all over the country and *don't quit your day job?* How about Aviva *made that shit her day job*, hmmm? How you like that, *Mom*?

The residents stalked one another online, this their reward for long days of immersive, solitary creative endeavor. *What are you working on? Where are you from? What are* you *working on? Do you know [fill in the blank]?* So went the dinnertime chitchat. Anne couldn't say for sure what her canvas was going to become, but it was huge, and she was staying for two months, and she was covered in paint splatter. Roxy was working on a memoir about her father. Sue was working on gorgeous assemblages made from crap her grandkids left around the house. "I tell them they'd better clean up after themselves or it's mine."

New arrival tonight: tall, broad-shouldered, slender, with a distinctly sweet set to his mouth, a sort of permanent smile in repose. He approached their table and stood behind an empty chair. His forearms were thickly veined. "Join you?"

"Sure," said Aviva and Rochelle and Anne and Sue and Hailey the poet and Roxy in unison.

"Well, *that* was beautiful." The new guy laughed, looking for a fraction of a second too long at Aviva. Score one for Aviva; *this* was potentially interesting. But the familiar dull ache unified her low belly and back. Storm clouds gathering for the inevitable downpour. She was going to bleed any minute. *Not pregnant*, the ache thundered. There was zero danger of a flirtation getting out of hand as luteal phase gave way to menstrual. A spark could easily ignite a wildfire in follicular or ovulatory, Lord knew, but in late luteal, sparks were hopeless: soggy kindling.

"Brooklyn," the new guy was saying, and Aviva nodded politely. Moved to Gowanus in the nineties when it was cheap, watched it slowly/suddenly change, sure, sure, whatever, yeah. All his friends had moved to the Hudson Valley, blah blah, and now he was surrounded by bankers, rich kids, tourists, wannabes, has-beens, almost-weres. Couldn't give up the excellent apartment, so short-term sublet it illegally while he traveled and did residencies half the year. He wore no ring. Aviva held her water glass in front of her face so that her own ring glinted.

She was completely faithful to her beloved husband in body, but spirit was another story. A rich, vibrant fantasy life was A-OK, according to the Rabbi. *More* than okay. Healthy. Necessary. Vital.

The new arrival turned out to be a composer.

"What are you working on?" Aviva asked.

"A song cycle."

"I love that it's called that."

"Me too."

"Aren't cycles the coolest? Nothingness, creation, existence, devolution, death, destruction, renewal . . ."

"'Bout sums it up!"

"Round and round we go."

Hailey the poet leaned forward. "What exactly *is* a song cycle, anyway?" Hailey was nakedly ambitious, dropped names like they were hot, so Aviva felt duty bound to ignore her completely.

"It's . . . a . . . cycle . . . of . . . songs," the composer said slowly. He met Aviva's eyes, and they traded smirks while Hailey waited for a more satisfactory answer. The composer took pity: "It's a series of songs that belong together, designed to be heard in a certain sequence, in the context of one another. Pink Floyd's *The Wall*, for example."

The way his lips moved around "context of one another" gave Aviva pelvic flutters, luteal be damned. This was the fun part. The game. The way the body responded. Soon enough it would be follicular again, and hope would reign. Round and round we go, where we stop, everybody knows (death!).

"So . . . like, a musical?" said Hailey.

"Or just a really good album of any genre."

"Didn't Schumann write some beautiful cycles?" said Anne.

"Ooh, ooh, wait, what about *Elegies for Angels, Punks, and Raging Queens?*"

"That changed my life," said the composer. "Heard it for the first time when I was seventeen."

Roxy pointed to Aviva. "*She's* a singer. She's got a new album coming out. She's big-time, this one."

"Wow," said the composer. "Cool. Your first?"

"Nope," Aviva said. Any asshole could put out one album! "Fourth."

He looked impressed. "What kind of stuff?"

"Good stuff," she said, not blinking.

"I love good stuff. What's your . . . *lineage?*"

"Folk. Jazz. Punk. Blues. Funk. Hip-hop. Psychedelic. Metal. No, not metal, not at all metal. I don't know. Bottomless need! Mortality! Desire. Romance. Immoderation. Heartbreak. Hope. Fear. Fuck if I know."

"Jesus, honey," said Sue. "Lean in."

"I'm already sick of my new stuff, but it's going to be a while before I have anything new-new."

That, everyone understood. Nods all around. The problem with "success," such as it was, was that the more of it you got, the fewer people there were to commiserate with you about it.

"I played covers all afternoon," Aviva said.

"Who?"

Aviva said Amy's name to a collective sigh.

"Ahhhhhh," said the composer.

"What a fucking *waste*," Hailey said.

"Unbelievable," Anne said.

"Whyyyyyy," Sue wailed.

"God, I love her," Roxy said. "I loved her the first second I heard her voice."

"Me too, oh my God, me too," said Anne. "That *voice*. That *voice*!"

"I don't know much about her," said the composer. "But there's the song about refusing to go to rehab, right? And she—what, overdosed?"

Hailey broke into the opening of the famous chorus. Wrong key, wrong tempo, wrong inflection. Anne and Roxy jumped in with *No, no, no*. Then Aviva finished out the lesser-known half of the chorus alone. Something happened when Aviva sang. She could irradiate space, suspend time, change the weather. For a moment, everyone sat in silence, then spoke all at once.

"Jesus *damn*."

"*Get* it."

"Yes!"

"She didn't overdose, by the way," Aviva said. "She just abused herself very committedly and determinedly to death. Misadventure at twenty-seven. Totally different."

"Suicide on the installment plan," said the composer.

"Which isn't easy. Takes real consistency over a long period of time to destroy your body that way. Hard work."

"How ironic," said Hailey. "I mean, what with the rehab song."

"Sing tomorrow night at the salon," said Roxy. "Will you?"

"Yeah," said the composer.

"Please," said Sue.

"You *have* to," said Roxy.

"Pretty please," said Anne.

"Don't *pressure* her," said Hailey.

Text from Sam: hey honeypie how's art camp?

She fished the negative pee stick out of the trash and sent him a pic— failed procreative sext.

Sad-face emoji.

Was he actually sad? He didn't seem like he cared that much. Correction: he didn't seem like he cared as much as Aviva cared. Adjustment: he didn't fall to fucking pieces at the end of every cycle, like it was the funeral of the whole goddamned world. He started another text, then stopped. Started again, stopped again. Finally: so sorry, babe. i love you. Which made her irate, the formality of "so" and the "i." She despised pity.

luv u 2, she forced.

He'd had his junk tested a year and a half ago. His junk was fine.

The mother of the world's very first "test-tube baby" had died, and Aviva read and reread the obituary, astonished to learn that doctors had not *informed* the woman that she was going to be the first of her kind. They had done IVF successfully with animals, but this working-class couple from Manchester, England, who had been struggling to conceive for a *decade*, were only told, "We think we can help you." So the woman signed all the paperwork, asked no questions. The wildest part? She was so happy to be getting her real live baby that she didn't even *mind* about having been used as an unwitting human experiment. She figured it out when she saw reporters camped outside her hospital window, and shrugged it off! Not aggrieved in the least to have been denied informed consent. On the contrary, she was proud. Because she had a baby to show for it. A baby! A BABY! Informed consent? Don't be ridiculous!

A generation or two later, now, and women of a certain age/caste were lining up to be juiced, jacked, mangled, manhandled—willingly, gladly, unquestioningly, at great cost—in the service of more and more absolutely *insisted*-upon babies, who always seemed to come out kind of like *FINE, FUCK, OKAY*, though maybe Aviva was projecting. Her feed was full to bursting of such babies.

Her favorite was Harmony Shmendrickson, the hard-won daughter of a bassist with whom Aviva had once done a southwest tour. They called her "Harmie" or sometimes, bizarrely, just "Harm." Aviva had run into Harmie's enormously pregnant mother in the ladies' room of a fancy downtown club at a mutual friend's birthday party a while back, and had offered rote congratulations. The woman had confided, shuddering, some "horrible fertility shit." Now baby Harmie was trussed up and paraded amidst beautifully aestheticized backgrounds and foregrounds, through winter and spring and summer and autumn, wearing vintage corduroy jumpers and adorable hats and teensy-weensy bathing suits and hand-knit sweaters. Here was little Harm in her first snowsuit. Here she was in her Halloween costume. Here she was under a rainbow umbrella. Here she was buck-ass naked in the bath.

Aviva did not *want* to get juiced, jacked, mangled, or manhandled in the service of an insisted-upon baby. It didn't seem like a nice thing to do to the *baby*. Forcing children to do much of *anything* seemed inherently exploitative, when you thought about it. Certainly you could *coax* them, maybe *convince* them, perhaps *bribe* them . . . but *force?*

How incredibly, soul-crushingly rude.

A documentarian made a roaring fire in the lounge. Wineglasses were filled.

"White or red?" Roxy asked.

"Neither, thanks."

Roxy froze, uncomprehending.

"I'm pregnant," Aviva whispered.

Roxy's hand flew to her mouth. "Sweetheart!" She gathered Aviva into a hug, stroked her hair, kissed her soft and full on the cheek.

Anne tapped her silver thumb ring against her glass and a hush fell over the room. Aviva sat on the floor alongside the composer, leaning up against a big leather sectional, all too aware of his hips near hers.

Hailey began with a poem about her father's once-upon-a-time new car, and the first trip they had taken in it. Then the father died and the car was sold. Everyone clapped.

"I liked how the seats were beige," Anne said. "And just by your saying that I could picture exactly the type of beige, and smell that new-car smell."

"It was, like, Proustian," Aviva muttered to the composer.

Next up was Roxy. Her writing was delicious and weird, and Aviva loved the way she read, intoning ever upward so that eventually the words hardly mattered, and you could be carried along on cadence alone.

"Okay," said Anne, tapping her ring against her wineglass again. "Now let's hear it for *Aviva*! I listened to some of her stuff this afternoon and *whoa*, you guys."

Lounge, club, concert hall, sitting room, it didn't matter: there was always the same fleeting damp panic, the same stomach drop, the heart-flutter flash. You'd think she'd be over it by now. Her fourth album! Someone tell her nervous system. She situated herself on the stool in front of the group, tuning the Epiphone.

"What was up with those mashed potatoes tonight? Sittin' a little heavy, or is it just me? Okay. Here we go. This here is my trusty Epiphone. I been hauling this bitch around for years. She was my destiny. She was sent to me to make the path clear. Shit could have gone another way. Any number of other ways. I was pretty burned out on music by the time I found this baby. Okay. Let's see . . . Okay. I'm gonna play you a song by an artist I adore. A ton of people adore her, but we mustn't hold that against her. She let things get out of hand. She didn't know when to say when. She dug in her heels in the wrong direction, know what I mean?"

It wasn't like Amy was obscure; not like she needed rescuing from the bowels of cultural history. And it wasn't like Aviva could replicate or approach Amy's voice. Aviva only had her own voice. So here went the barest rendition of the song, just a few chords, a minimalist offering. The first big love affair, over: sayonara to the older guy she could too easily dominate. She wanted to be *dominated*, see. A deceptively simple blues for when you need to be brought back to earth, reminded who you are. The song opened and opened and kept on opening. You could dance to it, drop down into your pelvis, let it make you funnier, funkier, smarter, skankier, snarkier, stankier. Listen to how smart this girl is! How self-aware and funny. A step ahead of everyone else. Borrow what she's got. *Well, I'd hate to be* your *boyfriend,* said a condescending TV host when the unknown first appeared

23

on his show to do this very song. Barely out of her teens, but she didn't give a fuck about that dumbass host. As if she would ever give a man like that so much as a *thought*. Not for all the money in the world. This was well before international super-fame, wigs, tattoos, paparazzi frenzy. This was when she was just a giddy child wearing too much makeup to cover up hormonal acne, high off her own immense gifts, a new tattoo of Betty Boop on her bum. Hard to remember now, how seriously transgressive tattoos used to be. She was going to be a roller-skating waitress if music didn't work out. Baby-faced teen with her tits and ass hanging out of a clingy dress, trying out those big tottering heels. Playing dress-up. Pierced lip. Total confidence plus staggering innocence, and she never once looked at the audience. Purely an inner trip. She knew how good she was, knew what her voice could do to a room. Didn't need to beg the audience for approval. She knew what she was giving them. Suffered fools not one bit. Lost already, sure, but life of the party wherever she went. Chubby, awkward, hairy little big-mouthed Jew. There's still such a thing as a Jew, like it or not: a full-on Jew, through and through. She hit puberty hard, like a car wrapped around a tree. They put her on antidepressants at fifteen; of course they did.

Why this particular song? Why this particular singer? Why not some unsung song? Some unsung singer? These things have a life of their own. Lotta great voices, lotta self-destructive bullshit, lotta untimely death, so why this girl? They were cut from the same cloth: sisters, cousins, all-seeing, all-knowing. Aviva knew a thing or two about addiction, about loyalty to the dark side. Aviva had given herself to the wrong people, too. There but for the grace of God. Nobody stands in between me and my whatever. How could you *not* follow lust and love down into the darkest halls of doom? Aviva had herself a good man now, a dear good angel of a man, and wasn't there a parallel universe in which Amy was at this very moment recording and touring and writing and building sandcastles on a St. Lucian beach with her wholesome brood? Amy had wanted babies very badly, too, and was likewise aggrieved by their failure to appear. When something takes hold of your imagination, you rise to meet it and do your utmost to serve it. No guarantees, no promises, just your full attention. And after all, wasn't everyone always talking about Aviva's *voice*? Hadn't she gotten that award, way back when, for *new voices*?

One good thing about music school, other than it having inoculated her against pretension of many flavors, had been her voice teacher, Sarah. *Nobody can teach what you got, honey. All I can do is help you use it and not lose it.* A special voice, an arresting voice, impossible to ignore. She didn't always hit precise notes—she wasn't some formalist, some *scientist*, some *striver*—but she sang from her gut and she meant it. Her voice a living organism: no song ever, ever the same twice.

What even *is* a voice? It's the sound one makes with one's larynx. The way one makes oneself heard. Breath, vibration, a style of narration. Phrasing. And when you're singing from your bones and bowels, these things don't need *explaining*. Everyone can feel it in *their* bones and bowels, animals and plants included. An unpasteurized experience. Honesty is the ultimate life giver. What would you do with all the energy you'd save if you never had to lie?

Knock on Aviva's studio door, late that night. Well, well, what did we have here?

The composer, sheepish, shuffling his feet. "Saw your light on."

She let him in.

"Nice space," he said.

"Where'd they put you?"

"Over behind the barn."

He stood there. She waited. Try to seduce her or don't, dude, one way or the other, but make up your mind.

"Hey, that was amazing tonight. You're really good, you know?"

"Yeah. I do know."

He laughed. How *funny*: a chick who knows how good she is.

She sat cross-legged on the bed while he circled the perimeter, picking things up and putting them back down, looking at stuff she'd taped to the walls, examining the list of previous studio inhabitants scrawled by the door. Finally he sat down in the one armchair. Aviva waited, amused, for this to play out, whatever it was. Not the worst approach to life in general. He sighed. "I haven't been with anybody since my divorce."

Oh *hell* no! Sad sack looking for mommy time? Screw that. The nerve of him, trying to sap her maternal energies. No, sir, she had no maternal energies to spare. Her maternal energies were on reserve. She had big plans for her maternal energies. It might have been interesting to find out how he'd worship her body, but no: a sob sesh was not in the cards. She got up off the bed and opened the door.

"I gotta call it a day," she said. "Thanks for coming by, though."

He was a little stunned, but he got up and out.

Find it elsewhere, pal. Mommies everywhere, bored off their tits, happy for any and all attention. Find it someplace else.

She woke the next morning bloated and numb and crampy and tired and insatiable and depressed. Bleeding was no less a bummer for being expected. Here it was. The humbling. Get cozy, be gentle. None of that absurd tampon/painkiller advertisement shit wherein you plug yourself up with some bleach/asbestos/formaldehyde-soaked scented cotton on a string and pop some pills and carry on upholding capitalism, running cross-country, riding your bike to work, kicking ass at doubles, and running for Congress, fuck that. Someone once asked Amy, on camera: "Do you ever feel like you get treated differently, being a female artist?"

"Only when I'm on my period," came the insouciant reply.

(Are we looking at a beautiful rebel, a visionary, a brilliant misfit for whom the world was not ready? Or the dumbest, most petulant little self-destructive twat to ever draw breath? The answer, of course, is both.)

On impulse, Aviva sent Amy's mother's account a direct message: *I write out of love for your daughter, from one heartsick Jewish girl to another.* That last bit a touch manipulative, but heartsick Jewish girls did have to look out for one another, across any and all divides.

Mum's response came immediately: *Do let me know when you're in London, darling, perhaps we can meet for tea.*

Holy shit.

She waited 'til breakfast was almost over so she wouldn't have to talk to anyone, blared some terminally ill Warren Zevon in the studio, lay around with tea, texted Sam, texted friends, eyeballed the feed, read schlock, watched videos, and texted everyone again. This was her "ladies' holiday," as the yogis called it. This was her adios, cruel world. Her biological Sabbath. Her uterine shiva.

Enter it into the app: day thirty-four. Not a terrible length of days for an Aviva cycle. She'd had longer, harder, worse. Never any easy-peasy twenty-eight-day cycle for this bitch, alas. But *hey* now! Would you look at *that*? She always forgot, and the app always reminded her: bleeding was *not* the end of the cycle. Nope: bleeding began a *new* cycle. The bleed is day one of the new cycle. Bleeding is not the finale, people. Bleeding is prologue. Bleeding is restart. Bleeding is just the beginning.

2.

FAME

Home from art camp, preparing to head off on tour, Aviva fell briefly under the sway of a self-proclaimed fertility guru whose marketing emails came hard and fast: *Click here for my Fertile Food Five! Click here for my Recipes for Righteous Reproductive Renewal! Click here for my Fabulous Fertility Facts!* The guru had obviously subjected herself to some serious branding/ life-coaching/manifestation seminars. *And if you sign up for personal coaching before the end of the month . . . !* This lady was gonna get your clicks or die tryin'. Join her mailing list and you'd be sure to access the secrets of "ferocious fecundity."

The guru's paleo recipes promised to be amazingly simple, once you got the hang, and her general message seemed wise: Respect the almighty cycle, or *else*. Food is the best medicine. An ounce of prevention is worth a pound of cure. Yes. Great. Okay. Good. Fine. There was inarguable truth to be had: the general health of any given menstruating person is reflected in the patterns and irregularities and challenges of her cycle. The cycle is the fifth vital sign, no less an indicator of general health than the pulse. If one treated only the *symptoms* and not the *root causes* of imbalance or disorder, one was being a moron, and one's problems would only get worse.

On the guru's recommendation, Aviva ordered a very special probiotic powder colonized from the feces of Australian aborigines. *You ARE Your*

Cycle was the title of the Goddess's self-published book, and Aviva went ahead and ordered that, too, but drew a hard line at the three-thousand-dollar private coaching offer.

Guru claimed to have cured her own severe endocrine disease using her proprietary protocol, and had, at age thirty-nine, conceived a daughter "at home, in bed, with my husband, on our third try!" Or so she crowed repeatedly via every established platform and a few in beta. So, what, lady, you don't have enough *business*? You wanna get *famous* for curing endocrine disorders with food? The work of curing endocrine disorders with food requires a fucking *glam shot*? You want to get *rich* off curing endocrine disorders with food?

A visit to the holistic MD in the guesthouse of a yellow Victorian in the 'burbs. Celtic symbols and aphoristic wood carvings all over the place. *There's More Than One Way. A Hint Is Sufficient For the Wise. Laughter Is the Best Medicine.*

The holistic MD had ordered some tests. Aviva's thyroid was fine, her fasting insulin was fine, her hormone levels were slightly higher or lower than they should be at whatever given point of her cycle, but not catastrophically so. She did not have celiac disease, but should still cut down on wheat (and *obviously* no dairy or sugar or caffeine or alcohol, *yes*, she *knew*) and maybe cut out legumes, too, for kicks. Also, get more sleep. And vitamin D. And purified water. And exercise. But not too much exercise. And couldn't hurt to carry rose quartz on her person at all times.

The holistic MD peered through reading glasses at Aviva's questionnaire.

"A singer, hmm? You know, singing has been shown to help the nervous system. Especially singing in groups, for some reason."

Well, of *course* singing helped the nervous system! Why had something so obvious and intuitive needed to be *shown*?

Health Is Better Than Wealth, read the wood carving above the exit.

* * *

The acupuncturist rested two fingers on Aviva's wrist to feel her pulse, which in Chinese medicine could be described as hollowed, tight, swift, scattered, hidden, knotted, slippery, hesitant, soggy, floating, or sinking, though presumably not all at once.

"How *are* you?" The acupuncturist seemed to really want to know.

"Last cycle wound up being thirty-four days, not the worst, but the week before I bled was a lot of fatigue, greasy hair, night sweats, *really* swollen tits, and the exact same three zits on my chin? And I hated everyone? I mean *hated*? With a passion?"

Why the uptick in her voice? Why was everything a question? Obsequious. Annoying. The power dynamic automatically wonky, everything an entreaty, as though any given caregiver might not otherwise find Aviva worthy of care.

"Where are we now?"

We. You had to love that.

"Day ten. Feeling good. Tip-top. Like a dude. Taking care of business."

"Let's see your tongue. Okay, and you're still"—the acupuncturist scanned her notes—"trying for a baby?"

"Yeah, but—I mean, not *trying*, you know? Just . . . hoping? I don't know. I gave up on the temperature charting. Just couldn't hack it? Really stressed me out? Anyway, the app malfunctioned and I lost like a year of data, and . . . I don't know. That thing fucked with my head, anyway. The temp-taking. Like, the minute I opened my eyes in the morning, there's this fucking thing I have to think about, you know?"

"Well, stress is the worst."

"Right. So. I stopped."

"How's your diet?"

"Not perfect, but pretty good? Once in a while I really want a donut, so I eat a donut, you know? Not like every day, but if I really want a donut I'm just going to have a donut, because life is fucking short. I mean, I'll have *half* a donut, you know? And, I mean, if half an occasional donut means

I can't have a baby, I guess I just have to accept that I can't have a baby? Because that's just, like, really a lot to handle?"

She was pleading; that's what she was doing. For care.

"Sugar is bad news for you, particularly. It's going to make ovulation tricky."

"I'm talking about like half a donut a week. Half a donut every *other* week. A donut a *month*."

"How are the herbs I gave you last time?"

"They made me pee a lot? And last cycle I had a monster headache the day I *finished* bleeding? In the past it's been the day or two *before* I bleed?"

She was asking to be cared for. It wasn't enough to have shown up here and to have gotten undressed. She was begging.

The acupuncturist slapped Aviva's folder shut. "Let's see your scalp. Okay. And tongue? Facedown today. Seems like a facedown kind of day. Are you all right with cupping?"

Aviva arranged her tits to either side and put her face in the cradle. She was quite all right with cupping.

"You're a musician, right? I keep meaning to check out your stuff. Is it, like, online?"

"Mmmmm-hmmmm."

"So, like, what kind of music?"

"The, like, groovy kind."

On went the cups.

"How do those feel?"

"Amazing? Thank you?"

"I'll be back in half an hour." Off went the lights.

Aviva's mind ran circles round the ol' prison yard. All the usual banal obsessive crap: what should she wear on tour, who'd popped up in her feed lately. The endless swirl of others. People she felt wounded by, people she wanted to wound. A sweet new image of wee Harmony Shmendrickson standing up all by herself and smiling *so* wide. Interviews. Things she should have said, shouldn't have said, planned on saying. Photo shoots.

Should she get a haircut? Some new boots? Nah, the old boots were the best, the old boots were trusty friends. Maybe this would be Aviva's last tour for a while because maybe she'd be busy having a baby, raising the baby. A swell of optimism: this was going to be a fun, good tour, and after this she was going to demur from tour! She and Sam would get a dog, paint the kitchen blue, get a hammock for the yard, plant themselves a garden, and have themselves a baby. Yap, yap, yap, went her mind, until eventually, whoosh, it surrendered to rest. Witness the miracle: she was transformed (temporarily) from a rickety bird feeder rocked by the swift arrival and departure of every finch on the block, into the dark and cool primordial forest itself, vast and majestic, impervious to the agendas of the hundred thousand creatures within and without.

She and Sam merged bodies as much as humanly possible without it becoming a bummer. You did *not* want to let sex become a bummer. You were *for sure* never supposed to let sex become a bummer. Rule number one: sex should be fun. She often passed out cold after getting it on with Sam, which is as good a sign as any that you should absolutely spend your life with a person (unless it's because they've drugged you).

"That was a good one," he said, a proprietary hand spread across the width of her belly. "I got my guys *way* up in there."

Cycle day twelve. *Definite* cervical changes. She hoisted her legs up the wall, wedged a pillow under her ass. If need be, she could start up again with the temp charting after tour, try having a better attitude about it. There was a groundbreaking, four-hundred-dollar digital thermometer from Sweden being heavily marketed in advance of its release. It connected to its own app, so that the temp chart would assemble itself *for* you, day by day, and the almighty app would get to *know* your specific, idiosyncratic cycle. Aviva was perhaps going to spring for this new groundbreaking digital-thermometer-plus-app. Let optimism reign. But first: thirty-five cities in forty days. Or maybe it was forty cities in thirty-five days? It was a lot of cities in a lot of days. It was Aviva's "moment," quoth Jerry and the Rabbi and the tarot queen and the booking agent and the label and industry friends and her demon hustler shadow.

Awake before dawn on departure day, she burrowed under the duvet, squeezing one of Sam's warm thighs up in between hers. "Don't make me go," she whimpered.

"Love you, baby. Proud of you."

It was still dark out when she loaded her stuff into the back of the cab.

The driver hated the night shift because it put his biological rhythms all out of whack. He was from Togo and used to be a gambler. A real addict, he said. No night or day in a casino. "Not healthy! Human body need night and day! Human body need fresh air! Human body need to be outside!"

He made a wrong turn. Aviva guided him back on track. He eyed her in the rearview.

"Married?"

"Yep."

"Children?"

"Not yet!" Let's give cheerful stoicism a try, why not.

"You should have! Children are best thing to have!" He glanced at her in the rearview again. "My children my best things!"

" 'Your children are not your children,' " she said.

"What you mean?"

" 'They come through you but not from you.' "

"What is that?"

"A famous poem. By Kahlil Gibran. An important poet." Fame and importance: not remotely the same, but could always be counted upon to bolster each other.

"I do not know this poet. But I wish you many children! Woman without children is like lake without fish!"

Aviva happened to completely goddamned motherfucking agree, but when they arrived at the airport she silently gathered her things and stiffed him on the tip, because he should learn to keep his motherfucking mouth shut.

* * *

She was flying to Vegas with her guitar. Deja, the tour manager, would meet her there, and the merch would be waiting for them. They'd do the first show, spend the night, and then set off in the van. Up through North Cali, into the Pacific Northwest, over into the mountains, down through the Southwest, into the Midwest, down across the South, up through the Mid-Atlantic, and back up into New England. Piece of cake. No one's first rodeo.

The security lines were long, but Aviva opted out of the full-body scan. She was a woman of childbearing age, dammit, and she would not be subjected to the newfangled scanner. Who knew what these jerks were doing to us with their big ugly machines?

"Need a female body check," a TSO mumbled into a walkie-talkie. His nametag read *Ed*. A minute ticked by. Aviva shifted her weight, stared daggers. "Sorry, ma'am," said Ed. "Shouldn't be too long."

People streamed past, putting their shoes back on, gathering up their stuff.

"Can *you* please just give me a pat-down?"

"Can't do that, ma'am. *Female body check. Do you copy. Over.* Scanner's the same amount of radiation as your cell phone, you know."

He glanced at Aviva's belongings, which sat piled at the end of the conveyor: boots, roller bag, guitar case, jacket, and massive trash Amy biography. The superstar was pictured on the cover all tough and sweet and scared and deep and vulnerable and used and fragile and doomed, in just the *cutest* little striped jumpsuit. The vacant look in her eyes meant it must have been taken after the first really bad overdose. Her "accident," Mum called it.

"What a voice," Ed said.

"Right?!"

"Why didn't she just go to rehab?"

"Well, she did, actually. A couple times, but . . . Dude, listen, please. I would love to have this conversation, but my flight is seriously *boarding* right now."

"Shouldn't be too much longer. *Female body check, over.*"

"I'm begging you. Gender is a construct. Pat me down, man."

"You just can go through the scanner, if you want."

"I'm pregnant," Aviva said.

And hey, look how that changed the dynamic. Suddenly Ed had a deferential edge, and seconds later a female TSO named Angel was roughly sliding the backs of her hands around Aviva's tits, up her inner thighs, and down her ass.

"Rehab was beside the point," Aviva told Ed as she shoved her feet back into her boots, hoisted her guitar, and tucked the biography under an arm. "'Cause she wanted to annihilate herself, see, and she was stubborn as fuck."

On the cover of the biography, Amy appeared unsure, her mouth ajar in an echo of snarl, muscle-memory snarl, but from the silence of her grave had no choice but to agree to this narrative. All narrative.

"Good luck with your baby," Ed said.

Aviva hustled to her gate and boarded the plane with mere minutes to spare.

Overpowering stench of perfume: Toilet cleaner? Air freshener? Fancy eau de toilette? Industrial sanitizer? No matter: exact hormone-disrupting synthetic fragrance compounds in all. She settled into the middle seat, row nine, lucky nine, sandwiched between a big young white guy with grimy fingernails and a stringy-haired white girl with long bony toes in flip-flops. Aviva had spent her formative years desperate for this white girl's precise hair: like Janice from the *Muppet Show* house band. You simply could not be cute without this exact stringy white-girl hair. It was a requirement. You might have an okay life without this kind of hair, but you would never be truly great, and ultimately no one would care if you just offed yourself.

Janice Muppet was flipping through a copy of last week's *People* magazine. There, fleetingly, on the Music page, Aviva caught sight of her own face, and allowed herself precisely two and a half seconds of satisfaction about being this quote-unquote success before she went back to feeling terrible about how gross it was to be packaged and sold, and how gross it was that *other* people might be impressed by the packaging and selling. Not impressed with the *work* Aviva had done, mind you. Not impressed with the *body* of work she was in the midst of making, no: just impressed with whatever *recognition* she got. Her dumb face in a dumb magazine.

The grimy guy was staring out the window, where the sun was rising spectacularly orange and purple amidst the roar of the jet engine gearing up for takeoff.

He leaned toward Aviva, keeping his eyes on the sky.

"This is my first flight," he said.

"Like, ever?"

"Like, ever."

"Are you . . . scared?"

"Naw. A little."

His name was Derrick. He had won this trip through a contest at work, a Valvoline in the Catskills. It included two nights in a hotel on the Vegas Strip, two tickets to a magic show, and two all-you-can-eat breakfasts. He was meeting his brother there, and they were going to live it *up*. He was twenty-five. He had a four-year-old son named Dominick, Dom for short. He was raising Dom alone because Dom's mother was a crazy bitch and he felt sorry for her, he really did, but she had a lot of work to do to get herself together, and sometimes it seemed she didn't have it in her to really make the effort. He tried not to badmouth her to Dom, who loved and missed her and saw her when she was straight enough to handle it, which wasn't too often.

"Boy needs a mother," Derrick said, shaking his head.

His hands were huge, shapely, and stained, and Aviva imagined them gripping her hips in the plane bathroom. Maybe *she* could step in and be Dom's mother. They could all live in the Catskills, in a shitty old ranch fronting the road but with acres of woods out back. Sourdough starter. Woodpile. She could raise the child as her own. Dom's mother would be a recurrent drag, but eventually she'd overdose and they'd throw her a nice, musical wake, and carry on. Grill a lot, grow weed, laugh long and hard, host friends. She'd be stoned and happy most of the time, sitting out on the back porch with her guitar, hollering dirges. Dom would call her Mama, and Derrick would drink beer, and once in a blue moon he might get a *tiny* bit violent, but not *too* violent, and she really *would* be asking for it, and he'd be sorry, and anyway it would sort of turn her on but she would *never* admit it on social media. Derrick would build her an addition onto the house for a music studio. But then one day, once Dom was grown, she'd run off with a last-chance lover to Guatemala, or Mérida, or maybe Tzfat, where she'd spend her crone years in long, silver braids on a cacao farm, practicing pranayama and occasionally leading seekers through therapeutic psychedelics and/or book club. Derrick would never forgive her, though she'd send him endless love and light in meditation.

"You got kids?" he asked.

Always a sucker punch, even when you saw it coming a mile up the road. "Nope."

"You'd be a great mom."

"How do you know that?"

"One of those things." He shrugged. "I can tell. You're a good listener." He took note of her wedding band.

"Husband doesn't want 'em?"

"Just hasn't happened yet." Aviva shrugged.

Derrick nodded, squinting at her.

"It'll happen," he said after a beat.

"Yeah."

"You want it to happen?"

"It's in the Lord's hands," she recited. "It is what it is."

"Sorry," Derrick said.

"It'll happen."

"Life's a bitch . . ."

"And then you die . . ."

"That's why we get high . . ."

They spoke the last lyric together: " 'Cuz you never know when you gonna go!"

They fist-bumped, friends for life (or the duration of the flight).

Before Amy died, she'd had some kind of platonic long-distance soulmate thing happening with Nas. They were planning on forming a supergroup, for real. She'd begun writing songs, even laid down a track or two. But then her meat ship sank.

The flight attendant brought drinks. Seltzer for Aviva, Jack Daniel's for Derrick, white wine for Janice Muppet. Aviva hauled out the biography and plopped it on her tray table. "Oh my *God*," said Janice Muppet, spilling a little of her Pinot Grigio. "I *love* her. So *sad!*"

"Yeah. She's my sister."

Janice's jaw dropped. "Your *sister*?!"

"Oh, no, not like actually, like: spiritually."

It was a fabulous biography: encyclopedic, exhaustive, unpretentious. Best of all, it had been published six months *before* the Tragic End, so there was no fake reverence, no variations on the poor doomed blessed martyr angel trope. Most interviewees thought she was a spoiled brat. One went so far as to call her a "filthy trash heap." Similar frustration and criticism were hurled from all directions throughout her life: She was a smart girl who did not apply herself. She was too smart for her own good. She would certainly do very well for herself if only she would fall in line. She was not living up to her *potential*.

They had no clue as to what her potential might *be*, but everyone could see that she definitely *had* some. Wild, unnerving, careless girl, called everyone's bluff. She seemed to have nothing to lose. She wanted to be "famous" when she grew up, because being famous meant everyone *saw* you, really and truly *saw* you, and couldn't look away. First guitar at thirteen: daughter of the commandments. Meanwhile, screw Jewish day school and screw all-girls' school and screw the tight-knit North London Jewish community. She wasn't *like* them. But then, oh dear, screw performing arts school, too, and screw the *other* performing arts school, as well. Nothing but cookie-cutter wannabes everywhere she went. Fucking *followers*. (Remember when that was a dirty word? A hard-core pejorative?) Hell, she wasn't like those performing arts twats, either. All *they* wanted was to be famous, and guess what? Fame's stupid. Fuck fame. All you had to have was the minutest taste of it to know it was shit. The performing arts school dolts didn't care about being *good*. They only wanted to be good enough to get *famous*. So go get your fame, you middling reality talent show twats. Have at your competitions, your Svengali producers, your fifteen minutes. Knock yourselves out. I'll be over here being freakin' amazing and singular, take me or leave me. She was truly gifted, so why should she have to lick ass? You only have to lick ass when you don't got the gift. She was exacting about music, and *exactitude* is what makes an artist; ambition is when you're satisfied with whatever the fuck people will buy. Everyone hated her, but she didn't care. She was so good, so sharp, so perceptive, so gifted, that she didn't *have* to care. And *that* is what infuriates people who are *not* so good or sharp or perceptive: they *do* have to care. Squeal, preen, elbow-flap, regurgitate received wisdom, beg for likes, maniacally bat their lashes. Confronting someone of her caliber reminds them of what they're not, makes them resentful. The T-shirt from her first UK tour bore huge lettering: *I HATE AMY*.

Anyway, yeah, she had a great voice, and yeah, she could dominate a stage, all fine and well, but what she really wanted, first and foremost, was to be a beloved wife and mum. Yeah, she could sing like a fucking boss. Yeah, she could write songs, easy-peasy. But so what?

Janice Muppet was asleep now, the magazine on her lap open to the cover story: a starlet, pregnant with twins, speaking out about her "infertility journey." *God has given me the greatest gift*, read the pull quote alongside a photo of the starlet all in white, gazing down at her swollen belly. Well, sure, "God" and the two hundred grand you paid some clinic. The starlet's boyfriend, a football hero, stood behind her with massive biceps and a hilariously uncomfortable expression on his face. Aviva slid the magazine off sleeping Muppet's lap, flipped the pages back to the Music section, and elbowed Derrick.

"Wanna see something funny?"

"Always."

She held up the page with her face on it.

"What the *fuck*?! You're *famous*?"

"In a way."

He took the magazine and read aloud: " 'In the singer-songwriter's fierce fourth album, she's ready to transition into a new phase of life, if only she can she get out of her own way. If Tom Waits and Fiona Apple had a baby who grew up to be a prickly, menstruation-obsessed feminist, she might sound like the intensely confrontational Aviva, whose lyrics are not for the faint of heart.' " Derrick let the magazine fall onto his tray table.

"Drop the mic, girl!"

She rolled her eyes: "Please."

"What the *fuuuuuuuck*? Do you know how cool this is? *Damn*, famous girl. 'Menstruation-obsessed feminist,' say *what*?!"

He flagged down the flight attendant, waving the magazine.

"Yo, hi, we got a *famous chick* on this flight."

The flight attendant nodded politely, examined Aviva—nope, not *that* famous—and continued on up the aisle. Derrick was still grinning like a fool.

"Uh, hey, famous chick."

"It's not like that."

"Uh, I don't know, dude. You're in *People* magazine!"

"Right, and next week it'll be someone else, and I'll be in the recycling bin. So it actually super-duper doesn't matter." She put her lips right up to his ear, scent of cigarettes and Ivory soap. "It's *ephemeral*," she said, real soft and slow. Derrick didn't move a muscle. He wasn't sure what "ephemeral" meant. "Never mind," she said, leaning back into her seat. "You're right. It's true. I am totally famous. Peel me a grape!"

They let their shoulders touch. Somewhere over Tennessee he let his hand experimentally brush up against the side of her thigh, just above her knee, so she felt it in her innermost. Aviva gestured toward the still-napping Muppet: "She's cute. Get her number."

"Not my type," Derrick said. "I need a woman like you."

"I'm old enough to be your mother."

He studied her. "Not true."

Possibly true, in extremis. But she switched tacks: "My husband benches two-fifty." Not a lie. Sam taught civics and history at Albany High, but he'd been a Divison I QB, and assisted the football coach on the side.

Derrick retreated into what passed for personal space.

"Listen," she told him, when they were buckling up for descent. "Look for someone a little offbeat, kind of a dork. Not the thinnest or prettiest or anything like that. A little different. Not overly concerned with fitting in. Someone with a passion, something she likes to do and is good at and works hard at, for her own satisfaction. You'll see it in her eyes. It's okay if she's a little depressed. A little depressed is okay, so long as she's got perspective and isn't too into drinking or drugs. Doesn't take herself too seriously. Interested in the world. Finds the humor in everything, especially the hard stuff. Likes to go places, explore. Curious. Likes her friends. Likes music. Into sex, for her own sake. Likes her body. Full pubes, okay? Do you hear me on this? Full pubes is important. The more body hair the better. Not afraid to dance or sing. Knows how to take a nap. Not afraid of confrontation. Okay with her lot in life. Not super impressed with money. Not afraid to get dirty. Literally dirty. Doesn't wear a ton of makeup. Not online all that much. Zero perfume. Mildly to moderately religious but doesn't need to talk about it, like, *ever*. Do you want to write this down?"

"I think I got it."

They parted ways with a handshake at the end of the jet bridge.

You forgot what it felt like, then you did it again and couldn't believe you'd forgotten: Roomfuls of faces in the dark, staring up at you in the light. Nevada City, San Fran, Oakland, Sacramento. All those faces! The proverbial sea of them. No band, no opener. The label's expectations were modest, because expenses were relatively low. Career sweet spot: just a girl and her guitar.

Deja was an ace right hand. Ten years younger than Aviva but she'd been touring practically her whole life with her old-school roots-legend father, and damn if she couldn't do it all: wrangle the sound techs and merch and engineers, sort out the cash. And *drive*, good God, the girl was tireless. Best of all, a person of few words. Verging on mute. They had an understanding, Deja and Aviva: an easy rapport, a groove.

Aviva had opted to play smaller prestige venues at or near capacity, rather than try to fill the bigger venues. You had to be nuts—or maybe just twelve years old—to covet fame. The actual greats were *tormented* if they *happened* to become famous; they had to join monasteries or commit suicide or wear huge sunglasses 24/7. Who wanted icon status? Maybe after you were dead. If rule number one was Don't Make Sex a Bummer, rule number two had to be Don't Make Music a Bummer.

"I think you're kidding yourself," said the Rabbi on the phone. "I think you *do* want the world at your feet, and I think you know you're good enough to have that, but I think you don't *want* to want that. And I think you're *right* not to want to want that. Because *that*, in reality, is a curse."

"What the fuck did you just say, and can you streamline it, please?"

"It's your internal conflict, darling."

"Wait, so I *should* want world domination? I *should* write some catchier two-minute repetitive pop shit and put my tits out on my feed? Do you know how amazing my tits are, for the record? I have insanely nice tits. Like, world's best, no joke. But I try *not* to put them out too much because they are so incredible I don't think it's *fair*. But you're telling me I'm wasting my tits? Should I get busy encouraging people to virtually jizz all over my tits?"

"That is not what I'm saying, no, but I appreciate the metaphor. You would hate that. And it would destroy your gift."

"It's not a metaphor, man. My tits are epic. But my gift! That's right, that's right: my gift. So am I okay to just play my fucking shows like the badass I am and otherwise duck and cover?"

"I'm saying both impulses live inside you and both impulses are correct and both impulses are also problematic."

"Awesome. How much for today's sesh, Doc?"

She opened Eugene with "Careless," in which she recollected every guy she'd ever fucked. In the chorus came the realization that she'd never worried about getting pregnant, and that she had, despite said carelessness, never wound *up* accidentally pregnant. The dawning realization in the bridge: *Why* had she never gotten accidentally pregnant?! She probably should have gotten accidentally pregnant. There had been that guy and that other guy and the one before that and after that and, oh, this other one, too . . . She'd intended it to be a perversely sorrowful song, a kind of tongue-in-cheek lament. All the cool witches got to sing about their abortions; infertility was intensely uncool. But in the studio—she had been stoned—the song had wound up almost peppy, borderline madcap, sarcastic. Now, on tour, she had the chance to strip it back down again.

At merch, a line of bashful, buzzing women and a handful of sensitive dudes. She signed all their CDs and tees with an extravagant, swooping "Love."

In Portland, Deja headed back to the hotel with a sound tech and Aviva decamped to a late-night cocktail/smoothie place with a gaggle of groupies. Each, in turn, detailed her distinct procreative struggles.

A former PR assistant from Aviva's first label, liberated for the evening from her young child, was wrecked on three vodkas with fresh-pressed kale juice, lemon, and blue-green algae from Lake Kamranth. She had recently had a miscarriage. Given that she hadn't been sure she *wanted* another baby so soon, she was more devastated than she thought she had any right to be.

A gifted slam poet Aviva had befriended eons ago at an open mic had suffered a brutally traumatic hospital birth and gained almost a hundred pounds in the three years since. She still didn't have any feeling in her abdomen or her right hip, and couldn't orgasm.

A friend of the slam poet's was talking about getting a sperm donor before time ran out.

A blogger who'd been championing Aviva's work for years had, in the past eighteen months, undergone nine unsuccessful rounds of IVF. She'd sold a memoir about the whole thing to a major publisher, but hadn't been able to make much progress writing it. Regular infertility *plus* creative infertility? Jeez-louise, tough break. At least Aviva could still birth a good song whenever the fuck she felt like it.

Halfway through her second virgin turmeric orange ginger, the ladies leaned in: it was Aviva's turn to dish. Here was the downside of creative fertility: everyone felt entitled to her, thought they already knew everything about her, lyric detectives every one. Yeah, yeah, Aviva had put out an album called *Womb Service*, sure, yeah, all about maternity, the cycle, the elusive baby, all that strangely inconsequential fucking she'd done. But they were just *songs*! She was not about to take up voluntary residence in some tidy little confessional *prison* for the rest of her goddamn life.

The ladies, however, all wore the same expression: Pony up, hon. It's only fair. What's your sob story?

Fine. It was important to tell the truth as much and as often as possible.

"I guess it's been about . . . a year?" (Two, actually. Going on three, but who's counting?)

The ladies gasped.

"You've been *trying* for a *year*?!"

Two, actually. Going on three! But what did "trying" even *mean*, anyway? Aviva had been "trying" to stay inverately chill. Going on three years of "trying" not to think too much about it, beyond all the acupuncture and massage and meditation and clean food and visualization and whatnot. But "trying," in these people's understanding, meant something else entirely. Something punitive, something uniquely twenty-first-century, something downright extraterrestrial. What a drag, to have to fully inhabit only the most obvious identity available to you at any given moment. Refuse if you want to maintain any kind of self-respect or freedom or creative juice whatsoever. Refuse!

"Not, I mean, not, like, *trying*. Just, like . . . waiting."

Then came the tense, all-important question. People always dropped their voices a full octave to ask it: How. Old. Are. You?

Her answer was pleasing to them. Yippee: still in the green half of her thirties.

"Okay," said the IVF veteran. "You have time."

Ah, time: the only thing still blessedly, completely outside our silly, sad, shortsighted affectations of control. (Well, that and weather.)

"Do I? Do I have time?" Aviva glanced at the fertility guru's ovulation phase menu on her phone. Lentils. Lentils would be beneficial right now. She needed food, and then she needed her hotel bed.

"You're a *baby*," said sperm-seeker.

"But time is *not* your friend," said miscarriage.

"I'm forty-three," said the IVF vet. "Started when I was thirty-nine. You have plenty of time."

"Yay," Aviva said weakly.

"My sister-in-law's sister had her first at forty-seven," said birth trauma.

"But not with her own egg, obviously," said miscarriage.

"No, obviously. You can't use your own eggs past forty or the kid will be stupid."

"Everyone always says they wish they'd started sooner," said sperm-seeker, "but at the same time you better be in a perfect relationship and financially stable and advanced in your career and own a fucking house."

"It's like . . . we . . . can't . . . win," said birth trauma.

Aviva cracked up. "Are you just realizing this right now?"

"So, congrats, right?" said miscarriage. "Now you're perfectly in love and financially stable and advanced in your career and you get to blow all of that to smithereens obsessively engineering pregnancies your fucking body doesn't fucking want."

"Your body has no clue," said the IVF vet. "Your body is an idiot asshole. Your body doesn't get a *vote*. Your body gets no say whatso*ever*. *Fuck your body*."

On their day off in Seattle, Aviva and Deja treated themselves to three hours at a Scandinavian-style spa and sauna. Wet heat, dry heat, cool plunge, massages, wet heat, dry heat, cool plunge again, then bamboo chaises under skylights, where they sipped artisanal kombucha. Deja dozed while Aviva perused a seventeen-pound women's magazine. Living it *up*. Rock and *roll*.

The sauna et al. were not a good idea if there was any chance she might (maybe? Possibly? Not *impossibly*??) be . . . ever so slightly pregnant? But she just wanted to not think about her reproductive potential for five minutes—was that so much to ask? Apparently so, because the music page of the seventeen-pound women's mag said *Womb Service* was an unlistenable screed. *Who wants to groove out to music about periods?! YUCK. We don't want to be defined by our bodies; feminism has moved way beyond that! We are so much more than our bodies! We deserve to be liberated from all those old ideas! We loved Aviva's last album, and she has a reputation for great live performances, but this album is the pits. Grade: D+*

The Boise venue had seen better days, but still had original plaster molding, plush lobby carpeting, chandeliers. Peter, Paul & Mary had played here. Woody Guthrie had played here. Ani had played here. Alan Lomax had paraded Lead Belly through here. On the marquee was Aviva's name. Look at it, up there. She fought back a swelling of something like . . . pride? A terrible sin. How did one exorcise it? She took a photo and sent it to her deadbeat dad, who had grown much more interested in his daughter since she'd become a "public figure."

Sold-out show. The venue manager flirted in the greenroom, but Aviva wanted to be alone with her guitar, wouldn't grant eye contact. Audience energy high. Bona fide roar when she hit the stage. She ripped right into the titular song, in which she was holding a friend's new baby and studying it curiously: it was a baby like any other, a lump of animate flesh, unspeakably precious, but, well, it had been forced. Coerced by the hands of man. It had *not* sprung spontaneously from the loins of its progenitors. What did this signify? One didn't wander the produce aisle obsessing over the difference between an apple that had emerged from heirloom seed deep in organic compost in its godly prescribed season versus an apple that had emerged from scientifically altered seed in chemically treated soil, indoors, without any regard for climate whatsoever. An apple was an apple, no? What was Aviva's *problem*?? Did apples *taste* different when they emerged from heirloom seed deep in organic compost in their godly proscribed season? (Well . . . yeah.) Were there cellular variations in the vibrations of the apples' *juices*, for heaven's sake? (Well . . . yeah.) At the end of the song the baby cried briefly, took a tremendous, thunderous dump, and fell into serene sleep.

"Wooooooo," went the crowd. Someone screamed, "I LOVE YOU." With a band, you could avoid taking in too much information from the audience. With a band, you could schmooze and engage to the exclusion of the audience. Without a band, you were up there pretty much open to whatever.

"I love you, too," she said. "Ain't love grand?" They hooted and hollered. "Don't love make the world go 'round?" More hooting, applause. Someone screamed out a request from the second album, and she took it.

In Missoula, a beautiful journalist from the local arts weekly: "Did these new songs come from your own life?"

"I wrote them, and I'm alive, so I suppose they must have, yeah!"

The journalist just sat there, expressionless, waiting for Aviva to elaborate.

Don't be difficult, Aviva: of course these songs came from your life. Just past the throes of early love with Sammy Sam, ready for everything. Bring it on. Aware of your wonky cycles. Vaguely nervous about your wonky cycles. All your relatives and friends and acquaintances and hardly a spontaneous conception in the lot; fibroids and PCOS and endometriosis, oh my! Clomid and IUI and IVF and frozen eggs and porno at the urologist's office and shots and coolers and weight gain and breakouts and donated eggs and retrievals and implantations and failures and failures and failures, oh my! Twins up the wazoo. All of it whispered artlessly when spoken about at all. You didn't know what lay in store for you, but you knew you didn't want any of *that*. And a year went by. Two. Going on three. You yearned for babies, but you weren't interested in forcing the issue. The ballyhooed/maligned intuition. Felt it in your *ovarios*. In your gut. Your microbiome. Your ancestral memory. Your mitochondria. And there was zero interpretation of this perspective to be found *anywhere*. None whatsoever. So you worked it out in your songs and you fucked your husband and you visited every goddamned acupuncturist in New England and you bore curious witness to little Harmie Shmendrickson as she gestated and was born and grew. You reaffirmed your faith and optimism at the start of each new cycle, and you waited patiently, ever so patiently, as cycle after cycle after cycle wound down, down, down, each in its own brutal way, sometimes longer and sometimes shorter but always the unholy nightmare, and you developed coping mechanisms and you bled and you bled and you bled. You suffered through these cycles and you learned from them and you withstood running shithead commentary, like Oh, do you guys want kids and Oh, you're not getting any younger you know and Oh, are you trying are you trying are you trying are you trying and you let the grief of it live inside you, made the pain a little bed to lie in, and meanwhile you went about your business like a fucking grown-up, because only an entitled twat thinks life is about getting exactly what you want exactly when you want it.

"I'm fascinated with fertility," Aviva said. "Aren't we all? I mean, back to, like, cave drawings?"

"I was particularly struck by the force of the rhyme in 'You Can't Make Me.' Are you anti-motherhood?"

"I'm anti-*selling* motherhood, I guess. I'm anti-*buying* motherhood. I'm anti-*capitalist* motherhood. I'm anti-*technocratic* motherhood."

"It just seems like you're pretty hostile to procreation."

"It *does* seem that way, doesn't it."

Another show, another hotel room, another hot shower at the end of another long night. Another remote control, another bedside lamp. Salt Lake City? Flagstaff? Tuscon? Deja was a freaking *animal* behind the wheel.

"Do you ever get sick of driving?"

"Never. I get sick of staying anywhere too long."

Feed feed feed: bobbing along on a sea of virtual high fives from people who otherwise wouldn't piss on Aviva if she were on fire. Who in fact had never bothered to piss on her when she *had* been on fire.

Emoji hearts and flowers from Sam: principal's wife saw u in a magazine! v impressed. wants us to come for din.

LOL NO THNX.

Links from the publicist. Interviews begat interviews begat social media mentions begat more mentions begat more of the same, leaving her clicking dutifully back and forth and back and forth and back and forth and round and round like an isolated lab rat with much to teach about neurology, addiction, and the self.

Some folks blessed Aviva; others snarled and slobbered, straining at their leashes. How dare she. She was a nasty bitch. She was solipsistic and self-indulgent and judgmental and unpleasant and disagreeable and depressed and negative and unlikable, and her songs sucked. And they didn't *like* her. So *there*. Maybe they had used assisted reproductive technologies or maybe they hadn't, but they goddamn well would if they wanted or needed to, crazy punk folk singer bitch and her shitty little songs be damned. Maybe their sisters had used assisted reproduction, or their mothers had, or their friends had, and anyway how *dare* this weirdo singer bitch, how *dare* she. It was funny how enraged people got about how *angry* Aviva was. This is very *angry* music, they said, enraged. Why are you so *angry*.

* * *

A local arts rag reporter with a buzz cut in Albuquerque: "The line *taking what you want by force just makes you the bad guy* really struck me. I mean, isn't that sort of harsh on people who just really, really want babies?"

"Far be it from me to judge," Aviva said sweetly. "I'm just performing some feelings and ideas in song, that's all. You're welcome."

She channeled the yoga teacher, Hanalei: eyes closed, find the breath, touch the tip of the tongue to the roof of the mouth, relax the shoulders, inhale fully, exhale fully. No problem, parasympathetic nervous system. Noooooo problem. Call off the dogs. Indeed, there were many millions of good and decent people with cherished offspring produced using chemically washed ejaculate injected into eggs extracted from chemically manipulated ovaries, for profit. Yes, there were many millions of beautiful, cherished beings whose existence had been thusly engineered. (That word, though! How *dare* she?) Oh, the children were all very precious, indeed. Just look at peachy lil' Harmie Shmendrickson!

"Why do you sing about things people generally don't like to talk about?" wondered someone from *Time*.

"Because, um, anything we're not supposed to talk about is de facto something that urgently needs talking about?"

A young podcaster with—really?—a huge Cabbage Patch Kid tattooed on her bicep: "It seems like you're kind of, like, judgmental of, like, other women's choices? Don't you think it's important for femmes to, like, support each other?"

"Supporting each other does not mean being silent about systemic forces that threaten our basic well-being," Aviva offered brightly, playacted cheer verging on melodic. "Said forces demand questioning, regardless of whether or not some women 'choose' to submit to them!"

The baritone of a national radio host out of Austin: "In your music you say what no one else is willing to say. Tell us why."

"Well, sir . . . why would anyone need more of what everyone else is already saying? Wouldn't that be kind of a . . . massive waste of time?"

* * *

It was unseemly to complain about "success." The Q&As and profiles and interviews and shows and requests and the biggest ongoing internet gangbang of her life: This was what an artist *wanted*, wasn't it? There was just something nasty and impossible about the way she was expected to cultivate and embroider it. Why, little old *me?* Why, *thank* you!

San Antonio. Dallas. Houston.

She habitually surfed over to late-stage Amy, wearing her beehive especially high on a celebrity game show, because costume was the only way to deal with the horrible problem of fame. You needed a persona to stand between you and the world.

Honey, said the host, *we're concerned about you.*

[no response]

Babe, is that your real hair?

Yeah, it's mine. Yeah, 'cos I bought *it, yeah.*

This was a mere, what, four years after her first appearance on that same game show—dial *that* up—back when she was still fresh, unknown, a bubbly, clever, raven-haired kid in her favorite pink argyle sweater, wearing way too much makeup. Hair blown out shiny, classic nice self-loathing Jewish girl next door. Wouldn't wanna offend anyone with that unpredictable, frizzy, unmanageable Jew hair, no *sir*, straighten that shit out, *regulate* that shit, nothing to see here, move along. Infectious grin. Not everyone's cup of tea, but no costume, not yet. Two totally different versions of this same person: one before fame and one after. Her response to fame—her *defense* against it—was pure theatrics. Toggle back and forth between these two different versions of this same girl. As often happened, the persona eventually took over, leaving the person . . . where, exactly? It was easier for everyone this way, though. No one wants to engage with a *person*. A persona just makes more *sense*. Knowable, simplistic, unchanging. An object for sale.

New Orleans. Tallahassee.

Can you believe your success? some bygone MTV dolt had asked Amy. *Is it what you've always wanted?!*

It's all right, Amy said, bored. *But it's not like I'd slit my throat or anything otherwise.*

"You use a lot of very blunt and unusual language to discuss the female body," said a guy with a British accent at the radio station in Atlanta.

"Do I."

"I like that line about your period being a death rehearsal. And the song 'Bellwethers,' which is about . . . your breasts, I believe? But some feminists are uncomfortable with your language."

"Are they."

"Yes, well, the line *feminists, man, what are you gonna do; they just don't make 'em like they used to,* in particular, seems provocative. I know there has been some debate online."

"You don't say."

"And then there's the word 'engineered' with regard to children conceived via IVF. Can you talk about why you chose that word? It's a bit pejorative."

"Seemed like the most precise word. In terms of, like, straight-up meaning. Of the word."

"Aviva Rosner, ladies and gentlemen. A singer-songwriter whose new release is generating a good deal of conversation, not just for her arresting sound but also because she tackles some contemporary taboos in a big way. Did you intend for the album to be controversial?"

"No. Maybe. Probably."

"Because reproduction is quite the sacred cow. And here you are—wham—tipping with impunity."

"I guess if we're totally fine with all this stuff, all this stuff we do to women, or whatever you want to call the vessels, to get the, like, baby prize, why do we need euphemism? There's nothing inherently pejorative about the word 'engineered.' We are in fact engineering human lives. And if we *can't* call it what it is, maybe that's because we're a little ambivalent. In which case, all the more reason to think a little harder about it, right? And, like, *conversely*, if we have no issue with it, why not just name it? Call it what it is."

"Well, 'engineered' certainly *sounds* pejorative."

"If so, now might be a real good time to get down and dirty thinking it through, huh? And by the way, breasts *are* bellwethers. That's just, um, exactly what they are, physiologically speaking. Anyway, there's, like, a whole hell of a lot we don't know about the female reproductive system, which seems kind of odd in light of the fact that we're so motherfucking practiced at fucking with it."

The guy flipped a switch, leaned back, interlaced his hands behind his head, and stared at Aviva like he wanted to fuck her or kill her or both, in whatever order.

"Let's back up and try that one more time, and no profanity, all right? Public radio."

"Sure. Sorry."

"And we're editing most of this out anyway, I'm betting. Back on in three . . . two . . . *Aviva!* An exciting new 'feminist' singer-songwriter."

No, she was not new. This was her fourth album. Any asshole could put out one album. But they kept calling you "new" until you got old, at which point they'd eagerly erase you and continue right on masturbating to some *new* new ones.

"I wanna go home," Aviva whined somewhere between Charlotte, Chapel Hill, and Virginia Beach. Cycle day twenty-nine. A normal person-with-a-womb would be starting the bleed now.

Deja wore a faint smile, and offered no response. She drove with good-humored efficiency bordering on total automation. When she wasn't touring, she was currently living in a trailer in rural Tennessee with her brother and his girlfriend and their kids. From Deja's extremely irregular posting, Aviva gathered that this was a joyful, muddy existence focused mainly around homeschooling, light farming, yoga, and ceremonial psychedelics.

"Don't you?!"

"Don't I what?"

"Wanna go home," Aviva whined again.

"I *am* home, babe."

"What year were you born?"

"Ninety-three."

"Fucking Christ."

On their way back to their neighboring motel rooms in Charlottesville, Aviva felt compelled to conduct some further research. "Come have tea with me," Aviva said. "Mugwort. Gives you lucid dreams."

Deja paused, key card poised at the mouth of her hotel room door.

"Okay," she said.

It was better than sex: they curled all up around each other, laughing and wrestling like kittens, littermates, twins, mouthing each other innocently, and fell asleep in a tangle. Neither could recall their dreams.

Rolling Stone wanted Aviva's thoughts on social media. They were doing a feature on some up-and-comers and especially loved her song "Buyin' Shit Online." How did she use social media? What effect did she think it was having on our culture, on music?

"Just take ten minutes," begged the publicist. "Don't overthink it."

Cycle day thirty-one. Time online begat still more time online, which begat a certain torpor that itself begat yet more time online. In the flash of a decade, social media had gone from a lark to a way of life. There was no arguing with it. It was neither bad nor good. It was both bad and good. Both/and, Sam liked to say: everything was both/and.

She took a walk through town (which town? Who cared?) and called the Rabbi.

"*Mein kind!* How's my favorite singer?"

"Over it. The road is *not* my home. Tell me: What do you think of social media?"

"I cannot tell you how destructive it's been to people's lives."

Oh, the things he saw parade through his wood-paneled office! Everyone was losing their minds over what went on in the virtual town square. We destroyed all the old town squares and built ourselves one big fat new one, with extra surveillance. *Meet the new boss, same as the old boss*, sang the Who.

"But tell me," he said. "Tell me, tell me: How's tour? I've been thinking about you, wondering how it's going."

"Rilke said something about fame just being a collection of misunderstandings accumulating around a name," she said. "It's fine. It's fun. It's fine. I'm tired. I'm hearing from everyone I've ever met. It's kind of nice and it's kind of horrible. Everyone wants a piece, you know? Smells good when you're cooking. Most of the time no one will piss on you if you're on fire, but get your picture in a fucking magazine and suddenly you're everyone's bestie. Suddenly you're *covered* in piss."

"You're going to have to get used to dealing with it, darling."

"Oh, and Sam almost got stabbed breaking up a fight in the cafeteria the other day. But hey! Arts and Leisure is running a piece on me this weekend."

"Wonderful! Mazel tov! I can't wait to see it. I'm not surprised. Well deserved, darling."

"And if Arts and Leisure doesn't give a fuck about me, then I'm supposed to be despondent?"

"But they *do* give a fuck about you. Rightfully."

"But they could very well *not* give a fuck about me. In which case we'd say screw Arts and Leisure. So I can't very well strut around all *pleased* about it. It's meaningless. It necessarily means nothing, either way."

"It will bring more people to your music, which is all that matters. Try to enjoy this, V."

"Enjoy it? Then I'd be complicit! Then I'd be part of it. This is the smallest taste of the mildest kind of exposure, freaking *punk folk singer* fame, and it's so, so lame. What must *real* fame be like? I've been online like ten hours a day by myself in hotel rooms and my eyes are seriously rotting out of my head and when I close them all I can see is the screen and I'm supposed to repeat the same bullshit a thousand times and find a way to arrange my face in photos for as long as anyone thinks I'm worth noticing and it *sucks*. I don't want to *explain* myself to anyone. It's *boring*."

"Good! That's intellectual honesty. If you loved doing media you'd be creatively stagnant. It's just part of your job. You just have to do your job."

"Okay," she said, eyeing a silver cuff bracelet in the window of a minimalist shop. Her own reflection in the glass gave her a jolt: hair massive and a mess, eyes rimmed with kohl. When had she begun to wear her hair so big, gathered on top of her head in such a great big bun? When had she begun to outline her eyes so heavily?

The more insecure I feel, the bigger my hair gets, Amy said.

Another day off, and they lunched at a popular DC bakery, where there was nothing on offer except refined carbs and sugar. Toxic, inflammatory no-nos, but the croissants were next-level flaky and Aviva was ravenous. She *wanted* to "partner with" her body, really she did, but meanwhile here was a case full of exquisite baked goods, and she was *hungry*, and the young person in the bowler hat behind the counter had the most hypnotic scribbly ovoid tattoos and the grayest-green eyes. The nearest fresh-pressed-juice place was a twenty-seven-minute walk across town. Cycle day thirty-four.

The fertility guru's menu depended on knowing which phase of the cycle you were in. But you had to be one of those careless, happy little bitches with perfect clockwork cycles to know what the hell was actually happening on any given day of your cycle. Aviva had had thirty-two-day cycles, forty-two-day cycles, thirty-five-day cycles, forty-nine-day cycles, fifty-two-day cycles, name it. Her average, according to the trusty old app, was thirty-seven. Did she have a long follicular phase? Did she have a defective luteal phase? Was she anovulatory? Why was there sometimes textbook ovulatory cervical serum on day seventeen and sometimes again on day thirty-two and sometimes not at all? Where were the oft-heralded patterns? The app was comprehensive, not diagnostic. The app had nothing to offer beyond the facts Aviva herself entered into it. The app revealed nothing. The endocrinologists could barely mask their disinterest. The online forums were inconclusive. You needed a goddamned doctorate to figure this crap out, yet none of the folks *with* doctorates seemed particularly *interested* in figuring any of it out. Well, screw the guru, and screw the app: she devoured what was surely one of the finest grilled cheese sandwiches in the world.

Deja had no qualms about carbs or sugar. "Hits the spot. I'm on the rag."

"Oh God, why am I *not* on the rag? It's supposed to be catching. We've been on the road for weeks. Come here and let me sniff you some more. You're probably fertile as fuck, too."

"I can get pregnant from saying the *word* 'pregnant.' And we are *not* making that mistake ever again."

"Any period issues?"

"Little crampy, I guess."

"What do you use for birth control?"

"IUD."

"You ever think about kids?"

"Someday. I guess. Dunno."

Aviva couldn't have conjured Deja if she'd tried. The agreeable little sister to accompany you wherever you went. Or maybe she was more like a daughter; maybe this was what it would be like to have a daughter: so close you barely needed to talk. Or mother. The kind of mother Aviva would like to have had, and would promise to work very hard at being, should she be deemed, finally, worthy. Or could it be that these were actually all the same relationship, in their ideal form?! Easy, nonjudgmental, unconditional?

Haters were incensed on perfectly understandable grounds: *My* babies are the best, and I wouldn't have gotten *my* babies without these miraculous scientific interventions! Queers were mad because they couldn't otherwise get the babies at all. The childless by choice were annoyed because Aviva was making feminism about reproduction *again*, and *enough* with reproduction already; who cared what stupid breeders did or didn't do with their stupid wombs! The youngs were offended because "women" were supposedly duty bound to *support* and *adore* one another's choices absolutely all the time, and never question what anyone else did with their own body.

"Maybe you don't have to say quite *so* much in interviews," said the publicist, in an about-face. "Maybe we wanna kinda let the album speak for itself."

"We." You had to love that.

So she had written some searching satirical songs about being a menstruating individual. That old beat. So she had made some jokes about assisted reproductive technology (ART, for short! Hahahaha. Art!) in which she had maybe sort of . . . embroidered her own infertility? Could her obsessive mocking maybe even be said to be a factor in her infertility? Had she *manifested* her own infertility? Magical thinking is perfectly allowable. *All* thinking is magical, when you think about it, and anyway the only thing that makes *sense* to Aviva is magic. Magical people this way, please, keep it moving, and rational people that way. Besides which, there was almost nothing that couldn't be said to be a factor in infertility, it being such a mysterious, mystical predicament, hell, *punishment*, sure, why not: *punishment*, though people always got *suuuuuuuper*-duper upset when she said this.

"What did you think was going to *happen*?" the Rabbi wondered.

"I thought no one would listen to my shit!" she said. "I thought it would be like the one before, and the one before that! I thought a small handful of devoted oddballs would adore me and the rest would ignore me, as per usual! I thought I'd sort of sneak in from the side. I thought I'd continue being this unmarketable freak!"

"Well," he said. "Oops."

She was having recurring dreams in which a furious schoolmarm army marched toward her, a thousand fingers sternly wagging, their footfalls her own pounding heartbeat. And she'd wake in a sweat, which indicated low progesterone, which rendered the womb inhospitable.

"You choose the path of most resistance," the tarot queen of the Berkshires had said. "You find the negative in everything."

Ohhhhh: Was *that* why she never got pregnant?

* * *

She attempted the *Rolling Stone* thing: *A huge commitment to social media is good for, like, if you are on a bunch of antidepressants and antianxiety meds but you still crave some sensation and you're curious about insomnia, and, like, really excited to try out some sleeping meds. It's good the same way really cheap imitation high fashion feels good, which is to say if you don't give a shit about the quality of the material or the tailoring or the fit or the longevity of the item or the lives of the people who make it possible. Or the consequences of having all that disposable crap piling up. Like FYI there's so much disposable fast fashion happening now that charitable organizations can't handle the volume of constant donations. They sell it in giant hundred-pound blocks to "developing" nations. And it's so cheap and disposable in those "developing" nations that there is in fact a line of clothing at a high-high-end shop in LA made up of vintage T-shirts that were donated to African countries decades ago, worn to holes but then bought back and affixed with rhinestones and patches and shit, so "authentic" that they're selling for like a hundred dollars apiece. A roiling seductive sea of waste with occasional sparkle, very occasional substance, and no end in sight, that's what social media is. And obviously just level-ten crack-addictive.*

Aviva had browsed that high-high-end shop last time she was in LA, incidentally, and contemplated buying a thusly bedazzled Joy Division tee. So much newly disposable income at her fingertips! In the nick of time she had realized the tee was horrible and gone next door to see what was happening at American Rag.

She tried again. Focus. What did she think of social media?

Okay: *At puberty, I was really horrified by my body hair, which was overwhelming and unacceptable. I developed a pretty close relationship with tweezers, and used to sit for hours pulling hair. Sad little hirsute bunny. I've since learned about trichotillomania, the obsessive pulling of hair from the body. I still find hair removal, on my own terms, to be quite amazingly soothing. When I'm tempted to spend time online I'll sometimes get out the tweezers and sit in my bathtub and just pull out leg hair, one at a time. I can do it for hours. Once I may have dislocated my hip, trying to get an ingrown on the back of my calf. It's kind of meditative and kind of escapist and kind of pathological and kind of fun and kind of psycho and kind of productive and an objectively huge waste of time.*

No. Again: *A steady stream of happy orange/red/yellow/blue validations. Likes begetting likes. Being into each other being into stuff. Being happy about each other liking each other's liking. You have to keep it up ("it": reminding people of your existence, or "it": reminding people how cool and accomplished you are, or "it": reminding people how funny and self-deprecating you are, or reminding people how sexy and alluring you are, or reminding people how happily ensconced in familial life you are, or reminding people how woke you are) in order to continue being the object of the orange-red-yellow-blue bling-blong ding-dongs. Everyone likes a gal who's into being liked. You have to want to be liked in order to be liked. If you don't care about being liked, you are unlikable, simple as that. What a buncha programmed fucking idiots we are, huh? Apocalypse cannot come soon enough.*

Try again: *Social media is affecting our language. Our evolving colloquial. Language is a living thing. I pretend to abhor social media but am actually studying it, watching it. A curious phenomenon, a fascinating monster. Admire deeply the people who keep it completely at bay; pity those who seem to have integrated it entirely; reside somewhere in between, ambivalently, with the rest of the jagoffs who comprise this dumbass race.*

She was overthinking it.

Both/and, she wrote. *It's a both/and thing.*

Could that suffice?

Finally she attempted a meditation on lovely little Harmie Shmendrickson, who had appeared today wearing a witty little purple satin hat made to look like a regal old-Hollywood head wrap, complete with rhinestone pin at the apex.

And in the end *Rolling Stone* killed the feature.

A high school classmate who'd never spoken to Aviva found her backstage in Baltimore: "OMG your album is *amazing*! You're, like, *huge*! Are you *thrilled?* I mean, are you just over the *moon?*" She leaned in close: "I can't talk to you or else I'll lose my shit. I can't listen to anything else right now. I'm obsessed with you. My twins are three. I love them so much. *So* much. But I haven't been right . . . since. I really haven't been okay. Everyone made it seem like no big deal. I thought it was no big deal. Everyone made it *seem* like no big deal. But I've never been the same. I think it really messed me up. I just haven't been . . . You are the biggest relief, dude, oh my *God*. Just to finally admit that I'm *not* crazy, you know? That it *wasn't* no big deal."

Aviva opened her arms to this woman, stood there hugging her, and— the absolute height of generosity—let the woman decide when the hug was over.

She caught a sad and terrible cold, though it did give her voice a nice raw edge. Deja was made of sturdier stuff and did not succumb to sickness. Aviva fell asleep to pay-per-view. She ate all the sugar, dairy, wheat, coffee. She failed to stay offline. She masturbated to sleep, thinking of Sam, of Derrick from the plane, of art camp composer (oh yeah, he was liking *all* her posts lately, wasn't he). So much for self-care.

Day thirty-seven: Philly. Day thirty-nine: Boston. The shows were getting rote. Her rings were too tight. Bowels, too. And the telltale chin zit, in full force. Her tits seemed to have doubled in density, and ached like motherfuckers.

The exhaustion was such that she began to entertain the possibility of actually being pregnant. It wasn't impossible: She had bid Sam farewell around day, what, twelve? She might really possibly be, like, for sure, maybe not-impossibly pregnant. She *felt* pregnant, maybe? She felt *totally* pregnant, in a way? Perhaps. And so she allowed herself to indulge in the possibility, allowed herself to *behave* as though she *might* actually be pregnant, which was crucial, and changed everything.

Casual browsing of chic organic cotton maternity basics. Cozier clothing, softer layers. She shut down her phone earlier and earlier at night. Drank herbal tea and turned off the lights. Most miraculously, she found she didn't want to murder everyone who popped up in her feed wrangling a baby or two or three or four.

Singer Aviva Rosner Doesn't Like Your "Engineered" Children was the headline of one of the national interviews, edited to make her sound unhinged. One thousand two hundred forty-two comments and counting.

You really stepped in it, Jerry said, with stars, bull's-eye, and the 100 emoji. The numbers are sooooo gooooood.

Here's a fucking number: day fucking forty. There's a number for you.

Ooooh, and lookie here, Aviva was an indie-rock magazine cover story. Forty thousand shares in nine days. Don't look at comments don't look at comments just a peek just a brief survey for curiosity's sake oh no, don't, don't, don't, oh shit fuck why *It's a good thing this miserable excuse for a human being can't have children / what an idiot science exists for a reason so that we can make use of it to get what we want and cure diseases and fix everything that's wrong with the world jeez / You're my spirit animal don't ever stop / hate her voice / Amazing cunt from hell / needs to go get some meds I used to be a judgmental bitch but now I am honestly so much happier everyone should get medicated / Disgusting / THANK YOU / Die.*

Day, what, forty-one? Her tits *killed*, but she allowed herself to revel in the specific nature of the kill. They killed *beautifully*. They killed *purposefully*. And hey! Harmie Shmendrickson had cut her first tooth. Bravo, Harmie Harm.

Another hotel room and one more show, then one more hotel room and one final show. Here came the exhaustion headache. Hey there, exhaustion headache, hey. Go to sleep, sweetheart, she told herself kindly (*maternally!*) and obeyed, because what if she *was* pregnant? Because she was definitely maybe possibly pregnant, yep, and so her exhaustion was sacred, and so *she* was sacred, and so sleep was sacred, and so she slept.

Day forty-three. *Definitely* pregnant. Maybe. Probably? For *sure*, possibly. Oh my God, lucky girl! She had herself a (possible?) secret. A *future*.

Lucky, lucky duck: she'd eaten the right combinations of guru-approved foods on the right days and she'd visualized properly and hoped hard enough and waited and waited and consumed the correct Chinese herbs in the correct dosages and put her legs up the wall after orgasm and done her time and now, now, at last, the magic had (maybe!?) taken place. At laaaaast . . . All those singers droning on about love and heartbreak and romance and death, cool; but give me any random tone-deaf soulless barren bitch any day for the real shit regarding the essence of yearning.

She bought pee sticks, which for some reason (the need to immediately confirm a positive or negative? Capitalism?) only came in packs of two. The first was negative. False negatives were legion. She peed on the second. Also negative. But pee sticks could be wrong, couldn't they? Especially in the early days.

An eleven-minute compilation of Amy "out and about" with the paparazzi in hot pursuit. There she was, leaning out of a parked car. There she was, going into a bodega for cigarettes and juice. There she was, stuck in traffic on a highway, wandering between the cars, bumming cigarettes off strangers and signing autographs. So thin and furious and bizarre, wearing those filthy pink ballet slippers. The ratty beehive. This was the persona entombed in collective memory. She's pissed at the paps, but she's also in conversation with them, performing for them. Insolent, haughty. She hikes up her top to sunbathe her midriff, leaning against a car. So, so thin. Working hard at proving her invulnerability. Talk about a losing game!

The paps were camped outside her front door, now, and she emerged holding a tank top, asking who had children, whose children might wear this tank top, because she did not need it. She handed it to one of them. *Cheers*, the pap said. *Awright*, she replied. Pranced back inside the house and closed the door.

Now she was coming home late at night with a girlfriend. They hurried in only to emerge shortly thereafter with steaming mugs, and Amy graciously served the paps some tea: *This one has sugar; this one no sugar.* Handed over a box of biscuits. Mothering them, her wayward charges.

Sometimes I feel like the mother of the world, as the Smog song went.

Aviva had *nothing* in common with Amy. Aviva was neither as gifted nor as self-destructive. What Aviva wanted was to curl up with a heating pad and take a weeklong nap.

In Maine the applause swelled and crashed; like the sea, it could carry you away. She wasn't shy about taking it. Yeah, that's right, let's hear it for *me*, people!

Tessa showed up backstage. Aviva's brother Rob already knew he was dying when he and Tessa started going out, but they'd had a few good years together before Rob bit the big one. Tessa had been there through all of it, right to the end. Tessa had stayed by his side.

These days, Tessa lived on a small farm with a bunch of animals, her perfectly nice husband, some almost-grown stepchildren. She wasn't on social media. You had to make a singular effort to connect with Tessa, and who really had time for singular effort at personal connection?

"Let's go get food," Aviva said.

"What do you feel like?"

"Some high vibrational stuff. Farm-to-table me, biznatch."

"You paying?" Always a money thing with Tessa.

"Yeah, I'm paying."

Soon enough they were eviscerating some delicious roast chicken the chef had raised and killed himself.

"I heard you on NPR! You sounded good. *Sexy.*"

"Aim to please."

"Are you enjoying all this?"

"I don't get off on it, if that's what you mean. The fun part is messing around in private, in secret, when the songs belong to *me*. The fun part is seeing what I can *do*. Finding out what the songs want to be. This part is bullshit. What matters is over."

"It could still be fun, I imagine. The . . . attention?"

"No, now I'm just a puppet or a punching bag, changes by the minute. Whatever. I'm glad things are going 'well,' but all that means is that I'm getting my chain yanked. Fame is the grossest thing in the world, Tess. Maybe I thought otherwise when I was a freaking child, but lemme tell you: anyone who gets a taste of it and still thinks it's the good stuff has got to be a fucking moron. And I'm just experiencing the smallest hint of it, here."

"What's going on with you and Sam?"

"Oh, you know." Aviva wasn't in the mood. But this was *Tessa*. Aviva had wept a thousand tears alongside Tessa. There was no need to be guarded with Tessa. "We are . . . available . . . for a child . . . Wide-open. Waiting patiently. Quietly hoping. It's been, uh . . . hard . . . that it hasn't . . . happened . . . yet. It's . . . yeah."

Rob had had his sperm frozen before the first round of chemo, but Tessa had not wanted to make use of it after his death. Barb and Chuck, the grieving parents, offered it to her repeatedly. Politely, at first, bashfully, almost, then increasingly insistently: USE OUR DEAD SON'S SPERM, GODDAMN IT. They had offered to *pay* Tessa, set up trust funds, take care of the child for life. And after they'd finally given up on Tessa, Barb had talked about hiring a surrogate. Chuck convinced her to drop it, on the reasonable grounds that Rob himself would have been appalled by the idea. "But Rob isn't *here*, is he," Barb had said, trying to get Aviva on her side. As long as his jizz remained in a state of suspended animation, Rob still sort of existed. Rob was still *theirs*, practically speaking. There was life in the dead boy yet! Hope never fully died until Rob's jizz was taken out with the biohazardous waste the month Chuck finally stopped paying the rent. Barb still couldn't speak of Rob or anything Rob-related without shaking—practically seizing—in anger. Chuck couldn't speak of Rob or anything Rob-related without choking up and having to immediately change the subject. Aviva's sad-sack psycho-sadist surviving brother, Mike, couldn't talk about Rob at all, or *anything* at all, with *anyone*. Tessa was officially the only person left in the world who had known Rob and with whom Aviva could actually discourse on the subject of Rob. Tessa was a good egg (so to speak).

"So what now? What next? Are you going to . . . do anything, or . . . ?"

"Like what? Oh, like hop on the fertility train? I would honestly rather eat literal shit, Tess. That game isn't for me. And as it turns out that's *such* an offensive thing to feel. Or think. I've lost track of which one I'm doing at any given moment. Thinking? Feeling? Whatever: the message is loud and clear that I'm not supposed to be doing either, at least publicly. They're indistinguishable, though, aren't they? Thinking and feeling? Braided up. At least in me. Or does owning that make me some kind of demonic witch who should be locked up somewhere and hosed down in a room with a drain?"

"I can see how the PR isn't your thing."

Aviva had woken up last night drenched in a particularly foul sweat. Her hair was greasy and limp. Textbook late-stage luteal. Extended, stagnant luteal. She wasn't pregnant. Of course she wasn't fucking pregnant. Screw the fertility guru's menu, screw the acupuncturist, screw the holistic MD in the suburban guesthouse, screw the app, screw everything.

She flagged their server.

"Can I have a vodka tonic with two limes, please?"

"Can I see some ID?"

"Wow, guy. Wow. Sure. Here you go."

Tessa was staring at Aviva with shining eyes. "Hon, you want kids, yes?"

"I do! I do. I can't help it. I do."

"You've *always* wanted kids."

"I want a lot of things, though. I want this one sack dress in every textile on earth. I want to live in Mexico City for a while. I want to have some bespoke two-tone cowgirl boots made in either red and white or tan and white or turquoise and white, I can't decide. I want so many things, Tess. I want some kind of killer modern Danish light fixture for the house. And maybe a tulip table. I want to be able to do a headstand without the wall. I want my enemies to fade into the hellfire of obscurity forever. I want to do a ten-day silent meditation retreat; I hear those things rearrange your *mind.* I want to go to Belize. I want to do ayahuasca in the jungle. I want my body worshipped by a different perfect anonymous brilliant disease-free stranger in a hotel room outside of time once or twice a year. I want all *kindsa* stuff, Tess."

"You told me when we met that you were going to have *five* kids. You wanted *me* to have *Rob's* baby after he was gone."

"I was fifteen, dude. And everybody wanted you to have Rob's baby."

"Except for Rob."

"Well, the dead are known for surrendering all want. That's what makes them so fascinating and terrifying and unknowable, right?"

"You even said you'd raise it with me."

"I would have. It would have been fun. It's not too late!"

"I'm forty-seven, babe. It's been too late for a long time."

"Forty-seven is *nothing* to fertility doctors. They'll fuck you *up* for the right price, honey pie. They'll fuck you *sideways* at forty-seven if you've got the cash. Come on. The NICUs have quintupled in size over the past couple decades because of this shit."

"What's a NICU?"

"Neonatal intensive care unit. The babies don't always come out so juicy and ripe when they're experimentally forced upon the unwilling bodies of the aged."

Tessa shook her head as though to dislodge this information. "You've always wanted kids, is my point."

"Yeah, well, want is not recognized as a great spiritual virtue, in my best understanding."

"Why not just see what your options are? You don't have to do anything you don't want to do. Just explore what's available. There's nothing wrong with getting a little help."

"I *am* getting help. There's this guru who tells you exactly what foods to eat at exactly which point in your menstrual cycle. I'm supposed to be eating lamb right now, but fuck it. Believe you me, I am getting *help.* I am getting like forty different *kinds* of help. Do I not seem *helped*? I go to acupuncture *constantly*. I go to like five *different* acupuncturists. I got a whole workup from this Celtic MD in her guesthouse. I have a Maya Abdominal therapist, Tess. I have a shrink. I have a midwife. There's an Ayurvedic nutritionist I might check out. There's a new app with a digital thermometer and it's, like, AI or something. Believe you me, I am getting *help*. Do you know how much my *probiotics* cost?"

A different server came by and replaced Aviva's empty with a fresh.

"On the house," she said with a wink. "Big fan."

Aviva was too stunned to respond.

"I'm just saying," Tessa said. "Maybe there's some simple medical thing that will make all the difference. How will you know if you don't try?"

"It doesn't work that way, believe me. You get on that train and it don't stop 'til you're broke, with cancer. It's a deal-with-the-devil sort of situation. The only decent path available here—and, arguably, in general—is to make peace with exactly what is. L'chaim!"

Day forty-five. Force of attention notwithstanding, there was still never any telling what was going on with her cycle, which was, at base, a flagrant bitch. You weren't supposed to badmouth it, though: your cells absorbed negative self-talk! Sorry, cells. Okay: not a flagrant bitch, per se. How about: a slowly but surely evolving *work in progress*.

Burlington, Vermont. End of the line.

In line for stupid-fancy coffee, a tap on the shoulder.

"Excuse me . . . ?"

She turned around. What offense had she caused? She was sorry, whatever it was. She was sorry, okay? She meant no offense. What. What.

"Excuse me, forgive me, but . . . aren't you . . . Aviva?"

Oh God, *what*.

"I'm really sorry to bother you, but I just have to tell you, I've been listening to your new album, like, nonstop, and I, I desperately needed it. I *love* you. I saw you last night. My best friend saw you in Texas. You're just—you're amazing."

"That's . . . nice to hear. Thank you."

"I'm so sorry to bother you; I just *had* to. This must get really annoying."

"Not at all."

"I can't believe it's you! Just—thank you, that's all. Your music makes me feel so much less alone."

Deja drove her home, and Aviva began to bleed on the way. The cycle had a sense of humor, at least. As was often said of "God." She met it with acceptance and resignation. She bought pads at a rest stop. "All righty," she sang into the cavernous, empty, white-tiled bathroom. Fabulous acoustics. According to the guru, a healthy flow started slowly and easily, bright red and consistent. This one was an immediately clotted dirty river of black death.

Aviva's reflection in the fluorescent light over the sink came a shock: matted hair, last week's eyeliner, greenish skin, sunken eyes.

But isn't it dangerous *to reduce women to their menstrual cycles?* the writers and critics and Twitt-heads demanded. *Isn't that what we've fought so hard against?!* Yes and no, Aviva had spent all these long, hard, pointless weeks repeating on stages and across tables and in hotel rooms and recording booths. No and yes. Maybe! Sort of! Not at all! Absolutely! Whatever! I don't know! But no matter: let it all drain out. This had been a bad one. A long and hard one. So be it. She had made it to the other side, and now she would bleed and bleed and bleed, and feel better and better and better, until it was all gone.

Then it would begin again.

3

BODY

Her train arrived at Penn Station, unholy fart box, from which she emerged up and out into the center of the universe. You couldn't help but work a swing into your step while walking through this exceptionally big shitty, and no one would give you a second glance. Unless they did, in which case, great! Worry a refrain over and over. Beat it into the pavement with your feet. Enlist unsuspecting bystanders. Orchestrate and art direct and let it flow around and through you. Whatever's stuck in your head, assuming you're the sort with music perpetually stuck in your head, which, if you're not, well, bless your heart and fare thee well. New York fuckin' City: jam sesh, dance party, musical theater. Every dorky, heartfelt show tune ballad that ever stirred the ball of muscle in her chest.

The streets, the bikes, the cars, the canopy of buildings: everything man-made! Feats of engineering, going back centuries. Testament to human ingenuity, for real, although a couple hijacked jets or a hurricane or a virus or an outsized lizard/ape/Stay Puft Marshmallow Man could make it cower and beg for mercy. Still: more could transpire over seventy-two hours here than was possible in a month, a year, a decade anywhere else. Notice the folks you're not supposed to notice, the ones who make the coffee and sling the cocktails and serve the food and answer the phones and suck the dicks and check the coats. Ignore the basic bitches in town for a day of shopping and leisure. That group of well-heeled women near Macy's shivering miserably in their new spring jackets. Mid-April, and everyone desperate for spring, but still an obnoxious chill in the air. Dress for the weather, people. The weather is in charge. The weather is God.

Follicular phase, and the world was Aviva's oyster. Aviva was her *own* oyster: the precious pearl of possibility within. She was unflappable. She was unstoppable. Her metabolism tip-top. She was practically a *dude* in follicular phase. Be a good girl, Aviva, play your cards right, no sugar no coffee no weed no bread no dairy no alcohol no negative thoughts no obsessive nostalgia, asleep before ten, plenty of sunshine and fresh air and movement and breath and relaxation and boundaries and positivity. *Be* the mother you wish to become; *earn* your precious progeny. Do right by the body and the body will do right by you.

Four hundred light-flooded prewar square feet in a quiet corner of the West Village. Of course she'd held on to her apartment, was she a fucking idiot? All well and good to fall in love with an Albany High School civics teacher and go play house and garden in the boonies, but let go of her *apartment*? Are you friggin' *nuts*? A room of her own. They'd have to pry it from her cold, dead hands.

Down payment from all the simultaneously dead grandparents plus good old Rob, who, obsessed with computers and sci-fi and "the future" and the stock market, had seen fit to invest his 1982 bar mitzvah money in a small computer company he liked, named for the forbidden fruit, on whose latest model Aviva was known to murder hours staring at the self-presentations of people she barely knew.

And! *Speaking* of easy money falling from the sky, five years ago there had appeared a massive check from her father. It was only fair, Chuck reasoned, given that he'd paid for Mike and What's-Her-Face's IVF, that he gift Aviva the same amount. He was meticulous about giving Mike and Aviva exactly the same resources, fair and square. Mike and Aviva needed no help despising each other; Chuck wasn't going to give them reason to fight over money, too. So shortly after the twins' blessed, preterm arrival,

Aviva had received a check for their *exact dollar value*. Mike and What's-Her-Face had gotten a perfectly engineered, portrait-ready family; Aviva had gotten some easy-breezy cash flow. The twins were cute and all, but easy-breezy cash flow was pretty fucking cute, too. So she owned the place outright and the monthly maintenance and co-op fees were perfectly do-able given that Sam had been paying off *his* little house for years. And let's not forget the nice check from the dumb TV dramedy over whose closing credits Aviva could be heard singing her dumb heart out. Thus, wonder of wonders, miracle of miracles, she was solvent. Be grateful for abundance when it comes, Hanalei always said, and grateful for scarcity when it comes, and learn from both, and do not get attached to either. Not the soundest money-management advice, but it sounded right when Hanalei said it.

The ceiling plaster had a couple new cracks. Construction noise from a huge new condo high-rise three blocks away rattled the gently sloping wide-plank floors, the tapestry over the mattress on the floor. Aviva lay with her legs up the wall and peered into the portal. Harmie Shmendrickson was at the playground, trying out a baby swing and laughing her ass off. Look at that pure, joyful smile. Look at the sparkle in those eyes. There was nothing remotely weird about Harmie. Harmie was perfect. A perfect little human spark. Who cared how she had gotten here?

Aviva's old bandmate Jameela in Toronto texted a torso selfie: nestled in her armpit was the small plastic container holding her husband's ejaculate; this was how she had been instructed to keep it warm while she took a car to the clinic to be inseminated.

Mommy, where do babies come from? Well, pumpkin, Mommy and Daddy loved each other very much and we kept buying furniture and clothes and going on vacations to cool places and getting shit-faced on the regular but that was getting surprisingly boring and we were kind of getting old, so we wanted to make sure you were born 'cause dogs don't always live super long and anyway we didn't really have any other vision for our middle years or old age and also when all your friends have kids you start to feel like a loser if you don't, so early one morning Daddy masturbated to this one particular sort of site about naked ladies who are missing different pieces of their bodies, like arms or fingers or legs or hands (everybody likes different kinds of sites, you see), and when he was very happy with the site he sort of peed happiness into a little container and Mommy put it in her armpit to keep it warm and drove straight to an office in a big tall building, where it was chemically treated by a lady with super-awesome purple glitter gel tips so that the weak ugly dumb sperm were burned up and thrown away and the strongest/best got sucked up into a giant needle, which then got inserted by an okay doctor with a comb-over who'd really wanted to be a sports doctor but his grades weren't competitive enough so he became a reproductive endocrinologist instead through Mommy's forcibly dilated cervix and into her womb, where we already knew there was an egg waiting because we saw it on the ultrasound, and also Mommy the day before got a shot of hormones synthesized from pregnant rat urine to trick the egg into coming out! And nine months later, there you were, a precious gift from a mysterious god. Life is miraculous, you see.

A trend piece about wealthy single older men arranging offspring for themselves using surrogates: *You reach a point in life and say, I have absolutely everything, but I don't have this.*

A starlet's confessional: *Why I Froze My Eggs.*

A story about scientists hashing out the ethics of ectogenesis: *Imagine, we could potentially free women from childbearing entirely!*

A congenial couple crowdfunding their fertility treatment: *We did it for our honeymoon, so we thought, "Why not?"*

Once you got hip to the through-line, it was everywhere, connecting everything. The through-line was money.

She had a lunch date, a podcast taping, an interview, appointments with the reproductive endocrinologist and the Rabbi, aaaaaaaand a two-night residency at a super-excellent, highbrow venue.

You manifested this, texted Hanalei.

More like worked my ass off for fifteen years, Aviva replied.

Same thing!!!!!!

Serena, the lunch date, texted to say she was having a *day*; could they push it back an hour?

No problem-o.

Hey, lady, called the stash of old cannabis mints over on the bookshelf. Hey, laaaaady, hey, pretty laaaady. How odd: the mints spoke in the same Australian voice as Aviva's robot concierge. Where you beeeeeen, pretty lady? I've missed you! Come over here and let me love you. The mints were ancient. Probably stale. A parting gift from an asshole ex—the Cracker—a few years back.

"I am concerned about your pretty little Jew lungs," Cracker had said, having recently quit smoking, himself. Aviva could get bronchitis from a strong breeze, so both vaping and smoking were increasingly out of the question. It was touching that Cracker cared about her well-being. "Can't have you messing up those precious Jew lungs," he said. "So *delicate*." She could still see him retrieving the little tin, his gift to her, from his overcoat pocket, an almost-imperceptible flourish in his wrist when he held it out to her, which she took as proof of his unspeakable everlasting loyalty and love. Which was moronic of her, and typical.

Do weed mints go bad? she asked her robot concierge.

No, they just became less potent. And she should leave them alone, regardless. Remember? The world was her oyster! She was her own oyster!

A story about human/pig chimeras being grown and experimented upon, using private funding: *It really raises questions about, you know, our humanity*, quoth a whistleblower who was roundly mocked by reproductive industry insiders.

A satiric op-ed by a TV writer: *Can You Keep My Embryos Frozen Until after They Go Through Puberty?*

If Aviva really wanted a baby so bad, she should absolutely, by this point, be giving herself hormone shots and letting lab coats regularly fuck her with ultrasound dildos. Because obviously it wasn't enough to cut out sugar and caffeine and weed and alcohol and dairy, and it wasn't enough to eat red meat once a month and pounds of veggies always and organic eggs constantly and unprocessed everything as much as possible, and it wasn't enough to slam avocados and turmeric ginger coconut lattes, and it wasn't enough to religiously take herbal tinctures and visit all the acupuncturists, and it wasn't enough to dutifully scour every fertility guru link not behind a paywall, and it wasn't enough to visualize and meditate and kvell over Harmie Shmendrickson, and it wasn't enough to carry rose quartz in her pocket.

Yoo-hoo, baaaaby, where *are* you? Baby, what the hell is *taking* you so long?? Are you in the ether? Can you hear me? I'm *waiting* for you, little one. Would you mind if I just have a tiny little nibble on one of these weak, old weed mints? It's plant medicine! Surely a little plant medicine won't dissuade you, darling. Come on: people get pregnant chain-smoking crack, scarfing antidepressants and benzos, pickled in booze, eating *all* the dairy and wheat and caffeine and sugar and canola oil and food dyes, nursing romantic and sexual obsession of the *very* worst kid, burning out their eyeballs on the *lamest* of feeds. Wouldn't desperate women with iffy access to birth control and abortion be overjoyed if a little junk food and weed and wallowing could block ovulation/conception/implantation?

She went ahead and popped a mint, then dialed up Rickie Lee Jones' *Naked Songs*. A raw, crooked voice in all its disheveled, piercing glory. Aviva and Sam had seen Rickie Lee in concert last year, fat and braless and laconic, bantering about having gotten addicted to online poker, and excoriating her guitar accompanist because he couldn't keep up.

Rickie Lee had managed to let go of vanity, or had maybe been forced to let go of vanity, and so she had survived, more or less (or less), artistically speaking, at least. Who might *Amy* have become if she'd let herself "go," given up on the industry or let the industry give up on her, cut it out with the wigs and costumes, reconciled herself to the indignities of time (and weather). Maybe she could have remained a conduit, like Rickie Lee, sitting there in her ugly stained T-shirt, with her big sagging tits and limp hair. Maybe she could have gone on to make weird, singular music that not everybody liked. Maybe she could have been free. No more hits! The biz would have forgotten about her *real* quick. Nobody went chasing after an artist who went her own way. "Because you don't want to fuck me anymore I don't matter?!" Rickie Lee laughed uproariously in a documentary nobody watched: *"Fuck you!"*

"What is the music you make if you don't have a *goal*?" Rickie Lee asked a Canadian radio host in a long filmed interview. The host, confounded and very possibly moved, said, simply: ". . . Huh."

What to wear to lunch? One couldn't dress for New York anyplace but New York. Serena would be wearing something obscure: whatever all the arty/rich girls were wearing right this minute and would abandon the moment the less-arty/less-rich girls caught on. How about: brown velvet drawstring pants, a shredded, ancient tank top with Courtney Love's deconstructed face on it, a nubby mustard-colored cardigan, and yellow clogs with socks, topped off with enormous fake gold hoops, purple lipstick, and dead Rob's jean jacket, worn paper-thin, coming apart at the seams. If you just went totally baroque-weird, you could often throw the arty/rich girls for a loop.

She marched up lower Fifth with Washington Square at her back. Rickie Lee had, alas, outlasted her utility. Dial up some Dinah Washington. Jazz, blues, pop, gospel: can't put ol' Dinah in a box. "Evil Gal Blues"! When the publicity was about Dinah's behavior, it was bad; when the publicity was about the music, it was good. Voice like that, you do as you please. Defiant Dinah. Loved her some Bessie, loved her some Billie. Only girl on the tour bus with the Lionel Hampton band before she struck out on her own. Nothing she couldn't sing: covered white music for Black audiences and brought Black music to white audiences. Voice that strong, she didn't even need a mic. First Black woman to cross all the way over: get a load of her in those 1950s Howard Johnson's jukeboxes. Awful taste in men, needless to say. Four husbands? One threw her down a flight of stairs, pregnant. Loved her furs. Even got a mink toilet seat cover when she made it huge. Would do anything to keep the weight off. Got real into pills. Speed, tranquilizers. Did her tough act onstage: don't you dare pity me; *I'm* the one telling *you* how it is.

"If I've had a bad day," Amy said, "I can still put on Dinah and say, you know what? It's nothing, it's *nothing*."

Aviva crossed Fourteenth Street, and damn, who says time travel isn't possible?

The autumn after college. Three roommates in a railroad apartment and a boring office job at an exclusive little management company between Seventeenth and Eighteenth, her boss an unrepentant sociopath. All the higher-ups very busy shitting themselves about staying ahead of "the web." (The Web! The industry's changing faster than anyone ever imagined! We need to stay ahead of The Web!) Aviva a lowly administrative assistant with *so* much time to kill, smoke breaks her only salvation. She met the Cracker under the tiny portico on Eighteenth, where the lowly assistants of the block congregated at ten forty-five a.m. and three forty-five p.m. on the dot. Cracker worked entry-level at a small but influential music magazine.

"Third floor," he told her by way of introduction.

"Fifth," she said.

He made a joke about Aviva being "on top," and thus began their demented little courtship.

Oh, shit, wait, Dinah, sorry. Pause. Apologies, Dinah, but your sonic granddaughter demands to take your place. That jaunty little horn overture: Oh, girl. Eighteen years old, with a boring office job, lusting after a guy at work, scolding herself for wasting her own time. Impossible not to strut to this. The winking twang of that one chord, and off we go, in full cahoots.

Cracker was just—as Amy warbled thrillingly over that excellent marching beat—*too hard to ignore*. Tall, skinny, knuckles not quite dragging on the floor but just about. White-trash punk from some godforsaken armpit of Alabama. Confederate drawl out in full force when he was drunk, which was nightly.

"Never met a real live Jew before," he said, expertly flicking his cig butt into the gutter. "In the flesh."

"I'm sure you have," she said. "A lot of us pass."

"Not you. You're *all* Jew."

"You do realize you're in New York."

"I'm new here," he said, awful twinkle in his eye.

That asshole made *all* Aviva's chakras light up. A drummer, it turned out. Moved to the city with his noise band when it looked like they might be on the verge, but nope: the lead singer jumped ship, went solo, got soft, and immediately hit it big. One night, that lead singer's dirge came on at the bar, and Cracker made a huge show of shuddering and writhing: *Turn this fucking miserable pussy tears bullshit OFF!*

No *way* was he going home to that Alabama armpit with his tail between his legs, so now he was living in Bushwick and fetching coffee at the small but influential music rag, going to shows, sorting through demo piles, writing arrogant little reviews, and drinking astonishing quantities of whiskey. Big Bukowski fan, and turned out to be pretty good at the industry job. Thinking about working his way up. Why the hell not? Buy an old typewriter, bang out a novel on the weekends with a burning cigarette dangling between his lips, how hard could it be? Aviva was pretty sure he was a genius, and greatly enjoyed torturing him with the probability that she was eventually going to sleep with him.

But—minor detail!—Aviva was concurrently engaged to marry a certain Jeff Lazar. Jeff Lazar, who'd been the basketball champion of Zionist summer camp. Jeff Lazar, who was getting his MBA and already had several job offers. Jeff Lazar, who was going to get filthy rich, and move back to LA with his bride, and buy a big house on a big hill with a big view. Jeff Lazar, who had a massive penis and keys to the castle. Their grandparents had been founding members of the same huge LA synagogue. *Of course* Aviva was going to marry Jeff Lazar.

She felt elderly already at twenty-two, felt the urgent need to set the course, "get things going" (read: begin having as many children as possible as soon as possible). Rob was fresh in the ground, Aviva's last two grandparents each had a foot in the grave, Mike was a sad-sack sadist zombie from hell, and her parents were all the way up their own assholes. It fell to Aviva to single-handedly repopulate the family, make the desert bloom. Jeff Lazar was the Answer. Some alcoholic antisemitic grease-stain drummer from the infected ass crack of Alabama was most certainly *not* the answer. (Unless the question was: Who's more likely to give you herpes?)

Aviva wore Jeff Lazar's big diamond ring with clear-eyed resolve and a sense of purpose. Marrying Jeff was akin to establishing a homeland. Do it for your people, beat the almost-insurmountable agricultural and military odds, don't worry about the ethical fallout from whatever has to be displaced. Press on, forge ahead, crush the opposition by any means necessary, the existence of a new homeland the only requirement. A moral imperative, even. She stopped taking the Pill months before the wedding, and they agreed on five children. The first three would be close in age, then a break before the last two. They kept a running list of names. Everything was going to be great.

Aviva worked her pointless nine-to-five, let her mother plan the wedding, flirted with Cracker on smoke breaks and instant messenger all day every day, tried and failed to keep up with him at the bar after work, then went home to Jeff's palatial apartment every night.

The cognitive dissonance inherent in this arrangement is perhaps the reason she also took up writing songs about growing up Jewish 'n' hirsute 'n' lusty 'n' lonesome. Jeff approved of her little hobby; thought her songs were "cute." *My folk singer*, he called her. She played open mics to which he invited all his bro friends. He wasn't a typical boring money guy; he was a *cool* money guy, with an arty wife-to-be. She applied to music school on a lark.

One night, Cracker came to see her at an ancient folk club in the village, revered by tourists, haunted by the ghosts of a thousand dead acts. "Oh, for fuck's sake, not another girl with a guitar," hollered Cracker when she got up. Jeff thought this hilarious, and they shared a heartwarming high five. But after her set, Cracker was strangely kind: "I don't know shit about whatever bullshit this is, but you awright, Jew-girl." This did way more for Aviva's confidence than the steady trickle of gig offers and scout business cards, the music school acceptance, and any amount of general applause. It was *Cracker* she was singing to and for, after all; *his* sensibility she cared about, *his* approval she craved. It was a *thing*. That guttersnipe just did it for her. The loins want what they want.

Jeff was consumed with school, unconcerned about his wife-to-be cavorting in bars and clubs with whomever, whenever. He didn't care about Aviva coming home smashed from drinks with "work friends," didn't notice her constant giggling at her computer. He *liked* that Aviva was a weird little musician freak with weird little musician freak friends. Jeff had quite the wandering eye of his own. They were *bashert* only in their longing for those five ghost babies.

Aviva lacked the guts to call off the wedding (and the existence of those babies), so she tried sabotage. She picked wicked fights, said horrible things to him, tried to make *him* dump *her*. One night, fresh off yet another knock-down-drag-out, she banished Jeff from the apartment, and went so far as to bring Cracker into their bed.

Alas, Cracker turned out to be a major disappointment in the sack. All that intense chemistry—where did it go? Without clothes on, there was *nothing* between them. His skin was pasty, he stank of liquor and cigarettes, and he was unable to sustain an erection.

"I'm just, uh, really into you," he muttered.

She assured him it was okay, but felt no mercy. When the sun came up there was this meek, skinny white dude in her apartment, wondering if perhaps she wanted to get *brunch*. Um, no, she did not want to get brunch. She ghosted him for a few days; he got the message. The incident scared her straight; she patched things up with Jeff and soon enough she and Cracker were back to cocktails and casual cruelties. Aviva even invited him to the doomed Malibu wedding that following summer. So magnanimous of her! He declined to attend.

She stormed City Bakery and hit the line like she owned it, too hungry to wait for Serena. The blood sugar wants what it wants. Spikes and crashes are disastrous for the nervous system, don'tcha know. Waiting for mac and cheese was an upstate weekender dude who occasionally subbed at Hanalei's studio. Intense older divorced guy, always a bit too keen to do forceful, unsolicited hands-on adjustments, but he'd actually helped Aviva quite a lot with her marichyasana D. He paused to move his messenger bag out of the way before giving her a too-strong hug.

"Hey, I listened to your album! You really don't hold back!" He was giving her an "I have your number" smirk. "I mean, don't get me wrong," he went on. "I liked it a lot; but I was just like, *damn* . . . All the stuff about your mother, and the sort of stream-of-consciousness stuff, and your whole . . . thought process. You're like: women are the *same as men*, they *think* about things and have . . . desire . . . and . . . anger . . . and *everything*!"

"Mmm."

"You're *something*! Got any shows coming up?"

"Doing a couple nights at the Knitting Factory this week."

Aviva spent so much energy downplaying it, so as not to get into sniffing her own shit. But it *was* an achievement, headlining a venue like that. It was, in fact, what lil' confused baby Aviva had once barely dared dream of. It was years of single-minded focus and work and commitment and sacrifice and desire and talent and craft and work and work and work. It was her life's fucking work. She had *manifested* it.

"Wow," the guy said. And then, after a beat, as if he were issuing a verdict: "Good for you."

She snared a prime table under the big front window. Serena texted: three blocks away! SORRY! There was an elderly gentleman at the next table. He leaned over with a flirtatious/menacing grin and gestured at Aviva's generously loaded food tray. "That all for you?"

"I'm pregnant," she told him brightly.

The old man *beamed*.

"Well!"

"With *triplets*, actually."

"Oh! Goodness! Wow! You look . . . great!"

"Don't I, though?"

Nothing better than shaming a shamer. O, glorious, sunshiny shame, most inveterately lucrative emotion that ever there was. She ate while pretending to read a memoir about anal sex and existentialism, eavesdropping on the elderly gentleman and the young colleague who soon joined him. They were discussing real estate deals in Iowa, Rhinebeck, Queens. The old man, it turned out, was a subordinate. He had messed something up in one of the deals, and was being chastised. The anal-sex-existentialism memoir was pretentious and boring, so she switched to the portal.

Ran into a bitch I hate and had to chat but rlly omw now, texted Serena.

A guy from elementary school marked his daughter's fourth birthday with nine photos and a long paean to his tagged wife: *the most incredible mommy in the whole wide world.* Kid looked all right. Wife looked all right. Good for them! Like! A girl from a literary agency on the ninth floor who had dated Cracker for a while (read: tried and failed to keep up with him at the bar) announced the publication of a "very personal" personal essay about the death of her dog. A bassist of whom Aviva was moderately fond showed off a new calf tattoo, all shiny with vitamin E: a pair of flaming dice rolled to two and three. Like! Several people were very upset about the political outrage of the day. Someone from college was raising money to make a documentary about her father, who had turned out to be a serial adulterer with at least one secret family. Someone was on vacation somewhere tropical. Someone was on vacation somewhere freezing. Someone was very glad she had gotten an IUD even though she was still bleeding six weeks later. The venue tagged Aviva in a publicity pic. Her tits looked awesome, but the thing about having big tits was that it was so much harder to be taken seriously. Someone went on a bender about how empty life had been before she got the precious gift of her perfect twins. Someone opined about why the new generation is dumb and useless. Someone's father was dying. Someone opined about why the old generation is dumb and useless. Someone's mother died five years ago today. Someone shared a list of the greatest dance albums of all time. Someone described her miscarriage in great detail, though she was unclear on the difference between a fetus and an embryo.

Serena finally showed up, emaciated in next year's jeans, and limited-edition sneakers.

"Fuck, did you already eat? No worries, I'm not even hungry. This *day*, fuck me, *fuck* me, this *day*. Fuck *me*, I'm so happy to see you!"

Her hair hung to her ass, brown to the shoulders and shocking-white blond the rest of the way. She had been junior art department at an ad agency on the twelfth floor at good old lower Fifth, and had been under the portico for all those smoke breaks, out for all those cocktails. She had confirmed, with conspiratorial glee, the foul sexual magnetism of the Cracker. And now, all these years later, she had two small, indistinguishable girl children, a loser trust-fund-baby husband, a jaw-dropping Williamsburg condo loft, a hugely successful "brand consulting company," an office of her own on lower Fifth, and a hundred thousand followers. She and Aviva had zero in common, needless to say, but it was supposed to be virtuous and right to hang on to old friends, wasn't that so?

The chastised old real estate gentleman at the next table agreed to watch their stuff while they went back up to get coffee. Aviva wound up with a shot of hot chocolate, an espresso, a marshmallow, *and* a cookie. The triplets were hungry.

"*Get it*, girl," Serena said. "I love how you just don't give a shit."

"Pretty . . . pretty . . . pretty stoned," Aviva said. "And the cookie's to share. And anyway, I'm follicular, so . . . fuck it!"

"What's follicular?"

"You're telling me you don't know the phases of the menstrual cycle?" Serena blinked.

"You're seriously telling me you're almost forty motherfucking years old and the biological mother of two *daughters* and you don't know the *phases of your menstrual cycle*?"

"Sue me, Menstrual Police. Jesus. And I am still a *ways* from forty, fuck you very much."

"You're telling me you posted a thousand selfies in a pink knit cap marching on fucking Washington for women's rights with your daughters in tow and you—"

"Fucking *okay*, V. Teach me."

"Your ovaries gear up to mature a new egg: follicular. Your ovaries release the mature egg: ovulation. Your egg travels down the fallopian tubes into the uterus, where it begins to rot and you feel increasingly like shit: luteal. You bleed: menstrual. And the cycle begins anew."

"Awesome, thanks. Consider me schooled."

"Don't be a twat; body literacy is hot!"

The chastised real estate subordinate did a double take, and Serena leaned in to whisper: "How stoned are you?"

"Long-expired edible. But I'm a *famous musician*, you know, so. 'Tis to be expected."

"Speaking of *which*! Saw you in Arts and Leisure. Crushing it. You have *arrived*, friend."

"*Hineini.*"

"Is that another menstrual cycle reference?"

"In a way, yes."

"It's good to see you but it's kind of hard to talk to you when you're stoned."

"Well, it's kind of hard to talk to you when I'm *not* stoned, Boob, so let's just split this cookie and get on with our lives."

Serena plastered a fake smile across her face. "What else are you up to while you're in town?"

"Couple of interviews. Shows. Shrink. And . . . a doctor's appointment tomorrow."

"What *kind* of doctor?"

"You know, the kind that . . . jacks you up . . . for childbearing."

"NYU?"

"Columbia."

"*Finally.* They'll have you pregnant in thirty seconds, then you have to have the second one as soon as possible—it's a hell ride but so *much* better to just have them back-to-back, get it over with—and you can be done *well* before you're forty. Which, trust me, is what you want. I'm so glad you're putting pedal to metal on this. *Love* that jacket, by the way."

"Dead brother," Aviva sang, preening. Serena's cue to take and tag a photo. What was the point of hanging out with Serena if Serena wasn't going to pimp Aviva to her hundred thousand followers?

"Is that a new label?"

"No . . . as in, it used to belong to my dead brother."

"Oh. Sorry. It's cute. I'm kind of out of it right now, between you and me. It's not public, but—Chad moved out." Chad was forever moving out and back in and back out. It would pass, and in no time Serena would be back to tagging him in posts about how great it was to be married to your best friend. "He's with some fucking performance artist this time." Serena said the woman's name, and Aviva giggled. Chad usually went for a simpler type. Interesting move, Chad.

"How are the girls?"

It took Serena a minute to realize Aviva was referring to her two small children. "Oh, fine. They're cuties. How's . . ." Serena legit could not recall the name of Aviva's husband.

"Sam?"

"Sam! Yes . . . the hot teacher from Syracuse."

"Albany. He's great."

Aviva left it at that, lest she arouse Serena's jealousy, also known as the evil eye. We downplay our blessings, we who are in touch with the demon forces. We keep our blessings at least partially hidden from view, lest the demon forces rise up to claim what we hold dear. You have to be clueless and untouched to wantonly parade your blessings. If Aviva were to tell Serena the truth—*Sam's a princely soul with an endless hard-on for me and only me; he is so obsessed with me that it actually gets slightly annoying sometimes; he thinks the sun shines out of my butthole, and he's endlessly patient and gentle and kind, or as gentle as a person with a constant raging hard-on for you can be*—Sam would surely drop immediately dead. The "universe" (or: "God") was a sick joker, so play it cool.

She really shouldn't see Serena anymore. Fuck what they said about hanging on to old friends. Throw your old friends onto the goddamned pyre.

"Are you still in touch with . . . you-know-who?"

Cracker. Had Serena been reading Aviva's mind?

"No," Aviva said, failing to affect airy indifference. "You?"

"You know we fucked once, right?"

"I did not know that, no."

"Sorry I never told you. I just . . . didn't want it to be weird between us."

"Why would it be weird between us?"

Aviva's marriage to Jeff had lasted all of six months. What a humiliating mess: massive wedding, piles of gifts, heavy custom leather-bound photo album. She fled the Malibu wreckage of Kitchen-Aid mixers and bath towels and hopes and dreams—their five unborn children, writhing in the void!—and washed back up on the shores of her old life in New York, where she had, good for her, gotten into music school. Jeff stayed in LA, where he was starting a business management firm catering to the entertainment industry.

Aviva found an outstanding, undermarket apartment in Boerum Hill and taught private guitar lessons to tween girls whose mothers were bummed to have missed out on riot grrrl. They flirted with Aviva in their freshly remodeled brownstone kitchens.

Inevitably, she wound up drunk in bed with Cracker once again.

They were more efficient this time. They had unresolved business. A score to settle. They took care of it, Aviva on top.

"This doesn't feel so . . . protected," Cracker calmly observed.

She made a dismissive gesture: they didn't have to worry about such quotidian matters. More than a year of unprotected sex with Jeff had yielded . . . nothing. The dawning awareness that unwanted pregnancy was not going to be her problem in this lifetime. Cracker maneuvered her onto her back and immediately came all over her tits. She lay there covered in it while he went to the bathroom and returned with a soaking-wet washcloth, which he held three feet above her, and, without comment, dropped. She flinched. It was cold. An unfriendly gesture, to say the least, but Aviva played it off as a joke. And this time it was *Aviva* who thought it might be the beginning of something between them, and this time it was *Cracker* who ghosted the shit out of her for a few weeks thereafter. And so the score was settled.

Turned out he had found himself a proper girlfriend while Aviva was out west having her wedding portrait taken in Vera Wang: an aging Swedish former model who did PR for a chain of yoga studios. The aging former model did Cracker good. He'd cut down on the booze and cigarettes and started going to the gym and discovered shampoo and gotten a promotion. It was serious with the model. Fine! Good. What did Aviva care? She could separate sex from emotion, thankyouverymuch! She considered Cracker a friend. An *old* friend. Make new friends but keep the old, both are bullshit and will leave you alone to die in the cold. The aging Swedish former model seemed like a decent-enough sort. And, anyway, soon thereafter, Aviva met her one and only Sammy-Sam, with whom she attended Cracker's wedding.

Serena was still talking: "Chad and I went to dinner with them a couple years ago, and man, is she a cold fish. They bought a house in Bed-Stuy, but they summer in the south of France. I think she's actually connected to the royal family of Sweden, or something. He really traded in his balls for a couple trips to Europe, huh?"

Aviva hadn't seen Cracker in years, now. They'd had that final meetup in the basement bar, when Cracker gifted Aviva the tin of now-stale (though still pretty strong!) weed mints, and they'd traded final confessions. Aviva's: maybe she wasn't cut out for this whole upstate-housewifery thing. Cracker's: he and the former model had been struggling to have a child. Every procedure, the best doctors in town, and nothing to show for it but piles of bills. "Alls I know is I'm not adopting one of those Russian orphans," he said. "Those little fuckers are *all* kinds of messed up."

And thereafter, he avoided Aviva every time she was in town, until gradually/suddenly she understood: he had eighty-sixed her entirely. Their friendship was no more. It stung worse than she expected it to. "Stagnation" was Aviva's usual Eastern medicine diagnosis: she couldn't let go of anything. Stagnation in the liver, the bowels, the lymph, the reproductive organs, and the contact list on her phone. Damp, swampy stasis. A tender heart grows bitter in the end. She had never been dumped so fully. She obsessed about it for a long time. Why?

"Because his wife doesn't like you," said Jerry.

"Because he's still in love with you," said the Rabbi.

"Because you represent something he's closed down in himself," said Hanalei.

"Because he's jealous of you," said Serena.

Cue the Shirelles: *Foolish little girl, fickle little girl, you didn't want him when he wanted you.* Cracker was now a high-up industry man, his drum kit a distant memory, maybe a dinner-party joke. The greasy, skinny, racist Alabama gutter punk had vanished; in his place was a well-married, well-traveled dandy, in tailored suits and expensive shoes, with high-end Brooklyn real estate. He had unceremoniously unfollowed Aviva, then she him. Make new friends and toss the old; don't waste your time pretending kidney stones are gold.

But she'd run into him one *last* last time, come to think of it: by chance, on the corner of Bleecker and Grove, outside a charming bistro. He was with the wife, waiting for a table. The wife was pale and gloomy and towering and complaining of an insidious sinus infection.

Aviva, earnest as a fucking puppy: "Ever tried a neti pot?"

The wife looked down from her great height, expressionless, save for a flare of her tiny nostrils: "I'm good with my antibiotics, thanks."

You'd sooner napalm your microbiome than rinse out your sinuses with warm distilled salt water? Okay, doll-face, okay. Let us not judge one another. All the best.

Serena downed the last of her latte.

"Oh, and did you *hear*? They finally had a *baby*."

"Holy shit. Like, a human baby?"

"I assume so."

"*Damn*, that must've taken some doing."

"Alllllllll the doings. That chick does not fuck around."

"How *old* is she?"

"Old. *Old*-old. *Old-old*-old."

Aviva hadn't stalked the Cracker's feed in a while. It was public, but he was an extremely judicious poster, sometimes went months. Lotta high-end cocktails and slow-cooked meat, some European landscapes, the former model's face artfully obscured by a windblown curtain of hair. And sure enough, wow, yes: a baby. Took a little more digging to find the child's name. Oh, but leave the child out of it. It's not the child's fault.

Just the thought of that slimeball fathering a child. Just the thought of the child's adoring eyes on him. Just the thought of their happy little family, a threesome. Just the fucking thought. Aviva felt ill. Maybe it was the huge lunch and hot chocolate and marshmallow and cookie. Maybe she didn't fully understand desperation and longing. Or maybe she just didn't want a baby that bad. Maybe her wanting was wanting.

There was time for a nap and a couple spoonfuls of Manuka to love up on her throat before she put on her costume and went to the venue. Tits out, legs in boots. No makeup. Hair artfully destroyed like she hadn't washed it in a week. Which in fact she had not. Take me as I am.

Love text from Sam. He wasn't interested in being her groupie. He didn't want to give up his job and his calling and his life to trail around after her, sitting in greenrooms and backstage and in VIP lounges. He'd be waiting patiently at home, waiting for her to come back and blow him and putter in his garden and bring forth his offspring. Which is exactly what

Aviva wanted, too, so no problem, right? Other than the gaping void of offspring.

Break a leg, baby, he added.

I'm not your baby! I don't wanna *be* your baby! I want to *have* your baby, you fucking prick.

For sound check, she did obscure early Amy, as Amy herself had done it in a random video shot outside under a hazy sky by the water in Miami. Amy had a mystical connection to Miami. That was during the time, right after the first album came out, wherein you no longer saw her playing her own instrument. She wasn't a wiz on guitar, just serviceable, and someone in management or at the label must have insisted she put the instrument down. Just sing, honey. Let yourself be *accompanied*. You just sing. Anyway, the guitar disappeared. But in Miami, before the dollar signs got quite so huge, she'd damn well played her own guitar. She looked so happy, so busy, so complete with that guitar in her arms. The way she tended to it! She wasn't good enough to just mindlessly play; she had to look down at it, check in with it, focus pretty intently as she plucked each chord. She wasn't making eye contact with her audience. It didn't work great in terms of showmanship. You didn't have an unobstructed view of her hips and her tits and her ass and her thighs and her big juicy mouth and her big sad deep dark flashing Jew eyes, and this was a problem, see? Because no one wanted to watch a sexy freak pluck her own painstaking accompaniment. The guitar had to go. Why did she concede, though? Why not hold on to your guitar? Why not keep it, if only to defy them? What, because then you might not get to become so rich and famous? Fucking please.

And it was only after the guitar disappeared that she'd begun costuming it up to such an absurd degree. She was *bored* without her guitar. Singing cost her absolutely nothing. Singing was like talking, like breathing. The disappearance of the guitar was the beginning of the end. Girl needed more to *do*. With her body: her arms, her eyes, that impressively busy brain. Girl needed something to hold on to, something to *tend*.

* * *

A finger of scotch from the promoter for a toast with Jerry and the house manager and a blue-haired journalist working on a profile and the label scout who had brought Aviva into the fold in the first place.

"I think we all knew this one was destined for greatness," said Jerry, holding up his glass.

"One of a kind," agreed the scout.

"She's not everybody's cup of tea," Jerry went on, "but fuck 'em if they can't take a joke, am I right or am I right?"

"*ROCK AND ROLL*," said the promoter.

The hum of the crowd, a buzz in the air. Aviva's guitar and amp sitting in a spotlight on the stage, awaiting her. She scanned her body for tension, let it go. The house lights went down and a roar went up. Jerry standing behind her: "You're big-time, Toots," he said. "Go get 'em, they're already yours."

She strode out onstage. They screamed her name. She was made for this. She owned this. The audience her disciples, her "followers." She picked up her guitar and ducked under the strap. Come to Mama.

"Hello, New York City!"

Woooooooooot.

"The theme of this evening, and of my entire fucking life, and of *your* entire fucking life, whether or not you realize it, is memento mori." And she slipped into the old favorite about Rob dying, the boring old favorite from the end credits of that dumb and lucrative TV show, which had netted her a sweet check and a thousand messages on however many platforms from people she had sort of known or used to know or barely knew, congratulating her on being such a "big deal."

"Even more important, though . . ." she said at the close of that song, tipsy on performance and lights and stale weed mint and preshow scotch. She was tuning for a cover of Rancid's "Nihilism" (this one goes out to that dumb asshole Cracker, wherever he may be): "MEMENTO CORPORIS!"

They hooted and hollered.

She missed the goddamned Cracker. They'd had *fun*. That old, underrated thing, fun. She wished she had a drummer onstage with her now. Someone to trade jokes with. Someone with whom to roll her eyes. Next tour, for sure: a drummer. She'd find a funny, nice one, make him her new best friend. Like Ani and Andy Stochansky.

She hadn't had liquor in such a long time. She'd pay for it tomorrow.

"That's right, bitches: the body! You can try to forget the body, but the *body don't like that*. The *body don't forget*. The body will *remind* you!"

For so long (stagnation!), Aviva had saved a voice memo Cracker had recorded on her very first smartphone, which he'd helped her set up. *Aviva's a Jew*, he'd singsonged. *Jew Jew Jew Jew Jew Jew Jew.* You could almost hear the sexy curve of his twisted, anemic smile. It had turned her on; it just had. She was sorry: it had.

"What a disgusting human being," the Rabbi had calmly observed when Aviva played the old voice memo for him.

Why was everything about Cracker today? Was it ovulatory? Was it flawed messaging from some throwback egg, busting out of a crusty cyst from years ago? Was it ceremonial? Were there traces of him in her body still, needing to be exorcised? (Was *that* why she couldn't get pregnant?) She had once done a shamanic ceremony with Hanalei to cut him loose. Afterward, she lay trembling and sobbing on the floor, and Hanalei had said: "Holy shit, you're a witch." But the ceremony hadn't worked. Or maybe things like that only worked gradually. Maybe a series of ceremonies was called for. Because when she least expected it, Cracker still occasionally turned up in her dreams. In the most recent, he and the wife were running to catch a train while Aviva sprinted after them, trying to get them to stay for dinner. Begging them. Pleading.

Stagnation is hideous. Wish stagnation on your worst enemy.

She did the song about all the (real and imagined) things that could compromise a person's fertility.

Shrieks of assent. She was preaching to the converted. The label wanted her to do a video for this song ASAP; they thought it had viral potential. More and more people are thinking about this stuff, said an exec. Paranoia about food, air, water, soap and shampoo and lotion and sunscreen and perfume and all the likely ways greedy unchecked corporate interests are poisoning us all. The old joke: just because I'm paranoid doesn't mean they're not out to get me.

For encore, the Amy dirge from sound check: minimalist chords, slowed to an absurd degree, the way Amy used to do it with her rudimentary guitar. Seventeen, eighteen years old: same age Aviva had been when she'd first worked up the nerve to play and sing for other people around a campfire ("You Had Time," by Ani), her right leg inexplicably shaking the entire time.

"I speak two languages," Mae West used to say, "Body and English."

She skipped out on postshow revelry for a late bite with Sarah, beloved voice teacher. Sixty-something observant Jew, never married, no kids, took care of her own parents through old age and death, not a bitter bone in her body. She'd taught Aviva how to find the deepest registers of her voice, how to sing from her gut, and how to breathe. She'd taught Aviva Alexander technique, vagus nerve stimulation. The woman had a smile made of the warmest benevolent light. Something like a fairy godmother.

They went to a dark, small French bistro, and Aviva ordered calf's liver, which, while utterly disgusting, was fertility-guru-approved for blood chi and general vitality in follicular phase.

"You were magnificent tonight, darling. I can't tell you how it feels to see you do your thing. You are beyond."

"I'm having a hard time getting pregnant."

No need for small talk with Sarah, no use for self-protection or urbanity. She appealed to Sarah as though Sarah was the gatekeeper, the mystical advocate.

"All the matriarchs had fertility issues, darling. *All* of them. The most special children don't come easily. The most special ones aren't given freely. Sarah, Rachel, Leah . . . All of them. We don't know what the big-picture plan is, but there's a reason for everything."

"Are you sure?"

"I know a woman who spent *years* trying to get pregnant, went to all the best doctors, tried everything. Then finally one doctor thought to check the husband. He was the problem all along."

"We checked. Sam's fine."

"So it'll happen. You are so young; you have no idea how young you are. Relax. You have to relax. Relaxation is the most important thing."

"Don't think of a pink elephant."

"What do you mean?"

"You know: whatever you do, don't think of a pink elephant. It's impossible. In order *not* to think of a pink elephant, you first have to think of the pink elephant. In order to then banish it from your thoughts."

"Very clever!"

"I'm cursed, is the truth. The blessing is that our descendants shall be as numerous as stars in the sky and grains of sand on the beach. The opposite is a curse."

"Life is mysterious, darling. We just go along and wait and see. We just don't know. It's not for us to know. The sun will come up tomorrow. Beyond that? Let's go back to how *magnificent* you were tonight. The power you've cultivated, it just keeps growing. Not just your voice. Your whole bearing. You should be so proud." Sarah's eyes were glassy, like a revelation had been granted. "I don't want to say too much because it's not good for you to hear it. It can mess you up, I know, but sweetheart! Time *stops* when you sing. I shouldn't say too much. You have a gift. From God. And you're using it. You're putting it to use. You should be so proud. Not everybody can do that. It's a very special thing to know what your gifts are and to use them."

"I'd rather have a baby."

"All in good time. You're juggling a lot. It's a lot. Just keep doing what you're doing."

First thing in the morning, the reproductive endocrinologist: Dr. Annabelle White, Lexington and Seventy-Third.

"It's been two years since your last pap smear," said the long-suffering receptionist, whose name, no joke, was Faith. Aviva was not huge on having her cervix scraped. Aviva was not huge on checkups in general. You go in for a checkup and suddenly need to have your tits lopped off, your moles dug out, your thyroid biopsied. Go to the doctor too often and find your-self . . . going to the doctor some more. Avoid doctors; die of old age. Or maybe avoid doctors; die young. But given that it's death either way, why not just avoid doctors?

Two years: enough time to have borne two babies. Or one and a half babies, realistically. Or two and a half babies, if she'd had twins, then gotten pregnant again right away.

She liked Dr. White all right. It wasn't impossible to at least attempt to "trust" Dr. White. Seventy-something, diminutive, resolutely unhip hair-cut, low-heeled beige pumps with nude stockings, smiled never. Surely one of only a few women in her medical school class. Couldn't have been easy. Aviva had been referred to Dr. White way, way back in the Jeff Lazar engagement days, after she'd gone off the Pill and been stumped by the wild menstrual inconsistencies that had lain in wait.

The exam was quick and horrible, then Aviva got dressed and went to wait in Dr. White's office, open notebook on her lap, pen at the ready. A good little student of whatever the doctor had to say.

White marched in, sat at her desk, and spoke at Aviva's file. "The results of your day-three blood test were good, but I don't think you're ovulating. I recommend a course of Femara."

"What's Femara?"

"A new ovulation drug. Preferable to Clomid."

"Why preferable? And why don't you think I'm ovulating?"

"It doesn't cause multiple ovulation, for one thing." She didn't answer the second question.

Aviva looked down at her notes.

"Have you heard of vitex? I've been taking that, and I wonder if you have any opinion on it?"

"What's vitex?"

"Um . . . chaste berry? An herb that helps regulate progesterone." (WHY DO YOU NOT KNOW THAT?)

"That's not going to make you ovulate."

"Um . . . okay." (HOW DO YOU KNOW?) "Do you have any thoughts on D-chiro-inositol?"

"What's that?"

"Um, a mineral supplement some people seem to have good responses to." (WHY DO YOU NOT KNOW THAT?)

"Oh yes, we did a study. It doesn't work."

"Oh," Aviva said. (MAY I SEE THE STUDY?)

"Do you have your temperature chart with you, please?" White scribbled something in Aviva's file. Still no eye contact.

"Um, unfortunately . . . I had this app, and I was keeping track of everything in there for the past few years, and I don't know what happened, but, like, somehow, recently, the entire thing just erased itself. Glitched out or something?"

Dr. White squinted at Aviva. Eye contact at last! Aviva felt this as a triumph, albeit a short-lived one.

"We should get you ovulating." White scribbled on her prescription pad, tore off the top sheet, and held it out, looking back down at Aviva's file. "Femara is the new thing."

"Okay. I mean. I guess. But. Um. Given the unfortunate history of, you know, like, 'the new thing,' regarding, you know . . . women's health . . . in particular, I wonder if . . . maybe I should just go ahead and take the, uh, old thing?"

"Are you always this anxious?"

"Well, I guess I'm, just, like, pretty . . . conscious. About my body. I mean, I try to be sort of, you know, 'woke'—ha ha ha—about what I do to my body."

Dr. White sighed. "If you want Clomid, I'll give you Clomid. But the chance of twins is much higher, and with your anxiety I'd hate to see you wind up with twins."

Oh, so now Aviva had *anxiety*. Well, as long as the ol' prescription pad was out, why not give her a lil' something for *that*, too?

"Look," Dr. White went on. "You just need to trust me. I am trained to assess the risks and benefits. Let *me* worry about you. You aren't qualified to be making these decisions."

Having started off sunny and mild, the day turned suddenly weird and wet, warm and humid. Abrupt change. Unseasonable. But there was less and less such a thing, wasn't there, as "seasonal" weather.

Aviva had an hour until her next thing: a meeting with the blue-haired journalist. She walked downtown, past a ritzy storefront gym, the windows of which showcased the gym's ad campaign: a young heiress, fifteen feet high, dripping couture and jewels, dramatically made-up, breastfeeding infant twins in tandem, under the words *MAKE THINGS HAPPEN*.

She texted a photo to Sam: A sign! A sign?

A block later, the minimalist window display at a children's boutique showcased a single organic cotton onesie that read: *All because two people fell in love.* The rest of what tended to result in a baby in this neighborhood was, of course, much too long to fit on a onesie.

Okay, so: Femara. The new thing. She Googled as she walked. A pill a day for five days to trick her pituitary gland into coaxing her ovaries to mature and release some eggs. What was the big deal? The big deal was that it was treating a symptom, not the cause. The big deal was what if it didn't work? The big deal was what if her ovaries didn't *appreciate* this "coaxing"? The big deal was what if what was going on between her pituitary and her ovaries was already complicated and fraught enough without this euphemized "coaxing"? What if this shit made her pituitary *angry*? Got her ovaries *upset*? The big deal was what were the consequences of the mechanism via which this "coaxing" actually took place? The big deal was what about the eggs that would be theoretically released with this metaphoric gun to their metaphoric heads? What an awful way for a new person's genetic material to begin to assemble itself. You don't pry open the petals of a flower, Hanalei always said. You tend to the plant and you wait.

But come on: one pill a day for five days. Aviva had snorted *how* much coke in *how* many club bathrooms on the Lower East Side pre–Whole Foods? She had blown how many purveyors of said coke without ever having learned their names? She had taken antibiotics for how many colds? She had swallowed how many birth control pills to "regulate" her menstrual cycle? She had forgone condoms with how many early internet meetups? She had smoked how many cigarettes in order to hang with the cool kids under the portico on lower Fifth? Swilled how much liquor in order to try and keep up with said cool kids after work? And in how many backstage lounges and at how many postshow parties? She had subsisted exclusively on Cheerios and white rice with soy sauce and SnackWell's Devil's Food Cookie Cakes and microwaved popcorn and Snapple peach iced tea and her mother's lentil soup (secret ingredient: ketchup) from roughly age ten to twenty, for fuck's sake! A pill a day for five days to "coax" her ovaries into maturing and releasing an egg or two was *not*, relatively speaking, that big a deal. A pill a day for five days to "coax" her ovaries into maturing and releasing an egg or two did not have to be a gateway drug. Or did it? Once you stepped onto this train, would you break your neck trying to jump back off again when it really got moving? If Femara didn't work, what was the next thing? And what was the thing after that?

The café looked like nothing from the outside, tucked away behind a brick wall on a quiet street. Inside, however, it was cavernous and skylit, with friendly staff and good coffee and fresh bagels and a ton of plants.

Aviva didn't want to do anything to force ovulation. If she wasn't ovulating on her own, tough titties. If her physiology wasn't primo for childbearing, then *okay*, maybe she was off the hook for childbearing. Or maybe Dr. White was wrong: maybe Aviva was ovulating just fine. Maybe she'd get pregnant with that prescription crumpled, unused, forgotten, at the bottom of her bag. Maybe she'd keep it as a souvenir, put it in the kid's baby book, or burn it at some future full-moon bonfire. Maybe she'd save it to use in a collage someday, or auction it off to benefit some reproductive rights charity, when coming generations needed to be reeducated about the possibility of "natural" conception.

A cute girl at the next table, deep in conversation with her friend, said: "Sure, these were warning signs, but if you never ignore warning signs, you have nobody to hang out with!"

The blue-haired journalist was late.

Jerry was all excited about the fabulous online chatter pertaining to last night's show. Tonight's show was sold out. And lookie-look, *Womb Service* was on some list. And lookie-look, everyone was happy with the streaming numbers. They're saying it could even get nominated for something!

Jer, I'm on a need-to-know basis. B my shelter, man. Shelter me.

Blue hair appeared. "SosorryImlateImsuchahugefanasyouknowLast-nightwasamazingohmyGodyouresobadassImfreakingoutrightnow. Holy shit, hi. Okay, sorry. I'm fine. Hi." There was some fumbling with the recording function on the device. The hair was a hypnotic, transporting, almost florescent blue. "So the theme of this issue is 'The Body.'"

"Ugh, not the *body*," Aviva said. "I actually prefer to think of myself as untethered consciousness."

"Your album seriously has me tied up in knots. Like, okay: I have two moms. They chose my donor out of a catalogue. Wait, I need coffee. Lemme be right back."

"I mean, it's not like I don't hate her, too," said the girl at the next table, "but you're supposed to at least pretend not to hate your friends."

"Okay," said Blue, returning with a latte. "Where were we?"

"Your moms. Donor catalogue."

"Right. My dad was tall, Jewish, played the piano, and went to the University of Pennsylvania—that's all I know. They got someone Jewish because one of my moms is Jewish and the other isn't, and the one who *isn't* carried me, so. My partner wants to get me a DNA test for my birthday, but I actually super-duper can't take another layer of complexity in my life, so I'm like: no."

"You know there've been a bunch of cases where the donor turns out to be a total fucking sociopath, right? Turns out a lot of clinics haven't been doing, like, any due diligence at all. For decades."

"Right. Yeah. Uncool! But anyway, as someone who wouldn't *exist* without reproductive technology, I am kind of surprised that you seem to want to, like, smash it."

"I don't want to smash it, I just want to fucking talk about it. Lift up the old rock and see what's crawling underneath."

"I'm such a big fan, from way back. Your first album got me through high school, not even kidding. 'Bearded Sophomore' blew my mind and, like, helped me come out."

Great old ditty about a regular lovelorn teen gal who just happens to be growing a fucking beard. All the popular kids are queer these days, but back in the day, goddamn, not so much. Had wee Aviva known that her facial hair could someday give her extreme cultural cachet, she might not have been quite so eager to have it all removed. Pay now or pay later, kids.

"But anyway," Blue went on, "come to think of it, there's a, like, this 'don't touch me' sentiment in so many of your songs, going way back. You seem to have long-standing issues with the idea that doctors are God."

Great work, young journalist!

"No God but God," Aviva said. "Well, that's Islam. But sure enough! We've replaced religion with medicine, have we not? *Opiates* are, in fact, the opiates of the masses. Humanity is really so freaking beautiful, from a tragicomic standpoint."

"What are your thoughts on hormonal birth control?"

"It fucking sucks. How did we get convinced to medicate the living shit out of ourselves in order to maintain the status quo everywhere else in society? We bought it, hook, line, and sinker. Short-circuit your entire metabolic system so no one else has to worry and nothing has to change?

How revolutionary. The very first pharmaceutical ever developed for people who are not sick. But not the last! Fun."

Blue tried a new tack: "Did you see the piece online yesterday by this girl who charged forty grand on her Visa to freeze her eggs at twenty-five? She mentions you in passing. Not a fan."

"Wait, don't tell me, lemme guess . . . she . . . froze her eggs because she's got things to do, places to go, people to fuck, and she wants to be . . . wait . . . wait . . . 'in control of her future'?"

"The kicker is that she wound up with, like, what's it called when your ovaries explode?"

"Hyperstimulation."

"Right. So she winds up losing one in emergency surgery, but says she would do it all over again in a heartbeat because she likes being *in charge*."

"Well, why on earth would we have two ovaries if we couldn't blow one up and keep on keeping on. You notice the charming ageist subtext in there, yeah? We don't want to waste our 'youth,' but when we're forty-five and used up, that'd be a perfect time to join the ranks of haggard used-up *moms*. That ordeal sounds *way* worse to me than just having a freaking baby in the physiologically prescribed season, but what the *fuck* do I know. Ask me where I get ideas for songs, will you? How the music industry has changed since I started out! How tour's been going! When I'm getting back in the studio again. Whether it's lonesome on the road."

"The body," Blue said, looking at some notes. "The body . . . the body . . ."

"There was this old rabbi at my yeshiva, okay?"

"You went to *yeshiva*?"

"Yeah, so, this old rabbi. He took the girls aside when we were like twelve and he gave us a Talk. In this Talk, he told us all about the declining birth rates amongst secular Jews worldwide. Because women were getting so *educated* and *empowered* and *accomplished* and waiting longer to get married because we had all these new ideas about personal fulfillment and freedom and independence, so we're like, oh, we'll just have a baby at thirty-five or forty, but then, oh, shit, that doesn't often pan out. So this rabbi—this super-well-respected old dude—he was *worried* about us girls. He wanted us to understand that it was really important to get married young and have babies, and put graduate school and career and adventure and self-knowledge and romance and travel and all that miraculous post-feminist shit on hold."

"Gross."

"Yes, gross, because we were twelve and I don't think he spoke to the boys this way, and, yeah: gross. I knew at twelve that it was gross. But I still absorbed it, you know? Like a little sponge. Cut to twenty-some years later. Same rabbi, new shtick! Dude is now going around giving talks about how the Jewish community needs to be subsidizing assisted reproductive technologies for any and all Jews who want or need it. He's raised a shitload of money. Hadassah has lobbyists in Washington on this issue, you get me? You see the absurdity?"

"I . . . No."

"He gave *up* on the first idea. He was shrewd enough to see that it was a loser idea. We *aren't* going to spend our twenties bearing children and keeping house; we'd prefer to fuck strangers in bars and hitchhike in Bali and get promoted at Google. But this guy's a pure realist. He just wants us to breed. It'd be simpler if we'd do it in accordance with our 'biology,' but that ship has *sailed*. So how can he make *absolutely* sure we breed? Sell us on the idea that technological conception is our birthright, entitlement, a *liberation*, if you will, and *pay us* to mess with ourselves. Never mind our bodies and their pesky rules. Never mind the lack of solid long-term data on what the fuck this shit does to us or to children or to *their* children, while we're at it. Never mind the creeping possibility of some epigenetic baggage we won't know about for a few generations. Never mind the total and utter lack of regulatory ethics. Override that shizz! Breed! Breed! Breeeeeeeed. By any means necessary. At any cost. With that beautiful illusion of 'control' like wind in our sails. Paid for by your friendly clergy and community overlords."

"Sounds like . . . an asshole."

"Yes. But that's not the point. The point is that intelligent women have to be vigilant, because in any given era we *have to say no*. To everything they try to normalize for us, everything they try to sell us, we have to say NO. Have twelve babies and die in childbirth before thirty? No. Take this magic pill to prevent pregnancy? No. Don't have abortions? No. Have de rigueur abortions? No. Get a device implanted in your body to prevent pregnancy? No. Get married in your teens? No. Wait for Mr. Perfect? No. Be an empowered whore? No. Be a pristine virgin? No. Suffer in childbirth? No. Be unconscious in childbirth? No. Let technology manipulate your body in the service of forced childbearing past innate biological capacity? No. Wear a veil? No. Wear a corset? No. Become sexually irrelevant as you age? Nope. Stay sexually relevant until you're a hundred and twelve? Nah. Don't vote? No. Get some liquid plastic tits? Thanks, but no. To *everything*!" The people at the next table were staring now. Aviva tried to lower her voice.

"Because whatever gets normalized for women, whatever gets taken from us and repackaged and sold back to us, up and down and round and round, back and forth, wherever, whenever, it's all so that we *keep having to mess with ourselves*, while everything else stays exactly the same. So to whatever's normative, whatever's expected, we must say . . ." She sung it, deep and slow: "No, no, no."

Slow clap from the the next table. Blue laughed.

Who cared about what sweet old Davey Foster Wallace had said about artists being at their worst when beating a drum? Please. The body: Aviva would beat this drum 'til she could beat no more, and she'd do so the only way possible: *using her body*. Beat it, repeat it, inhabit it, because the drum *was* her body. The body: Beat it 'til it lay vacant and still, 'til you could beat and repeat no more, at which point it would fall into the deepest of silence forever. And incidentally, pity goddamn DFW, with his mountains of junk food and pills. Who *wouldn't* hang themselves on all that junk food and all those pills?

"I think I have what I need for now," Blue said. "I'm looking forward to your show tonight. One last question. Wikipedia has you at thirty-four, and I see you're wearing a wedding ring and everything, so, ah . . . what's your deal?"

"My deal?"

"You have kids? You want kids? What's your story?"

Pause.

Relax, Aviva. Let your shoulders drop. Feel your hips rooted in this here chair. "Kids are cool," she said. "What an awesome privilege and responsibility, huh?"

She blacked out most of the second show—not a bad thing, more like an extreme meditative state. She slept like a baby, no dreams or memory of dreams, and woke to a bright, breezy day shimmering with sunshine and chirping birds and fruit trees in bud.

A video had been posted of Aviva holding forth between songs, giggling and growling, sweaty and elated, all the way in on her own groove. "A lot is invested in us being body illiterate," she said. Her hair looked amazing and the lighting was great and she was doing some intuitive, authoritative finger picking while she held forth, using the guitar for punctuation.

"Think of the industries that would fall if women were invulnerable to bullshit about our own bodies! And by 'woman,' I mean: entity deriving from the ovaries of the ovaries of ovaries, which themselves derived organically from ancestral ovaries; future ovaries existing within the ovaries from whence they came, and so on and so forth back and forth and back all the way to the mysterious leap out from the mud and the muck and the mire, which might itself be understood as some sort of original ovary, controlled by the pituitary of some unknowable entity, tales of Adam and Eve and the snake and the tree and the temptation and the forbidden fruit and the banishment notwithstanding, or perhaps *withstanding*, we'll never know. All of which is to say: put me down as queer. Pronouns 'fuck'/'you.'"

People are pissed about that little rant, texted Jer. You can't joke about pronouns.

Wasn't joking, she replied.

She walked the thirty beautiful blocks up to the Rabbi's office. It doesn't matter what was in her headphones. It was a woman's voice in her headphones. It was a woman's voice singing said woman's own original songs.

"*Mein kind!*" said the Rabbi. "Mazel tov on the shows! My sources tell me you were outstanding, which doesn't surprise me at all."

She took off her shoes and curled up on his big leather couch.

"I'm having fun. Second show might have been better than the first. I like being a lone wolf, but I kept thinking about how fun it would be to get a drummer next time around. Anyway, I'm follicular, so everything's fine."

He took note of her outfit: a bit more over-the-top than usual. "How you doing with the shopping?"

"Amazing. This designer in West Texas is making these insanely detailed vintage reproductions in the most delicate cotton voiles and silks with lace trim and crocheting and they look like what your formerly wealthy refugee great-grandmother wore in layers so she wouldn't have to carry everything when she fled."

"So . . ." He laughed. ". . . not great. The problem with addictive behavior is that it requires more. Always. More and more to accomplish the same temporary satisfaction."

"I know."

"And how about the weed?"

"It's . . . helpful? Every now and again. Every once in a while."

"Just so long as it's a side dish, not the main course. How's Sam?"

"Sam. Sam! Sam is Sam. I got home from tour last month, like limping, deflated, *wrecked*, and he's waiting for me at home with a bouquet of the world's ugliest dyed blue carnations, *so* happy to see me. He has no idea what it's like on the road or in general, and he doesn't really want to know. His life is so . . . *set*. He goes to work, he goes to the gym, he watches sports, he eats whatever I make, he enjoys his cereal and frozen ravioli if I don't cook, he farts, tells me he loves me, grabs my ass, and he's snoring immediately. He's so *simple*. For him everything is *fine*. He's, like, from a different planet. How did we wind up together?"

"You're everything he's not, and he's everything you're not. Which is exactly why you belong together. Together you are whole."

He clasped his hands to make the point.

"I saw the endocrinologist yesterday."

"Oh?"

"She is totally committed to figuring out what's going on with me. She's *determined* to puzzle out the connection between insulin resistance and hormone imbalance and environmental toxins and progesterone deficiency and orgasm and PCOS and long cycles and my not having been breastfed and having post-Pill syndrome, and wants to see me daily so as to meticulously unravel the singular mystery of my particular body and metabolism before she would dream of exposing me to any pharmaceutical intervention."

"Really?"

"No. She told me to take a new forced-ovulation drug."

"And what do you think?"

"I think it's a terrible, horrible, no-good, very bad idea."

"Mm-hmm."

"But . . . maybe it's a perfectly fine idea?"

"Okay."

"Answer me this: Why are doctors such arrogant, hubristic know-nothings?"

"That's a little strong."

"Present company excluded, of course."

"Thank you."

"I mean, you have to be *completely* unfamiliar with the history of medicine to think of doctors as gods. *Oooh, guess what? We're doing this amazing new thing, try it! Oh, sorry, never mind, that doesn't work at all, and actually it totally fucks you in the ass, but wait, wait, we've got something amazing for you now,* truly *miraculous, a wonderful advance, we'll fix you right up!* I mean. Where's the humility? Where's the *I don't know?* Where's the *First, do no harm?* Where's the making peace with the way shit is? I mean, thalidomide! I mean, antibiotics for acne! I mean, pelvic mesh!"

"What you're saying is not untrue. You're not wrong."

"*That* is what I like to hear, Doc. Thank you. How much for today's session?"

"We used to say in medical school: you don't know what you don't know. And anything you think you know will be overturned eventually. The idea that neurons cannot regenerate was absolutely sacrosanct when I was in medical school."

"So where are the good doctors? The ones who say *I don't know?*"

"Few and far between."

"Humility and decency are rarities in every profession, though, who are we kidding."

"If all you have is a hammer, everything looks like a nail."

"Yeah, well, *I'm* a hammer. And everything I see is a goddamn nail. All I do is hammer, hammer, hammer. No time for ambiguity. *Everything* is a goddamn nail."

"Why do you think that is?"

"You tell me, dude. Wait, wait: something about my mother."

"Go on."

"She had her head so far up her own ass. She sold me down the river. *Marry a Jew! Marry a Jew! Have lots of babies! Have lots of babies!* Meanwhile she can't be bothered to help me figure out *my body.* Puts me on the Pill at fourteen. Puts me on the toxic acne medication that literally changes your DNA. Cooks absolute shit food in margarined nonstick pans all the time. Lives on cottage cheese like a good skinny bitch. Takes me to the Russian spa to have my hairy teen *asshole* waxed. I still have literal burn scars all over my upper thighs."

"You deserved better."

"*She* had no problem getting pregnant. *She* had *three* babies. She got pregnant *four* times, actually. She lost one between Mike and me. She fell off a bike and miscarried."

"That's terrible."

Aviva shrugged, her sympathy for Barb long exhausted.

"Protocol changes," the Rabbi said. "We do the best we can with what we know."

"No," Aviva said. "No. That's not right. That's not sufficient. Putting children on hormones. How dare they."

"You're upset at your mother."

She rolled her eyes.

"We don't know what we don't know," he repeated.

"Exactly! So if you're an endocrinologist, why not know everything you can possibly know about hormone disorders? Why not educate yourself beyond the beyond? Take a freaking *interest*. Make it your business to understand everything herbalism and Ayurveda and freaking *energy healing* has to say on the subject while you're at it. Why not be *obsessed* with the problems you're trying to address? Why not go further, and further, and further still? Or else just *admit* you don't know, *admit* that you're helpless, and leave children *the fuck alone*."

"I don't disagree with you," he said gently.

"Good! Thank you!" She was crying. She always wound up crying in there. "On the way over here? Walking through Madison Square Park and up Third Avenue? I passed no fewer than *four* sets of twins, dude. White twins, needless to say. In top-of-the-line strollers pushed by brown women, *of course*. I mean, seriously. Why does nobody but me *mind* this shit? I jotted lyrics for a new song I'm gonna call 'Rich White Twins.' The chorus just goes: 'Is there any other kind?'"

"Why are you crying?" he asked, handing her the roll of toilet paper he kept on a shelf behind him.

"Because this shit is *sad*!"

"I think you're upset at your mother for not protecting you."

She stopped crying immediately. He was a good shrink.

When Aviva and Sam were first getting to know each other, Sam had given her his favorite book, a Tobias Wolff memoir. She never forgot the scene in which all the neighborhood fathers take their sons to the bus for basic training. The sons are all going to be shipped off to Vietnam thereafter. They should have been standing in front of that bus, Wolff wrote. They should have been physically blocking that bus. Why were they putting us on that bus? They should have been lying down in front of that bus.

"And I think you're very conflicted about what to do, here," the Rabbi said.

"Do I go ahead and force ovulation? Shut up and take it like a woman?"

"I can't answer that for you."

"When I was a kid I used to have this rule where I never turned down a dare."

"I know how much you want children."

"Yeah," she said, with zero affect.

"I know, sweetheart," he said, and again she started to cry.

"What is *wrong* with me?"

"Nothing's wrong with you, sweetheart."

"*Something's* wrong with me."

"Well, *something's* wrong with everybody."

"But not everybody's *stagnant*. Not everybody's a *swamp*."

"Actually," he said, smiling, "you'd be surprised."

The train home was packed and rickety. She got a window seat on the river side. A passing rain fell soft then hard then soft again. The old train clunked along, AC cranked. There's no modulating the temperature on these old trains. The AC's either on or it's off. Ditto the heat. So you reliably freeze in summer and roast in winter. So much effort and energy wasted, when you could just as well roast in summer and freeze in winter.

A pop star had welcomed twins and there was speculation that she'd used a surrogate so as to avoid "wrecking" her body; people were yelling at one another about whether or not this was anyone's business. Someone was thrilled at signs of spring starting to pop up in his neighborhood. Someone was frustrated with the way the media was treating a political candidate. Someone was praising their kid on the occasion of a birthday. Someone was wishing more people would watch a great TV show not enough people knew about. Harmie Shmendrickson was trying riced cauliflower for the first time, and *loving* it. Serena's two girls exuded effortless chic playing a memory card game on a ten-thousand-dollar shag rug. Someone was "exhausted" by the effort it took to consume news about a mass shooting. Someone was promoting their new album, someone else was promoting their new album, and another someone else was promoting *their* new album.

Ani was doing some spoken-word bit about *mister limp dick, up to his old tricks*. Ani knew what to do with the psychic vestiges of someone like, say, Cracker. Ani's pissed, but that's why she's going to be okay. You put on your shit-kickers and you get yourself together and you write as many songs as it takes to move *on*. Aviva switched to Amy bootlegs, demos made toward the end, ideas for when she finally got back into the studio. There was increasing pressure to make a follow-up record. She needed to make another album; she knew that, she wasn't stupid. But she didn't live long enough to do so. Stagnant as hell, this girl. She'll never get over a damn thing. She's got survival probs. Impractical shoes. You can't *run* in those shoes. The whole demented Betty Boop death cult thing is sort of cute, for a minute. Until it isn't.

("It's not cute at all," Aviva could hear the Rabbi say.)

You know what the appeal of a fuck-doll is? She is hyperfertile. That is the whole implication. You can fuck her and fuck her and she'll be waiting for you without a word of protest or complaint, corralling the kids and scrubbing the floors in a bustier, *loving* her lot in life, so long as she knows she's your girl. So long as she knows you're coming home to fuck her again tonight. So long as she can make it to the beauty parlor once a week. A simple girl. And who are we to tell her to want something different? How automatic it is to revile and condemn those whose wants are different from our own. But you have to respect a person who knows what they want. Is there anything more badass than knowing what you want?

Badass or no, she was an embodied symphony of shit. Raven-haired Fuckup Freak Jew Barbie. She knew full well she let men wreck her life. She got *off* on letting men wreck her life. Something perversely romantic about giving the person you fancy full license to wreck your life. All that "nobody stands in between me and my man" crap. Burn yourself to the ground in honor of the one you love. *I love him, I love him, I love him, and where he goes I'll follow, I'll follow, I'll follow.* She just wanted to be his *girl.* Let me *love* you. Hold me *tight.* I could be *real* good to you. Any old dude with a nice dick and a swagger would do. Don't knock it 'til you've tried it, being a big man's adoring whore. It has a lot going for it. Keep your ass perpetually cocked. Some *fine* consolations to be had in that pose.

There had been hard drugs, but she'd gotten over that stuff. The hard drugs were *well* behind her. There was an autopsy, although Jews are not supposed to autopsy (something about respect for the body?). Anyway, she did *not* overdose. She was clean. She was still drinking pretty hard, and everyone knew the drinking wasn't good, everyone knew that she was not in a great place with the drinking, but as long as she was off the hard drugs, the hope was that the drinking could be dealt with in due course. She was still performing, but only intermittently, because it was uncertain up until the moment she opened her mouth onstage whether or not she'd be able to deliver.

These demos are fragments, shadows, hints. She's just fucking around. She's trying to have fun. Please don't let all the joy have been sapped from this process. It's *her*, and she's riveting, but there's nothing cohesive here. Nothing that points toward anything.

There was the eating disorder, too. She loved her fast-food fried chicken, but she'd just masticate it to bits and then spit it out. Her kitchen cupboards were fully stocked with Haribo gummies. One of the bodyguards said that was all she ever did eat during those last few months.

ELISA ALBERT

Big bro tried to call her out: *You're going to die, you understand? You're not going to make it to thirty, you know that, right?*

But she laughed him off. Silly. You take everything so *seriously*, God. She was already half-gone.

Daddy was handling her financials, overseeing the business stuff. Daddy was a big macher, now, what with his daughter being a global superstar and all. More money than he'd ever seen in his life flowing through his hands on the daily. Like winning the flippin' lottery.

Mum was dealing with chronic autoimmune disease, the end of a relationship, the beginning of a new relationship. Mum was a tough cookie. She had every reason to give up, lie down, and wait to die, but that's not how Mum played. Mum had a positive outlook. Mum couldn't very well sit in the dark wringing her hands about her addled superstar daughter. Mum couldn't do anything about her addled superstar daughter. She loved her addled superstar daughter, but her addled superstar daughter wasn't exactly asking for maternal advice.

Don't worry about me, Mum. I'm fine. Call you next week.

When she felt "run-down," Daddy would have her check in to the London Clinic—*not* a rehabilitation facility, mind you—and "rest up" for a few days, ordering off the menu like room service, drinking champagne as she pleased.

The doctors warned that the drinking was unsustainable. She needed to gain weight. She was showing early signs of emphysema. Her vocal cords were compromised. But no one could tell her what to do. Not her parents, not big bro, not the team of bodyguards rotating through her house 24/7, not the throngs of wild, screaming fans spanning the globe, and not her manager, though eventually he did get tough and start canceling gigs, because gigs were the one thing she seemed to care about. No one could inspire her to take her health seriously. Not even her beloved Specials, with their good old refrain: *Stop your messing around / better think of your future.*

The drugs, the drinking, the eating disorder, the smoking, the love-object obsession: addictions are *symptoms*. The disease is . . . Loneliness? Disconnection? Broken family? Late capitalism? Birth trauma? We all know how the rat studies work: When the rodents are isolated and bored and without purpose, they fuck themselves up on whatever's available, just to activate their desperate starving pleasure centers, squeeze out even the tiniest trickle of that yummy pleasure hormone. But! When the rats have access to rat *community* and *purpose* and *connection* and *nourishment*, they voluntarily leave any/all kinds of toxic shit alone.

People are not rats, though (rats might be smarter). And however fucked up she was doesn't matter, because out of her suffering used to come, and might still have come, music. Something good out of something bad.

One of the bodyguards told the press that what she'd really, desperately wanted was a baby. But she had stopped menstruating, and couldn't figure out why. *Why don't I get my period no more? Why can't I get pregnant?* Because you've demolished your body, you sick, sorry girl. Because you've thrown yourself away. Because you've aged a hundred years in a quarter of that time, and because you are mortal.

This sense of connection with a famous person is like the feeling of connection with your ancestors. You don't know the famous person, but you feel connected (*are* connected). You don't know your ancestors, but you feel connected (*are* connected). Just because it's a one-way thing doesn't make it any less meaningful. The famous person doesn't know you. They know you're *out there*, in some vague sense. They know "you" exist, and others like you. Your ancestors didn't know you. They may have hoped you'd exist. But it wasn't for them to know.

But we carry them in our bodies, our ancestors. Perhaps this was the key to the mystery of Aviva's poor embattled ovaries, struggling to do their work. Her empty, useless womb. Trapped eggs, wasted eggs, growing stale. Perhaps already stale. The root of the word for "mother" in most languages is the word for "mud." Out of the muck and the mire, out of the sludge of the earth, something new takes form and struggles to grow, emerge, gargle, crawl, survive, draw breath, exist, exert itself.

Maybe Aviva's problem was resisting change. Swimming upstream. Maybe she should work harder to embrace the *now*, the future. Maybe bodies *are* mere suggestions. Maybe if you have enough money and access, everything *can* be had for a price. Swab the inside of your cheek and be connected within days to the whole of your ancestry. Hollow out some unlucky bitch's expensive eggs and insert your own DNA. Clone your favorite pet in a country without regulatory laws about experimental science on sentient beings. Swap out your inherited propensity for nearsightedness, for gloom, for eyes the color of literal shit.

Maybe the old rules no longer applied if you had enough money and access.

Aviva *had* money. Aviva *had* access. The story should end there.

Why doesn't the story end there?

4

BREATH

Her father was gravely ill. One of his all-too-frequent colds had become the usual sinus infection and bronchial trouble, and things had devolved from there. His "concierge" doctor, via text message from a golf course somewhere, had advised Chuck to take the random course of antibiotics he always kept handy, because who doesn't keep a random course of antibiotics handy? Yeah, well, wrong call, concierge shit-for-brains. Unable to breathe and greatly panicked in the middle of the night, Chuck had almost died in an ambulance to the hospital, where he'd landed on a ventilator and an IV drip with the "right" antibiotics for double staph pneumonia. No guarantee the "right" antibiotics would even work at this point, Chuck having built up quite the resistance. Twentieth-century miracle drug, nature has outsmarted you.

Charlene (Chuck's latest soon-to-be ex-girlfriend) called, and Aviva dropped everything.

Chuck had been sickly from birth—asthma, allergies—and the dude simply *adored* doctors, followed allergists around on his knees, scarfed prescription drugs like candy, was never without the very latest over-the-counter decongestants. For a time in the late eighties, he had become addicted to Afrin. If you were going to abuse drugs to such an extent, why not at least *party* drugs? Have a bit of fun while you destroy yourself!

Sam couldn't take time off so close to the end of the school year; his seniors having worked so hard, he really wanted to see them through, plus Aviva's family of origin seriously freaked him out. Anyway, they weren't one of those tied-at-the-hip couples, one of those closed-ranks, can't-take-a-solo-shit, conjoined-twin couples. She loved him, he loved her, but they had their own lives, their own independent stuff to do, and let's face it: they were an odd couple. Apart from the love—and maybe a smidge of karmic destiny, time would tell—they had no obvious reason to be together.

So! Zero possibility of conception this cycle. A breather. Which everyone said was healthy. A reprieve from the oh-so-trying trying.

"How about doing a small surprise gig while you're out there," Jer said. "We'll get someone to video, low-key, slide it right onto the web. I love you in clubs."

"Jer, my dad is, like, dying."

"Okay, well: if he lives."

On the plane, incessant yelps from a tiny, smelly dog in a bag under the next seat. After takeoff the dog's owner settled the trembling animal on his lap, and everyone oohed and aahed: "what a cutie" and "oh my goddddd" and "what kind of dog is that" and "boy or girl" and "how old."

Meanwhile, a few rows back, an inconsolable human infant was shrieking.

"God," the same people grumbled. "Shut that fucking baby up already."

Mortal illness notwithstanding, the rule was ironclad: never more than five consecutive days in LA. More than five consecutive days in LA was certain disaster. The familiar ghosts lay in wait. But it was her hometown, and she loved it dearly: that sweet mix of Pacific air and car exhaust, unparalleled salads and smoothies and sunshine and shopping. The Sunset Boulevard curves she could drive from muscle memory, backward, forward, blind-folded, high. Let the Red Hot Chili Peppers and Tom Petty and Jane's Addiction and Counting Crows serenade her in traffic on Wilshire/Sunset/Olympic/Pico or looking for parking by the pier or trying not to get killed on the 405 or the 101 or the 10. She was a girl again here, forever and ever a third-generation LA girl, whose adventurous forebears had left behind first the shtetl and then the rust belt, and struck out for the West Coast dream factory to gobble up a good amount of bargain real estate *decades* before there was so much as the *hope* of multiplatform media synergy, *forget* about a philharmonic or a proper art museum, and let us say: amen. The fact that Aviva, living dream of said forebears, had now chosen to make her home back in the rusty armpit of New England was a sick joke. Her poor forebears, all their adventuring undone! She might as well take it a step *further* back and start summering in a dirt-floor Romanian cottage with a kitchen garden. Not the worst idea, come to think of it. Can't keep a good Jew down.

Anyone who complains about the driving in LA just doesn't love music. In her earliest memories it was Barb's Chopin, Beethoven, Bach. And Chuck's *shboom if I could take you up to paradise up above shboom if you would tell me I'm the only one that you love life would be a dream sweetheart hello hello again.* And Rob's Toto and Billy Joel and Bruce Hornsby and Journey. And Mike's U2 and the Band and Dylan and the Cars. The Cars! Always on the radio in all the cars. At sixteen, when Aviva finally got her license, she constructed obsessive car mixes: Shawn Colvin and the Indigo Girls and Ani and Ani and Ani and Ben Folds Five and Jellyfish and early Dave Matthews and 10,000 Maniacs and Luscious Jackson and Joan Armatrading and Ani and Ani and Ani and Joni and Fleetwood Mac and okay maybe a *tiny* bit of Phish and did we already say Indigo Girls? All that dorky, plaintive, unabashed shit. Took her until college to get into hip-hop, alas. You had to love *music* to love LA.

She put down the rental car windows and sang along to the radio, letting the wind whip her hair. People weren't *snobs* in LA. People wanted to *relax* in LA. People weren't so *cynical* in LA. People didn't *overthink* everything in LA. People were *beautiful* in LA, wrapped in easy-breezy layers of fine cottons and linens and cashmeres and canvas. People spoke in *italics* in LA. The air was like a *drug*. Home sweet *home*.

You don't scare me, Aviva hotly informed Cedars-Sinai as she took a ticket to enter the parking lot. Her last visit to this particular hospital complex had been to be with dying Rob. He had died for a long-ass time, poor Rob, each treatment more brutal and futile than the preceding. Cedars was the least of it: Aviva had spent her adolescence wandering the hallways and cafeterias of many a big, important, ugly hospital where Rob had been voluntarily tortured. Finest terminal cancer torture money could buy, you betcha, nothing but the best for Chuck and Barb's doomed firstborn: Mass General, MD Anderson, NYU, and finally back home to Cedars. Hideous postmodern bullshit churches, all of 'em, full of terrified little mortals willing to believe in and perform any punishing ritual demanded of them by the pseudo-holy gods in charge.

YOU DON'T SCARE ME, she informed the lobby and the gift shop and the elevators. You. Don't. Fucking. Scare. Me.

They'd all been born here, incidentally: first Rob then Mike then Aviva, one-two-three perfect, pretty babies for Mr. and Mrs. Chuck and Barb Rosner. Rob had been born on the sixth floor, and he'd expired on the tenth—how quaint was that?

Charlene was doing calisthenics in the hallway while on hold with the insurance company. Charlene had had a supporting role on a classic late 1970s show, playing the dumb bosomy next-door neighbor, hair profoundly afeather. Some genius agent had written residuals into her contract, and she was thusly set for life. She mostly went to the gym and researched longevity diets. Aviva liked Charlene okay, as Chuck's soon-to-be exgirlfriends went, but it was generally hard to get attached. Chuck had been through so many women over the years that it made no sense to bond. Desperate little Aviva had gotten ill-advisedly attached to the first half dozen—Diane and Jody and Janeen and Anita and Batsheva and Laurie—and after that, enough was enough. *Dayenu* on the would-be stepmothers. Aviva's actual mother was more than Aviva could handle, anyway. Barbara! The Barb. Barbed Wire. Uncle on the mothers.

Mike was slouched in the farthest corner of the waiting room, staring into his portal. He glanced up long enough to identify Aviva, offered a clipped "hello," and was gone again. He hated Aviva, yes, but hated her so ardently, and with such commitment, that he couldn't ever seem to get *enough* of hating her. A paradox.

You had to put on a mask to enter Chuck's room. He was emaciated and unconscious, wearing five-day silver stubble, cocooned in a nest of wires and beeping devices attached to one big machine, which appeared to have its arms stretched protectively over him. Mike followed, soundless as a vampire, and stood opposite Aviva. They stared down at their unconscious father.

"He's old," Mike muttered.

"But he's stable, right? Charlene said stable."

"This is her fault."

"How is this her fault?"

Mike rage-shuddered, turned, and sat violently in the corner chair. The machines beeped. Aviva reached around the wires for her father's hand and leaned in to press her lips to his scruffy cheek. Dad. Daddy. Notwithstanding the fact that Chuck had withdrawn eye contact pretty much the nanosecond she had sprouted her lopsided little teen titties, there was a special bond between fathers and daughters. Or so said people who had no clue what the fuck was going on in general.

"How was your trip," Mike muttered, meaning: *I wish you were dead.* Aviva let go of Chuck's hand, lest it receive any of the foul energy Mike elicited.

"Fine," she said. Meaning: *I am so much more authentic and happy and successful than you are!*

Mike, Mike, what had happened to Mike? Life had happened to Mike. He couldn't take it. He'd been a sweet kid. Probably too sweet. So now he was exactly the opposite. A property of physics Rob could have explained: polarity. A tender heart grows bitter in the end.

Charlene came in and stood near the foot of the bed.

"CHUCK," she yelled. "CHUCK! YOUR DAUGHTER IS HERE, CHUCK."

Chuck startled awake and struggled to remove his oxygen mask.

"That's a long way to travel," he gasped. Dear old Daddy–est Dad, at least until his little beauty hit puberty and became a beast. His breath was jagged and terrible. The machine beeped differently for a moment, then settled back into steady rhythm. Aviva perched on the edge of the bed and made her own breath nice and long.

"Hey, Dad."

"Great article about you last week," he gasped. Ever since Aviva's "career" had "taken off," he'd begun to forgive her for having tits and body hair. He was proud of her, now. Turned out, all you had to do to reverse paternal abandonment was get a mention or two in the paper of record.

"Daddy, please don't read that stuff."

"I love it! I can't believe my daughter's a famous singer! You really make people think! And feel! You're provocative! You're special! I love that!"

Mike stormed out of the room, thrashing the curtain behind him.

Chuck felt around on the bed, agitated: "Where's my phone?"

"Daddy, you don't need your phone right now."

Charlene got the phone off a shelf above the sink, handed it to him, then washed her hands for a solid minute and went back out to the hall.

"I just have some emails . . ."

And into the glowing light he went.

"Let me see the phone, Daddy."

He protested weakly as Aviva put it back up on the shelf. She stood at the end of the bed, took gentle hold of his blanketed feet, and inhaled deeply for them both. Chuck sighed happily and closed his eyes. Just taking your own deep breath while touching or in close proximity to another person will often prompt them to take a deep breath of their own. Sarah had taught Aviva so many fascinating tools and tricks. Breathing, breath work, the breath. Psychic brain surgery. The diaphragm and pelvic floor like mirror-image hammocks. Another long, slow, deep inhale, and another long, slow deep exhale, and Chuck involuntarily imitated her. (See how great a mom she'd be?)

"I must have done something right," he murmured.

"You did a lot right, Daddy."

"No," he shook his head. "No, I really screwed up."

"Shhhh, Daddy. Shhh."

Five days in LA: she could do this.

Seems like he's gonna be okay, she texted Sam. Girlfriend not worth discussing. Mike a demonic shitheel. Pacific air DELISH.

Her Airbnb was an unrenovated bungalow guesthouse by the beach. Proper old-school sexy murder Venice. Last remaining unrenovated structure for blocks around. She treated herself to dinner on Rose and a stop at the weed collective for the mildest tincture they had.

"Gimme some grandma shit," she told the girl at the counter. "Just need a little extra swing in my hips."

She set up camp by Chuck's bed the next day, reading a scintillating memoir about the end of a crushing love affair. What made it especially readable was the fact that the narrative's heartbreak facilitator, the Crusher-in-Question, was, Aviva knew for a fact, a former lover of *hers*. Love Fiend! A musician and art-party fixture, well known for leaving a long, illustrious trail of destroyed women in his wake. Almost as famous for reducing smart women to quivering piles of lit crit as he was for sexy/obscure stoner anthems and indie film cameos. Aviva's time with the Fiend had been brief, just a few weeks of insanely powerful encounters: first in the squalid basement bathroom of a gallery in Chelsea, then in her apartment, a midtown hotel room after a film festival, the bathroom of a loft party in Greenpoint, her apartment, a hotel room in Philly for a weekend while he did a couple shows, then her apartment, and, last, oh God, what a ridiculous screaming woman–scorned scene she had made, her apartment.

In spite of herself, Aviva had developed "feelings" for the Fiend. Certain men, they just awaken an animal response; it's impossible not to develop "feelings" for such men, even when you know they don't have "feelings" for you. Or, more to the point, that they have "feelings" for many, many others. Or, perhaps even *more* to the point, that they do not have "feelings" for anyone at all. She had never once set foot in *his* apartment.

She still had regrets about that final scene at her place. What an embarrassment. She had played it reasonably cool thereafter, only very casually stalked him. He'd briefly moved to Montana to be with a poet whose scowling black-and-white author photo had obviously been staged to ape early Patti Smith. He and the poet had had a child and moved to Kyoto for a spell. Then he'd left the poet for an artist in London. Then Aviva lost track of him, by which is meant: he ceased posting shit online. Then a pianist with whom he had *also* been sleeping committed suicide, and rumor had it she'd addressed the suicide note to him.

Now this memoir, by someone else entirely, was all the rage.

Aviva had gotten over the Love Fiend relatively quickly—no memoir, no suicide attempt—though probably too much weed and wallowing for a minute there, and Lord, let's not dwell on how badly she'd degraded herself in that final scene. Cried so hard she couldn't breathe. *Begged* him to stay with her for just one more night. But he had walked out without looking back; Aviva was a pain in the ass, and the Love Fiend was not about carrying anybody else's baggage.

Within the week Aviva had hooked up with some rebound she'd met on Craigslist, for the love of everything holy, but against all odds Craigslist had turned out to be a decent guy. In any event, Aviva's Love Fiend fallout had been small potatoes, comparatively. She'd gotten a good song out of it, on the third album. It enjoyed heavy rotation on a few algorithms ("pissed-off women," "breakup music," "hell hath no fury like a woman scorned").

In any case, this memoir was bringing her *back*. Men like the Love Fiend, hypnotic bad-news sexual magnetism buffets . . . people who fall for them are sort-of sisters. Sister-dick-witch. Sister-dick-wife.

The sun rose higher, breaking through the clouds and bathing the institutional room in brightness. Chuck's machines beeped and whirred while he slept and slept. Aviva put a weird slow Amy remix on speaker and began to dance ever so slightly, furtively, around the room.

Then Mike showed up: party over.

Mike side-eyed her, but Aviva just minded her business, and danced on. Nothing obvious, only the smallest movements, that promised swing in her hips, some openness in her shoulders while she busied herself refilling the water pitcher, rinsing out the bedpan, freshening up the room's energy as best she could.

From all her great teachers, Sarah and Hanalei and the Rabbi, Aviva learned that you don't teach by instruction, and you don't teach by insisting, and you don't teach by forcing, and you don't teach by announcing. You teach by demonstrating, inhabiting, embodying. See what happens next time you're standing around in conversation with someone and you drop your shoulders, lift your head, open your heart-center, plant your feet. You need not say a word. See what happens when you do all of that, and then you take a deep breath.

Sure enough, Mike cleared his throat, stood up a little straighter. He shook out his shoulders, rolled his neck. Mike loathed Aviva, yes, but he was always *watching* Aviva, nevertheless, always keeping this weirdly intensive *eye* on her. A hateful, competitive eye, but an eye nevertheless.

The curtain swept open, and a nurse entered, Charlene close on her heels.

"Best to let him rest, and you guys go get out of here and rest, too," the nurse said. "Everybody needs rest."

"CHUCK," Charlene yelled. "CHUCK, WE'RE GOING NOW."

Chuck startled awake, mumbled something unintelligible, then drifted back under.

"You guys go ahead," Aviva told them. "I'll just be another minute."

She switched to Millie Jackson for a couple upbeat songs. Then some mellow, groovy Ani about being happily married, a new mother, struggling toward wholeness, with the understanding that to *be* a decent mother one had to make real peace with oneself, put one's lies and striving and negativity and insecurity to *bed*. Radical ideas. Creation and destruction: both tremendously hard work. Pick your hard work. Pick your struggle. Which are you going to work toward? Going with the flow or against it? But going with the flow wasn't as fun, nor as cool, nor as riveting.

"They sicken of the calm, who knew the storm," said Dorothy Parker.

Dinner. Italian place. Brentwood. Barb.

Aviva stood a full foot taller than her progenitor, but Barb hooked an arm around Aviva's neck and yanked her down into the kind of embrace that necessitates immediate and extended chiropractic care.

"Isn't this place *cool*?" Barb demanded. "I only take you to the *coolest* places, because you're *so cool*. Let's order before we talk; I'm starving. How's your dad? What an idiot. Joint venture on a bottle of wine?"

There were two Barbs. Charismatic, charming Barb, who read everything and knew everything and could cut to the heart of any matter, make the world seem deeper and richer and weirder and more interesting than anyone else. Then, unpredictably, a swift change, a hostile takeover, and you faced the other Barb: a door blown off its hinges. You'd be having a nice time, a good talk, some adventure, everything fine and good, but then the other Barb, a kind of weather pattern, would cover the day, the week, the year, your life, with such total darkness you couldn't even *recall* the feel of sun on your skin. This brand of mothering had shattered Mike completely. It had only cracked Aviva. And Rob . . . ? Who could say what it had done to Rob? Once you've been dead awhile, you become as mysterious and theoretical as before you existed.

"Okay," Barb said, closing her menu and squaring off. "So what's the story?"

"He's really sick. He was really sort of on the brink, they said. But he's coming through it. They say he's going to pull through."

"Who's his flavor of the month? Is she as dumb as the last one? Couldn't possibly be!"

"I don't think you get to hate on the love interest of a dude you threw in the garbage, Barb."

"Here's your seltzer," said the waiter. "And your Montalcino."

"I asked for the Cabernet," Barb said. "I don't want this. I didn't ask for Montalcino. I asked for the Cabernet."

She had, in fact, ordered the Montalcino, but the waiter was too smart to argue. He whisked away the offending glass and replaced it in record time with the Cabernet. Aviva tried to catch his eye and telepath apologies.

"L'chaim," Barb said. "So! Dad's fine. Good for him. He's always fine. That man should have been dead a hundred times over. But more important, Aviva: What is going on with *you*? Let's cut the bullshit. You are getting a little long in the tooth. What's the deal. What are you waiting for? You're going to run out of *time*."

Barb had raised Aviva on continuous insistence that people without children are the most pitiable losers on earth. This is officially known as "pronatalism" and unofficially known as "being an asshole." At least she had ceased the elaborate Sturm und Drang about Sam being a Gentile, however. Small mercies.

"Time and weather, right? Fucking relentless."

"What's your *plan*, Aviva?"

"I'm not in *charge*, Mom."

"Who's in charge, if not you?"

"Who do you *think*?"

"Oh, you're suddenly devout now? Give me a break."

"You think it's right, forcing kids?"

"I think people want children, Aviva. It's a very deep want. It's a very deep thing."

"Is that why you're so, like, 'religious'? To remind you that what you *want* matters most of all?"

"Well."

"If I remember correctly—and you'll have to forgive me here, because we were all working *very* hard at yeshiva and Zionist sleepaway camp to get ourselves voluntarily molested by all the cute rabbis-in-training, so I wasn't paying *super*-close attention to the Talmudic discourse—but if I remember correctly, there were some salient points about how we are *not* supreme or in charge. I have some vague recollections about how human beings aren't the end-all, be-all. Like: something-something humility something-something acceptance of our place in the universe, something-something respect the natural world, something-something? Like, something about being grateful for what we have and doing the best we can with whatever's allotted us? Don't quote me on any of this."

"Did you guys want bread or no bread?" the waiter wanted to know.

"No bread, thanks," Aviva said.

"*Definitely* bread," Barb said. "Aviva! What is the *point* of *life* if you don't have *children*? Life is *nothing* without children."

"I would *love* to have children, Barb. We have been *hoping* for that, as you *well know*. We have been hoping like *hell*, as it happens, but we have not been so blessed, and if we are never so blessed, I guess I'll just have to find another way of attempting a meaningful life. What else can I tell you."

"Don't be so sure your husband isn't going to have a change of heart and dump you someday for a young lady who's all too happy to have his babies. Happens all the time, honey. Men can do whatever they want. Ohhhhhh, this bread, my God, why are you not eating bread? And by the *way*! You talk like you have no *resources*. You have *resources*! *Avail* yourself, for heaven's sake. Go see a *doctor*. You have *options*. There are things they can *do*. Don't *worry* about the money."

"I'm not interested in getting *done*, Mom, get it? And I seem to be the *only woman I know* who feels this way. I might even be the only woman in the fucking *world* who feels this way, for all I can tell. I don't *want to*. I just don't freaking *want* to. I don't trust it, I don't like it, I think it's weird and violating and gross and just really . . . gross and weird and upsetting and I'm sorry, but no. Just no. Not for me."

"You had the risotto—be careful, that's a hot plate—and you had the chef salad, hold the bacon! Right? Good? Yes? Enjoy!"

"Excuse me, this is *way* too much dressing. I need the dressing on the *side*. Why would anyone want this much dressing? You should always let people dress their *own salads*."

The waiter wordlessly swept the offending salad off and away. What a pro. Aviva took a deep breath and leaned in to speak low.

"Mom, can I ask you a question? Seriously. Why are you so religious if you don't believe in God? What is the *point*, exactly?"

Barb smiled behind her wineglass. "I don't see what *God* has to do with anything. Religion is about community."

"Well . . . if there *is* a God, it sort of seems like these little matters of life and death would fall within God's purview, no?"

"Why do you have to *think* about everything so much? It's tiresome. Honestly."

"See what happens when you educate girls? There's this danger that they might actually start to think for themselves. Really inconvenient when women start to cultivate independent thought, I know, because it's way simpler for everyone if we pretty much just exist to be manipulated, right?"

The waiter returned with a naked salad and a ramekin of dressing.

"Thank you," Aviva told him on her mother's behalf.

"Aviva, for heaven's *sake*. *How* can it be that big a deal? Go see a *doctor*. You're being *ridiculous*." Barb violently stabbed her salad in time with the "doc" in "doctor" and the "dick" in "ridiculous."

"There's nothing *wrong* with me, Mom. I don't *need* a doctor. I'm not *sick*. You want me to *make* myself sick?"

"How do you know Sam isn't the problem?"

"Oh, wouldn't you love that. He's not."

"I don't think a doctor would do anything to *hurt* you."

"Oh, sure, *there's* the abridged history of western medicine. Uh-huh. Right. Do you remember the paper I won that award for in high school? About the founder of gynecology?"

"Everything is not a *conspiracy*, Aviva. Why do you have to *exaggerate* everything?"

"Because I value my heath? Because I've learned the hard way not to trust authorities managing my body for me? Because I've read some *his-*

tory? *Books*, Mom, remember *books*? You used to *love* books! Anyway, I've *been* to doctors. And I'm not *impressed*."

"Everyone wouldn't be doing this stuff if it were a bad thing."

"Okay, is that what they told you when they gave you full routine episiotomies before yanking your children out with forceps? 'Don't worry, everyone does it'? Or when they ordered you to formula feed, keep it classy? Is that what they said when your kids were being stuffed to the gills with antibiotics for viruses twice a year? Is that the jingle from the douche commercials in the seventies? 'Everyone wouldn't be doing it if it were a bad thing'? Was that the ad campaign for the baby powder that gave everyone ovarian cancer? Is that the official statement from the legal department at the chemical companies responsible for literally shrinking all the penises *in the world*?"

Barb munched her lettuce while Aviva kept on.

"Bodies are a *mystery*, you know? Bodies are *sacred*, in theory. Mortals are supposed to be *humble* before the great mysteries. Genesis, remember? You sent me to so much fucking *yeshiva*, Barb. Was there an 'unless you just really, really, *really* wanna artificially engineer an adorable little human pet of your very own' coda I *missed*?"

"But don't you want a *baby*? A few pills, some injections, whatever! You won't even *remember*. It'll get you a *baby*. A *baby*. Ooooh, or maybe *twins*. Then you're done. Like your brother, or that *mieskeit* from Temple Emanuel who married the actor. Wouldn't that would be *fun*? I'll help you. I'll come stay with you. Anything you need. We'll get you a nanny. A night nurse! I had the best night nurse with you guys. I barely had to touch you after you were born; it was fabulous. You won't even *remember* anything about any of this nonsense once have your precious babies." Barb made a sweeping gesture that meant no memory, no history. Any and every ordeal gone, forgotten, blown away as if by magic, or extreme weather.

"You wrote your master's thesis on *Frankenstein*, Barb. I plagiarized heavily from it in college. How does the part about the shortsighted doctor's single-minded pursuit of power inappropriate to his status as a lowly fallible human not *resonate*? The bit about Prometheus stealing fire from the gods? 'Penetrating' the secrets of nature? Lacking foresight and tormented beyond his wildest nightmares by his ill-advised creation, whom he is ill-prepared to *love*?"

Aviva was not breathing properly. Aviva could not get enough air in.

Barb had been headed for a stellar career in academia when she met Chuck, but by the time she was done having kids, academia had forgotten her, so Barb sank her teeth into elite hard-core recreational Judaism instead. A damn shame, because that thesis had been *righteous*. But bringing up Barb's aborted academic career was the surest way to piss Barb off.

"Okay, you know what? I'm sick of talking about this," Barb spat. "Do what you want. What do I care? So *don't* see a doctor, *don't* have a baby, *don't* give me more grandchildren. But I think that's incredibly sad. What a waste. What a terrible, terrible waste. It's your loss. It's our whole family's loss, actually. A tragedy. What on earth do you plan to *do* with yourself if you have no kids? Keep dressing like you're twenty, going around singing stupid songs? It's not gonna be so cute in another ten years, sweetie, let me tell you, and by that point the ship will have *sailed*. If you never have children you're just a child your whole life. How pathetic is *that*."

"How is everything, ladies? Can I get anyone another glass?"

"Just the check," Aviva said. Her songs *were* stupid; it was true.

Barb downed the last of her cabernet. "Children are the only game in town, honeypie."

"Well, let's hope I'm so blessed." Aviva laid her napkin delicately over her bowed head and held her hands out open on the table. "Let us join hands. Let us pray."

"Oh, cut it out," Barb hissed. "You want a baby, *get to work*. You're playing around with time, here, honey, and time is *not* your friend. Why do you have to take things so *far*?"

"I learned it from watching *you*!" Aviva mock-hollered.

Barbara. The Barb. Mother of Rob, then Mike, then a baby she lost at five months' gestation after falling off a bike, then Aviva. Four pregnancies! How could anyone *be* that lucky? That lost baby does not get mentioned because Jews do not mourn the unborn. We'd be in mourning our whole lives if we did, Barb always said, but she would never, ever get on a bike again. She was maybe bipolar or maybe manic-depressive or maybe a borderline or maybe a narcissist or maybe all of the above or maybe none of the above, maybe something no one had yet managed to classify in any shitty old diagnostic manual. Maybe, quite simply: a cunt. She had been in therapy once, briefly, but had quit, she said, because she and the therapist "ran out of things to talk about." Isn't it funny that the shitty diagnostic manual still has no entry for "cunt"?

"My mother had a *terrible* time getting pregnant," Barb said, signing the bill. "Seven years, they were married, and nothing. They even went to New York City to see a Polish doctor."

Aviva had heard this story many times. She had searched "Polish fertility doctor NYC 1940" to no end.

"What did the Polish doctor *do* to them?"

"God only knows. Apparently, my father only had one testicle. He was told to wear boxer shorts, I know that much."

How they must have despaired! How superstitious and desperate they must have gotten! No rich twins or bargain foreign surrogates or desperate egg donors or hundred-thousand-dollar dog clones from South Korea back then. 1938, '39, '40 . . . A war unfolding across the ocean, but war wasn't their problem. And everyone else always so worried about *preventing* pregnancy at any cost. Cackle.

"Thank you so much, ladies! Come back and see us again real soon!" The waiter avoided Aviva's eyes, refusing to bond over the awfulness of Barb. Aviva was alone in the world.

"So you're a product of early fertility medicine, Mom."

"Guess so! And would you prefer if they hadn't had me? Don't answer that."

Back to staring at her screen in Venice. There was a sweet-dreams dick pic from Sam, a positive pee stick pic from Jameela in Toronto, sweet sunshiny

Harmie Shmendrickson in the bathtub, and Hanalei, wondering if Aviva wanted to try a special psychedelic at a retreat center in Central America in a couple months, with a shaman.

Really good group, Hana wrote. Safe space.

I've never even properly tripped, Aviva replied.

Didn't you microdose, like, all of last summer?

Indeed, she had: outstanding.

Grandmother plant will show you exactly what you're holding. She'll show you exactly how to let go of whatever's got hold of you. Stuff that's not even yours. Stuff you inherited. Stuff you maybe don't even know you're carrying. Like a really good internal scrubbing.

Aviva tried to summon her actual grandmother, Barb's mother, subfertile in the early- to mid-twentieth century, and with so little recourse. What had the Polish doctor in the big city *done* to her? Meanwhile, Grandmother plant medicine, scrubber of secrets, addresser of ancestral trauma? Aviva told Hana she'd think about it.

In one (symbolic) hand Aviva held a prescription for the exciting new forced-ovulation pharmaceutical, and in the other, an invitation to join a circle of practitioners for ancient ceremonial plant medicine.

She had been open to many drugs over the years. Fun drugs. Alcohol and caffeine and lots of cannabis and some cocaine and kratom and mushrooms and Molly that one time and the LSD microdose bender last summer. So why would she draw the line at fertility drugs? Or ceremonial psychedelics? What, after all, was her *problem*? Let's do allllllll the drugs, shall we? You never know if you never try.

The feed of a nascent songstress everyone followed, better known for her emaciated frame in diaphanous dresses than her music, was currently talking up her accidental pregnancy like Oh, hey, wow, guess I got knocked up! Because hark: Getting pregnant accidentally at this point in time, on this continent, in this caste, was some sort of funky/punky win. "Trying" was the ultimate uncoolest. Finding oneself—*OOPS*—with child? Inveterately cool. The songstress was talking up her unplanned-but-welcome pregnancy with twee annoyance, like Oh well, guess now I'm having a baby or whatever! Translation: I'm not a desperate loser like alla youse who *want* to breed; I'm just an effortlessly fun gal with an irresistible womb! It was fascinating as an indicator of possible cultural shift: fertility treatment was conventionally bougie/entitled/lame, like summering on the Cape or mall shopping or fake tits or a destination wedding. Might this attitude signal a glimmer of rebellion on the horizon? A status-conscious class of women who might come to view assisted reproduction as a trapping of convention, lending it the same cultural distaste as, say, a McMansion lawn in the 'burbs crawling with whatever mutant insects survived the deforestation and insecticide?

Someone with whom Aviva had gone to school spent years posting about her repeated miscarriages and secondary infertility, and now here's the announcement that she's pregnant. Everyone thrilled for her, absolutely over the moon: *YOU DID IT!*

A label-mate, total weirdo with amazing style, married to an oddball-chic producer twenty years her senior, adorably bloated in her second trimester, just under the wire; she's past forty if she's a day.

Someone with whom Aviva had partied hard on tour years ago cuddled twins. The caption: "Thank you, ovaries!"

A powerful forty-nine-year-old music exec captioned a very, very tiny newborn in an isolette: "Today is a beautiful, beautiful day! The most beautiful day! Today I get to hold my daughter in my arms. Finally. For years I held her in my heart, but she wasn't real to anyone else. She was only real to me. She was always real to me. Thank you for choosing me, finally, my beautiful girl. You are the most wonderful thing I ever dared hope for. I'm finally a mother! I never stopped believing!"

A fertility columnist had a new piece up: Were Jewish women "doing battle with" infertility aware that if they moved to Israel they could get at least two rounds of IVF paid for by the government? A thrilling, progressive perk of aliyah! The US should consider subsidizing fertility treatment, too! The whole *world* should subsidize fertility treatment! It's, like, the *awesome* version of eugenics! Margaret Sanger would be so super delighted, wouldn't she? *When motherhood becomes the fruit of a deep yearning, not the result of ignorance or accident, its children will become the foundation of a new race*, Sanger had written. Yeah, Margie, word: The old races aren't really working out, maybe you're right, let's start a new one. It'll all be entitled, rich, elderly people for whom offspring can best be understood as . . . property. Utopia awaits!

Over in the tabloids, meanwhile, a midwestern dude cradled his cata-strophically premature infant quintuplets alongside a crowdfunding plea: his wife, the mother of the litter, had died tragically in childbirth, though no mention, and perhaps no real comprehension, of what the fuck had transpired to set *that* particular shitshow in motion.

The female body our perennial favorite object for manipulation, and always the righteously suffering rule-followers who violently reject any sug-gestion that they might be complicit. *You might be complicit*, Aviva tried out, rap-style. *You might be the problem. You might be sucking the dick of a system you're a cog in.*

What did it *mean* to force ovulation? What did it *mean* to inject massive quantities of synthetic hormones? To chemically bathe sperm? To inject them directly into the womb, or into an egg. To freeze an embryo. To de-frost the embryo. To implant the embryo. To buy eggs. To buy embryos. To manipulate the endocrine system in order to support an embryo. Oh! And did everyone know that artificial gestation was on its way? Did everyone know that embryos were being routinely created and experimented on and discarded? But that's where you started to overlap with the anti-choice folk, which was uncomfortable, to say the least. Regardless: Was everyone aware of the study about long-term vascular degeneration in people created in this way? Was everyone really comfortable living in a society that believes it has the right to buy and sell life *itself*? Did the biological reprogramming of female bodies in the service of reproduction *at any cost* mean *nothing*?

No, Aviva did not want to hop on the fertility drug train. Still, it whistled its comings and goings day and night. Next stop: forced-ovulation station! Choo-choo!

* * *

She began the day with her bare feet in the Pacific surf, then finished the Love Fiend memoir over a delicious solitary breakfast at the best vegan diner in the world. A relief to be done with that Fiend, yet again. Adios, amigo. She left the waiter a big cash tip inside the memoir and headed off to an artisanal donut place, where she picked up a dirty dozen for the nursing staff on Chuck's floor.

Mike was already in the corner chair, staring at his computer.

"Morning," Aviva said.

He grunted, but didn't look up.

"Donut?"

"No thanks."

"Where's Charlene?"

Mike shrugged. The machines beeped. Chuck slept. There was a little more color in his face today.

"How is he?"

"They're going to help him get out of bed later, maybe let him try to stand and walk around a little."

To be born at all is to be blessed, but to be born with older brothers is to be especially blessed. Or maybe to be born at all is to be *cursed*, but that line of thinking doesn't get us very far, so let's go with "blessed," for the sake of argument.

"Tell me about your family," new therapists always said, and Aviva would invariably start weeping.

"They're terrible people," she'd sob. Not strictly true: Chuck was a deadbeat pussy hound, fine, but he was also fundamentally kind, and Barb was . . . well, Barb was somewhat manageable approximately twice a year at dinner or a movie or a one-size-fits-most linen garment shop. But Aviva had lost both of her beloved big brothers—one was dead, and the other was living dead. And yeah, she had managed to busy herself with music and yoga and friends and men and music and clothes and music and books and songs and art and parties and weed and touring and Sam (and . . .

eventually a baby, right? Where was the goddamn baby? It seemed extra fucking unfair that there was not yet a baby!), but it was a pretty sizable void. The bitter lack of baby was like *compounded* void. Did one howling grief simply replace another over the course of a person's lifetime? Was that how things worked? Anyway, one of her beloved big brothers was dead and the other was living dead, and here was the awful truth: the latter hurt more, by *far*.

They sat around all day. Aviva drank tea and doodled in her notebook. Lyrics and fragments and hearts and faces and a sketch of Mike slumped horribly in his chair, gnarled around his screen. She had no idea what Mike thought about in general, or who Mike even *was* at this point, their break having been so thorough that the stump of former connection felt only occasional phantom pain. He had been an unremitting sadist for years—her first love, her first abuser—and she had finally, finally gotten him out of her system. She adored this colloquial. This was what you did if you valued yourself: you kept your system tip-top. You refused to be stuck with stuff you didn't want, ruinous stuff. You got it *out* of your *system*, by whatever means necessary. But something about Mike's grim posture and bearing still made her sad.

"How're the twins?" she ventured. One was said to "break" a silence, wasn't that interesting? Silence a world unto itself, an intact entity; to make sound was to break it.

Mike held up his phone, displaying a recent photo.

Aviva loved the twins. It wasn't their fault their parents were assholes. Who amongst us is to blame for the fact of our parents being assholes? They were five now, little sweeties. Jasmine Justine and James Jackson. Aviva had attempted to bond with What's-Her-Face postpartum: "Into alliteration, huh?"

"No," What's-Her-Face had said. "I just really love the letter 'J.'"

What's-Her-Face had been a teenage east-side self-identified "gangbanger ho" who remade herself first into an exclusive west-side wedding planner and then into Mike's ferociously perfect wifey. She had converted to Judaism (Reform, of course), though she still wore a tiny diamond cross around her neck, out of respect for her still-living *abuela*. Her life was a tightly scheduled orgy of manicures and orchids and gray-palette interior design like a cutting-edge W Hotel lobby circa 1999 and specific enormous pristine leather purses and high-end takeout for dinner every single night because she refused to engage with food in any way whatsoever and an elderly Guatemalan maid polishing the Sub-Zero and a bored white-girl nanny schlepping the kids to and from school and lessons and play dates. Which was, more or less, a precise re-creation of how Aviva and Mike and Rob had been raised, until it had all collapsed into a radioactive trash fire. Aviva had the sense that she might have quite liked the original What's-Her-Face.

Later in the afternoon, the hospital chaplain came by. Short, sensible haircut, pretty craft fair blue stone earrings, solid eye contact, wide-toe-box shoes.

"I wanted to check in, say hello, see how you're doing," the chaplain murmured, offering a soft hand. "May I sit down?"

"Gotta go," Mike said, packing up and vanishing in record time.

Aviva and the chaplain sat staring at the unconscious old man.

"He doesn't take *care* of himself, is the thing," Aviva said.

The chaplain nodded.

"He's never taken *care* of himself. He isn't *honest* with himself."

The chaplain nodded.

"It's an incredibly fucked-up family. They say all families are fucked up, but, you know, some are, like, more fucked up than others. Like: fine line between routine dysfunction and Greek tragedy, am I right or am I right?" She did a burlesque wink, hoping to get a laugh. But no: the chaplain just stared at her hands.

Then the chaplain seemed to remember why she was here. She pulled a binder from her tote bag. "Do you or your family follow any particular religious tradition? I have lots of material here . . . Protestant, Catholic, Episcopal, Hindu, Muslim . . ."

Chuck was the kind of Jew who identified as a Jew mostly because he had a huge schnoz, and because growing up in Inglewood, none of his shithead classmates would let him forget for five fucking minutes that he was a Jew. Therefore: he was a Jew. That the mother of his children had had a surprise midlife return to the fold was a bit awkward for him, but what can you do.

"Jews," Aviva said. "Full-on Jews. Extra Jewy Jews. With nuts!"

Again, no laugh. The chaplain flipped to the appropriate tab and scanned the pages, seeming lost. Aviva helped her out.

"It's called the Mi Sheberach. May I? Here, lemme see. Yeah. Right here. Prayer for the sick. Jews believe that physical and spiritual health are linked, and that you really need both to, ideally, like, live a full and happy life."

"Would you like to say it with me?"

They read the transliteration together, halting and hollow. The chaplain wasn't into it. You have to be into it, is the secret.

"Amen," the chaplain said, beaming, as though they had accomplished something wonderful together.

"Sooooo, what's the chaplaincy biz like? How long you been in it?"

"I'm somewhat new, but I find it very fulfilling."

"Do you yourself have a favorite spiritual tradition?"

"Well, actually, my grandparents were Jewish. But I was raised Universalist, so."

See you on the trains, Barb would say.

"Just curious, sort of off topic . . . but clergy's clergy, right? What do you think about . . . infertility? Do you think it's a sort of celestial punishment?"

"Well—that's—I don't—"

"I'm asking for a friend."

"How— Well, very challenging to even—"

"No, you're right, I'm sorry, no worries, beside the point, what with the old man in such bad shape. But you must see *everything*, huh? Every kind of corporeal suffering imaginable, right? And isn't it all, like, metaphysical at the end of the day? The sufferings of the body? People's approaches to the sufferings of the body? I mean: What even is a body without breath? The *person* is the *breath*, do you know what I mean? The body is just the shell. The encasement. Whatever. I dunno."

Amidst the machines, the ever-present beeping, the smell of bleach, and the squeaking of nurses' clogs on the polished hallway floor beyond the curtain, the chaplain remained blessedly, mercifully silent.

"Anyway," Aviva went on, "there's pretty much only one approach to the sufferings of the body around here. Does it ever get you down?"

"Sometimes."

"Do you think it's worth praying to the ancestors?"

"Well, I—"

"For my friend."

The chaplain stared at her hands again. Maybe her silence was mandated by nature or by training. There was a lot to be said for silence. Aviva could take a lesson. Pretty much everyone Aviva knew could take a lesson. But by the same token, keep your flaccid transliterated Mi Sheberach and get the fuck out of here with your weak-ass watered-down Universalist bullshit, hon.

"Thank you so much for stopping by," Aviva said. "We really appreciate it. It's really very noble work you do."

The chaplain gave Aviva her card.

In the car, Amy served as a ferocious corrective. Art is a *corrective*, that's what it is. Entertainment is distraction, vacation, and that's fine, too, for kicks. But art is something else. Aviva drove directly back to the vegan diner, and what do you know? As she walked in, there was Amy, *still singing*! Ha! The very same *song*, even! Picking up almost exactly where she'd left off when Aviva had turned off the car.

She claimed a spot at the counter and made no effort to hide her joy.

A girl sitting kitty-corner elbowed her friend: "Look, dude, she's grooving, too! Hey girl, hey! I see you grooving! Oh yeah."

The girl's friend grinned: "How can you not? This fucking chick, I mean . . . Once in a lifetime."

And without another word they all got up and danced for the rest of the song.

"This girl I know says she's still alive," said the girl when they sat back down. Her excellent white canvas pseudo-work-wear set off a deep tan and mood-ring eyes. "They were in rehab together in Malibu."

"I would so fucking buy that," Aviva said. "That would be *perfect*. She only ever wanted to be a wife and a mum. Singing was just something she loved to do for herself. Faking her own death is exactly the kind of shit she'd pull."

"I *KNOW!*" the girl shrieked. "Nobody would even *recognize* her if she took off the wig and eyeliner and gained a few. I'll bet you *anything* she's still alive. She faked the fuck out of that shit and got the hell on with her life."

"Yeah. But alive, not alive, what's the difference, when you get right down to it?"

"Archie," the girl said to her friend. "Arch, we got a philosopher, here. We got ourselves a total fucking philosopher, here. Are you an artist? You must be an artist."

"I'm definitely not *not* an artist. I mean, who can *say* what's up with existence versus nonexistence? Who's got a conclusive *answer* to that? No one, that's who! So I'm a big believer in everyone just shutting the fuck up. Except for me. Does that make me an artist?"

"Whoa," the girl said, grinning. "Whoa."

"*Yes*," said Archie.

"She's alive because we *say* she's alive," Aviva said. "And she's dead because it's none of our business anyway."

"My fucking piece-of-shit brother made my parents send me to rehab," the girl said. "Amy wasn't there, though."

Aviva held up both hands for double high five: "I have a piece-of-shit brother, too!"

The girl slid off her stool, came and sat next to Aviva. "You have a really cool, loving vibe about you." She scrawled her number on a piece of paper. "Call me. We have to stick together. People like us."

"*So* true," Aviva said, and handed the girl the chaplain's card.

Everyone at the label was so "pleased," Jerry kept saying—festival bookings were robust, and there was talk of another tour, maybe just New England, maybe the Northwest, plus interest from the UK and elsewhere in Europe. *Womb Service* had surpassed expectations. People continuously tap-tappety-tapped at their machines about it. "There's a momentum happening, babe. Things are happening. People are talking. The higher-ups are *happy*."

"Happy enough to let me record some crazy-expensive covers next?!"

"Simmer down. Let's enjoy this. It's a nice plateau. They are *pleased*, V. Let's continue to *please* them. They can be generous when they are pleased. Point of fact: the A&R guy heard you're in LA and wants to give you their box at the Hollywood Bowl tomorrow night."

Classical night, and last-minute, but still.

Alone with her father in the late afternoon, Aviva put her hands on him. Kind touch. Caring touch. Breathing steadily around and through and for him. She found some kind of tarp in a cabinet and laid it down on the floor: enough with the infernal chairs. She got down, stretched, loosened up, moved energy around and out and through. This was how you reconciled yourself to yourself.

Chuck slept and slept. Aviva dropped weed tincture under her tongue.

"I wouldn't sit on the floor in here," said a nurse who stopped in to push buttons and check monitors. Aviva didn't care. You had to get down on the floor if you had any hope of cutting any shit whatsoever; those were the rules.

Mike showed up to slump in the corner chair and doomscroll. But see, she could *stomach* Mike on a little weed tincture; she felt legitimately *sorry* for Mike on a little weed tincture, really and truly and compassionately *sorry* for the guy. On a little weed tincture, she felt like *his* big sister, and then the whole nightmare of existing in relation to him made a different kind of *sense*. Stoned, she could process it all via *italics*. Stoned, she could, in essence, be like: "It's *okay*, sweetie, it's *okay*, there, *there*," and she could back away slowly, as if from an angry dog. You cannot turn and run like hell from an angry dog, because the angry dog would chase you. You had to make peace with the angry dog, let it "win." Okay, angry dog, you win. Yes, angry dog, you are very powerful, indeed. I surrender. And *then* you could back away, inch by blessed inch. She'd had it all wrong in the past. She'd been startled by and scared of the angry dog. She'd berated it, yelled at it, tried to fight it, and demanded, loudly, repeatedly, to know what the fuck its *problem* was. Now she knew better: Don't *yell* at an angry dog, for God's sake. Just back *away*, slowly, slowly, slowly, and be *gone*. It would forget all about you in due course.

"How's Sam?" Mike said out of nowhere, like the word "Sam" was, itself, an insult.

"He's good."

"You ever gonna have kids, or what?"

Breathe, Aviva. Breathe.

To admit to Mike that she was in fact desperately hoping to be blessed with children but had thus far been cruelly denied for some mysterious reason(s) was to tear out and devour her own heart. Do you know what it's like to find yourself in the company of a person who is quite interested in your deep and prolonged suffering? It's bad. Impossible to have any sort of decent interaction with Mike. Dangerous and pointless even to attempt. The Rabbi's many-hundreds-of-dollars-an-hour advice was simple: ignore Mike. No reaction whatsoever. Withdraw the oh-so-precious gift of your attention, and that is all. Peace out. See you in another life, motherfucker.

"We'd love to have kids," she said, working on evenness and detachment. Fabulous miracle, to live within the fortress of "we." So *righteous*, belonging to a "we." It had its own upbeat tenor, the "we." How she loved her "we."

"Well, what are you waiting for? You know how it works, right?"

Probably the longest continuous string of words he had spoken to her since the late eighties. She aimed her mildest approximation of smile at the space just above the top of his head. Be caaaaaareful, she could hear the Rabbi say. Tighten the hammock of your pelvic floor, she could hear Hana say. Let your breath expand your ribs horizontally, she could hear Sarah say. Music school had been absurd, spilling over with diseased egos and ferocious climbers, but Aviva had badly needed to learn to breathe, and Sarah had taught her. Breathing well could be a kind of rebellion, resistance, like growing and canning your own food. She let her arms fall open. Claim the space. Fill the lungs to capacity (more, more, full, fuller, fullest), hold, and then release, slow and steady, past where you think you're done (out, out, empty, emptier, emptiest). All disease and disorder come from improper breathing, Sarah believed. All the way in, all the way out. The diaphragm a huge balloon, the pelvic floor its mirror. Over and over again until consciousness is altered, then rejoin the external world changed. What if we could teach this to guerilla armies. What if we could teach this to middle schoolers. What if we could teach this in mental hospitals, prisons, detention centers, police stations, refugee camps, city councils, House, Senate. Mike went back to pretending to read his screen. Mike mattered not at all.

"You know," he said, with an odd, strangled note of authenticity creeping into his voice, "we wouldn't have the twins without help."

Oh-ho, but let us call bullshit on that narrative! The best fertility doctors were no less a status symbol than one's car, address, shoes, manicure, follower count, and handbag. What's-Her-Face wouldn't have *dreamt* of leaving the commodity of *offspring* to something as low-class as *fate*. According to Barb, they had "tried" to get pregnant for about three months, then gone directly to the biggest guns in town. At Barb's insistence, those idiots were still paying rent on nine frozen embryos. Barb was obsessed with those frozen embryos. They had officially taken the place of Rob's long-lost frozen sperm. Household gods, if you will. Screw ancestors: we have our *descendants* on ice.

"Cool," Aviva said, and gathered up her stuff to go.

She treated herself to a quilted jacket from some stupid-gorgeous shop on Abbot Kinney. And a new nontoxic pigment lipstick. And a fresh-pressed juice. Then a strip-mall Thai massage. Right neck and shoulder were all fucked up, as per usual. "Everything connected," the masseur kept whispering. "Everything connected." She made the most lovely, sympathetic noises. "Ooh," she crooned at Aviva. "Ooh, yes— Ooh, yes. Everything connected. Everything connected." Then a fourteen-dollar gold-flake pomegranate smoothie from a Persian wellness café. Then sunset on the beach by the skate park, toes in the sand. A quinoa bowl with toasted coconut flakes and maca for dinner. A shot of algae, a seventy-five-dollar probiotic supplement, a self-administered orgasm, and, last but not least, sleep.

A dream: she left Sam and their baby at home and went to a party at the Love Fiend's. (Not him again! She was done with him! Wasn't she?!) The Fiend's girlfriend wasn't around. Aviva connected with him instantly, deeply, and soon they were kissing. She was aware of it being "wrong," but she wanted him. It predated Sam, that want, and therefore could not be said to be a violation of her loyalty to Sam. In the dream, however, the Fiend was a terrible kisser. He slobbered all over her face, and she found him not enjoyable in the least. She no longer wanted him. She disentangled herself and offered a friendly embrace, instead. He vanished to tend to his party, which was not going well. She gathered her things and prepared to leave. But then the party started to thrum with life and music and energy, and soon it looked like a rave, the Fiend's apartment transformed to a cavernous warehouse full of writhing bodies. She put down her things. And then it was Cracker beside her, grinning a mischievous grin. "What do you think, darlin'," Cracker said. She was so glad to see him! (*Him?*

Really?! Enough with him!) She looked anxiously out a window, hoping she could get away with staying a little longer before going home to Sam and the baby. Oh my God! She had a baby at home! A husband and a baby! Fuck it, she thought, and stayed to party. Cracker displayed what looked like candy: strips of red gummy coated with sour sugar. She watched him light a match and blow one into a bubble or something, sucking out the air and then immediately collapsing into an exaggerated intoxicated haze. Suddenly it all seemed harrowing and creepy: this drug, this party, these men. But she continued to sit there, entranced, and she forgot all about the baby, and—oh no! Oh shit! No!—at home Sam was nowhere to be found, and the baby had cried and cried and cried until it died.

Chuck came to with a start the next morning, like he'd been dreaming of falling.

"You're here," he said.

"I'm here, Daddy."

"How's the album selling?"

"Oh my God, Daddy, who gives a shit?"

"Where's my phone?"

"You don't need your phone, Daddy."

He glanced around at the room, his IV, the tubes and wires. He didn't remember his time on the ventilator.

"I got myself pretty fucked up, huh?"

She managed to wrangle some quality time with the twins, Jazzy and Jamie, negotiated at great length with the nanny, who negotiated at great length with What's-Her-Face, who negotiated at great length with a foundational emptiness Aviva could not begin to fathom.

In the car, Aviva put on Pete Seeger.

"He's singing about social justice," she told the twins.

"What's social justice?"

"It's that we all have to work together to take care of each other, not just ourselves, and that no one should be able get rich off anyone else's suffering, or anyone else's work, or anyone else's lack of anything."

At the playground, Jamie scaled the heights. Top of the slide, top of the climbing tower, back and forth on the little rope bridge between the two. He shouted down at Jazzy and Aviva, who preferred chillin' on the swings: "How's it going down there?"

Their job was to reply: "Good, how's it going up there?" "Good!" Jamie would holler back, and then again, a minute later: "How's it going down there?" And so on. Awesome little rhythm.

The twins loved their Auntie V, all the more so because it sounded like "Aunt TV," which was just about the funniest thing in the world. Jazz, especially, clung *so* tight that she seemed to want to crawl *inside* Aviva. She constantly tried to get up into Aviva's lap, obsessively clutched Aviva's hand, and wrapped her sweet little arms around Aviva's neck every chance she got, nuzzling right on in. It was adorable and flattering, sure, but soon Aviva grew concerned that Jazzy was just bereft of basic affection in general. Suffice it to say, What's-Her-Face wasn't big on "attachment" parenting, that wacky philosophy of caring for one's young like a mammal.

Soon the twins got involved in a game of hide-and-seek with some other kids, and a random, tiny child marched up to Aviva: "Whose mom are you?"

The child had wide-set eyes and a missing front tooth. She seemed a little small for her age, or a little wise for her years, or both.

"No one," Aviva told her. "None of them. I don't have a kid. Yet."

"Well, then why are you here? You're not allowed to be here unless you're with a kid."

"That's my niece and nephew, over there. I'm with them."

"They twins?"

"Yes."

"So that means you're their auntie."

"Yup."

"I have triplets at my school."

"I bet you do."

"So where is your daughter?"

"I don't have a daughter."

"You don't?"

"Nope."

"Are you *sure*?"

"Pretty sure, yeah."

"Yes, you do!"

"*Do* I?"

"Definitely." The tiny child nodded.

"I mean, I hope so. I'm kind of waiting for her."

"She's coming on a Wednesday. Or maybe a Friday."

"*Really?*"

"Yes. Definitely a Wednesday, I think."

"What's her name?"

"She doesn't *have* one," the child said, rolling her eyes at Aviva's stupidity. "You have to *name* her, silly. You're her *mom*."

A woman called out: "*Tribeca!* Stop bothering the nice lady. It's time to go!"

"Bye," the child said, and skipped away with an assured little wave.

After the playground, Aviva took the twins to a *The Little Mermaid* matinee at one of the beautiful old theaters in Westwood. Jazzy was riveted by Ursula, the villain, but Jamie was pretty unmoved by the whole thing. Afterward, over steamers and cookies, Aviva threw out a thought experiment.

"What would you give up your voice for?"

"Maybe a puppy," Jazzy said. "Something to love."

"Nothing," said Jamie. "I would *never* give up my voice."

Attaboy.

"What about you, Auntie V? What would you give up your voice for?"

"A baby."

"But then you wouldn't be able to *sing*," said Jamie. "You *have* to be able to sing, Auntie V, it's your *job*!"

"Good point."

"How about *I'll* be your baby," Jazzy said. "And then you don't have to give up anything."

"How come you have to give anything up to have a baby, anyway?" wondered Jamie. "Can't you just . . . have a baby?"

Jazzy piped up: "*Mommy* says babies come from when a mommy and a daddy go see a special *doctor* and the *doctor* mixes up special *parts* of the mommy and daddy and then pops it into the mommy's *stomach* to cook for a while!"

"Oh yeah," said Jamie. "And then when it's all cooked the doctor takes it out and it's a baby-cake!"

Much giggling.

"No," Aviva said. "That's not right, darlings. I mean, it may be *increasingly* right, and by the time you're all grown-up it might actually be *mostly* right, but *usually* there's a big sort of special, hug-dance that a mommy and daddy do. It's really fun and nice, and they put all their happiness and fun into the special hug-dance, and if they're very, very lucky it can sometimes make a kind of a spark, or connection, and start a baby growing in the mommy's *womb*. Stomach is where *food* goes, my love, before it turns into *poop*. A baby can't grow in a stomach. Babies can only grow in a very cool part of a person called a *womb*. And, like, fake plastic wombs in laboratories if you're *super* rich and patriarchal and just, like, think it's cool trying to exert personal supremacy over biology."

"What's biology?" Jamie wondered.

"It's the science of how things are."

"What's 'personal su-far-macy'?"

"It's when you think you're the boss of everything that is, was, and ever will be."

"So, Auntie V?"

"Yes, darling?"

"Why don't you have any babies? I would like you to have a baby so I could have a baby cousin."

"I would like that, too. You would be a great big cousin."

"You would be a great mommy!"

"Our mom says you don't really like babies, otherwise you'd ask the doctor to make you some."

Well, darling, sorry to break it to you, but your mommy is a truly epic shit-for-brains.

After she dropped them back with the nanny, Aviva posted a selfie from the playground. See? See?? She loved kids! She was a beloved auntie! Not one of those cold, brittle, barren bitches who hate children, no: Aviva was soft and nurturing and selfless and adoring and adored. See how the little ones clung to her? She was worthy. She was a complete and total member of the human race, goddamn it. Goddamn it. Goddamn it. Goddamn it.

She invited three high school friends to the Hollywood Bowl: Nikki, Jenn, and Holly.

Nikki had a girl and a boy (Zadie, six; Dylan, three), no problem. She'd been spared reproductive troubles but not marital ones: her husband had ditched out. She ran an art gallery out of the formerly derelict mixed-use nine-story downtown loft building her parents had bought for a song when no one wanted to go anywhere *near* downtown.

Jenn had one son (Homer), aged four, from her first round of Clomid. She was bored out of her mind, half-heartedly trying for another baby, and just into her second decade of managing a wildly expensive boutique on Larchmont.

Holly had "twiblings" (Scarlett and Berlin) born two years apart from the same batch of frozen embryos. She'd had a swank job as an event planner at a talent agency 'til the girls were born; now she was starting a company whose mission was impossible to parse but had something to do with disseminating a precise and costly bohemian-chic home décor aesthetic on sosh meed. Her husband was an agent. Holly wasn't dumb, per se, but she did seem to be getting slightly less coherent over time. Occasionally she read a memoir by a television personality, but otherwise, if it didn't come up on her feed, she had absolutely no idea it existed.

"Jesus, V," Nikki said over macrobiotic small plates, "maybe *not* having kids is the smart move, here. My life is really just, like, I mean: *Mom. Mom. Mom. Mom. Mom. Mom. Mom.*"

"They're everything to you but, like, they *can't* be everything to you," Jenn said.

"You're everything to *them*, but you *can't* be everything to them," Nikki said.

"The other moms are beyond lame," Jenn said. "I have never met such lame asses in my fucking life. It's like a whole undiscovered lame country."

"Well, get the fuck out of Larchmont," Nikki said. "What did you expect? Punk rock?"

"Some of the dads are kind of hot. Anyway, it's true," Jenn said. "Kids are not a good hobby. You still need, like, hobbies."

"Stop scaring her, you guys!" said Holly. "V, motherhood is *amazing*."

"Oh my God, shut the fuck up, Holly."

"You shut the fuck up, Nikki."

"I just . . . never imagined myself as childless," Aviva said.

"Well, la-di-da," Nikki said. "I just . . . never imagined myself as a divorcée."

Jenn nodded: "I never imagined Homer being an only child."

"I never imagined myself as being victimized by a corrupt political system," Nikki said.

"I never imagined myself having an intimate relationship with a machine," Jenn said.

"I never imagined myself as a climate refugee."

"I never imagined myself as a corpse."

"They think they figured out why I can't get pregnant again, you guys," Jenn said. "Ready for this? Excessive scarring caused by the C-section. Apparently not uncommon."

"Are you serious?!"

"Dead."

"I've never even *heard* of that."

"Right?"

"I've had some really rough pap smears," Aviva said. "You think I could have, like, cervical scarring?"

Jenn shrugged.

"God*damn* it; I *knew* I shouldn't have gotten all those pap smears. I fucking *hate* pap smears. And now they're saying we don't even *need* regular pap smears. 'Get yearly pap smears! We need to scrape off bits of your cervix on the regular!' 'Just kidding! Don't get yearly pap smears! Every three to five years is fine! Sorry your cervix is all fucked up now!'"

"So last month the OB recommends IVF," Jenn said, "and sends me to the clinic at UCLA. They *love* me there, I'm *super* young compared to all the dowagers in the waiting room, everyone's gung-ho, I'm a *great candidate*, the *perfect candidate*, they just *love* me, they're all seriously like *grinning* at me, there's pictures of babies *everywhere*, you could cut the tension in the waiting room with a *knife*. I'm like, okay, bring it on, if we're doing this let's do this. Then a huge box of stuff comes via FedEx two days later. Literally seven thousand dollars' worth of ovary 'roids via FedEx. Brent's insurance covered *all* of it. It sat in my fridge for a day, syringes and hormones and all *kindsa* shit. An instructional DVD. A fucking *DVD*. I didn't sleep."

"Why did the DVD need to be in the fridge?" Holly wondered.

"Oh my God, Holly, shut the fuck up," Nikki said.

"So then what?"

"Well, I'll tell you, friend," Jenn said. "I changed my mind. I found some chick on a message board—some unfortunate lady whose insurance won't cover any more of that shit—and she came to pick up the whole box like the *moment* the sun rose. I can't even tell you how hysterical with gratitude she was. She was, like, *sobbing*. Like *thank you, you're an angel, you're an angel, thank you*. I'm like, lady, I don't think I'm doing you much of a solid here, but good luck, you know? Knock yourself out."

"Knock yourself *up*."

"Way to make someone's day," said Nikki. "Maybe there's, like, an underground sisterhood thing you could get going, like get all the savvy ladies working at Apple or wherever all the fertility shit is covered to funnel ovary 'roids to the needy. Robin Hood–style."

"She sent me *roses*."

"Everyone has to do whatever they're comfortable with," Holly said whilst art-directing a photo of their champagne glasses looming in the foreground, with the famous stage backlit by the setting sun.

"I'm not comfortable with any of it," Aviva said. "It *all* sounds bad. I'm supposed to take some new thing. Forgot what it's called. Femara! Though by now there's probably a *new* new thing."

"Ooooh," Nikki said. "The new thing! Gimme the new thing! I want the new thing! The new thing must be better than the old thing!"

"I mean, *should* I?"

"I don't see why not," Holly said. "Everyone does it."

Holly had no concerns whatsoever about the new shit, the old shit, the future shit, whatever shit anyone cooked up in whatever lab within whatever compound within whatever vast network of highways.

"It's going to make regular PMS feel like doing ecstasy with unicorns in a meadow on a sunny day by a babbling brook," said Jenn. "That much I can promise you."

"Clomid didn't bother me at all," said Holly.

"At *all* at all?!"

"I mean, maybe a little? I might have been a *teensy* bit emotional? But I barely remember." Holly was a true-blue woman, the genuine article: she put everyone else first, bore her suffering without complaint, asked no questions, told only aesthetically compelling Instagram lies. She also had a full-time nanny and a live-in housekeeper, but leave that aside for now.

The stage lights came on, and butlers began to clear away the remnants of dinner.

"Yuja Wang," Nikki read from the program.

"Use your *wang*?!"

"Don't be an ass: *Yuja Wang*. The pianist's name."

"The *penis's* name?!"

"Wow," Aviva said, too loudly. "That has to be a sign, right there! You guys! I should *not* force ovulation and get artificially inseminated. *Use your wang!* I should use my *wang*. A message!"

The elderly folks double-dating in the next box turned and stared.

"That's fucking racist," Nikki hissed.

"Nikki's right, babe," Jenn said. "Watch it."

Holly knocked back the last of her champagne, and Aviva poured most of hers into Holly's empty glass.

"A toast, you guys," Aviva said. "To all the things we don't have. I, for one, don't have a baby."

"I don't have a fulfilling career," Jenn offered.

"I don't have a husband," Nikki said.

"I don't have a son," Holly said.

"I don't have a daughter," Jenn added.

"We all don't have something!" Aviva sang. "Keep it *going* . . ."

"I don't have a strong jawline," Jenn said.

"I don't have that many followers," Holly said.

"I don't have any feeling in my pelvis," said Nikki, who had, as a matter of course, ripped to her butthole under the inept supervision of LA's finest OB. A lot of LA glitterati ripped to their buttholes under the inept supervision of this particular OB, then joked about it in *People* magazine, scaring the living shit out of brainwashed mass-market consumers in Nowheresville, who became thusly convinced that C-sections were, just, like, "easier."

"I don't have any memory of the years 2000 to 2010," Aviva said.

"L'chaim!"

Onstage, the musicians were warming up.

"You guys, oh my God, Yuja Wang is twenty-fucking-eight years old!"

"So's the conductor," Aviva said

Wang emerged to thunderous applause, in a dazzling disco ball of a gown. She took a bow, sat at the piano, and proceeded to shred on some Prokofiev. From the box, and via the high-def monitors on either side of the stage, you could see every shimmering sequin, every dancing finger, every bead of sweat running down her nude back.

"You don't *have* to get artificially inseminated, you know," Holly whispered to Aviva as the applause roared at intermission. "You can just take the drugs and then just get it on like usual."

"But if you *are* going to take the stuff you probably *should* get inseminated," Jenn leaned in to add. "Just 'cause: Why leave room for error? If it's not happening by itself in the first place, and you're gonna take the drugs anyway, don't leave it to chance. Insemination is your safest bet."

"Or you could just leave *out* the drugs entirely, and try insemination *without* any drugs," Holly realized.

"Or," Nikki added, "just be fucking glad you get to sleep eight hours a night for the rest of your life. Just be fucking *glad* you get to have twenty fucking minutes to your goddamn self before bed. Just be glad you can watch TV whenever you feel like it. Be grateful you don't have to go back-to-school shopping at Old fucking Navy. Thank your lucky fucking *stars* you don't have to pretend to be interested in making friends with the other mommies."

"That attitude doesn't really line up with the, like, *brand* you're putting out there on your feed, Nik," said Holly.

"Eat a bag of dicks, Holly," said Nikki.

The internet can be a good resource (How *do* you cook navy beans?), but it's no comfort at all. Good morning! It was Mother's Day.

An insufferable girl from college posed beatifically with twins: *Today I'm thinking of all the women who are not mothers, who are suffering on this day the way that I suffered for so long! Until my perfect precious angels arrived.*

DIE IN A FIRE.

The portal was hell. Everyone and all their fucking kids and their fucking #gratitude and babies and throwbacks and vintage moms and it just didn't. Fucking. Stop. Why couldn't Aviva simply disengage, erase the apps, power down? Why indeed. WHY INDEED.

A review in the *Los Angeles Times* said Yuja Wang's "nonchalant, brilliant keyboard virtuosity . . . would have made Prokofiev and even the fabled Horowitz jealous." And here was the best part: "You get the feeling that her *body*, not *her*, *is* the music, that the connection with the keys is a force greater than mere willpower." How great was that? "A force greater than *mere willpower*"! You had to love any acknowledgment that our bodies are more sophisticated than our intelligence. So subversive, and right there in the paper! "Mere" willpower.

Brunch: a noisy restaurant crammed with women being taken out to brunch. What's-Her-Face got the twins settled with their little custom baby screens and headphones, so they could thoroughly ignore and be ignored for the duration. Barb got immediately shit-faced and verbally abusive toward the waitstaff. Aviva tried a new approach with What's-Her-Face: when the inevitable feelings of contempt came up, she would just hold the tip of her tongue to the roof of her mouth, relax her jaw, and think *victim of the system, victim of the system* until the contempt passed. It was working okay, and it was too loud to pretend to want to talk, anyway.

Mike was seething even more than usual, and he cornered Aviva near the bathrooms before it was time to go.

"What the *fuck* did you tell the twins about where babies come from?"

Aviva's heart slammed around in its cage. "Uh . . . where babies come from."

"Well, you are fucking done. That's it. You really fucked up this time. You just can't control yourself, can you? You and your little *outbursts*. You are a fucking nightmare, and you're *done*. Crazy fucking bitch. You're not going to be seeing them again for a *very* long time."

He was literally spitting mad. He was spitting on her. This was what the Rabbi would call "displaced anger."

"I'm sorry; they're not supposed to know where *babies* come from?"

"Oh, *fuck* you. You knew exactly what you were doing. You know it's more complicated than that."

"Lemme get this straight. You not only deny them spontaneous biological reproduction but *knowledge* of spontaneous biological reproduction? That is some fascist bullshit, right there."

"*You*," he said, vibrating with rage, his face so scarily close to hers that she could see the oil in his pores, the fillings in his teeth, spittle accumulating at the corners of his mouth, "are *mentally ill*."

She breathed. She walked away slowly. She said, over her shoulder: "Keep telling yourself that, you fuckin' idiot."

And she went back to the hospital to say farewell to the pitiful man who had fathered them both.

Charlene was flossing her teeth in the waiting room. Aviva chose the farthest possible chair.

"I don't like to sit in the room with him because I don't want to bring any germs in," Charlene explained, unbidden.

"Aha," Aviva said.

"The doctor came by earlier and said he's responding well to the antibiotics. And his lung function is improving, too. They're thinking they can release him to rehab tomorrow or the next day. He'll be weak. He'll need to gain back weight and muscle. But the infection is under control and he's getting enough oxygen now. So we can all breathe a sigh of relief."

Charlene did seem to care about Chuck, which was sweet. She had no kids of her own, and Aviva had overheard her, talking to a nurse, refer to the twins as "our grandchildren," which had a sort of poignancy, even if it was wishful as fuck. Maybe Mother's Day was unpleasant for Charlene, too.

"Hey, Happy Mother's Day," Aviva offered.

Charlene smiled. "And to you."

"I'm not a mother," Aviva said.

"Neither am I," Charlene said, as though that settled the matter. She went back to flossing.

Chuck was reading the news on his phone, relishing the juice and pudding on the tray in front of him.

"Hey, Dad," Aviva said.

"My girl! Are you going to write a song about what a dummy your father is for getting himself into this mess?"

"No, Daddy."

"Thank you for being here, my girl."

I'm not your fucking girl.

"You're welcome, Daddy."

He looked at her like he was seeing her for the first time, which, who knew? Maybe he was.

"How's my girl?"

It was now or never. You had to try to be honest sometimes, didn't you?

"I haven't been . . . able . . . to. . ." Just out with it, say the words. "I'm still not . . . pregnant, Dad."

She burst into tears and buried her face in her hands.

"I know, honey," Chuck said. "I know."

Crying felt pretty good for a second. But when she got ahold of herself and shook it off and looked up at her father, he was staring at his phone, poking at the screen.

She picked up a few gifts. Incense for Hanalei, a set of plant-dyed linen napkins for Sam and herself. A beet-juice-and-mica lip gloss for Sarah. A single gold chain earring, for herself. A vintage oversized cropped Wrangler jacket, also for herself.

The shopgirl—lovely in 1970s Big Sur sex-cult herbalist costume—was syrupy: "Did you have a nice Mother's Day?"

"Oh, yes, thanks! And you?"

"Yeah, me and my sisters are taking our mom out tonight. Do you have kids?"

"I do," Aviva said.

"How many?"

"A beautiful baby girl."

"Awwwwwww. Do you have a picture?"

"Lemme see . . ." Aviva found a photo of Amy as a baby, all big smooshy soft dark eyes and perfect rosebud mouth. "Yeah, here's my babe."

"Oh my God, she's *gorgeous*! Those *eyes*!"

"Right? I know. Insane."

"Do you guys have fun plans for the rest of the day?"

"Oh, no, 'cause unfortunately . . . she died."

The shopgirl gasped.

The thing about being blighted and miserable and cursed is that you actually *do* feel slightly better when you can make someone else feel terrible. It actually *does* lift a bit of the weight. Misery doesn't just like company, the Rabbi always said; misery *demands* company.

Dinner with good old ex-husband Jeff Lazar at their old favorite jukebox joint in Santa Monica. He was still single, still sucking on a vape pen. He showed her some profile pictures of the diverse array of women he'd been fucking. Over a decade since they'd stood under the chuppah.

Aviva put Amy on the juke. An essentially fun jingle, but listen to the words, to how she breathes around each line. Smart girl. Faithless. With a bad case of the bottomless needs. A good band name: the Bottomless Needs. God, listen to her! So dumb and romantic, an arrested pubescent. Why couldn't she have gotten into yoga, or hiking, or gone on Birthright? But there we go again, shaking our fists at the sky, taking issue with the way things are. She didn't *want* to grow up. She wanted to stay pure. Puerile. Which was her prerogative. Compromise and acceptance are the price of growing old happy. You either simmer down or boil over. She chose the latter.

"Makes sense," Jeff said. "You and her. I get it. You gonna see the documentary?"

"Fuck the documentary."

"I liked the cover you did in Denver. Super good."

"Shit, is that online?" Aviva knew perfectly well it was online.

"I shouldn't be hanging out with you. My therapist always says: 'Jeff, do you want life to be easy or do you want life to be hard?'"

"And what's the answer? What do you say?"

"Easy." He laughed. "I want life to be easy! Life is hard enough even *when* it's easy."

"That's evolved of you."

"Right, right."

"If either one of us had been this evolved when we were together, we probably could've made it work, Jeffie."

"Believe me, darlin', I think about that a lot."

She was no longer even slightly attracted to Jeff. Had she ever been? No matter. She took out her phone and began to brazenly scroll: passive-aggressive subject change.

"I follow all these, like, wellness feeds? And I'm starting to think the fundamental revelation of the internet age is that a really astonishing number of people totally do not know the difference between the words 'breath' and 'breathe.'"

"Sounds like you're following some shitty shit."

"Probably so."

"Also, stop being such a snob. Fly with the times, babe. Who cares if people know the difference between 'breath' and 'breathe'?"

"You're right. New is good. More is better. Old is bad. Wrong is right! Obscurity is nothingness!"

"Don't look back, only forward. The little children will lead us. And *speaking* of which! What is your *deal*, anyway? I thought you'd have like a hundred babies by now. Your dude shooting blanks, or what?"

"Naw, he's good. I'm the janky one. Seems I'll have to get jacked seven ways to Sunday if I want those babies. It's on me. And I don't wanna. Get jacked."

"So you don't want babies?"

"I want babies so fucking bad, Jeffie Pie."

"Badly."

"No, actually: bad. But you know what? Badly, too! I want babies both bad *and* badly. My wanting is awful in both senses. Bravo, dude: poetry."

She went around to his side of the booth, slid in beside him, and leaned up against him. Anywhere she could get a little sugar. "It's not *fair*. Wouldn't I be a great mom? I want to birth them in a bathtub and then walk around with my tits out for *years*."

"You're making me hard."

"But it ain't happening, so I'm supposed to take drugs to force ovulation and get artificially inseminated."

"That makes me less hard."

"My feelings exactly. But it's super common. Everyone who's systemically screwed and doesn't *want* babies gets pregnant immediately, and everyone privileged and overeducated who desperately wants babies has to put a fucking gun to their ovaries."

"You're not that old."

"It might have more to do with being too highly educated. Like, if the blood gets directed too much toward a woman's brain instead of the ovaries and uterus, her junk dries the fuck up."

"For real?"

"So what do you think? Should I force it?"

"I guess. If you want kids, do what you gotta do." He looked at her with puppy dog eyes. "It could have been our baby. What if it was our baby."

"Nah, our chemistry was off, honey. You got better things coming."

"You remember my cousin Jenny? She went somewhere, some special clinic in, I dunno, Seattle? Kid's six now. I am fascinated by it. No one can relax around that kid; it's *such* a nightmare. Feel awful for that kid. All I know is the egg was from a very diminutive woman of Southeast Asian extraction. According to my mom. So you're looking at the kid's seven-foot-tall bald string-bean Jewish father and trying to imagine him fucking some like four-foot-nine girl from a village in Thailand, two individuals who never *laid eyes on each other*, and it's like . . . yeah . . . I . . . dunno."

"Yum, like war babies. 'Children of war,' they used to be called. Nice euphemism, right? Sounds way better than 'Raped by Imperialism.' Wonder what the girl used the money for. Hope it was something good. Probably had to just hand it over to a fertility pimp."

"This from a chick who used to tell everyone marriage is by definition prostitution."

"Touché!"

Jeff put his hand on her thigh. A line, crossed. She let it be. Who was it hurting? She loved Jeff like . . . a cousin. A *second* cousin. Maybe third. And everyone messed around with their (preferably distant) cousins in the throes of emergent sexuality, did they not? Everyone *certainly* had ancestors who'd married their cousins. Isn't that why all the Ashkenazim had to get their junk genetically tested? So as to avoid potential inbred monsters? God forbid the Ashkenazim have imperfect offspring! So many alumni magazines to fill up, no time for terminally ill Fragile X schizos. Nip that shizz in the bud, winners. Win!

Jeff looked at his watch. "There's a party at Randy's. Wanna go?"

His college bestie, a TV writer with four kids and a chipper wife from a prominent Republican family. House of glass, way up in the Palisades. You could see the whole city from the eastern side and the whole ocean from the western. He'd had a massive hit with an odd-couple sitcom about a West Coast Jew married to a chipper WASP Republican from the Deep South.

"Absofuckinglutely, yes."

They drove in easy silence, windows down, through the balmy night. What *if* she had stayed married to Jeff? What if she had gotten oops-pregnant and been forced to stay with Jeff? What if they had "made it work" the way two reasonable and committed people usually could? What if they were coasting along Sunset right now on their way to this party with a brood of their own being tucked in by a sitter back at home?

Upon arrival, they were feted a bit excessively by their hosts, whom Aviva hadn't seen since that fateful day under the chuppah. They congratulated her on all her success, and she congratulated them on their network residuals and their four beautiful children, all off somewhere writing code or going viral on some platform you haven't heard of yet.

"Oh man, I'd love to have a fifth," Randy said. "Trying to convince the boss."

The wife issued a rehearsed smirk: "The shop is *closed*, babe."

"I know, babe, I know, I just always think: Who are the ones we haven't met yet? There's someone else we *haven't met yet*. I'm just so curious about who that *is*."

"I can show you an app where you can meet all the new people you please," said the wife. You could almost hear the laugh track. She was one of those women who somehow remain thin and energetic and emotionally even-keeled no matter how many new souls pass through her body. It had something to do with an inexhaustible supply of money and something to do with excellent luck and solid genes and *maybe* even something to do with having been excellently mothered, herself, but let's not get *too* radical.

"We've pretty much given up on this asshole," Randy told Aviva, gesturing at Jeff. "I still can't believe he let *you* slip through his fingers. I hear you up and married some guy who teaches, what, *middle school*? In, like, Buffalo or some shit? Are you atoning for something? Fixin' to have yourself some kids right about yesterday, or what?"

Aviva worked extremely hard to relax. No spillage! No tell! Lying well is extremely difficult work. Almost no one can do it. Changes in breath are a sure tell.

"It's in the Lord's hands," she said.

Randy laughed. "Well, you know how it works, right?"

The wife shot him a look of death, and everyone got good and quiet real fast.

Aviva excused herself in search of a bathroom, and to see what was of interest along the way, maybe steal something. It was just large enough a party (and house) that you could disappear and wander around and take something small, a memento.

The door to the master suite was open, and all four kids were piled like puppies on the bed.

"Hey," Aviva said, and eight eyeballs looked up at her from four different screens.

"Hey," said the eldest, after a beat, and all the eyeballs went back to their screens.

The lighting in the hall bath was intensely beautiful. Aviva flirted with herself in the mirror for a while. She was fucking gorgeous. A skeevy critic had recently called her "luminous." Behold! It was true.

When she reentered the main room—open plan, lofted beams, some sort of entirely newfangled track lighting, capital "M" capital "A" Modern Art—she immediately locked eyes with a hot guy across the room, and froze.

Holy shit: it was Marcus Copeland.

He smiled.

She smiled.

The noise of the party was suddenly muted, and the room itself seemed to darken, except for two spotlights: one on her and one on him. They stared at each other like in the bit from the old *West Side Story*, at the dance, where Tony and Maria lay eyes on each other for the first time. The scene, the people, the din . . . it all fades into shadow. The world is reduced to two people, locked into each other's eyes.

Copeland's mother had been the great Jewish folk singer Susie Goldman, whose interpretations of traditional liturgy had lifted up generations of young Yids in melodious celebration and prayer, especially at Zionist sleepaway camp. If you happened to be the child of twentieth-century American Jews whose assimilation into Gentile culture was not yet complete, you knew your Susie Goldman like you knew the beating of your very own heart. *And the old shall dream dreams, and the youth shall see visions* . . . Copeland's father was the great New Orleans jazz clarinetist Erasmus Copeland, who'd died tragically young.

He'd grown up in pre-condo Brooklyn, belonging to every culture and to no culture, a glorious misfit. He'd found refuge in music, where the hell else? Hip-hop, punk: he'd been perfectly situated to absorb and enact it all. Came of age at the right place at the right time. A DJ before anyone understood what a DJ really was, or could be. A big-time producer now, though every few years he put out an album of his own original stuff on some obscure label under a different name. It didn't get any cooler than Marcus Copeland.

He smiled at Aviva like he knew who she was. Did Marcus Copeland know who she was?! His hair was gray at the temples now. His eyes were intent.

They drew closer, slowly—Aviva could swear she heard the overture, the at-first-glance melody, those playful, unadorned notes, after which Tony and Maria both hold up their arms and snap, twice. Leonard Bernstein at the top of his game.

They circled, helpless to look away, before they finally came to rest, facing each other.

"Hi."

"Hi."

There was no one else in the room. They couldn't take their eyes off each other. They sat on a couch and forgot all about the party. They leaned in close, closer. They talked about Lauryn Hill and Heart and PJ Harvey and Erykah Badu. They talked about the dick producer who had steered Aviva toward a more upbeat vibe than the last album had called for. They spoke of industry bullshit and longevity and what it took to define yourself. They giggled; they batted their lashes. Aviva's undies were soaked. They talked about New Orleans music culture, and New York, and LA, and upstate, and Europe. They talked about tour and they talked about studios they liked and disliked, and they talked about people they both knew. And they fell silent, and smiled crookedly, and blushed.

"I was a huge fan of your mom's, by the way," Aviva said.

"Are you serious?" He did not tend to move in circles where his mom's oeuvre held a whole lot of relevance.

"'We must live for today we must build for tomorrow; give us time give us strength give us liiiiiiiiiiife.'" The Book of Joel. It still knocked the wind out of her.

"I'll be goddamned," he said. "I don't meet a lot of people who know my mom's stuff. And I could listen to your voice all night long."

Jeff made his way over and plopped down on the couch next to Aviva, staking his claim.

"Here you are," he said. "And you . . . you're Marcus Copeland, aren't you?"

Jeff knew very well that Marcus Copeland was Marcus Copeland! Marcus fucking *Copeland*!

"Dude," Aviva said, "*you're* the one who gave me *Green Light Go* when I was twenty-two! Also, you need to lose that vest immediately if you want to hook up with anyone at this party."

Poor Jeff looked down at his pleather vest, wounded, then got up and slunk off.

"We were married for five minutes a hundred years ago," she explained.

"He misses you," Copeland observed.

"Our wedding invitation was ringed with 'Wedding Song' lyrics."

"Dylan's biggest lie is in that song, you know."

"There are no lies in that song."

"Huge, blatant lie."

She narrowed her eyes at him, and waited.

"'Now that the past is gone,'" he said.

Marcus Copeland!!

Ooooh, but Aviva was safely married, see? See her nice sparkly ring from Sammy-Sam, her manny-man? She was ambivalent about wearing it—so conventional! So sparkly!—but she was ever so satisfied with and fond of her Sam. She was happily married! She was off the market! She was preparing to become the mother of Sam's children! She was *readying* herself, so that said children might find her worthy!

But flirtation was healthy, according to the Rabbi. Only dangerous if you started complaining about your spouse, and neither Aviva nor Copeland breathed a word about their spouses.

The party wound down. It became past time to go. Jeff was her ride, and Jeff was out of patience. He stood by the door, jangling his keys and glaring.

"Good night," Aviva whispered to Copeland. And in slo-mo, Copeland reached up and gave her this insane little face caress, then kissed her very, very softly on her right cheek. A secret, the precise measurements of that kiss. A softly screaming secret message, right there in the middle of the room, while Jeff and the hosts and a smattering of others watched.

"Until we meet again," Copeland said quietly.

Holy shit, that little caress. That small, echoing kiss. That was going to last her a *real* good long while.

Jeff was sulky driving her home. She thought she felt that telltale twisty twinge in her left ovary. Mittelschmerz! Maybe Copeland's hand on her face, his lips grazing her cheek an inch from her own lips, had made her ovulate. Her pituitary screaming his name. She was flying home tomorrow. Maybe she'd make it back in time for Sam to seed her. Maybe the past really was prologue. Maybe she was going to get to *have it all*, after all: be a homemaker *and* have the freedom to roam the world singing and making new friends and liaising with new lovers and playing to new audiences *and* perfecting her wardrobe *and* downward dogging *and* drinking psychedelic tea with Hana *and* coming home again to Sam and their adorable offspring.

(Except, um, *having* it all didn't mean you had to actually, like, *do* it all, right?! Because "it all" sounded like a gosh-awful lot. Wasn't that what nannies were for? Surrogates? Housekeepers? Wet nurses?)

Departure day, hallelujah.

She packed her bags and put everything in the rental car, then set off on foot to find her old pal, the washed-up producer who had made possible her first album: Mr. Man! It was a buzzkill to make a plan with the Man. You had to just sort of seek him, find him. Texting was passé even before it existed.

He was holding court on the boardwalk, wearing a Santa suit at the Sidewalk Cafe, nibbling on psychedelic sour gummy worms with a ragtag gaggle of buddies at ten thirty in the morning. His eyes grew wide when he saw her.

"Aviva Rosner, as I live and breathe!"

"Hey, hey, hey!"

"Fuck, I must be *real* stoned. Am I having a flashback? Is it really *you*?"

Time-travel to Aviva at twenty-three, playing her beloved Epiphone near the skate park for tips. *Who is this biblical maiden wandering my village*, the Man had boomed. *From whence comes this melodious sound?!*

Godfather of Venice. Did voter registration in the Deep South back when you could get murdered for it, was a roadie with the Grateful Dead, slept with Joan Baez, got arrested protesting the war, helped hide Abbie Hoffman, played bass in a million bands, hit bottom with the bottle, became a storied producer with a tiny, crusty, disorganized, beloved Santa Monica studio. In the early eighties, the big labels had paid him huge money to mix their shitty pop hits. A cult-classic movie about a lovable loser/philosopher/stoner with a heart of gold had been based on him. He'd helped promote the very first Burning Man, which had, in fact, been named for him.

These days he wasn't much in demand, his shaggy guesthouse studio having fallen out of fashion, so now he held court at a variety of cafés in flowing robes and his dead mother's costume jewelry, letting tourists in the know take selfies with him. That the guy actually lived in semisqualor, not in the best of health, sort of addled, and more than a little worse for the wear, was beside the point: He was always up for a party. As open and free and worn and messy and cheerful and decaying as the dream itself.

"Join us, baby! You know Dave and Artie and Carlos?"

Aviva did not know Dave and Artie and Carlos, but they all clasped hands like old friends, because that's how it worked if you were in with the Man.

He had listened to her earliest songs and told her she was special and good. Told her to keep going, keep going, keep going! He had taught her more complex chord progressions and helped her record her first EP. He had kept her in weed and parties. He had introduced her to everyone. What else you got, cutie? Keep *going*. Get up and play every chance you get. Play for yourself, for joy, for fun. Play for tourists, play for four people at an open mic. Play all day every day, and all night, too. Play! Play! It's called *playing* because it's supposed to be fun, baby. He had given her a place to crash more times than she could remember. He had shown her what a creative life actually looked like. That you had to inhabit it and live it; you couldn't just claim it by standing near it. He was darling and avuncular, although he *did* occasionally politely check in about whether she'd like him to make her come like she'd never come before or would ever come again in her whole goddamn life. To which she'd respond that that was the grossest fucking thing she'd ever heard. To which he'd shrug and tell her she was missing out.

"You see this chick?" he asked Dave and Artie and Carlos. "This chick . . . *This chick*! This chick swims in the deep end of the pool, my friends. This chick's voice will break your fuckin' *heart* and blow your fuckin' *mind*. This chick is the real deal, gentlemen. This chick could have any man or woman she wants and you know what she went and did? She went and married a *schoolteacher* in some godforsaken armpit of upstate New York. This chick doesn't *give a fuck*, you guys. You have never *met* a chick like this. How long you in town, babe? You wanna swing by the studio? Have a jam?"

Dave had a meeting with some Koreans who were maybe going to finance his film. Artie had to go take his mother to physical therapy. Carlos, Carlos was kind of hot; Carlos turned out to be the personal assistant to a television star who was texting him maniacally about what he should pick up on his way home. Aviva and the Man walked out to the shoreline and put their feet in the water. It was like no time had passed. Time meant nothing to the Man. Time was an illusion. Time was absurd. Time was a trap.

"Why are you here?"

"Unexpected," she said. "Dealing with some shit. Flying out tonight."

"And can you explain why you refuse to play LA while you're touring all up and down the entire fucking West Coast?"

"I'm in exile."

"What's-a matter, you? Why you look-a so sad? It's-a not so bad!"

"I'm barren," she confessed. "My pussy is a gateway to the void."

"Please. I never seen such a fertile woman in my life. Fuckin a, Look at you! Those tits? That ass? Come *on*. I could knock you up *today*. Give me a shot, baby. Just one shot, you'll be pregnant up to your eyeballs. Jane Fonda once asked me to knock her up, but I couldn't get involved with that. Tom Hayden was a good friend. Just one shot, baby. One shot's all I need."

Truthfully sounded more fun by half than taking pregnant-cow-piss pills and asking Sam to jerk off into a cup then getting inseminated via plastic and metal wielded by a technician in an office park. Or having blue dye injected into her ovaries to blow out her tubes for the X-ray machine. Or the D&C to scrape out her uterus in order to make it more, like, hospitable? Like tilled soil or something? Or . . . No. No. Stop. No. No. No.

"God hates me," she said, by way of passive refusal.

"Oh jeez, not that *God* bullshit. God doesn't give a fuck. God doesn't intervene."

"So who giveth? Who taketh away?"

"We had a scare, you know, way back before Elsie was born, when nothing was happening. I ran to go get my junk tested, but my junk was good. You know there's only like four *hours* a month when you can hit it just right, though, yeah? You have to time it right to the goddamned *minute*. Where *is* that husband of yours, anyway? I don't think I've ever laid *eyes* on the guy. If he doesn't exist he's gonna have a helluva time knocking you up, you know."

He put his arm around her, and she rested her head against his enormous shoulder. He smelled like laundry detergent and piss. They wiggled their toes in the sand.

"Just one whack at you, baby," he crooned. "Please. My genes are the best. My grandfather rode into Jerusalem on a fucking horse after the siege in forty-eight. Look it up."

"I do have a new song we could record, if you have time."

"Time! Do I have time. Of course I have time." He broke into a coughing fit so long and rough it made her own lungs burn. "But think about it, flower. Give me one shot at your perfect Hebraic pussy before some goddamn baby wrecks it. Let me just *see* it. I just want to give it a *kiss* before I *die*."

"I will think about it," she promised. "Meanwhile, let's go lay down this track."

"I'd like to lay you down. But okay."

The cemetery out by the airport was famous for containing the remains of Al Jolson, Dinah Shore, Leonard Nimoy, and many other bygone celebrity kikes. Jolson's monument was a garish fountain, a graphic rendering of which also served as the place's logo. Nobody was around aboveground. Aviva lay in the grass by her grandfather's headstone and texted Sam a sunny/goth LA cemetery tit pic. The sky was cloudless, jet stream blue.

Reasonable minds can differ as to what death means and what happens to our consciousness or "soul" when we're dead, but there's no arguing the fact that right now you are alive and one day you will be dead.

"Grampy," she sang to her grandfather. "Grampy Gramp, I love you. Send me a baby. C'mon, Poppy. Hook me *up*."

Rob was a few plots over. She crawled over on hands and knees.

"Rob*bie*," she said. "What is *up*, bruh. Robbie-Rob! The Rob-ster." July 1969 to August 1998. Death can't be a catastrophe. It simply cannot. That is all.

She stretched out in the grass under the huge tree at the edge of the meadow, counted four jets passing overhead, and almost fell asleep. Probably still working through a contact high from being with the Man.

Her phone rattled: it was her appointed time to talk to the Rabbi.

"*Mein kind*," he said. "How are you?"

"At my ancestral burial ground: the cemetery near LAX. Rolling around in the grass under a creepy blue sky. Gorgeous day. Very tempted to sun-bathe the yoni."

"Sounds . . . excellent."

"Best-kept secret in town. I have the place entirely to myself. Well, corpses excluded."

"You think you'll be buried there one day?"

"Hadn't given it much thought, to be honest! Interesting. But no, I hope not. But also, might be kind of nice? But no: terrible. Mike would find some way to harass and despise me from the next plot over. Fuck, now I know what I'll be worried about for the rest of my life. Great! How much for today's sesh, Doc?"

"How's the trip been?"

"Chuck's out of the woods. He will live to read the news on his phone another day! Barb's awful. Twins are adorable. I told them where babies come from—or, like, where babies *used* to come from, pretechnocracy—so now I won't be seeing *them* for a while. Mike's a piece of shit. Robbie's swell, real peaceful here in the ground. So good to hang with the dead. They're so nonjudgmental. And I have been doing a *lot* of thinking about the forced-ovulation drugs."

"Ah yes, the ovulation drugs."

"Way I see it, I take this junk and then I probably take more of this junk and next thing you know I'm taking different junk, *stronger* junk, and then, you know, jump cut to me buying eggs off some working-class bitch who's going to get cancer in ten years because of it."

"You're scared that once you start down this road there's no end to it."

"Precisely."

"Who's to say you can't draw the line wherever you want to draw the line?"

"I don't think it works that way, dude. Seems pretty obvious that the whole deal just gets more and more heartbreaking and more and more inva-sive while you get more and more *invested*—literally and emotionally—and I think it's just too hard. I mean maybe you wind up with a baby, maybe you don't, but either way, what the *fucking fuck*, you know? I'm fucking *scared* of it."

"I don't blame you," he said.

"These pills are the first step. Fine. These pills are *nothing*, relatively speaking. But where do they lead? Where does it end, you know? Maybe forcing ovulation isn't a big deal, but then if it doesn't work you do it *again*, and then if that doesn't work you do it *again* and they inseminate you, and then if *that* doesn't work you shoot up using, like, veterinary needles, and they give you general anesthesia and remove insane numbers of forced eggs from your inflamed ovaries, and then sift through them and, like—no. Just: no! I'm not fucking doing this. I'm not doing it! Once you start, there's no end. What's the next thing, you know? You've come all this way, haven't you? And meanwhile what are you *doing* to yourself? But of course *you* don't matter, right? Because you have to sacrifice yourself to the *possibility* of a child. Isn't that the whole point? Isn't that what motherhood *is*? Lay yourself down in the road: Isn't that what makes a woman a *woman*?"

"Let's pause and take a deep breath," said the Rabbi.

Never not a good idea.

"Look," he said. "Aviva. You'll second-guess it either way. You can take the drug and maybe it won't work or maybe there will be side effects or maybe you'll have problems or maybe your baby will have problems, and you'll second-guess having taken the drug. Or you can *not* take the drug and feel like you missed out. Either way, you'll have doubts. All you can do is make your choice and don't second-guess it."

"It just seems like the la-la-la *good girl* thing to do, you know? Such a fucking good little fucking good girl thing to do. It's like: this is what you have to do. You give in. You say, 'I'm broken! I'm not enough! Fix me! Fertilize me!' And you get juiced up and taken over and forced to do what you're 'supposed' to do. Aren't I allowed to say 'no'? All that *reproductive choice* people *love* to go on about? I don't want to stop anybody else from getting all jacked up, I'm not looking to like *enact legislation* against this shit. But *I* don't wanna get jacked up! All those signs at the women's marches with the personified uterus and the fallopian tubes giving the finger, you know? Right, right, sure, great, fuck off and get out of my reproductive system, sure, great, I mean, unless I'm suddenly a HOLY VESSEL for procreation, in which case all bets are *off*, man! Come *right* the fuck on IN, do whatever the fuck you *want*. Get rich having a fucking experimental *party* in my uterus; I'll just busy myself shopping for the most elaborate stroller on the market, *please* come right in and jack my shit *up*. Force ovulation! Inseminate! Scrape out the endometrium! Shoot the dye through the tubes! Force more ovulation! Remove the eggs! Put the eggs back in! Buy some new eggs! Fuck my shit *up*, please and thank you and, oh, here's a huge pile of unregulated money! It's like, what's up, rich Brooklyn feminists in *The Future Is Female* shirts busy buying eggs off impoverished teenagers while pretending to read *The Handmaid's Tale* for wine book club. I mean, just *no*. Why am I not allowed to say 'no'? Why is 'no' not *allowed*?"

She needed to breathe. She tried to breathe. It was hard to breathe.

"I think your point of view *is* allowed," the Rabbi said. "But you're not necessarily allowed . . . to . . . say it out loud."

"THEN IT'S NOT ALLOWED!"

"Yeah, it's probably not allowed."

"It's just weird to me that it's so *unheard-of* these days for a person of privilege to want children, not be automatically granted children, and then not subsequently, like, *demand* to acquire children at any cost. Whatever happened to the idea that it might be, like, spiritually profitable or beneficial to just sit with not getting what we want, even if we happen to be affluent and therefore fully and totally conditioned to getting what we want?! Was that ever a thing?"

"Was what ever a thing?"

"Making peace with not getting what we want!"

"Not so much in the popular imagination, no."

"Well. That's fucked *up*!" And . . . she was crying.

"You're articulating a big internal conflict, sweetheart."

"But I'm *not* conflicted! I don't want any *part* of this shit."

"So don't take the drugs."

"But I want a fucking *baby*," she fairly shouted, hoping maybe the dead could hear.

"You're in a tough spot."

"Oh, *thank you*, Doc. *How* much for today's sesh?"

"You're reminding me of an old joke. You want to hear it?"

"Better be good."

"A great flood washes away a town," he began. "And a deeply devout man survives by clinging to a piece of wood. He's floating through the wreckage, but he can't go on this way. God will save me, he thinks. Soon a rowboat comes along. The rower stops. 'Need some help? Hop in!'

"'No thank you,' replies the man. 'God will save me.' The rower shrugs and the rowboat continues away. Soon a motorboat comes along.

"'Hey! I'm here to help, plenty of room,' says the motorboat driver.

"'Oh no, no need,' replies the devout man. 'God will save me.'

"The motorboat driver shrugs and motors away. Soon a helicopter spots the man floating amidst the wreckage and lowers a line for him.

"'No thanks,' shouts the man, waving the helicopter off. 'God will save me!' Very soon after that, the man drowns. When he gets to heaven he demands to see God. Standing before the Master of the Universe, the man is irate: 'I thought you would save me! I believed in you! I had faith!'

"God sighs. 'I sent you a rowboat. I sent you a motorboat. I sent you a helicopter. What else do you want from me?'"

5.

PUFF

Fine: One pill a day for the first week of her cycle, meant to fool the pituitary into forcing the ovaries to mature and release an egg or two or three or more. Trickery. Fuckery. Force. Farce.

The drug may be inhaled or absorbed through the skin, so pregnant women should not handle or be near it. Inform your doctor right away if your condition worsens or new symptoms appear. Side effects may include ovarian hyperstimulation, ovarian rupture, sweating, joint pain, extreme fatigue. Developed for use as an estrogen inhibitor in hormonally responsive breast cancer patients, postsurgery. Estrogen: the feel-good hormone! The hormone known to make us happy, pliable, agreeable, satisfied. The hormone of cooperation and community, acceptance and compliance. The drug will halt estrogen in the body. The manufacturer has not applied for FDA approval for use of this drug with infertility. A 2005 Canadian study showed higher incidence of birth defects associated with use of this drug. The manufacturer heavily criticized the study for its "improper design," but let's assume the mothers of those "defective" babies don't give a fuck about the study design. Fun fact: the drug can also be used in combination with the abortion pill to help terminate a first-trimester pregnancy! Also: banned in India.

How bad could it be? Everyone did it.

"Sorry," Aviva said out loud before she knocked back the first dose. Sorry for what? Sorry for whom?

* * *

Perfect, exquisite horror, obvious within half a day. Absolute disaster. She could not stop crying. Convulsive, corrosive sobbing. Gasping. Shredded. Zero catharsis to be had.

Ah, the descriptive limitations of physical/emotional overwhelm: It was like, it was like, it was like. It was like someone fisting her throat. It was like her heart being ground under a boot heel. It was like getting knifed in the stomach by someone you trust. It was like a powerful punch to the solar plexus. It was like a poke right in the tender titty the very day you got your first period. It was like being kicked directly in the shin, only the shin was yourself and the kick was yourself and the shin was life and the kick was death and it was time for all of it to end, now, *please, end, now, please,* end, end, end, now, now now, please. Death was the only answer. A gun, please. Where could she procure a gun? She didn't know. She didn't want to know. She was terrified of guns. And she wanted one. Now.

There was generalized pain, which melted into exhaustion, which melted into a sorrow so bottomless she could think of nothing but a gun. A gun: agent of pure annihilation. Gun in her mouth. Gun at her temple. Gun between her eyes. She wanted a *gun.* She was thinking about *guns.* She wanted to be ripped apart by a *gun.*

Then there was specific, acute pain located around her left ovary, but it radiated out across her lower back and hips and up into her shoulders and neck and into her face and jaw.

It was *fascinating* to feel this bad. She was so heavy; glued to the bed. Abundantly rich in tears. Such a great abundance of tears. So fertile, her tear ducts!

Sam went to work. High school civics stops for no pituitary terrorism. She was going to have to take care of herself. A modern woman. Translation: alone, fucked.

She called Dr. White.

The doctor was unavailable at this time.

"Is this *normal?*" she asked Faith, the receptionist, not even trying to keep her voice level. Faith promised that Dr. White would call her back as soon as possible.

"Well," said Dr. White an hour later. "It does sound like you're having an extreme reaction."

"Oh, do you *think*?"

"It does sound that way, yes."

"I mean, does this *happen* to people?"

"Occasionally."

"Are you *fucking kidding* me?"

The rustling of paper.

"I'm in *so much pain*," Aviva whimpered. "I'm really *scared*."

"You can always go to the emergency room if it's that bad. The ovaries sometimes react badly. But if you think you can handle the pain, try to take it easy and let's wait and see."

Take it *easy*?! Aviva was really more in the market for some oh dear, I'm so sorry, oh you poor thing, oh sweetie, how terrible for you, I'm so very sorry, how awful. Care: it necessitates *care*, see?!

Night sweats, dizziness, shortness of breath. She wanted to *fuck a gun*. Her body was no place to be. She wanted out.

The Rabbi, at least, was sympathetic: "Do you want to continue with the whole course? You can stop now. It should pass in forty-eight hours. The half-life shouldn't be more than forty-eight hours. This is a bad reaction. You're having a bad reaction. You don't have to continue."

"I have three more pills."

"You can stop now."

"No fucking way." She was no quitter! Cue the old joke: I considered giving up drugs/alcohol/gambling/casual sex, but I hate quitters! "Absolutely fucking *not*. This is a test. This is what it *takes*. This is what you have to *do*. To be rewarded with a baby, which is how you know you're a valid *woman*. This is mere *preparation* for the pain and suffering to come. I make it through *this* to prove I'm worthy."

"Nobody is worthy of a baby, sweetheart."

More tears. She was a well of tears.

"How could I have done this to myself? I walked right into it. I *fell* for it. I did this to my goddamned *self*."

"Why wouldn't you? It's a commonly prescribed drug. You trusted your doctor."

"Here's a theory! Women don't question feeling like shit! Women are accustomed to feeling like total fucking shit all the time! Women walk around feeling like incredible shit, and volunteering to feel ever more like shit, because on some level we know it's *required* of us! Hurting ourselves is how we know we *exist*. It's how we belong to the human *race*."

"This drug might not bother some women. No two metabolisms are the same."

"Oh, I just take everything harder than everyone else, is that it?"

"You might be somewhat more sensitive in general, don't you think?"

"Oh-ho! Wait for it! Here it comes! Let's hear it, bring it on: my greatest burden is also my greatest gift, right? Right? Oh yes, let's do that number, what a crowd-pleaser."

"It's the truth."

"Fuck you."

"I'm sorry you're going through this. You don't deserve this."

"Feet to the flames," she muttered. "Feet to the motherfucking flames."

"You are having an extreme reaction," the Rav reminded her again. "It is going to pass. It will pass."

It was soul death, a bad trip, being nailed to a cross. It was a blade at her throat. It was being sliced from collarbone to cunt and left to die, open to the elements, birds of prey circling above. It was a body hurled from a twentieth-story window. It was every kind of profanity in every possible order. Headaches and hot flashes and bloat and tears and tears and how, please, explain: How could there *possibly* be still more tears? *How?* Please. It was a five-day menopause, the body in sudden total estrogen deprivation. Who came *up* with this shit? Well, no matter, because apparently all the *other* women didn't mind it one bit. All the normal good nice mommies-to-be could ride this shit out just *fine*, no complaints, compliance and co-operation to spare. Ho-hum. Witches, though: witches fucking minded. Which is maybe how you knew you were one.

She couldn't listen to music. Nothing. Not jazz, not Chopin, not blues. Not folk, not hard-core, not rap, not reggae. Music made no sense. Music was noise. Her guitars hung on the wall like sculpture. She imagined smashing them into a vibrating heap. She imagined setting them on fire. So much for creative fertility. She wanted to leave Dr. White a shrieking, unhinged message: ARE YOU "WORRIED" ABOUT ME, BITCH? ARE YOU COMING TO TAKE CARE OF ME?!

She drew the literal and metaphoric curtains, watched a dozen episodes of a show, online shopped for a very special fleece hoodie, and ate a carton of chocolate peanut butter cup gelato, phenomenally unstinting on the peanut butter. She took her daily dose. She wept and wept and wept. She was no quitter.

Her father's name on caller ID. Might she share her predicament? Might he offer a spot of comfort or perspective? Might he hold space for her pain? For even just a moment?

"Hi, my girl!" (I'm not your fucking girl.) "Just read that great new piece they wrote about you! You're such a star!" (Oh my fucking God who gives a shit you narcissistic freak.) "Everyone is so impressed with you! You're *famous*, my girl! You're really *something*!" (No shit I'm something; who the fuck isn't *something*?!)

"Thanks, Dad."

"I always knew you were special." (Um, you refused to make eye contact from the nanosecond I sprouted titties until, like, yesterday.) "Your mother was always trying to tell me you weren't going to amount to anything, but I knew you were incredibly special." (If you say so, bro.)

"How you feeling, Dad? Gaining some weight?"

"Stronger by the day! I did fifty push-ups with my trainer yesterday! And you should see what good care Charlene takes of me. She is *amazing*.

Here she is with my morning smoothie! Mmmm, vanilla protein powder and bananas, wow! What a lucky guy!"

"Good for you, Dad."

"So what else is new with you?"

Well, as you well fucking know, I haven't been blessed with the children I feel so desperately called to bear, which has been pretty unremittingly cruel and searing for a couple years now, but I guess that hasn't come up in your fucking Google Alerts. Anyway, now I'm finally trying this demonic ovulation drug they give out like candy to barren bitches, which my pituitary and/or ovaries do *not* seem to appreciate! So I'm in complete and utter agony! Which actually makes the psychic pain of my ongoing predicament seem preferable by comparison! Sooooo I guess that's goodbye and good luck to this crappy branch of your shitty fucking bloodline, old man!

"Not much, Dad. Gotta run."

Albany was the kind of place you *left*, if you could. If you lived here it was because your family lived here or because you grew up here or because you went to school here or because you had a job here. Behold: a "real" place, not a fine-tuned theme park of money and status and style.

"I *like* it here," Sam told her that night they first met at the club on Central where Aviva was playing on tour with a folk-ska band. A defensive edge in his voice: "It's beautiful if you know where to look."

Yes, Sam was the kind of shy, adorable, hot, built high school teacher from a huge townie family who said shit like "beautiful if you know where to look."

Where were they again? Rochester? Geneva? Ithaca? Scranton? Utica? *Albany.*

But this guy chatting her up, he was hella sweet, *damn.* He seemed like he . . . wasn't an asshole? Something about the twinkle in his eyes. Unmistakable. The eyes have it. A *ridiculously* cute shy twinkly-eyed high school teacher from a family of fourth-generation local Polack cops. Yikes. The very last thing Aviva thought she needed, what with her songs and shows and album release parties and industry inside baseball and big-city bonhomie and perfect cheap Boerum Hill walk-up and rotating crops of lovers and scowling at people on the street. What could she possibly want with some (adorable) high school teacher from *Albany*, even if he *did* happen to play a wicked mandolin and haunt the local club to hear new music and volunteer with the fire department? She had her charming alcoholic friends and her kind weed dealer and some great buzz brewing around her upcoming third album and her beloved harness boots and Wednesday-night yoga class on Atlantic when she wasn't on tour. Which she most often *was*, anyway, so easy come and easy go, in theory. What did she need with some cute Polack from *Albany*?

But good God, was he adorable. After the show, she took him back to her motel, and that, as they say, was that. Sam! Aviva was a goner. It wasn't a great habit, fucking near-strangers on tour, but even a broken clock is right twice a day.

He came to visit her in Brooklyn soon thereafter, and she brought him to a friend's show, where a ton of preening music school people were out in force.

"Who's your *bodyguard*?" snarled Lee, the occasional lover whose first and only album had been cruelly ignored.

"He's cute," Julie declared in monotone. "*Real* cute." Julie, an awful singer who sexed it up onstage for whatever crumbs she could get (spoiler: it worked!).

"Oh my God," Ana said, "you teach inner-city *high* school?! That sounds kind of scary. Isn't that kind of scary? V, you're dating a *teacher*? You're so *funny*." Ana, a keyboardist, the most brilliant and successful and unhinged of their crew, had toured with David Byrne, gotten a huge international arts grant, and was always having a nervous breakdown.

This was the music school cohort in all their petty, pretentious insularity, their fake liberal glory. Lee flicked his cigarette into the gutter and hocked a loogie a few inches from Sam's shoe. "So how does one decide to *become* a high school teacher? You into teens?"

"Sorry about my friends," Aviva told Sam. "I've been meaning to get some new ones."

"They're all right," he said. But he didn't complain when Aviva suggested they vamoose.

They eloped six months later. It felt a little reckless. But people are allowed to be complicated. The way they held each other was so decent. It didn't matter where they were from or what kinds of vacations their families took growing up (Hawaiian resorts; Adirondack camp). They were both rabid Jonathan Richman fans. They both liked to read. Sam was the star of the local over-thirty flag football league, and the guy to call when a student was violent or suicidal or needed a place to sleep. The delinquents all went to him for advice, called him Sammy, the Samster, Sam the Man. Gentle as a summer breeze, though he was almost comically ripped from hours spent at the gym. Perfect gentleman with a noble soul, a musical bent, a wry sense of humor, the brightest eyes, and an insatiable hard-on for Aviva.

They married without ceremony, a civil servant at city hall serving as witness. Aviva knew she'd lose her nerve otherwise. And that is how she came to play lady of a nineteenth-century row house on a rough block in Albany. Oh, Albany: delicious exemplar of failed urban planning. Prime case study of American decline. Was she really married to a townie Gentile, and living in a dilapidated fixer-upper on a rough block in Albany? She was. No one had seen *that* coming.

Barb refused to speak to her for an entire blessed year.

Chuck acted a little hurt about the whole nonevent thing (translation: any man who wanted to take ownership of his daughter should have come to kneel and swear fealty first), but he got over it. When they finally met a few months later, Chuck and Sam "took a walk" together—literally, like, around the neighborhood. And presumably Sam had been fully deferential, because when they returned from the walk, Chuck declared Sam "a solid guy." And that was what passed for a blessing, after the fact.

Aviva threw herself into her new life. She went to neighborhood association meetings. She volunteered at the soup kitchen. She frequented the thrift shop, and signed up to be a Big Sister, for which there turned out to be a two-year wait list. Things were going to work out great in Albany. She was going to get involved, befriend her neighbors, have armloads of babies, and raise them in community! Urban Homesteading 101. And concurrently, of course, she was going to get a tour bus outfitted to bring said babies on the road. Then, when gentrification came creeping in, a decade or two hence, they'd sell the row house and get an old cottage on a bunch of land out in Voorheesville or Petersburgh or Poestenkill or some such. Wherever the wells weren't all contaminated with PFOAs. Meanwhile: bring on the babies.

She sought out mom friends. She wanted that mom dust. She made it her business to befriend all the capital-"M" Moms she could find.

There was the cloying one on Dove Street, who owned a toxic-fragrance candle shop and was having number two. She was given to greeting Aviva with a burlesque "Hey, *Mama*. What's up, *Mama*? How you doing, *Mama*?"

There was the aspiring influencer, always in a Facebook fight with someone. Her barely concealed rage about Aviva's career/travel/wardrobe gave rise to frequent, clenched utterances such as: "I guess that's the kind of thing you can *do* when *you have no kids*." (Aviva will *trade* you, bitch. Snap your fingers, count backward from three.)

There was the unhinged woman with four small boys too close in age, in way over her head, and constantly spiraling.

"What am I supposed to *do* with these kids? Beau won't wear a diaper and he thinks it's funny to piss everywhere! Arturo's eczema seems to be getting *worse* on the steroids. The twins won't go to sleep! Carlo's had a fever of 102 since Friday! I'm losing my mind! And I think Aron is masturbating already—he's only nine! Do you think he's homosexual? I think maybe he's homosexual. We're taking him to a therapist."

At first, Aviva thought Unhinged was hilarious. Gradually it dawned on her that Unhinged was not funny at all. The kids were lost, wild, unfocused, deranged, filthy. Except for the eldest, whose silent watchfulness felt like a curse.

Cloying and Aspiring Influencer liked to intermittently freeze out Unhinged, who did not, as they put it, *have her shit together*.

"Why did she *have* those kids if she wasn't going to, like, get good at it," Aspiring Influencer would hiss. "It's not rocket science. It's just a fucking trade. Learn the tools of your trade and organize your stupid life and just fucking deal. She's just so, like, *bad* at it. Learn your freaking trade, woman. She's just doing a sloppy-ass job. It's just shoddy work. Get better at your job, lady."

"Maybe she didn't really want kids in the first place," Cloying would say.

"Wouldn't she have figured that out after the first one? It's called birth control, hello."

"She does seem kind of . . . fucked up. It's just, like, too many kids. She probably would've been okay with one. Or two. It's just too many."

These women scared the shit out of Aviva. And because she lacked even the faintest notion of boundaries or self-protection, she offered up her eagerness to join their ranks. She made it known that she was keen to become one of them. She wanted to learn their rhythms, their language. She wanted to know who the good midwives and doulas were. She walked past the playground in Washington Park, and felt rage that the slide was still broken after almost a year, because most people with money got out of this neighborhood as soon as they had kids, and no doubt the suburban playgrounds were all pristine.

But time passed, and passed. And passed. And Aviva was still not pregnant.

And the moms began to pity her.

"I'm sure it will work out eventually," said Aspiring Influencer, overjoyed at the opportunity to feel superior. Childbearing is the third-most-common distinction in the history of the world (dying and shitting being the first and second), but sure: take your opportunity to feel superior.

"Listen," said Unhinged. "You have to have sex *every single day*. Are you having sex *every single day*?"

And thereafter, Unhinged brought it up every time they interacted.

"How's it *going*?" she always asked, her face grave, eyes darting down to Aviva's midsection.

"Do you want the number of a good doctor?" Cloying always wanted to know. "He's very good. It's a huge company, clinics all over the country. Reputable."

"Meaning what, like, he doesn't use the wrong sperm by accident or on purpose?"

When Aviva drove the back way to the mall (who doesn't love the mall once in a blue moon), down Everett Road and up Albany Shaker Road (Sam always argued with her on this route, but why would you want to take some gray psychotic murderous dystopian highway when you could just sail down a two-lane in what was essentially farmland, though it was still forever being divided and assaulted by developers?), she sat at the long red light facing the impeccably maintained office park, where the clinic's "I" and "V" and "F" menaced her from the topmost corner. The parking lot was always full of Teslas and Mercedes SUVs, and once, wowee, a Porsche.

And then there was Yasmin, a veiled Pakistani who ran the "healthy" convenience shop with her husband on Clinton Avenue, a once-grand boulevard now lined with abandoned zombie Victorians. The convenience shop had kombucha on tap, and some obscure mushroom supplements. Yasmin's two small kids played in the storeroom or on the floor behind the register, which brought to mind Aviva's great-grandmother, a refugee who'd married a boy she met at an immigrant dance on the Lower East Side, and moved out to the coal-mining butt crack of Pennsylvania to run a general store and put four daughters through college during the Depression. Perhaps these small children playing on the floor behind the register would someday be the proud grandparents of genre-defying, provocative singer-songwriters whose streaming numbers gave label execs boners.

Aviva very much wished to experience, via Yasmin, some of the love and care and wisdom and resilience of her great-grandmother. Was that unfair emotional labor? Yasmin was certainly more Aviva's people than Cloying, Aspiring Influencer, or Unhinged, is the point.

Avvia and Yasmin traded silent smiles, which eventually gave way to nods, which eventually gave way to hellos, which, at long last, gave way to how-are-yous.

"You are married?" Yasmin asked today.

Aviva nodded.

"Kids?"

Aviva shook her head and tried not to cry. Probably a mistake to have left the house under the influence of the demon drug.

"Why not?"

Aviva shrugged.

"You are *lucky*," Yasmin whispered so her kids wouldn't hear. (The kids still heard.) "You are so *lucky*. Children are hard. You're free. I wish I was like you. I would like to travel, see the world. You take trips a lot, yes?"

"I do take trips a lot. But I wish I was *you*. I want babies."

"In my culture," Yasmin said, "you have to hold babies if you want a baby. Hold someone else's baby all day, all day, for many many days. That's how you awaken your baby to come and find you. You have job?"

"I'm a musician," Aviva said.

Yasmin gasped.

"You make money from this?"

"Some."

Yasmin launched into a few lines of a Pashto song. Her voice was thin, but the two small children froze in their play, spellbound, and turned their faces up toward their mother's voice like little plants to the sun. The moment Yasmin stopped, the children went back to their play as though nothing had happened.

"Beautiful. What does it mean?"

" 'I'll die for the wind of the mountains. I'll die for the wind. I can't cry. The rivers don't bring water. They don't bring any news from you.' "

* * *

"Let's go to the farmers' market," Sam said. Saturday. He remained chipper while Aviva lost her goddamn mind.

The weather was psychedelic nice. So much for the pathetic fallacy. The market was a big, joyous affair. Bluegrass band, a hundred different kinds of greens, and families, so many families, everyone a freaking family. The holy life cycle playing out everywhere you looked. The gorgeous dreadlocked girl who ran a sprout CSA and made jewelry, a baby on her back and one playing at her feet. The bearded man who cultivated mushrooms with his teenage son learning the business beside him. The hipster mom with the letterpress shop looking murderous and sunk. The fundamentalist family of six, all those serious little girls in their identical bonnets and dresses and sandals.

Aviva was a wounded animal. Aviva was death, plague, destruction, chaos, darkness, malevolence. She let Sam lead her around. She had left her glasses at home, and was not wearing contacts. She liked being in this, her "true" state: a person with terrible vision, a person who quite literally *could not see*, a person utterly dependent on someone else to lead her around. It was useful. An interesting practice. A form of surrender. Perhaps she had been designed this way so that she could make her way through the world without worrying about whatever was more than, say, a foot from her face. Perhaps she was designed to move slowly, carefully, and to focus only on what was right in front of her. Perhaps, when wearing contacts or glasses, she was just getting ahead of herself. Overwhelming herself. Perhaps vision correction was a kind of overstimulation. Why should Aviva have to *see* everything? Why did everyone have to *see* everything? Those with perfect vision could guard the perimeter while the impaired looked inward, sang songs, tended the fire.

They sat on a bench by the lagoon so Aviva could remain discreetly catatonic in between stuffing fresh pastry into her face and offering fake pleasant hellos to random acquaintances. The problem with living in what amounted to a small town was that you couldn't leave your house in a foul mood. In a big city you could at least indulge a bad mood, in public, to the absolute fullest: what luxury!

Here came the busybody wife of Sam's principal. Big fish in a small pond, but her energy wasn't the worst. Aviva could sense things differently—better!—in half blindness.

"Hey, you guys," said the principal's wife. "Did you hear the *news*?!"

"No," Sam said. "What's the news?"

"We. Are. Having. *Twins!*"

This would be the third set of twins recently welcomed in the community. The woman winked at Aviva. "Be careful! I think there's something in the *water!*"

"Oh, there's *absolutely* something in the water," Aviva said. "Absofreak-ing*lutely*, babe, the water supply is *definitely* affected. Fish in Lake Michigan are displaying secondary sex characteristics, you've heard? And their brains are full of Prozac. There's a *ton* of shit in the water. You can forget about water *altogether*."

The woman's grin faded as she backed away.

"Calm down," Sam said quietly.

"I am so calm. I am so fucking calm. Fuck you, how calm I am."

The Rabbi was right: the demon drug had a half-life of forty-eight hours. It passed. The minute it was out of her system, she was fine. The very moment. Restored. Homecoming. Thank God. Thank Gods. Thank Goddesses. Thank No-God. Thank science!

Now a solid week to ten days of dutiful, no-nonsense intercourse. Let the Sex March begin. Some advised every *other* day, since daily could deplete the troops, and healthy sperm could live in the folds of the cervix ("sperm hotels"!) for several days. But Aviva was taking no chances.

The first day was fun. The next two days were fine. The deed got done. Thereafter it became a dreaded chore. And on the seventh day, Sam could not get it up. He was apologetic, but Aviva was having none of it.

"We need to *fuck*, Sam. You have *literally* one job."

"I'm sorry, baby."

"Don't be fucking *sorry*! I don't *need* 'sorry'! Just do your fucking job!"

"Give me a minute."

"Are you *serious*?"

"My dick doesn't like hostility. I'm cool with hostility, but my dick really doesn't like it."

"I did *not* take those motherfucking *drugs* for your *boner* to go on vacation!"

What a mess. The wild radius of her mood! Sam pleaded with her: "It's okay, baby. Tomorrow is another day. Let's just go to bed angry. It will be okay."

Sam the Man. Her good Sammy-Sam. Indeed, she was too exhausted to stay up and continue weeping. She let him pull her close. She rested her head on his chest. She stopped crying. She let her hand drift down to cup his balls. She had to liberate her baby! She had to be nice to its daddy. She had to change tactics.

"Sorry, babe," she said.

He was immediately hard. She kissed him, no stress, nice and slow. She summoned the yin. When you're safe, and only when you're safe, is it okay to privilege sadness over anger.

They got it on, quiet and strong.

"We did all right, baby," Sam murmured when they were both almost unconscious from orgasm. "And it's not even midnight yet."

He farted a satisfied fart.

"The fart wants what it wants," she mumbled, and was out like a light.

She dreamt that Mike was dead. She dreamt that Mike had died suddenly, catching her by surprise. She was weirdly devastated.

Sam was not around. Aviva found herself being comforted, randomly, by Mike's high school girlfriend, the self-aggrandizing dolt who often assaulted Aviva's feed, one of those people who haphazardly start lifestyle companies around every life cycle event they experience. Go overboard planning your own wedding, become a wedding consultant. Have a baby, initiate some sort of breeder-focused start-up. Send the child off to school, put up a website offering consulting services for organizing the home and disciplining the children. This lady had shown up backstage a few months ago, hollering: "WHO IS DOING YOUR PR? MY GOD, YOU'RE EVERYWHERE."

Anyway, Mike was dead, and Aviva's first thought was: What a relief. Which then melted into confusion, grief: What day of the week was it? Where were her shoes? She was sitting in the high school girlfriend's Spanish-style West Hollywood bungalow, which was resplendent in tile. Then Aviva was sobbing in the arms of the girlfriend's *husband*, an affable guy she had met maybe once, in passing.

"Sing me a song," Aviva begged the husband. He tried to oblige, but the words made no sense.

Then she was driving a wacky miniature car through some kind of giant abandoned maze. The steering was bonkers, and the brakes didn't work. If only she had a dollar for that old classic, the brakes not working!

She woke in a ferocious sweat. Which meant something about the liver, the adrenals, the metabolism, the hormones, the estrogen, the progesterone, the heart, the body, the mind, the spirit.

Sam was asleep beside her. Sam: the first person in her whole life to really and truly love her back. Her whole godforsaken life she'd been throwing herself madly, passionately, at people who quite simply didn't requite. Starting, alas, it was true, with her parents. Even Rob had been kind of detached, though never cruel. And Mike, ugh, the less said about hate-sick Mike the better. And a hundred different boys and girls, women and men, to whom Aviva had offered her heart, only to be left in the lurch with a bleeding chest cavity.

She stared at the ceiling until it became dawn.

The demon drug had felt exactly like trying to force someone to love you. Someone who simply and plainly did not, could not, would not love you. No point in trying to force it.

Backyard birthday party for one of Sam's million nephews and nieces. Huge suburban house in a brand-new subdivision twenty minutes away.

Top-of-the-line finishes, all the latest-model pickup trucks in the driveway, room-sized flat screen, leather-upholstered furniture, and otherwise barren. Barren of art, music, plants, books. A few mass-produced faux-wood signs hung on the walls, to be fair: *Home = Love* in the dining room. *Eat Light, Eat Right, Stay Tight* in the kitchen.

Aviva handled her involvement with Sam's relatives exactly as the Rabbi had advised her from the get-go: she showed up, behaved herself, and pleasantly agreed with everything anyone said. Politics, television programs, gardening: all good! Whatever! Sure! Yeppers! She staggered her attendance at these events—the holidays, the birthday parties, the barbecues—showing up just often enough to assert general goodwill and marital solidity, but not often enough to make her want to perform seppuku. Every third family event she attended, she allowed herself to get stoned. Not today, alas.

There's always at least one pitiful childless couple in every extended family. And it doesn't matter whether they're physicists or architects or academics or CEOs; they're pitied and shamed. They're the losers, because children are how you enact your immortality. Die without children, and no one will miss you.

"What about people whose children die before them?" wondered the Rabbi.

"Losers," Aviva told him. "Sorry. Total fucking losers."

"What about people who foster or adopt or mentor and help raise other people's children?"

"Touché," Aviva said. "But marginal."

So there they were, this clan's resident childless couple. The weird, sad standouts: Aviva and Sam. Everyone had mostly cut it out by now with the sickly sweet queries about when they were going to procreate, either because word had gotten around that there was trouble and/or because enough time had passed without a bundle of joy that it was safe to assume Aviva was a withholding career-obsessed bitch and Sam couldn't or wouldn't take charge, hold her down, and seed her anyway. But these folks didn't ultimately care whether Sam and his weird Jew wife ever had kids; these folks had plenty of kids. One outlier barren bitch didn't threaten *this* bloodline.

"You okay?" Sam asked, seeking permission to go stand around the grill, speaking in code grunt with the brothers and cousins. The capital-"D" Dudes.

"All good," Aviva told him—permission granted.

This left Aviva with the women and children. Some kids bounced high on a massive trampoline. Others shrieked in the aboveground pool and played cornhole.

The women perched on the deck. They were incapable of basic honesty, one symptom of which was the tenor of their voices, which originated and died in their sinuses. They talked mostly about shit they'd recently purchased or were planning to purchase, and trips from which they had recently returned or were planning. Consumerism and passive-aggression: the very best life had to offer. Aviva felt as numb and strange around these people as if she'd found herself deposited in another solar system, in the company of impenetrable, if nominally friendly, aliens. Aviva caught Sam's eye from across an expanse of poisoned lawn, and smiled like she was having a lovely time.

One of the cousins was sitting on the all-weather sectional with her infant, the newest member of the clan. Aviva beamed at mother and child, trying not to be creepy, and said, faux-casually, of the baby: "She's beautiful, wow."

"Thanks," said the mother in her teeny-weeny voice. She crinkled her eyes, but the rest of her face did something tight and awful that meant: kindly keep your distance from the epitome of decency that is myself with this precious newborn in my arms.

But Aviva was a glutton for punishment, and Yasmin's advice was at the fore of her mind: "Do you think . . . it might be . . . okay if I . . . could, maybe, like, hold her?"

The conversation on the deck ground to a halt, so everyone could watch this scene unfold, and Aviva knew she had made a mistake.

"Oh," said the mother, "I'm sorry, but she just ate."

Was that a thing? Could babies not be held by strangers immediately after eating?

Aviva went in to the kitchen, where gallons of soda and aluminum tubs of shit food covered the gleaming granite island. Can you believe there are still people living on God's green earth who buy and use disposable plastic cutlery?

Sam's niece Mackayla appeared from around the side of the massive stainless steel fridge, all cute and bashful.

"What up, Auntie V?"

"Cutie pie!"

A sixteen-year-old in her arms wasn't the same as a baby, but maternal love was maternal love, was it not?

When Aviva had first begun to visit regularly, Sam had arranged a special mall date with his favorite niece. Mackayla was eleven at the time. They saw a delightful rom-com. The giggling was contagious.

"How are you, baby girl?"

"Dunno. Whatever. But, like, hi, crushing it much on YouTube, lately? Like forty thousand followers, last time I checked."

"Don't you *dare* give a fuck about that bullshit," Aviva said. "I will fucking *end* you."

Mackayla busted out the chorus from "Womb Service": " 'Hey, bitches, you're so blind, you're so blind you blow my mind, hey bitches, hey, hey, hey, bitches.' " Aviva didn't always consider the effect of her lyrics on the, ahem, children. Was it possible she was a bad influence?

Mackayla looked around and reached into her pocket to produce a fat, dank joint.

"Let's go out front and smoke this. I found it in Uncle Lenny's jacket, but he's already probably too stoned to miss it."

"Your parents would have me arrested, dude. You're a child. I'm a mess, but I'm not a get-high-with-a-fourteen-year-old mess. What are you, like, Little Girl Lost?"

"Gonna be seventeen in the fall. And you're supposed to be my cool aunt."

Mackayla's arms were stacked with bracelets, a ring on every finger. Her long hair hung as it pleased in a wild, frizzy tangle. Her jeans were nineties vintage. She was dressed a lot like Aviva during the first-album era, the boardwalk era, the tiny-club-in-the-Marina era, the Man's-unkempt-vibrating-magic-garden-garage-studio era. What was this warm feeling in Aviva's chest? Was it pride?

"Swear to me you'll lay off this shit until after college and I won't say anything to anyone, but if you're going to be a degenerate I *will* go straight to your parents, you get me?"

"Buzzkill, oh my God!"

"Love you, too. I'm confiscating this."

"Auntie V."

"What?"

"I just really love saying that. 'Auntie V.'"

"Do you have headphones on you?"

Mackayla pulled them from another pocket, like: of course.

Aviva rummaged through her bag and held up a splitter.

Into the guest room off the kitchen they went. They closed the door, took off their shoes, lay backward on the bed with their legs up on the wall, taking turns picking songs.

Mackayla played Juice WRLD. Haunted, tragic, violent dead boy on drugs.

Aviva played one off Amy's first album. The record company had been so condescending and dismissive; Amy was just a sexy little *child* and couldn't *possibly* know what was good for her or her songs. They kept sending industry songwriters into the studio to write with her. Hacks, the lot of them. They laughed her off when she tried to exert creative control. "It's *jazz*," she tried to insist. "There *is* no chorus, don't you *get* it?"

"You're a teenage nobody! And people don't *buy* jazz records, sweetie."

Contractually, she'd had to cooperate. Hated the record company, hated the marketing, hated the industry. Kept talking smack in the press about inferior contemporary female vocalists. She wasn't going to play nice; she was going to be *honest*. And sometimes honest isn't nice. What's worse: Meanness or lies? Lies! Lies are worse. Lies, lies, lies! Are! Worse! (And *that*, right there, was the start of a new song: behold the miracle of creation.)

Amy was an intrepid girl who turned her suffering into songs, and what did that get her? Attention! Fame! Money! Which she did not manage to turn into anything, because she let it destroy her instead. Maybe it would have been better to be mediocre from the get-go. Better to have been like the singers she mocked, the ones with nothing real to say. Better to have the songs written for you. Better to filter your voice through a machine. Better to sing each song exactly the same way every single time. Better, maybe, not even to sing at all. Just lip-synch.

They switched back and forth between Juice WRLD and Amy, tenderhearted addicts who wrote memorable songs before dying young, having all but predicted their own downfalls. The speed of Juice WRLD's meteoric rise and fall made Amy seem like David Crosby by comparison, but the truth inside the music was the same: you can tell when an artist has no *choice*.

Then Mackayla queued up a Taylor Swift, which Aviva thought was some kind of joke. Taylor *Swift*? Wasn't she a widget Barbie Frankenstein? Creation of a Svengali production team? Another dumb girl in a leotard shaking her hot ass for stadiums of shrieking tweens? Aviva had never bothered. Why would she?!

"No, Auntie V. No, listen, she does do stadium tours and stuff, but she's actually amazing, and she writes all her own stuff, she totally does, and she's grown up in public, like, singing about it. Just listen."

At which Mackayla's mom threw open the door.

They yanked out their earbuds, blushing like they had been doing something naughty.

"She's in *here*," the mom hollered over her shoulder. "She's in *here*, with Sam's *wife*." The mom stood there for a moment, her face twisted with confusion, staring at her problematic daughter and her husband's brother's weird barren wife. What was Sam's *wife* doing hanging out in here with a *teenager?* With the door closed. Fishy. You couldn't trust a woman without kids. A woman without kids had too much time on her hands, and could get up to all kinds of trouble.

Mackayla rolled her eyes. "Mom! God! *Chill!*"

In any case, reverie over. Aviva went back into the kitchen to stand around the gallons of soda and the disposable aluminum tubs of slop, making small talk until it was time to go.

The slow descent into luteal. The hardest time. The wait-wait-wait-wait-wait-and-see. Wait to bleed, or wait not to bleed. Nothing to do but wait. Buy the same ol' two-pack of pee sticks as the days wore on. Be hopeful. Be scared. Be disappointed. Be furious. Be defeated. Start again.

Days and days of rain. The park all muddy. She sat in the window at the coffee shop, messing around in her notebook and responding to messages and staring at her feeds.

An arresting, passionate young Australian street performer, gone viral on guitar with a shitload of gadgetry and special effects, managing to sound as though she had a full band. Cool beans.

A big article in the paper of record about there being zero long-term studies of ovarian stimulation as used for egg donation as well as IVF. Half-page illustration of a woman standing by the edge of a cliff. Stories of once-healthy young donors and all their myriad problems.

A flaccid magazine piece about the author's two pregnancies: the first, which she'd terminated at five months when "the doctor noticed something worrisome," and the second, resulting in "crossing the finish line" (aka a live, full-term, "perfect" infant birth). *We lost our first baby*, the writer repeated several times. But the subtext was clear; that the writer didn't have the temerity to articulate it didn't make it any less so: they had been informed that the first baby was deformed in some way, and so they had terminated. A *choice*, a part of *reproductive freedom*, yay, great, congrats. But just cop to it: You didn't *want* a potentially deformed baby. A potentially damaged or ill or terminal baby. You didn't want *just any baby*. You don't "cross the finish line" with some congenitally deformed *thing*, fuck *that*.

An article about the exponential decline in male fertility. Plummeting sperm counts all over the developed world. Researchers shocked and concerned. A chemical in sunscreen? Syntehtic hormones in the water supply? Microplastic everywhere, in everything? Cosmetics? Food additives?! Perfumes?

The moon was moving farther and farther away from the earth at the alarming rate of three centimeters per year, which couldn't mean nothing. It couldn't possibly. For, like, the tides. The tides! The cycles. Water. Women. Women! Whatever those were.

A billionaire industrialist, his infant son having died tragically of SIDS, immediately went and engineered himself not one but *two* sets of boy *triplets* to replace the lost child. Six brand-new boy children, born on schedule to two different wombs for hire, to soothe the ache of losing the first son. Who says money can't buy everything?

The elderly veterinary scientist responsible for crossing poodles with Labrador retrievers to create the Labradoodle was speaking out against his creation. Yes, it had seemed like a good idea at the time—a blind person whose spouse was allergic to dogs was in dire need of a guide dog, so the Labradoodle had been a "godsend"—but lo and behold, some decades later it had become clear that this crossbreed suffered a host of health problems. Ditto the bichon frise, which people adored for their "humanoid"-looking faces: unfortunately, their engineered genetics meant that their eyes watered more or less constantly their whole lives, causing them ostensibly hellish discomfort. Well! Discomfort was to be expected from life. Who were nonexistent creatures to complain about a little discomfort in exchange for existence?

And hark: news of Amy. Oh, algorithm, you know Aviva *so well*! The announcement that she was set to be brought back to life via hologram, and sent on an international tour. AI was going to make it possible to interact with her—the mirage would be built based on everything she had ever said or done on record, every photo and video.

A local person Aviva vaguely knew approached. She stood there grinning, seeking audience. Aviva reluctantly took out one earbud, then the other. The local had babysat for Aspiring Influencer all last summer, and had been fangirling out on Aviva's feed.

"Sorry for interrupting," the local said. "I'm so excited to listen to your new album, but I keep putting it off because I'm nervous I might get, like triggered by it, because I actually just got married, don't know if you heard, and we are at the very . . . beginning . . . of this . . . whole . . . journey!"

Aviva stared blankly until the girl patted her belly. "I mean, we're *trying*. We're *trying*! And we find out next Tuesday whether or not it's happening!" Oh, riiiight, because "trying" for a baby involved God knew who doing God knew what to you for God knew how long or how much, and you would be informed whether or not "it" was happening on an appointed day next week.

"Good luck," Aviva said brightly, and put her earbuds back in, only to be assaulted by Unhinged on the feed, a photo of the disastrous brood captioned thusly: *Lately I've heard about a woman I know struggling with #infertility and I just feel so #grateful to have my beautiful #babies! As hard as it is some days, at least we are a #blessed #family.*

Here's the problem with living in what amounts to a small town (and by "small town" is meant both the literal place in which Aviva made her home and the small town of the feed): you couldn't just mind your own damn business.

Oh, do you have to be tortured to be a great artist? people always wanted to know. Oh, do you think great artists are more fucked up than the rest of us?

Yes, assholes, yes. You don't get something for nothing.

Before bed, Aviva read a derivative dystopian novel about an alien planet on which women are reproductive slaves, and Sam read a history of the First World War.

"Isn't it kind of obnoxious to call it the 'First' World War?"

Witty banter, aka foreplay! He looked at her over the top of his sexy reading glasses.

"I mean," she went on, "since war has been a fact of life since, like, the dawn of civilization."

"Never on such a large scale, though," he said, with utmost seriousness.

"But, like, if you were fighting in a war before mass media, it probably *felt* like *your* entire world was at war. Every war *was* the whole world, as it could be perceived, at war. Seems like kind of a cheap marketing ploy to make war seem bigger and better every time, like to awe the spectators or something. 'Ladies and Gentlemen, it's the *First-Ever Wooooorrrrrrld War*! Check it *out*!'"

"What would you prefer they call it?"

"How about 'Most Terrible War Yet'? They could just call every war that, and just, like, number them. Most Terrible War Yet number 24,8469." She cracked herself up, got a case of the hiccups, and couldn't stop.

Hiccupping irritated Sam. He had some deep-seated problem with hiccupping. He could not stand hiccupping. It was a bit dickish, the way he responded to her hiccupping.

"It's not like I'm doing it on *purpose*," she said, then hiccupped again, and cracked herself up again. He went back to his book. Her hiccups got kind of painful and upsetting. And then she got the giggles again, which only made everything worse.

Sam's clenched jaw gave him away.

"Dude, I'm *trying*," she told him.

"Can I get you a glass of water, baby?"

"Don't call me 'baby.' I'm not your fucking baby."

She did occasionally like being called "baby." In follicular phase, "baby" was A-OK. In ovulatory phase, "baby" was acceptable. But in luteal phase, "baby" was grounds for divorce.

"Okay, *sweetheart*. So you do want me to bring you a glass of water or not?"

"Just bring me a fucking glass of water! Isn't that obvious? Jeez. I can get my own glass of water if I want some water. But bringing it to me might be a nice way to mitigate your irritation at the involuntary spasming of my *diaphragm*, don't you think?"

He sighed mightily and went to go get her the water.

She stopped being a cunt for a moment: "Thanks."

Then she hiccupped again, painfully.

"FUCK."

Now Sam got the giggles. A relief.

The nonexistent baby had this obnoxious way of calling everything about their relationship into question. Fuck you, nonexistent baby, for fucking up their marriage even *before* assenting to your own goddamned *conception*. Aren't you supposed to wait until you're *born* to undermine your parents' relationship?! Precocious little shit, aren't you.

Sam had Springsteen tickets. Aviva had never seen Springsteen. She wasn't opposed to Springsteen; she just didn't get the big deal about Springsteen. They walked down to the stadium through Empire Plaza, and she tried to be excited and have fun, because Sam loved Springsteen, and Aviva loved Sam.

The sun was just beginning to set. Skateboarders crisscrossed the dramatic brutalist expanse under the watchful eye of the Egg. Middle-school kids did wheelies on their bikes. Magic hour. And the childless couple walked, hand in hand, down to the bro-crammed stadium to see an old white kazillionaire with a facelift and hair plugs do his working-class-savior act for twenty thousand people.

They sat way up in the nosebleeds. The crowd screamed, "Bruuuuuuuuuuuuce. Bruuuuuuuuuce."

"Why do they call it the nosebleeds, again?"

"Propensity for nasal hemorrhage at high altitudes," Sam screamed.

There was no opener. The working-class hero came out right on time. A beautiful man, she had to admit, even from way up there. He emanated an undeniable *something*. Black jeans, black shirt, black vest. Big silver cross at his throat. In his sixties, but he worked that stage like a stallion in his prime. Grinning, radiant, beaming. You couldn't resist. There was nothing to resist. He radiated joy. You forgot yourself a little, so you could enjoy yourself a little. (How were there still tears to be shed?! Music was so close.) There was no heaviness in this performance. It was buoyant. The music wasn't a vehicle for carting around all your heavy shit. The music was catharsis, a way to *unload* all your heavy shit. It was a break from ambivalence. He was earnest and up-front. He wasn't bothered by what all these people wanted from him, these tens of thousands of screaming, cheering, laughing, dancing, crying people. It was a revival, that's what it was. People need to gather en masse and scream and sing and shake their hips and shoulders and nod their heads: yes, yes, yes. *Someone* had to enact this essential primal leadership role, and best for it not to be someone evil or political. *Someone* had to do this work for the masses. Here and now, it was Springsteen. He walked out on a platform into the crowd, shook hands, high-fived, grinned, offered eye contact, took requests, and brought a delirious teenage boy up onstage to jam. Played for *four straight hours.*

When Aviva looked over at Sam, he shrugged and laughed and screamed: "THE BOSS!" And he slipped a hand around her waist, danced with her, squeezed her ass. This was one way to banish ghosts: frighten them with commotion, spirited noise! When it was over, Aviva was so wrecked she laid out forty-five American dollars for a *Two Hearts Are Better Than One* T-shirt. They only had 2XXL left, but she would cut the neck and sleeves and wear it as a dress. It would be beautiful when it got worn soft and thin, years down the road (with her babies clinging to it).

Walking back up the hill amongst throngs of people singing "Glory Days," Aviva felt washed. Conversion complete.

Back to the acupuncturist. Day what, now? Twenty-four. Tits getting heavy and sore. Insomnia in full force. Bloating. She couldn't wear a bra.

"I'm trying this new mantra," she told the acupuncturist. "It goes: *There is nothing wrong with my body. There is nothing wrong with my body.*"

"How about 'everything is *right* with my body,'" the acupuncturist suggested. "Not 'nothing is wrong.' Take out the negative. 'Everything is *right.*'"

A business card on the bulletin board at the co-op: *Kirsten Tabowski. Full-Spectrum Doula. Pregnancy, Birth, Postpartum, Infertility, Stillbirth, Miscarriage, Abortion, Menopause.* Black lettering underneath a plain circle. The circle was complete, but empty. Or full? Or both empty and full at the same *time*? A sun, or a moon. Or a void. Or a world.

Aviva sat in the parking lot.

A cheerful voice answered on the second ring. "Kirsten Tabowski!"

"Hi. I found your card at the co-op? I'm looking for a . . . doula?"

"The co-op!" said Kirsten Tabowski with a great honking laugh. "I can't believe my card's still up there! They must not clear those things too often. I moved to the Adirondacks like four years ago and sort of hung up my hat. No one's called me in a *very* long time. I'm sort of retired. But hello! I'm glad you found me. Maybe I can help."

"Okay . . ."

"It's really weird you found my card, I have to tell you. I'm not . . . for everyone. My circle has . . . shrunk. I only do this work when it's . . . right. I don't have the same energy I had twenty years ago."

"Is this, like, a get-turned-away-from-the-witch's-hut-three-times-before-you're-accepted-in thing?"

"Ha. I'm not explaining very well. What I'm telling you is, I can *totally* recommend someone really great who can hold your hand nonjudgmentally. Because everyone deserves that. But I don't do that anymore. I used to. But not anymore. How deep and in what kind of shit are you?"

"I'd say like knee-deep?"

"So let me just tell you my deal. I was an abortion companion back in the day, that's how I started. I went with people to their abortions, 'cause I had had an abortion myself, so I was the friend who went with everyone to their abortions. I cared for people before and after. There wasn't really a name for it, back then. I didn't hang out a sign or anything. I was just that friend who'd hold the space for you when you had an abortion. Then I started having babies, I had a whole *bunch* of babies, wham-bam, four in ten years. I was really into babies. I was, like, good at having babies. So then I became a birth doula, obviously, because I got to know a fuck of a lot about how that whole process goes. And there was a name for *that*, and I could make a little money. It was awesome, all that warrior-woman shit, felt like a real calling. Then I sort of got tired and more into gardening. What else can I tell you? Who are you? What's your story? Tell me. I'm at your cervix."

"Well. I've . . . never been pregnant."

A moment of silence bounced off a satellite somewhere in outer space.

"Okay," said Kirsten Tabowski. "But . . . you'd like to be?"

"Yep."

"*Well*. I got into the fertility stuff the same way I got into all the other stuff: suddenly everyone I knew was dealing with it. It's funny: people come out of the woodwork. It's wild. One of my sisters had a real hard time getting pregnant. Then a cousin, then a friend from college, then a neighbor. And it was just, like, message board message board message board clinic clinic clinic anecdote anecdote. This vast underworld people are just sort of let loose in, to wander alone and go quietly insane. I got curious, what can I tell you. It interested me. I wanted to learn more, so I could understand more. I wanted to be a good sister, cousin, friend. I spent like two years *straight* on the blogs. I got my, like, *PhD* on the blogs. And anyway, I don't know what to tell you, I don't know what you want to hear, but shit just started to smell real bad. Maybe you don't want to know. Maybe you already know. I don't know *what* you want to know. What do you want to know?"

"So you're like a jack-of-all-reproductive-ordeals."

"Yes! That's exactly what I am. But I kind of ran out of steam, is the thing. Burnout is real. It's a little freaky you found my card. I mean, I still mentor a few people, I'm still *here* in whatever sense, but honestly? There's no amount of money anyone could pay me at this point."

"You sound like the doula for me."

"At some point I saw enough, and I got real tired. My sister got colon cancer at forty-one, when her daughter was two. My college bestie got breast cancer at forty-seven, when her twins were six. My neighbor's baby was born at thirty-two weeks gestation and spent two months in the NICU. My cousin mortgaged her whole life on nine rounds of IVF, which resulted in seven miscarriages and game over, but she'll be paying off that debt until she drops dead of whatever's in store for *her*. Oh, and let's not forget about my *other* friend, whose twins are struggling with developmental delays and pretty severe metabolic disorder *at nine*. Listen, I'm sorry, I'm not trying to offend anyone. People hold this shit sacred, and it's their business, you know?"

"I do know."

"Raise any concerns about industrial fertility and you're immediately a monster who wants to reinforce biological destiny and deny queers reproduction. But fuck that, you know: I served for a long time. I have *served*. I've been there for anyone and everyone who wanted my support, because people deserve that, straight up. But what I've seen, and I mean, like, over and over, in these clinics, the money, the drugs, the doctors, the desperate people in this giant sinkhole of suffering for profit, is . . . I have never seen so much suffering *in my entire fucking life*, not with *all* the abortions and *all* the unmedicated labor and, oh, by the way, I had a stillbirth, which was, you know, a story for another time, but *all* the shit I have ever seen, combined, doesn't *touch* the suffering in those clinics, man. And I am *concerned* about all that suffering. And I don't know *why* exactly I am called to hold this concern, but for whatever reason, here we are. It's freaking me out that you found my card, hon. *Here's* an interesting detail a lot of people don't know: Conception in a lab involves 'disabling' the lucky chosen sperm. The sperm gets its *tail* snipped off after it's been centrifuged and bathed in a chemical solution. Then the tech basically *rapes* the egg with a disabled sperm in a hair-sized needle. And the egg does *not* appreciate this. The egg actually physically *resists* it. The egg is actually *designed* to *resist* it, because the egg very much wants to choose her *own* winner sperm."

"Oh God."

"Yeah. We got our violation on the cellular scale and we got our violation on the planetary scale and we got our violation everywhere in between, and I say let's stop pretending we're worried about destruction on a planetary scale when we're goddamned *thrilled* to override it on the cellular scale. I'm sorry. I'll stop now. Hell of a coincidence you found my card, hon."

"I took Femara a few weeks ago?"

"How'd that go?"

"Horrible."

"Yeah. I'm sorry."

"But, like: Am I just a wimp? Shouldn't I just, like, woman up?"

"Oh, hon. I don't even know you. But . . . no."

"I mean, do I just not want it bad enough? Should I just learn to bite the bullet? Isn't that what childbearing entails?"

Kirsten Tabowski sighed like the world's final exhale.

"In the abortion realm, we talk a lot about how *not* having the baby you don't want, the baby you aren't able to care for at this juncture . . . that *is* being a good mother. Because it constitutes acting in the child's best interest. It's merciful. And living with grief is something a good mother sometimes has to do. It's very selfless, in its way."

"I'm waiting for some kind of miracle. I am just trying to follow the signs." (I'm looking for some answers/trying not to lose my mind. Witness the magic: another song seedling, pushing up through the dirt.)

"I think it's pretty cool that you found my card, actually. I'm sorry for what you're going through. I don't have a fix. But what I can tell you is: I have four grown kids. I have a solid marriage and we worked our asses off and got through it and did the best we could and there's a lot to be said for letting things run their course, but it sure as shit wasn't a picnic. Or a cure for loneliness, by the way. That much I can tell you. You exist to be replaced, that's all I know. Having kids taught me that it's not remotely about me. Kids are not the answer to *anything*, hon. The answer is surrender. It's not even a little bit about you or what you want. Which is maybe why people who think it's cool to want to force it . . . tend to be . . . by and large . . . you don't, like, write for Twitter, do you? How can I put this delicately? All I can tell you is that being able to have or acquire kids doesn't mean shit. You can have a hundred kids and fuck 'em alllll up. How many happy families do you know? How many well-adjusted people do you know? How many people have you ever known *in your life* who aren't broken? In your life. A dozen? Out of the maybe ten thousand people you've ever met?"

"So what's your, like, fee structure? You charge by the hour or what?"

Her laugh sounded hoarse and elderly, like Kirsten Tabowski was about two hundred years old, and had long since given all her shits. "It's more like a volunteer thing," she said, still laughing. And as she laughed she reverse-aged and started to sound young again. "It's more like a nonprofit thing. It's pro bono. It's free. It ain't for sale. It's off the record. Pass it on. It's open-source. You're welcome."

Peals of laughter, like a prepubescent girl who believed she was going to live forever and write her own story, a very young and bright-eyed girl who had not yet seen much.

"So what do you do now, if I may ask?"

"Well, I went back to school! I got my master's. I figured, I'm pretty good at learning. There was this classic Paula Fox novel about a middle-aged married couple and no one who had ever written about it seemed to get that it's all about the fact that this middle-aged couple hasn't been able to have children. Plain as day, but no one ever talked about it. I wrote about it for my thesis, and now I'm looking at a ton of other contemporary literature through that lens. Fertility, I mean. I might go all the way for a PhD, but I might not; depends when it stops being fun. It's still fun right now. And I'm getting ready to be a grandma for the first time! My eldest is having her first next month! Listen, hon, I wish you the best of luck. Please don't put me online. But feel free to call again if you want. I could consider coming out of retirement for you. Which I guess I sort of just did, didn't I?"

* * *

Dr. White had ordered blood tests on days twenty-three and twenty-five, to see where the progesterone levels were, see if Aviva had ovulated, see if she was maybe, possibly, even . . . ?

A bored, gorgeous, zaftig early-middle-aged woman with a flawless top-knot did the honors. Her nametag read *Opal*. She wore enormous hammered brass earrings and jaunty eyeliner wings with her scrubs, looking like she belonged in a girl group straight out of 1959.

Recurrent pregnancy loss, said Aviva's paperwork, which made her feel worse and better, because losing pregnancies had to be better than never conceiving at all.

"Did you eat today?" Opal wondered.

"Yeah. They didn't say not to."

"It's fine. I just have to press a button." Opal looked at the paperwork and saw the diagnosis. "Aww," she said.

In an instant, Aviva was full-on sobbing.

"It's okay," Opal said, opening her arms and holding Aviva tight against her big bosom.

The sobbing passed as quickly as it had come on. Weather.

Opal was a righteous queen about the whole thing: "Everything is going to work out just fine, sweetheart. Wait and see. Everything is going to work out just fine. Happens all the time. I'm sure you're in good hands. These docs really know what they're doing."

Not pregnant.

And the blood tests showed no progesterone spike at all. Which meant that the forced-ovulation drug had not, in the end, forced ovulation. Dr. White suggested she come back in. Aviva declined. She called the Rabbi, instead, and produced a fresh batch of hot tears.

"My progesterone levels are in the toilet. That horrible shit didn't even *work*."

"You're angry. I don't blame you."

"I am *never* messing with that stuff, *ever* again. *Never*."

"You taking the full course of those drugs was one of the bravest things I've ever seen."

"Try 'dumbest.'"

"You made a difficult choice and you stuck with it. That's bravery."

"No, I went against my instinct. That's called 'stupidity.' That's called 'soul death.' No one wants to be my fucking kid because I am a shitty person in a shitty body with shitty ancestry, okay? Let's just be straightforward about this. The spirits are *shunning* me. The spirits are better off wherever they are in the underworld than coming through the likes of *me*. Addicts, prostitutes, murderers, liars, thieves, people who live all day every day on their phones: the spirits show *no* compunction about coming through *them*. But not *me*, no *thank* you. Not *this* bitch. Anyone is preferable to *me*. Anything is preferable to me! Even formlessness, even nonexistence."

"We'll get through this."

"Yeah, yeah."

"I really thought you had a shot with this one," Jerry said.

"What are you talking about?"

"I really thought this album was gonna get nominated for something."

"I take it the album didn't get nominated for anything."

"It's a long game, sweetheart. It's one album in a long line of albums. That's what counts. You'll wind up getting nominated down the road for something you don't even expect, you'll see. That's how it works. You just keep on keeping on. You mean a lot to people."

"Just not the right people."

"Ah, well, fuck people. Every album takes you a little further on the journey. And anyway, the UK tour is coming together beautifully. Everyone is really excited."

Aviva messaged Amy's mum: *Gonna be in London in a couple months! Let's meet up! Heard about this hologram thing! Is it true??*

Will be lovely to meet you in person, Mum replied (there was no way she was for real). *And re: hologram, who knows. He's working on it.*

Him: Pops. The big bad dad. Anything to make a buck.

But speaking of which! It was Father's Day. Who made this shit up, anyway? Sorry, Sammy. Sam-the-Man. He pretended not to notice or care, but Aviva noticed. Aviva cared.

She placed the requisite call to Chuck, who was busy celebrating his grandpaternity with the twins, and said he'd call her back later, which he didn't do.

And now, ladies and gents and nonbinaries: the bleed.

She smoked the entirety of the stolen joint she'd lifted off Mackayla. A lot of joint for one person. Meant for sharing, a joint that size. Weed and feed, feed and weed. And bleed! Weed and feed and bleed and weed and feed. And bleed. And feed. And weed.

First time Aviva ever got high was in the eighth grade. She was in a locally famous Jewish adolescent performing arts group, pleased as punch to stand before the Jews of greater Los Angeles singing and dancing. Rollicking, exclamatory, feel-good Hebrew-English anthems with happy beats, unforgettable harmonies, twee choreography, quasireligious lyrics. Many of which were written by Susie Goldman, Marcus Copeland's mother! Like the Carpenters on an acid trip at the Wailing Wall.

You had to audition to be admitted. A rumor circulated that they might get to record an album. Aviva wanted very much for her family to see her onstage and cease ignoring her. She had incredible hope that this might happen. She wanted to belt these anthems from rooftops. It would be like the sun shining again after a freakish decade of rain. She was sure that if she stood onstage and sang her heart out, they'd *see* her, really *see* her. She fantasized about it constantly. She practiced the songs and choreography all day every day. What would it be like to be truly valued by her family?! Baring her soul to the applause and adoration of Barb and Chuck and Rob and Mike. They would finally realize Aviva existed, and unite in celebration of their forsaken baby girl. And never again would the fractured wreck of their family lose sight of what mattered: one another!

The older girls were goddesses with French manicures and side ponies, rehearsing the Running Man in parachute pants. The older boys were all dashing and kind. The younger girls made up the chorus, and dreamt of the day when they would develop secondary sex characteristics and star in the show. The younger boys would have to wait longest of all, but they were in it for the long haul. They were like their own little family, these performing arts kids, under the inspired direction of a locally famous singer-songwriter, whose winning smile was a balm to the aching souls of the San Fernando Valley housewives who worshipped him.

Aviva was in love with Brent, a senior. Brent had been in the troupe for years. He wore Lennon glasses and stonewashed jeans. He had shoulder-length brown hair and wore brightly patterned rayon button-downs. He was a wonderful dancer. He went to public school. He was always nice to her, but never really took her seriously. She was just an eighth grader, after all, and it remained to be seen whether she was simply tall, mildly big-boned, or unacceptably oversized. Aviva ate Brent's indifference like love. (Family lessons: 1. Absence of cruelty = love. 2. Cruelty = work harder for love.)

They went on an overnight. Thirty kids, staying a couple hours north of LA at the same camp where Aviva and Rob and Mike spent all their summers. Saturday night they sat around a campfire: Brent and Aviva and her best friend Jessica and one of the "adults," Simon, a twenty-something assistant musical director with his *own* Jewish singer-songwriter aspirations. Everyone else had gone to sleep. They were drinking beer. The time had come. Aviva was prepared to engage in any sexual behavior requested of her. This was her moment. Life was *starting*.

A game of Truth or Dare commenced. Jessica wound up on Simon's lap, grinding against what she later told Aviva was a "serious boner." Aviva accepted Brent's sluggish tongue in her mouth. There were shrieks and giggles and everyone got even more drunk, impossibly.

In the wee hours, a joint was passed, and behold Brent's cinematic offering, the slo-mo extension of his arm, the eagerness of her first inhale, her eyes closed, the shadows in her cheeks. A moment of calm and then her violent cough, then her laughter at the cough, then her laughter at the laughter at the cough, then the laughter at the laughter at the . . . and so on. Aviva was stoned, had always been stoned, would always be stoned. She couldn't believe her luck.

Jessica was now a makeup artist, working mostly in TV. Her feed was very Stepford fame-whore. Simon had become *ba'al teshuva*, and lived in LA with his wife and dozen children. Brent, let's have a look-see, here . . . Brent appears to be the county coroner in Las Cruces, New Mexico.

Aviva had tried absolutely everything to get Sam to dump her back in their early courtship, but for some strange reason, he'd refused to dump her.

"I used to sometimes slice my arms up with a razor," she told him, and he kissed her scars. "I don't shave my legs, like, ever," she told him, and he grabbed a furry thigh, Bernini-style, and kissed her some more. "My mother's a religious fundamentalist alcoholic." Kissed her. "My father's a pathological pussy hound." Kissed her. "I have never saved any money whatsoever." Kisses and kisses. "I cheated on my first love." Kiss. "I'm divorced." More kisses. "I'm pretty sure I've been in perimenopause since I was like sixteen." Kissed her, kissed her, kissed her.

He himself was no perfect prince, of course. He'd been rigorously trained to avoid conflict, had a *ridiculously* outmoded understanding of foreplay, tended toward antisocial, refused to see shitty character traits in the people he loved, descended from flavorless people, and wasn't always instinctively up for dancing. But she could certainly work with his bullshit if he was willing to work with hers, and maybe *that* was the secret of happy coupling.

"I'd rather be stoned than not," she added to her laundry list, as an afterthought.

"Well, *that's* a little bit of an issue, don't you think?" he said.

"I do," she admitted. "It is."

* * *

Random call from the guy she'd met on Craigslist (post–Love Fiend, for shame). He was flourishing, in love, living in New Orleans, and finishing up a PhD in neuroscience. Good for him.

Carroll Gardens, Brooklyn, summer of 2003. He'd come over with weed and go down on her, the perfect gentleman. Helped her get over the Fiend, but not, alas, Cracker. Crumbs of Cracker clung to her. There was nothing you could do about those kinds of crumbs. Weather was no help. Time was the only thing for it. Lots and lots and lots of time. And then still more time.

"So hey," she said to Craigslist guy. "I've been wondering: Do you think pot slows you down and fucks with your head, long term?"

"I don't know," he said, "but my head works a little differently than most to begin with. So it kind of brings me down to the level where I feel like I can be in the world with everyone else. Does that make sense?"

"Yeah," she said. "That makes perfect sense."

Later the same day, the regular homeless dude was loitering on the corner of Spring and Lark, holding court for two college kids, a guy and a girl. He seemed to be amusing them; they were smiling wide.

"Hey, how you doin, miss?" the homeless dude said to Aviva. The college kids just stood there, grinning. Aviva reached for her wallet to give him money, but he wasn't asking for money.

"Let me ask you something," he said. "What's your name?" He asked her this at least twice a week. Before she could answer, he apologized: "You see, I smoked a lot of the, um, what they call ganja, back in the day, you know, 1972, and that was some different shit they had back then. So my mind don't *work* the same."

The kids giggled. "Yeah," they said. "Yeah, the *ganja*."

They weren't making fun of him, exactly. Aviva wasn't sure what was going on.

"Mister," Aviva said. "Can I ask you a question? Do you think pot messes with your head, long term? Like, in general?"

She wanted him to tell her, Yes, as a matter of fact, I do. She wanted him to say, Miss, please do yourself a favor and lay off that ganja, else you gonna end up just like me: addled and irrelevant, discarded and forgotten.

But the guy just shrugged. "Nah, you see, it was some different shit back in those days, and I wasn't starting out from such a good place in the head, you know?"

She knew.

Fun fact of the day: seeds, eaten by animals and processed through said animals' digestive systems and then shit out in due course, are most perfectly primed for sprouting in the spring. No planting or cultivating or industrial agriculture necessary.

She watched old footage of herself online, radiating an intense, defensive energy. God, she's horrid. She couldn't blame any of those spirits in the void for declining to become her offspring.

"'Fuck it' is not an acceptable response to life," said the Love Fiend in one of his rare online appearances, in response to a celebrity's heroin death. But fuck him and his too-little-too-late AA aphorisms. Why *isn't* "fuck it" an acceptable response to life? Aviva really would like to know. Because honestly: fuck it.

Someone else on the feed with a little boy and a little girl. How did she know this person? She didn't remember. He was rich as the devil, this guy, always sunning in Mallorca or skydiving in Morocco or skiing the Alps with his fam. Here I am with my boy! Here I am with my girl! But he happened to have fathered another family before this one, by the way. Another girl and another boy, as luck would have it. He had ditched out on that previous family. Didn't bother to stick around to raise that family. And now this man vaunts and venerates his second set of kids (and their mother) like his life depends on it: my girl on the beach! My boy in the hills! My girl and I at the summit! Dinner with my boy! Or sometimes "our": Our boy! Our girl! Ours! Mine! Ours! Mine! Meanwhile, the first set of kids was nowhere to be found. For the purposes of the feed, the first boy and girl did not exist.

You tended to notice stuff like this, if you were someone whose capacity for noticing had not by now been sanded clean away.

A girl she barely knew always posted her fiancé with captions like *look at this dumbass* or *what a goober* or *dorkface* or *hi from this nerd!* The guy seemed guileless and genuinely happy to be marrying this girl. Aviva thought about him often, angry on his behalf, although it was true that he did look like a dorkface. Tonight's post: the announcement that they are expecting a child. *This LOSER is gonna be a DAD*, was the caption.

Here was Amy doing a huge outdoor concert in Argentina, exceptionally thin and exceptionally mad. Contempt oozing from every gesture, every intonation. *Screw this.* Screw all of you losers, sheep, undulating hordes, followers, wouldn't know what's good if it bit you in the ass. Screaming all my songs back up at me. Shut up, won't you *please*.

In the studio she was great; in front of small audiences she was great; in front of massive crowds she was a mess.

"It's more than a business, because you're singing your heart out," she told a VJ backstage in the next video. Of making peace with her hits, she said: "They're still really good songs."

And here she was at nine or so, before puberty did its thing, at big bro's bar mitzvah. Bro looking dapper, so grown-up. Pops still pretty good-looking himself. Mum sweet and svelte, all done up. Nan all proud and blowsy. You can see how aligned Pops and Nan are, mother and son, lives of the party, dominant personalities. The kids understood the dynamic at play. Kids know everything. Kids know *precisely* who their parents are.

If they could reanimate Amy via holographic interface and artificial intelligence, shouldn't it be possible in the near future to use the same type of programming to enliven one of those weighted silicone baby dolls, the therapeutic dolls that cost thousands of dollars? What if they could give you one of those weighted realistic silicone babies loaded with an algorithm that you could *raise up from infancy*—you'd trade in the baby for successively bigger realistic weighted silicone dolls, and you'd *teach* it things. You could raise it the same way you might raise a flesh-and-blood child: with religious beliefs, ancestral memory, family history, folk songs and stories, values, mythologies of your choosing . . . except an AI-enlivened hunk of whatever wouldn't ever disappoint or devastate you by, say, marrying a Gentile or being functionally illiterate or sliding into culturally sanctioned alcoholism. But no: the algorithm would absolutely *have to* be programmed to include some kind of fundamental betrayal, because isn't that what the whole deal was actually about? New generations rise up and lay waste to the values and mythologies and rituals of the generations that precede them. It's called progress!

In this manner, with weed and feed, she managed to make it through yet another bleed. Weed plus feed plus bleed successfully eradicated both time and weather. She floated herself right on through, like a ghost, off the hook, until the bleeding subsided, at which precise point she found herself outside, in her little urban garden, sitting in the sun listening to some birdsong and an argument being had by the neighbors. She watched the light play through the leaves of the big birch tree, entirely unbothered by her circumstances, and what do you know? Like a miracle *she* was new, reborn yet again from her old damn self.

6.

DRINK

Even the best marriages have issues, but unintentionally barren marriages?
Really tough. Aviva's insistence on yoking reproduction to sexual congress
only made things between herself and Sam more difficult. To say nothing
of the violence recently enacted by the demon drug upon her pituitary.

Sex had become stressful and boring and compulsory and repetitive
and sad. A familiar story. The stakes had gotten too high. The mind and
body are connected, or haven't you heard? Aviva got turned off by the way
Sam's hands got clammy during foreplay. She could practically smell his
fear, and he tended to repeat all the same old moves by rote.

When Aviva bitched to the Rabbi, he said, simply: "It's on you, too, you
know." Asshole! Traitor! He was right.

Meanwhile, Marcus Copeland had been emailing.

Hello, yes. He suggested she watch a soon-to-be-ubiquitous British
series that "reminded" him of her. She replied with a witty line from the
series, of which she was already a fan. He sent her a song he was working
on. She replied with a joke about his enormous oeuvre. He recommended
a band he was into. She recommended a band *she* was into. He said that
they should get a drink next time he was in New York. She said yeah, for
sure. He said he would let her know when he was in town. She said cool,
great. He said it would be nice to spend some quality time. She said *while
we're young*.

These emails lit her up cunt to crown. She woke from a dream in which she was reaching orgasm with Copeland only to find herself reaching actual orgasm in actual time/space, with Sam snoring beside her. Oh my *God*, sexual *desire*, riiiiight: procreation theoretically/traditionally/ideally had something to *do* with sexual desire, if that isn't *way* too insanely retrograde to even *suggest* at this point in the history of human/machine interface. Take it a step further: What if spontaneous healthy reproduction works best if we do simply follow our genitals around like animals? Given the fact that we *are still* animals, all due respect to the scientific and industrial revolutions. Dear God in heaven: even fleeting *recall* of Copeland's small farewell face caress at the end of that party back in LA still had the power to give Aviva full-body shivers. Surely it would be foolish to ignore anything so intense as that.

But the marriage. The marriage. The marriage needed some support. The marriage was not fruitful. The marriage hung in the balance. So here they sat in the teeny-tiny waiting room of a sex therapist's office on the second floor of a building on the main drag in Kingston.

"The cunt doesn't lie," Aviva murmured, a lyric in search of a tune.

"Nor the cock," Sam agreed, his face breaking into one of his massive firework-display grins. Dear funny man! Get your head on straight, Aviva: Here is your dear funny adorable man. You love the way his armpits smell. You can't get enough of the light in his eyes. You don't mind his morning breath. He is smart and brave and true.

The sex therapist flung open her office door so it almost banged Aviva and Sam in the knees. She was short and wide in head-to-toe crushed burgundy velvet. A sort of sex Buddha on leave from the circus, with a wild tangle of silver hair and round, unblinking eyes. She'd published a book about sexual renewal in long-term relationships. An interesting book, though Aviva also quite liked the *other* sex advice book she'd read concurrently, all about how monogamy in mammals is not only unnatural but also spiritually damaging.

"Welcome," said the sex witch. "I'd like to speak with each of you individually first, if that's okay." She leaned on the door frame, making bedroom eyes at them. One of those every-interaction-is-a-seduction types.

Sam went first. He was game. At the door, he turned to give Aviva a funny little salute. His hands were trembling ever so slightly. What a man, what a man, what a mighty good man. How could she even *entertain* the idea of Marcus Copeland with a man like Sam in her corner? Sam! He had taken a bite of a dog biscuit at Thanksgiving last year, on a dare, to make Mackayla laugh. He could sit in companionable silence for *hours*. He kept a book of the Born-Einstein letters by the shitter. He was a goddamn *volunteer firefighter* when he wasn't urging inner-city kids to run for office someday. He was sincerely grossed out by porn. Mighty, mighty good man. Worth a hundred Copelands. A thousand Copelands. Aviva was going to tell her cunt what the hell was what. You couldn't let the cunt decide! What kind of bullshit was that?! The inmates cannot run the asylum.

The trash magazines in the waiting room were up-to-the-minute. A middle-aged talk-show host, expecting her third baby via surrogate, thanked God for the "beautiful choice" of surrogacy. Her first two pregnancies had been "difficult," but she had always wanted a big family, so she was grateful to the working-class woman who was making this "dream" possible. It was all very shiny and good. The official political stance of the left was that women are not walking uteruses. If you were rich enough to be able to pay a desperate woman to cook you up a baby, however, the whole uterus as commodity thing was "beautiful."

A serious actress, elsewhere, shared her harrowing story of multiple miscarriages, accompanied by a series of arty photos in which she modeled luxe looks for fall. The official political stance of the left was that human life does not begin at conception. From the perspective of the "brave" forty-six-year-old actress who'd bled out a bunch of primo top-dollar lab-produced blastocysts, however: "The grief of losing my babies is unimaginable."

Trash mags could really be quite clarifying: If you *wanted* a baby, pregnancy was a precious entitlement, the very essence and meaning of life itself.

If you *didn't* want a baby, pregnancy was expendable inconvenient garbage. There *was* no inherent value independent of desire. How mind-blowingly strange was that? Potential life having no innate value whatsoever; any perceived value, or lack thereof, simply a reflection of personal desire, or lack thereof.

Within Aviva's portal awaited a cache of likes and some juicy email. Festival season around the corner, and the booking agent full of details. Would Aviva rather fly into Miami the night before or the morning of? Did the rider look okay? She could play with the house band if she wanted; sound check would be it for rehearsal, though.

Out the window, on the brick wall of a neighboring building, a graffito had painted a magnificent pair of juicy pink lips, four stories high. Aviva posted an arty shot, filtered up so the colors really popped. She captioned it "lips/vulva," because only the absurdly privileged ever got to bring forth anything remotely viable from between either.

Sam emerged wearing a bemused, indulgent expression. They made eye contact about the fact that this was kind of dumb so let's at least look forward to getting lunch at that great place down the street afterward. Perhaps the primary benefit of any kind of couples' therapy was that it could give the couple a common enemy.

She got up and offered him her chair. They were in this together.

"Mmm," he whispered, sitting where she had been. "Still warm."

See? Good. Playful. Gross. Sexy.

The witch's inner sanctum was decked out in swaths of cheap black velvet bunting and smelled of mildew. The many floor pillows, scattered on industrial gray carpeting, had seen better days.

"Make yourself comfortable," the witch said from her perch atop the only chair in the room. Her feet did not quite reach the floor. She had a satisfied, superior air, like she had already had more orgasms in her lifetime than everyone else on the planet combined. Grandiose. Numinous.

"So," she said. "Tell me why you're here."

Aviva had already filled out and emailed back the fourteen-page questionnaire, but okay. "The . . . ahhhhhh . . . lack. Of . . . children."

Do not cry, Aviva, do *not*. Drop the shoulders, lift the pelvic hammock, raise your chin, relax your jaw, and take possession of yourself. Smile. This is all a joke, and you are above it. The old stage armor.

"The, uh, absence . . . of . . . yeah."

The witch kept waiting, staring impassively at Aviva, waiting, until, *fuck*, Aviva broke down into huge, wracking sobs.

"Take your time," the witch said with a little smirk, handing over a box of tissues. It really was best when the clients broke down. Then you could build them back up, and they worshipped you.

"You start to feel like you're some kind of blighted *freak*," Aviva managed at last. "Everybody else has *babies*."

The witch nodded slowly, with a mix of pity and pleasure. God, she loved her job.

"You set up camp in that void, and the wind just *howls*," Aviva continued, getting her lyrical shit together. "The world spins on and on and on while ancient third-rate celebrities and ancient aspiring third-rate celebrities and tabloid urchins and dumbass rich bitches you went on teen tour with have *babies* and *babies* and *babies*. Constantly. *Constantly*. Harmie fucking *Shmendrickson* is getting on toward *two*. Everyone gets their little fucking trophies by whatever means necessary, and you pretty much stop even *wanting* a fucking baby if that's what it's about because who the fuck can even *think* about life that way in the first place? And you sorta start to wonder why you're even *alive* if you're such a blighted fucking *void*. And there's just this . . . creeping . . . *deadness* that starts to overtake everything, this heinous *wrongness* everywhere, so it gets to where you can't really be around anyone at all, like *anyone*, like *at all*, because they're either, like, unspeakably lucky or morally repugnant or, like, *both*? And either way *you're* just . . . this . . . blighted . . . *organism* . . . who can't take part? This, like, cursed animal in this, like, perpetual winter?! Like you might as well be the very last human being left on a dystopian earth?!"

This was pretty good shit. She should write this shit down. Sadness was a pathetic dead end. Sadness was for losers. Rage was at least entertaining, Jesus *damn.*

"That's hard." The sex witch stage-nodded.

"That's what *she* said."

"You're describing *grief*," the witch went on. "That's *grief.*"

Oh, sex witch gonna sex-witch-splain *grief* to Aviva, now?

Out the window, on the side of the neighboring building, the huge pink graffiti lips seemed to shift, so they appeared to smirk slightly and proffer a kiss.

"Trying to conceive can be very stressful."

"You know, I have *heard* that, yeah. Thanks."

"Let's talk about ways to help you guys transcend that stress."

"Oh, you mean like 'relax'?"

"Exactly."

"Cool. Totally."

What a waste of time. What even was time. Why, it was the only thing human beings had thus far been unable to even *attempt* to *pretend* to control. Also: weather! Tiiiiiime and weather. Unless it was true that the Jews controlled both.

"Let's work toward a place where you're having intercourse for its own sake," said the sex witch. "Not as a means to an end. We want to put conception out of our minds. Conception is not our concern. Instead, let's talk about how you and Sam can hold space for each other's vulnerabilities, get back to making each other feel good again. Real connection. No agenda."

"Yeah, sounds good. Is there some way you could, like, suggest to him that he be, like, a smidge more . . . aggressive? He's, like, excessively polite. I think he'd hear it better from you. Like a prescription. A girl wants to be sorta thrown down every once in a while, know what I mean? Also, he's kind of an ass man? And my tits are, like, legendary. So we're a bit of a mismatch."

"It sounds like we want to encourage him to be more yang, and in order to do that, we need to strengthen your yin. You have a lot of yang going on.

Which I suspect makes him instinctively more yin. So we need to change the balance, here. Let him be yang. You be yin."

"Yin" meant receptive, welcoming, passive: feminine. "Yang" meant aggressive, penetrative, intrusive: masculine. This was a cornerstone of the sex witch's book.

"So, the reason our sexual connection is in a coma and I'm barren—or, like, the other way around—is that I'm too masculine and he's too feminine."

"Pretty much."

"Do you get a lot of shit for that line of thinking?"

The sex witch shrugged the carefree shrug of a late-middle-aged cis woman who never, ever read the internet.

"Anytime we're talking about fertility, we're talking about blood flow to the pelvic region, so the attraction and the receptivity have to be exceptionally strong."

"So, barren women . . . we're just, sort of . . . frigid, in a sense?"

"We want to get you aroused to the fullest extent. When was the last time you felt that strong electrical current of desire?"

When a married superstar I idolize emailed me to say he'd like us to have twenty-four hours alone in a hotel room next time he comes through town, Aviva did not say, but felt in her pants, sure enough, there it was: a steady, insistent throb that said COPELAND, COPELAND, COPELAND.

"I completely understand why artificial reproduction doesn't appeal to you, by the way," said the witch. "It's very unnatural."

Unnatural! OMG! Ha! Had this bitch ever even been *online*? The plague was natural. Poisonous mushrooms were natural. Predator eating prey was natural. War was natural. The deadly sins, man's inhumanity to man, poverty, groupthink: all *super totally* natural. Local! Organic!

"I would like to think," the witch went on, "that there are many of us who hope that reproduction can remain something of a metaphysical phenomenon taking place between two consenting, healthy bodies whose biology has evolved to best suit the process."

"Sing it. 'Biology,' *yeah*, bit of a dirty word these days, but intelligent far beyond what we can comprehend. Do you know about the evidence suggesting that the unmolested egg actually exerts influence and choice and *control* over which sperm she *allows* to penetrate her?"

"Doesn't surprise me at all," said the sex witch.

"She *chooses*."

"Beautiful."

"But, if that's true, stay with me here, why doesn't forced conception qualify as a kind of sexual assault? And given that I personally am sort of into slightly, like, for lack of better word, 'aggressive' foreplay, I wonder if maybe I just need to shut the fuck up and embrace technocratic conception. Like maybe I could get hot and bothered about transvaginal ultrasounds and fallopian tube Drano and all the shots and drugs and the, like, overriding my body's basic integrity. Like what if people who go all in for that shit are on some level sort of *aroused* by it, you know? Like 'oooh yeah, Doctor, give it to me, I deserve it, I've been a bad, *baaaaad* barren girl, lemme have it, harder, up my dosage, ooooh this syringe is sooooo biiiiig, *yeah* . . .'"

The witch struggled to stay on script. There was no getting a laugh out of her.

"It says here you've been charting your temps for a few years?"

"Yeah, but the temps made no sense, so the charts were kinda useless. And then the app malfunctioned or, I don't know, but anyway everything wound up getting somehow erased and I wound up losing like two years of data?"

The witch plucked an onyx yoni egg off an altar full of dusty crystals.

"Do you know what this is?"

"Absolutely! Mine's Tiger's Eye. Good times. And I do make sure to wash it very thoroughly before using it. You know they try to discourage women from using them by suggesting we can't be trusted to properly clean them. Hilarious, right, given that women used to routinely die from infections following childbirth because first-generation OBs just ran around sticking their hands into cadavers and then up vaginas, and the dude who initially suggested hand-washing in medical contexts was made a laughing-stock and died alone in a mental institution, but what can you do."

"And what about the yoni steam, are you open to trying that? It can be a wonderful way to clear out holding patterns and emotional baggage."

"All in."

"Excellent. I'll give you some herbs. Let's shift gears for a moment. Why don't you tell me about the first time you had intercourse."

"I was freakishly old. Twenty. And I wept after."

"Was it traumatic?"

"Not at all. But it was like . . . a dam broke."

"Say more," said the sex witch.

The blessed event had occurred in college, very soon after Rob's death. The Gentle Giant had stayed calm while Aviva wept uncontrollably. He went to get her a glass of water, and he knelt by the bed and spoke softly: "Here, have a sip." He hadn't tried to talk her out of her tears, hadn't seemed alarmed, hadn't tried to fix anything. He had seemed to perfectly understand, somehow.

"It wasn't—I wasn't upset about the sex. I was upset about sort of—breaking with myself, you know? I felt it as a very sudden—sort of abrupt—farewell to the girl I had been all my life, up to that point. She was no more in that moment. She was, like, very suddenly *gone*, that girl. I experienced it as a sort of death. But a welcome one, you know? Perfectly fine. A relief. Overdue. Like she had been on life support, so it was merciful to let her go. But still: a loss. I really loved her and I was going to miss her. Or maybe I hadn't loved her enough, you know? But anyway, it was all over, and now she was gone. For good."

"So it was a tender experience."

"Very! Yes. Very tender, indeed. And he was the best. We had *such* a good time together for a few years. You're only twenty once, you know?"

They would orgasm together, laughing, entwined, joyful as can be, and thirty seconds later he would be hard again, and they'd start over.

She could still picture the rapturous look on his face, a certain angle of leg, the exceptionally appreciative yet authoritative way he held her. She couldn't have asked for a better partner in young love. They'd had no future, though, because Aviva didn't want to get married and live in rural Oregon and drink beer and hunt and watch TV and barbecue and attend church with his people. So after college she had callously broken his heart by moving to New York and getting engaged to Jeff and fucking a long line of scumbag musicians (Hi there, Cracker!) and being a generally reckless idiot. She had passed up true love on grounds of superficial bullshit, and now, all these years later, here she was, living in rust-belt upstate New York, married to a different decent and kind man whose relatives did pretty much nothing but drink beer and hunt and watch TV and barbecue and attend church. At least the universe, such as it was, had given her a second chance.

"Why don't we invite Sam back in," the witch said.

She instructed them to sit facing each other on the floor with their legs extended in mirror Vs. Aviva's thighs rested on top of Sam's, their clothed genitals inches apart. They giggled apologetically at each other. How had it come to this? The witch instructed them to look into each other's eyes and breathe slowly, in unison, for a count of one hundred. Much more difficult than it sounded. Eye contact is the home of the brave. The giggles ebbed and flowed, then took hold.

"Let it pass," said the witch. "Keep going. Let all that nervous energy burn itself up. Twenty-seven. Twenty-eight . . ."

And there! Yes!! There! Aviva felt it, unmistakably: a stirring. The giggles vanished. Sam. The familiar light behind his eyes, the ease and grace she found there, the sweetness of his breath, the warmth of his skin. How safe and happy she was with him! Soon enough they were going to get out of this ugly little office and away from this strange therapist. They were going to get lunch down the street, and then they were going to get the hell on with their lives, come what may.

"That yang energy," the witch whispered to Aviva. "Call it in. Thirty-four. Feel that? Welcome it. Thirty-five. *Lure* it. Thirty-six. Accept it, accommodate it. Sam, hold back, make her wait, hold back until you can feel her begging. Present yourself and don't back away, but just stay at the door. Hold your space. Wait for her to draw you in. You are the *essence* of yang, Sam, and you stay steady and strong and *decide* when you will give yourself to her. *You* decide. Once she has offered herself to you, *she* will wait. *You* wait until she is ready to yield *entirely* to you. Thirty-seven. And then you hold back slightly, still. Focus. Be persistent, stay focused on her, only her, do not look away. Thirty-eight. The gateway is where it *all* happens. The dance. Thirty-nine. Breathe. Don't look away. Forty."

At which point Aviva got distracted, thinking about how forty was too fucking old to have a baby anyway, and by forty-three, forty-four, fifty, sixty, seventy, she kept thinking *too late, too late, nope, nope, nope*. She saw herself and Sam aging peacefully in their empty, quiet house, the two of them alone in a fading twilight, massive heavy silence blanketing them like a dozen feet of freshly fallen snow, while the bright clamorous world beyond blossomed and opened and spun and continually, wildly, noisily, joyously renewed itself. Aviva and Sam holding hands amidst the ticktock of a dozen clocks, a hundred clocks, a thousand clocks, time seeming to slow and slow and slow so that an eternity passed between each tick and each tock, and by the time the witch finally reached one hundred and the exercise was over, it was as though the whole arc of a human lifetime had come to its meaningless end.

In the kitchen, she squatted over a huge steaming stainless steel pot full of hot water and herbs. Incredible, a whole new sensation, warmth radiating into her physical and energetic body in ways that felt altogether novel and unequivocally fabulous.

"This is insane, Sam. This is, like, wow. This is, like, holy *shit*. Wow. Just wow."

He was sitting at the table icing his knee, which he had tweaked playing tennis. "Look at us, baby. Fire and ice. Yin and yang."

"Everything I've ever heard about this is people squabbling on the internet about how it's dangerous and stupid and you could burn yourself by accident so don't do it. What a load of crap. This is, like, oh my *God*."

"Capital 'G'?"

"Capital 'G.'"

And hey: postwitch/poststeam sexual congress was righteous, too. They retired to the attic, where the early-evening light was spectacular. There was a big plush antique rug Aviva had scored at an estate sale in Menands, and a turntable hooked up to her best speakers. It had originally been envisioned as a nursery, and then gradually became a haunted space. Their reclamation of it was swift and complete. They rolled around on the rug every night that week, languid in the breeze from the open window, fucking and laughing and listening to records.

What day of her cycle was it?! Who knew? Who cared? She was going to cultivate some ignorance, for a change. She was *not going to think about her goddamn cycle*. The realization that they might get it on for no other reason than that *it could be fun to get it on* was a calm and shimmering lake atop which they bobbed peacefully in their exclusive vessel, the promise of never having to go back to that dingy little sex therapy office more than enough to float them a ways.

(It was, in fact, the sixteenth day of her cycle. The cervical serum happened to be primo, the good stuff, top-notch, heaven-sent. Probably it was going to be a girl, because XX sperm swam slower but lived longer, while XY sperm swam faster but died sooner. Aviva was not *thinking* about any of this, however. Not at all. Nope. Who cared?! Not she.)

Van Morrison was singing about the corruption and fatuousness of the music industry. Got to love Van, and not just those same three songs everyone wore down to dust. Tough break about his politics, but politics are personal, or the personal is political, or whatever.

"I'd listen to Van sing the phone book," Sam said.

Aviva's cue to do her impression of Van singing the phone book: "Auto mechanic—UUH-HUH—auto insurance—OOO—Automat—HEH!" She lifted her head from Sam's chest and put her lips up to his cock: "Is this thing on?"

"Please speak directly into the microphone," he said.

"Testing," she said. "Testing. Check."

"Loud and clear."

And then Aviva was off on an honest-to-goodness vacation. To the psychedelic yoga retreat in a relatively tourist-friendly third-world country near the equator, led by a famous elder yogi, with Hanalei assisting. She was going for it. Just when everything at home with Sam felt so nice again: timing's a bitch. There was in fact no way to have it all or do it all, because there was no technocratic workaround for the fact of *time*, was there, now.

Day eighteen, however. And *maybe* she was carrying a little bit of Sam with her on her travels? Regardless, bring on a week of asana and clean food in a jungle abutting a beach, bare feet in sand, sun on her naked ass, salt water in her hair. The retreat culminated in the ceremonial psychedelic ritual for whoever chose to partake. Aviva still wasn't sure whether she was going to partake, but it was probably a bad idea if there was any chance she was . . . carrying a little bit of Sam with her.

On the first of three planes, from within the earbuds of the person in the next seat, a tinny voice was belting out a song, really going for it. How robust the voice must sound in the ear of the listener, how powerful and large. But to Aviva, five inches away, the voice was absurd chipmunk noise. No telling who it was or what it was singing about. Perspective is everything. There came a shift in the beat, a change in the key, and Aviva realized that this particular chipmunk was her very own Amy, Amy, Amy: Say her name three times to cast a spell. Say *anything* three times to cast a spell.

Truth be told, however, Amy was starting to get a little boring. Aviva had listened to the two albums and the one live compilation and the hidden tracks album about a thousand times each, and that was all there was, unless you started in with the remixes. That self-destructive bitch had robbed

Aviva of so much more music. She had taken her singularity and she had absconded with it into the next world.

Aviva was growing likewise inured to all the available clips and the interviews and the live footage. Okay, okay, we know, we know: you're funny and irreverent and provocative and careless and cool. Something vital escaped with repetition, something leaked away. Repeat anything too much and it becomes shtick, and there's nothing less interesting than shtick.

So give the poor doomed superstar a rest. Let the poor girl be dead and gone. Let her return to the great energetic oneness from whence she came, belonging to everybody and to nobody. Let her rest in her grave, cremation notwithstanding.

On layover Aviva read about: how female astronauts stop their periods while in space ("We're curious to see what it does to their bone density and cardiac health!"), a couple who were suing their fertility clinic because they had given birth to a baby derived from the wrong embryo ("Not our child!"), and a man who'd discovered he had more than four dozen offspring scattered across the country as a result of his "donated" (read: sold for cash) sperm decades ago. This man was now—rom-com alert!—involved with a single mother who had given birth to one of his biological offspring. It was all very adorable, though there *was* also the brief, sobering footnote of a daughter amongst the dozens who turned out to have killed herself at some point, but oh well, can't make an omelet without breaking a few eggs.

An older dude in the waiting area was eyeing Aviva, she realized, and within a minute of her noticing, the dude sauntered on over. She took out an earbud. Was this, like, a fan interaction? Attempted pickup? What.

"Saw you sitting over here," the guy said.

"Um-hmm?"

"I thought you must be listening to music," the guy went on. "But I didn't see those headphones. You just look like there's always music playing in your head. You just look like that kind of person."

"I am exactly that kind of person," Aviva offered, smiling. "And it's awesome. But it's also a lot to handle and you have to be really fluent in your own flow and boundaries because it's actually a pretty huge responsibility. You have to serve your gift, you know, not the other way around. So if you'll excuse me."

The guy backed away.

Jerry was giving her shit for social media ineptitude, meanwhile. She had recently tweeted, for the first time in weeks, apropos of nothing: *hey cuntrags, what personal struggle of vital importance are you ignoring whilst you sit on this site jerking off your diseased ego?*

She felt this was "authentic" and "socially conscious" and "seeking true connection," which were the top three Rules for Cultivating a Strong Following according to the PDF a label exec had send over.

But Jer wasn't pleased, not at all.

Aspirational, honey. The key word is ASPIRATIONAL. You want to make people feel GOOD about themselves, so they'll LIKE you. That's how it works. It's not that fucking hard. They're all fucking lobotomized chimps at this point. KEEP IT SIMPLE and POSITIVE and ASPIRATIONAL, babe. Show them your outfits. Don't be a pain in everyone's ass. Hate to be the bad guy, here, but this is why you didn't get nominated for anything.

Another jet and a terrifying eight-seat prop plane and half-hour truck ride from the regional airport, and there, at last, was the retreat center.

Hana came bounding over, cheerful as a kid whose best birthday party guest has arrived. "Hey, girl, hey! They put us in a special little platform jungle hut way off on the edge of the property. It's amazing, wait 'til you see! I already got us a couple microdoses for tomorrow, and Juanita is going to get us whatever we need for the rest of the time. I'm soooo happy you're here! Are you good? The group is . . . interesting, but we'll all jibe, I'm sure."

"Hi! Who's Juanita? Hi!"

Juanita was the juice bartender in the main pagoda. The one to see for booking spa appointments and also scoring drugs: dark chocolate cannabis, hash, mushrooms, and the famous, all-important ceremonial psyche-delic tea. If you wanted the tea you had to tell her no later than sundown tomorrow, so she could be sure to source enough. Psychedelic tea was not on the official itinerary, but everyone in the know knew it to be the culmi-nation of the week's practice, if not your whole life thus far.

It was sweltering, but Aviva was still shivering from the three airports and airplanes.

Weather and time, time and weather.

The story of Aviva and yoga (or, ahem, "union with God") began at seven-teen years of age at a shitty gym in a Culver City strip mall. Barb had given her a membership for Hanukkah, because Barb was embarrassed by the size of Aviva's ass. Well, Barb was embarrassed by the size of her *own* ass, more like it, but what was the point of having a daughter if you couldn't load her up with all your own baggage and force her to follow in your de-ranged footsteps, mirror you, and be, in her living essence, a sort of positive reflection and reinforcement of yourself?!

Step aerobics was all the rage back then. A plastic and rubber-matted step could be adjusted a few inches higher or lower, depending on just how fat your ass, and you . . . stepped onto and off of it for an hour. Up, down, up, down in a windowless, mirror-walled room, while an instructor blasted techno and shouted at you about how much better life was going to be when your ass wasn't so fat.

Step failed to captivate Aviva's fat ass. There was, however, a *yoga* class held twice per week in the same windowless mirrored room, and even though Barb mocked this all to shit ("Yoga! Ha! Only you, my dear, could go to the gym and still find a way to sit on your ass!"), Aviva discovered, after her first-ever class, a vibrating kaleidoscopic nest of butterflies living in her goddamn *soul*.

The teacher was a forty-something failed actress with a thick Texas drawl and dyed flame-red hair. Too late to be a movie star now, poor darlin', but she was funny and disarming and unpretentious and chill. Made it okay to learn. Made it safe to learn. Made it possible to truly relax and absorb, the way only the rarest true teachers can. Aviva felt, in yoga, a bizarre and curious stillness. A distance, a reprieve, more room to exist freely inside her body. *So freaking weird.* Like she'd cleaned out the closets, reorganized, decluttered. Everything in its place and a place for everything. She could inhale a little deeper, and exhale a little longer. It felt . . . good. Which was a new and somewhat unfamiliar sensation for young Aviva Rosner, with her shallow careless parents and her sweet dying brother and her sadist monster brother and her Pill-ravaged endocrine system and her habit of dragging razor blades down her arms so she bled just enough to be relieved.

Years followed in which she availed herself of whatever yoga she could find, wherever she could find it. Stumbling upon a decent teacher turned out not to be so easy. Ms. Texas had been an unsung master. Yoga wasn't omnipresent in those days; there didn't yet exist a bull market for the material trappings of vinyasa and pranayama and meditation and kirtan, but Aviva sniffed out many a studio, many a teacher. Fine teachers, okay teachers, harmless teachers, awful teachers. Teachers who loved watching themselves in studio mirrors, teachers who didn't seem to give much of a shit about how any particular student fared in any particular pose or sequence, teachers whose egos were bound up in demonstrating only the most complicated, advanced poses, teachers who seemed to get off performing "yoga teacher" for the "audience" of students, teachers who didn't seem to care that much about alignment or breath, teachers who needed you to comply, or *else.* That one freak show at the corporate chain studio in Brentwood who'd kicked Aviva out for not "following" his "orders." Screw automatic reverence for the teacher. Fuck that shit. Reverence for the *teachings*, sure. But *never* for the teacher, *never*, *ever* for the teacher, and screw teachers who *want* reverence. Huge red flag. Fetishizing the messenger is some dangerous shit. Watch out for the ones who dig being fetishized, and we're not just talking about yoga anymore. The teacher—the singer, the storyteller, the spiritual advisor, the artist, the orator—is merely a humble messenger, at best, no matter *how* fine the message.

And so it was that, after having "done" yoga for all those years, after having dropped in at studios all over the world, Aviva wandered into Hana's tiny studio in the ski resort town an hour from Albany, and bingo: a real teacher, a soft-spoken expert with a barely there ego. A teacher who taught by example, who spoke knowledgeably about poses and alignment and intention and progression not half so much as she simply *embodied* it all, reminding you to soften, to back off, to breathe, to smile through it even when it was hard, to laugh, to check in with yourself, to chill, to stay present.

"Hardness is not the goal," Hana liked to say. "Softness is the goal. Something rigid cannot open. It can be forced, maybe. It can be broken, certainly. But patience and softness are how you open, and openness is how you get truly strong."

Strong, soft, and open: gotta be all three, all together, or no dice. Do you know how difficult that is? "Strong" don't mean shit. "Soft" don't mean shit. "Open" don't mean shit. You have to be all three, at once. Only then might you get somewhere, in your dealings with yourself and with the world.

Hana had served as a mountain guide on programs for troubled teens, then spent a year in Mysore, working on the primary series. She had studied and apprenticed with Big Names. She was legit. But she never traded on that shit. It came down to this: Aviva stood taller and breathed deeper in Hana's presence. A teacher is someone whose goose is fully cooked, as Ram Dass said. Someone who lives the principles. A teacher might never have to say a word. Aviva felt lighthearted and sure-footed and grounded and nice and easy around Hana. She felt safe and open, in perpetual bloom.

"You're my teacher, too," Hana always said. "You give *me* that, also. It's a chemistry thing. We're mirrors for each other, baby. Mirrors, that's all."

Opening circle.

A graduate student with severe anorexia. A middle-aged playboy from Abu Dhabi with his nineteen-year-old model girlfriend. A Broadway chorus dancer. A phalanx of forty-something hard-bod housewives. A wan, unsmiling civil rights attorney with a hacking cough. A lookalike mother and daughter from Miami, on a bonding trip. A thirty-something female investment banker with a botched face and an obvious pill problem. A retired couple from Queens, still madly in love, traveling the world. A towering young raw-foods guy who looked precisely like cliché White Jesus.

Aviva side-eyed them all, eager to embroider some little beef with everyone. Preemptive, or something. Luteal undercurrent: the least charitable take on everything and everyone—except maybe it wasn't luteal phase, maybe she was just a total bitch. Anyway, everyone sucked, and they were all out to get her.

("I'm not trying to be negative about anyone; I just think some people waste their potential," Amy said.)

"He's kind of hot," Hana whispered, indicating White Jesus.

"Nah," Aviva whispered back. "It'd be like fucking a donkey."

"Welcome, everyone," said Theresa, lead teacher. "Let's *arrive*."

Ugh, that patented performative/cultish/condescending tone, the way it sought to legitimize the practice, lend credibility to the gathering. Lady, we're already *here*. We need not be *convinced*. We've already *paid*.

Theresa was a big deal in the yoga world, had been amongst the earliest group of westerners to study with Guruji, the old molester creep. Real apprenticeship, none of this two-hundred-hour certification bullshit wherein you memorize a little Sanskrit and a few sequences and wax banal philosophical about gratitude on your feed and call it a day, no, ma'am.

She brandished a piece of driftwood. "Let's introduce ourselves and share something about where we are in our practice and in our lives right now."

Oh, shit, nooooo, not the talking stick! Anything but the talking stick!

"I'll go first. My name is Theresa March Mayflower, and I have been practicing yoga for forty-seven years, ever since I suffered a cheerleading injury in college. I studied in with Guruji for nine years, beginning in 1974, and have been privileged to share his teachings ever since."

"Did he ever happen to finger you during asana?" Aviva whispered, and Hana choked back a laugh.

"I've written four books on yoga and continue learning from my students every day. I have a little tendonitis in my left wrist, so I'm working around that at the moment. It's a pleasure and a privilege to be here in this beautiful place with all of you."

Theresa handed the driftwood to the woman on her left, one of the hard-bods, who teared up immediately, because her youngest kid was leaving for college in the fall and she didn't know what she was going to do with herself thereafter. Her biceps were quite impressive.

"I guess I'm just pretty lost," the hard-bod said. She handed the stick to her neighbor and dried her tears with a corner of her block-printed cotton-linen sarong.

The civil rights attorney shrugged and said, barely audibly, that she had nothing to say, then had a coughing fit.

The investment banker was so addled she could hardly finish a sentence. "I suppose . . . I'm . . . here to . . . have a nice . . . rest and relax." Her lips looked like a very serious allergic reaction.

"I'm Hana," said Hana. "Hello! Theresa was kind enough to ask me to assist her this week, and I'm looking forward to getting to know you all and deepening our practice together."

"Hey, I'm Aviva. I'm interested in the way my practice dovetails with my menstrual cycle, and as I continue to get to know myself and my cycle better, I'm working to support each phase of the cycle by adjusting my practice accordingly."

"Hoooo-boy," Theresa said. The group tittered. "That's maybe a little *too* much information there, Aviva. Might be best to save that kind of thing for *private* space so we don't make our *male friends* uncomfortable. And actually, in Ashtanga our practice is *suspended* during the menstrual cycle, but we can talk more about that another time."

Unfrigginbelievable: the elder yogi didn't know what "menstrual cycle" even meant. A seventy-something-year-old woman who'd spent her life studying and theoretically honoring the human body and spirit, and not only was she not conversant in the *language* of menstruation, she was embarrassed to be talking about it in public.

"Ruh-roh," whispered Hana.

Aviva withheld the talking stick from the anorectic. "Um, no, sorry? The menstrual cycle is an *ongoing* phenomenon. People with female reproductive organs exist continuously within the phases of the menstrual cycle? There are four phases, and the cycle repeats itself from puberty until menopause unless it is disabled by severe endocrine disruption or organ removal or ingestion or implantation of synthetic hormones."

It would be cool to do that whole bit spoken-word-style, layered underneath a song.

Theresa squinted at Aviva, and addressed herself to the males in the circle: "Sorry, you guys, it seems our new friend has a *lot* to say about this stuff! I hope you aren't going to bail on us!"

More tittering.

Aviva smiled her fakest yogi smile. "That's not giving them much credit, now, is it?"

Eat a bag of dicks, elder yogi.

"Interesting stuff," said White Jesus. "Never thought about it much, to be honest."

"Oh, I had four sisters," said Retired Husband with a shrug.

Middle Eastern Playboy appeared lost.

"Gosh, it sure is nice to hear some male voices," Theresa said.

"Oh yes, because that's such a *rarity*," Aviva said, and shoved the talking stick at the anorectic, whose main concern was whether or not she was going to be "allowed" to close her eyes during asana.

They did a short meditation, just twenty minutes of sitting in silence, but witness how even that brief exercise struck panic and dread into Aviva's heart. You were supposed to let whatever came up come up, acknowledge it, let it go, not get attached to any thought. Just observe. Oh, look at this thought. Oh, look at that thought. Oh, look at me looking at my thoughts. Oh, look at me *looking* at looking at my thoughts. Oh, look at me *looking* at *looking* at looking at . . . Fuck. Fuck fuck fuck fuck fuck I wish I was high right now fuck fuck fuck this fuck all these hard-bods and fuck the playboy and fuck the teenage prostitute and fuck the anorexic and God why am I here God why did I come here God I want to get out of here God I want to sit in my garden with my guitar and fuck my foot is falling asleep fuck I don't want to make friends with these people, my neck hurts I want to lie down my nose itches lemme outta here lemme out out ouuuuut.

She tried a body scan. That usually worked. Top of the head, good. Ears. Eyes. Jaw. Shoulders. Solar plexus, stomach. Abs. Hips.

In her pelvis, there was still some remnant of Sam. She alighted briefly upon their time on the attic floor, her legs around him, his hands in her hair, lips on lips on skin on skin, with that breeze wafting through the windows. She lingered there, in her pelvis, feeling the tingles, the radiance, the joy.

And there, right there, in the pelvic thrum, the aftershocks still accessible, Aviva felt sudden certainty that the elusive magic was unfurling. Microscopic nautilus. A spark. A chiming of bells. A life. Alive. (Did you know that hope never, ever dies?)

She felt illuminated, vital. She felt like she could manifest an orgasm without moving a muscle. (Was this nirvana?!)

For real, this time. The seed had been planted. The seed was taking root.

(Don't get attached to that thought . . .)

This was it. This was really and truly *it*.

(Uh-oh: *very* attached to that thought.)

It was summer now, which meant a late-winter or early-springtime child. She was going to birth at home. The photographs would be explicitly radical, and she would defy the feed overlords to censor them.

(Quite attached, oh dear.)

It would be a public *service* to post the birth photos, to normalize the heroic fact of unmediated childbirth at home. She had always wanted to be one of those types. Hana could be there as her doula or whatever. And Kirsten Tabowski! And maybe she'd invite Mackayla. Well, she'd feel it out, and invite Mackayla if and only if Mackayla unambivalently wanted to be there. It could change the course of Mackayla's life, give her a window into another world, a real feminist awakening, a true understanding of the primordial power of the body. And Sarah! Sarah had to be there, too: the more elders the merrier. A circle of women from across the life spectrum to welcome the new baby girl. Maidens and mothers and crones to surround and uplift Aviva in her transition. A wheel of women, with Aviva and her newborn daughter—one person giving way to two—at its center.

(Just observe; observe your thoughts!)

She was going to raise her baby on the road, kangaroo-style, get some of those noise-canceling headphones all the musicians' kids wore. The child was going to grow up roaming the globe with a hundred godparents, a *thousand* godparents. The childbearing-inspired songs were going to melt hearts, and simultaneously radicalize the shit out of them all. See? She needn't have worried, all this time. Everything will have unfolded perfectly, in its own good time and in its own good way. All her fretting and grief had been for naught. Or, no: all her worrying and fretting and grief would come to serve as a reminder not to take life so seriously. A reminder to chill the fuck out. A lesson in how to be a more positive, empathic person *because* of the struggle. The waiting had been school. A person couldn't fully appreciate what came easy. One season had to follow another, and sometimes it was cold in summer and warm in winter, but you had to ride it out, find a way to trust, have faith, wait, be patient, all that Hebrew Bible Steinbeck shit. Turn, turn, turn. All that Pete Seeger shit.

By the end of the twenty-minute meditation, the baby was a toddler with a head of wild dark curls, a funky little attitude, and a strong sense of self, in a retro floral reversible jumper with corduroy detailing and jaunty buttons, and Sam was throwing her high into the air on a cloudless day, and catching her in his big strong arms as she laughed and shrieked, while Aviva snapped a perfect, gravity-defying photo that went directly online and then later into a frame on the mantel, to be admired for generations to come. Suck it, Harmony Shmendrickson!

Theresa rang the medicine bowl and led the closing chant. Aviva was at peace. A little more space in her chest; a little more room to breathe.

For the anorexic, she found tenderness and sympathy in spades. She lowered her eyes in deference to the playboy and the model, because they were hardier creatures than she, and probably better suited to the world as it was. She forgave the banker with the botched face for harming herself in such a way as to punish all who had to look at her. She deferred to Theresa, who was simply a mixed bag, like all of us, and a product of her time. And she namasted the hard-bods, because she aspired to become one of them, didn't she, and now she was well on her way. Ommmmmm.

Hana was way into hallucinogens. She had done the ceremonial tea no fewer than fourteen times over the past decade, and raved about its utility in helping shed the unnecessary bonds of self.

"It's like a good internal scrubbing," she kept saying.

Fourteen times seemed a bit excessive for an internal scrubbing, but who was Aviva to judge? She'd been open to the idea of the ceremonial tea. She'd been interested in doing it. She'd been leaning toward doing it. She was tempted. But things were different now, considering the possibility that she was maybe probably definitely likely not impossibly With Child. A mother couldn't do whatever the hell she felt like doing, whenever the hell she felt like doing it. You had to put the child first.

The banker with the botched face was sitting at the juice bar, chin in hand, waiting for a smoothie. She spoke with great care, like she was re-learning how to operate her face.

"Hello, menstruation girl. Are you going to do this . . . drug ceremony thing? I don't think I am. It seems . . . risky."

Her lips looked like twin glistening pink plastic turds shat out the anus of a giant Barbie. She could have been twenty; she could have been sixty. Her eyes were penetrating, dark, and rife with sorrow, unless Aviva was projecting.

"I dunno. I kind of want to. But . . ." Aviva lowered her voice: "I'm *pregnant*. Don't tell anyone, okay?"

The banker tried to convey surprise and delight, but her face would not comply.

Juanita sashayed over with the banker's smoothie.

"Overheard, sorry," Juanita said. "Don't worry! Grandmother plant will *not* hurt the baby."

"Excuse me!" said the banker. "You don't know that!"

"I've worked with Grandmother throughout *all* my pregnancies, and my babies are all absolutely perfect," Juanita said.

"Well! That's . . . not . . . scientific," the banker stammered.

They looked to Aviva for her verdict. On the one hand, a pale, pill-wracked depressive with a face beyond Mary Shelley's worst nightmares, scowling to beat the band. On the other, a sun-kissed goddess rocking a majestic head wrap and halter top with harem pants, exemplifying high-vibrational nutrition and perfectly spinning chakras. If these were the archetypes, Aviva's choice was clear.

"Put me down for yeah," she told Juanita.

The banker shook her head in disgust and took her smoothie to the pool.

"It's so totally fine," said Juanita with a wink. "Grandmother *adores* babies. Grandmother would *never* hurt a baby. Grandmother takes care of babies. You'll see. Mamas gotta look out for mamas."

Whatever the fuck that meant.

"Hey," Aviva said, "while I'm at it, can I book a massage?"

"Oh hells yeah, I'm gonna put you with Pascale. She's amazing. She does chakra clearing? It's just the thing to prepare for Grandmother. Such a transformational time for you. The perfect time."

"I really liked what you had to say about the menstrual cycle," said the civil rights attorney. They were in line for dinner. "I'd like to know more about that."

Her eyes darted left and right: frightening to say such things out loud, notwithstanding the law degree and the civil rights work. So much for "educating women."

She lowered her voice even further, so she was barely audible: "I think that whole . . . thing . . . is really interesting."

"So why are we whispering," Aviva said.

"There are five *yamas*, or ways of interacting with the outside world," Theresa said at the beginning of her evening dharma talk.

The playboy and model had skipped. The empty-nest hard-bod was already wiping away tears. The civil rights attorney took notes. The anorectic picked obsessively at loose threads on a corner of her shawl.

"The five *yamas* are: nonharming, truthfulness, nonstealing, nonexcess, and nonpossessiveness. And then we have the five *niyamas*, or ways of dealing with the inner world, with *ourselves*: purity, contentment, self-discipline, self-study, and devotion, or surrender. *Yamas* are about regulation of our outward behavior, and *niyamas* are about how we guide ourselves *within* ourselves. Given that we are *not* our thoughts, how do we strengthen our true nature? How do we not get thrown off course? How do we comfort and soothe ourselves? *That's* the business of the *niyamas*."

They partnered up to discuss how they themselves were sometimes immoderate. With what particular intemperance did they struggle?

God, just *one*? And only *sometimes*? The endless uphill climb of moderation. How often did she take something positive—fantastic style, receptivity to medicinal plants, intensity of innate sexual desire—and engage with it immoderately, as though trying to obliterate herself in the process? Intemperance: a lack of moderation or restraint. From the Latin for "regulate." Used in Old English to refer to the climate. Weather, baby: it all comes back to weather. Internal, external: everything just a question of the weather.

White Jesus was Aviva's partner. She confessed to shopping immoderation:

"I buy myself shit, like, all the time."

"Doesn't, like, all of America do that?"

"I guess. What about you?"

"I'm real strict on food stuff," Jesus said. "Like since I went vegan and more so since I went completely raw, I've convinced myself that a bite of cooked food is going to rot in my bowels forever. Like I've taken this good thing—food awareness—and turned it into something that kinda alienates me from my family and friends and stuff."

"Yoga attracts a lot of addicts, have you noticed?"

"For sure. And depressed people."

"But people who make fun of yoga are just so fucking scared of yoga, you know?"

" 'Depression is just anger turned inward,' " he recited.

"All the type A go-getters wind up getting injured in asana. Like, even yoga can be used destructively."

"Everything can be turned into a negative if you're excessive about it."

Their eyes wandered over to the anorexic.

"How can they let her be here practicing in that condition?"

"Hurts to see," he agreed.

"You think it's better to have your fucked-up shit visible on the outside or not?"

"Don't know."

"Can you tell from looking at me that I care too much about clothes and shit?"

"Kinda. Now that you mention it. Yeah."

People went into town and came back with beer and tequila, Juanita supplied hash chocolates and tiny grains of LSD and itty-bitty pieces of magic mushrooms for microdosing, and everyone was more or less shit-faced all the time starting on day three. Grandmother plant was said to dislike other substances, and according to Hana you were supposed to be on a "cleanse" before you approached Grandmother, but no one seemed too concerned.

One of the hard-bods sidled up to Aviva over lunch. She didn't have kids, but was married to a much older, wealthier man with grandchildren. "I love them all so much," she said under the twinkly lights in the pavilion, sneaking a swig from a flask. "But I didn't realize how it was going to feel, fucking an old man. I mean, when we met I was thirty-four and he was fifty-one and in *great* shape. *So* hot. But now he's sixty-eight, and honey, it is *rough* at this point. I am fucking an old *man*. I mean, I love him, and I love the kids and grandkids so much, I really do, they're my family, you know? But the truth is, I've been fucking this guy from work. Younger than me. I can't believe I'm telling you this. Do people confide in you a lot? You sort of have a vibe. Anyway, I feel like such shit about it, but the sex is insane, and I am sorry, but life is short. I love my husband and I will stay with him 'til death do us part, no question. I'm devoted to him. I am never leaving him, but life is so fucking *short*, you know?" She took another swig. "Fuck, I think I just got my period. Hold on."

She got up and ran to the bathroom, her blue muumuu billowing behind her. Upon return, she was jubilant. "I am bleeding *everywhere*; it is like Stephen *King* up in here. I keep thinking I'm done with this whole thing, and I will be soon, I mean, I have to be, right? No one just keeps going forever, do they?" She laughed her ass off. "You know all about this shit, right? You're, like, the period girl. Anyway, I haven't exactly been using *birth control,* if you know what I mean." Here came more intense snorts of laughter. "Always a relief when Auntie Flo comes to town, know what I mean? Dodged another bullet! Please don't tell a soul what I said about the guy from work. Please. It would kill my husband."

Aviva tongued a few specks of LSD with Jesus on the beach at dawn on day four. Literal specks, not much bigger than the period at the end of this sentence. Size of human ovum.

She held her hands over her low belly during shavasana, microdose in effect, increasingly aware of a particular hum. A buzz, vibration. Yes, OMG. The LSD speck only enhanced the Speck. All her yearning and suffering and grief and waiting was behind her. The torture, the hell, the limbo: it was in the past.

After practice, she and Jesus and Hana took a long walk down the beach to where there was said to be a swimming hole. They spun and twirled along the shore like children, skipping, laughing. They couldn't find the swimming hole, but who cared. On the way back, the sun higher and higher, they came upon a hard-bod.

"Hey y'all," she said. "Check out these seashells I found!" She unfolded her sarong to reveal a stash: white and red and purple and pink, spirals and horns and clams galore. "My kids are going to adore these."

"You cannot take those shells," Aviva said, in total seriousness. Gone was the carefree joy of being fertile on specks of LSD with her friends at the beach. "You cannot take what belongs to this beach and take it home to put in a jar. You can't do that. You just cannot."

The woman closed up her sarong stash, took a step back, and giggled. "Um, yes, I can?"

"Maybe just not quite so *many*?" said Jesus, his face the seat of all concern and mediation in the history of the world.

Hana said nothing. Hana walked off into the surf and began to hum a shamanic *niggun*.

The hard-bod set her mouth. Aviva wanted to rip her face off.

"Do you not read the *newspaper*? Do you not understand what's happened to our beaches because of everyone taking shells for hundreds of years? Why don't you take a *picture* to show your kids and explain to them that these shells were not yours to *take*. Tell your kids about how shells on beaches belong on beaches, and beaches belong to everyone. Maybe someday *your* kids will have kids of their *own* and come to this very same beach and be *overjoyed* to find that there are actually still some *shells* here because entitled neocolonialists like *yourself* didn't feel entitled to *take* them all. If the *fucking oceans* haven't all *died* by then."

Rage! Not good for the baby. A hot storm, out of nowhere. Temperature: the degree or intensity of heat present in a substance or object, especially as expressed according to a comparative scale. Temperamental: of a person liable to unreasonable changes of mood. Temporal: of or relating to time, from the Latin. Synonyms include: secular, nonspiritual, worldly, profane, material, mundane, earthly, terrestrial.

"Um, thanks," said the hard-bod. "I'll give that some thought."

The anorectic was avoiding communal meals, and this bothered Aviva. She wanted the anorectic forced to load up a plate at the buffet, forced to at least playact at carrying food back and forth from plate to mouth with a utensil. She wanted this retreat, this practice, to live up to its ideals. The anorectic needed help. What good was any of this if the anorectic could slip through its cracks? What was the use of these philosophies, these practices, this community, if it could not help someone whose immoderation was so desperate, so blatant?

"You would have made an absolutely perfect anorexic," the Rabbi told Aviva at one of their early meetings.

"What the fuck, dude?"

He was amazed, he explained, that she had escaped that particular pathology, given every precise prerequisite: high intelligence, distant, materialistic, appearance-obsessed parents, expectations of excellence, family toxicity, traumatic pubescence . . . all of which perfectly primed her for an eating disorder.

"You were an ideal candidate, is all I'm saying."

"Points for extreme suicidal ideation? I, like, literally *invented* cutting."

Probably it had been lucky for Aviva that an absurd number of her schoolmates had nurtured moderate to severe eating disorders, so of course she'd come to consider eating disorders passé. Had everyone else been a cutter, Aviva might have become interested in starving herself. The only thing she knew for sure, even then, was this: whatever everyone was doing, do something—*anything*—else.

Tonight's dharma talk was about Ahimsa. Nonviolence. Aviva tuned out immediately.

Her daughter would need a name. There was plenty of time, and she wouldn't dream of naming a child before it was born, but starting now there would of course come messages about what the child should be named, and Aviva resolved to pay attention. Not a simple or basic name, for the child would not be simple or basic. A handful of a name for a handful of a girl. A character, a witchy little imp. It would be hard not to devote the feed to the delightful singular impishness of this glorious darling dark-eyed daughter, but Aviva would hold the line, refrain from using the child for content. Just stick to, say, one or two posts a year.

She left the dharma talk, and went to ask Juanita for some celery juice and a square of date-quinoa fudge lightly laced with hash.

"Make that two," said Hana, right behind her.

Juanita set down their treats with a wink and moved off again with a happy little shake of her ass.

Hana and Aviva held up their treats and toasted.

"What's up with the chick who's starving herself to death?"

"She's in a bad way, I know."

"It's some concentration camp shit. You can't let her practice like that. She shouldn't be practicing in that condition. How can you guys let her be here?"

"It's not really our place to say anything. Though Theresa did have a student in the eighties who died of an eating disorder, so I guess she'd want to be more on top of it."

"It's really fucked up that everyone is pretending it's fine."

"No one's pretending it's fine."

"Saying nothing and doing nothing is pretending it's fine."

"What are we supposed to do?"

"Force-feed her! Confront her! Intervene! Send her home!"

"You want to fix the world, V, but the world doesn't necessarily want to be fixed."

Time for the massage. Open-air hut at the end of a short stone path through the jungle, roar of the ocean just beyond swaying palms. Pascale was sitting on the massage table, wearing a white crochet bikini top, a long delicate necklace strung with tiny crystals, and shortest denim short-shorts. She looked to be in her late forties, her scowl having ceased to be cute. She sat spread-eagled on the massage table, so Aviva could see her hairless, gray-pink vulva through the frayed crotch of the short-shorts.

She was busy scribbling on a yellow legal pad and didn't acknowledge Aviva for an uncomfortably long time. Aviva stood there until Pascale looked up at her. Hard face, leathery skin. Aviva disliked Pascale immediately, but there she was standing at the end of a short stone path in the jungle, at the entrance to an open-air hut in which stood a massage table, with the roar of the ocean just beyond.

"What is your diet?" Pascale wanted to know. French accent. No "hello."

"Militant vegetarian for many years? Some of them vegan? Now I eat ethically sourced meat a couple times a month, which I never in a million years thought I'd want but seems extremely helpful in regulating my menstrual cycle, I have to admit? File under: Militant anything tends to be unproductive, right?"

Pascale looked up at Aviva with icy eyes. "No. You do not need meat. You take prescription medication?"

"No."

"Good. History of depression?"

"You can say that again."

"History of depression?"

"Uh, yeah."

"Anger?"

"Absolutely."

"Family history?"

"Oh yes, quite a lot of depression and anger there, too."

All those years they had paid rent on Rob's frozen jizz, and all those years Aviva had tried to talk sense into her ridiculous parents: "You really think anyone is going to benefit from engineering the offspring of a dead guy with a long family history of cancer and mental illness?"

Chuck was more or less incapable of having that conversation (or, to be frank, any conversation), and would just stare off into the middle distance, unreachable. But Barb would laugh herself silly: "Honey, *every* family history is full of cancer and mental illness!"

Pascale looked back up at Aviva, eyes like slits.

"No," she said. "It is not anybody else's fault. Do not blame anyone but yourself for your problems. It is yours alone, and you must face it."

Aviva was quick to agree, yes, of course, sure, yes, all that tough-love self-help personal responsibility shit, sure, sure, whatever you say, lady. She kept nodding too long, cowed.

"Get on the table, facedown."

She did as she was told.

Pascale held some ylang-ylang under Aviva's face for an inhale, and Aviva ventured one final piece of pertinent information.

"Um, also, by the way? I am . . . just at the beginning of being pregnant. It's very new. Very early."

"No, you're not. I can tell."

Oh?

Oh.

Pascale began angrily pummeling Aviva's spine. It was like punishment. For what? For occasionally eating meat? For identifying her family of origin as a source of depression and grief and rage and poorly dividing cells? For wanting to believe in the possibility of pregnancy?

Aviva supposed she deserved this punishment, and did her best to accept it.

"You're very blocked," Pascale said.

Yeah, no shit. So bring it on. Unblock her, why don't you. She was ready for it; she could take it. Harsh pressure down her spine, into both hips, down the hamstrings and calves, back up into the neck and shoulders. Aviva was determined to benefit from whatever pummeling this sinister clairvoyant bitch had to offer. Break her *open*, lady. No *shit* she was blocked. She'd left her devoted husband thousands of miles away. She avoided most of her living relatives. She had hurt people she loved and tried to love people who didn't love her. She'd hated everyone in this retreat group on sight. She wasn't making the most of her professional opportunities. She smoked weed and microdosed and ate dairy and carbs and sugar. She was carrying on a flirtation with a married womanizer. She looked at her phone while driving *all the time*. So unblock her, you fucking bitch, let's go. *Break* her. *Harder.*

"You need to breathe," Pascale said. "You are not breathing."

Aviva tried to be worthy of whatever this was, whatever needed to play out on this table in this hut with the roar of the ocean nearby, but her breath came ragged under the harsh, harsh touch. Pascale found a part of Aviva's armpit that could not withstand pressure, and pressed so hard Aviva let out some crazy burst of laughter that was not laughter at all. It did feel sort of good, though, the laughter that was not laughter.

"There," Pascale said. "*That's* where you keep your lies."

When it was time to turn over, Pascale focused punitive pressure around Aviva's right ovary while Aviva gasped, sobbed, and laughed more of the laughter that was not laughter. It was crying, too, but it was also not crying. What was it? What should it be called, the crying that was more like laughter, the laughter that was more like sobbing? An entirely new form of expression. What language or cultural tradition had a name for this?

"Stop," Aviva gasped. "Please. Too much! Please!"

"The river moves around the stones. Be the river, the water. You are not the stones. You are the water. *Breathe.*"

"Please! Please! No!"

But Pascale would not stop. She pressed on and on and on and on. She did as she pleased. Aviva gasped and moaned and sobbed and giggled and pleaded and laughed the not-laugh.

"You're very blocked," Pascale said.

Aviva's right ovary was the locus of all suffering. Here was where life was thwarted, trapped, denied. Here was where life came up against itself in all-out war. Here was where birth, death, the will to live, and the necessity of death originated. Aviva was a bad person, the descendant of bad people. Okay: so unblock her, do it, do it, she can take it. She will take it. Do what needs to be done. Clear the way. Wash those stones.

"Sit up."

Aviva did as she was told.

Now Pascale wrapped her hands around Aviva's neck and began to choke her. She compressed until Aviva sputtered and gasped, until Aviva could no longer laugh or cry, her eyes bulging, unable to breathe even enough to say no. Stop. No. Stop.

"Yes," Pascale said, "yes, that is good. If you need to choke, you can go ahead and choke. It's good for you."

Aviva's panic reached fever pitch, and she understood that this crazy bitch might actually kill her right now, right here.

Then it was over.

She lay on the table, shaking. The sun, it seemed, had set.

Pascale yanked the chain on the overhead light, a single bulb suspended inside a wicker pendant hanging a few feet over Aviva's face.

Aviva hated this crazy bitch very, very, very much.

"Turn the light off, please," Aviva said.

Pascale yanked the chain again, and the light went out.

Aviva made no movement.

"Are you okay?" Pascale asked.

"No," Aviva said slowly, with a brittle, hollow laugh. A different laugh that was not laughter. "Not at all."

"Well," Pascale said. She wiped her hands on a towel, then disappeared.

Aviva got up slowly, dressed, and hobbled away as fast as her jellied legs would carry her.

She was curled on the bed in the tree house when Hana found her.

"You weren't at dinner."

Aviva made a sound. She had no words. Her body was closed like a fist.

There was no sleep that night. There were vague, terrible nightmares. Writhing and apologizing and begging some invisible entity for help. *I'm sorry I'm sorry I'm sorry*, she wept in the general direction of her lower belly, which throbbed and cramped, sending shock waves throughout the hips. *I'm so sorry I'm so sorry, please, please, please, I'm so sorry, so sorry.*

Had there, in fact, ever been any possibility of a pregnancy? Or was this just a new wind howling in the vacancy? The Nothing, awakened from slumber, looking to avenge itself?

Hana stayed close, held her like a mother might hold you, like a sister, like a friend. Hana stroked her head, her back, her shoulders. Hana whispered kindly. Hana stayed and stayed. How rare that someone's there to hold us when we are in need. What simple grace. It was almost enough.

No, Aviva cried, in dreams of writhing and in actual writhing, not that she could tell them apart. *Please. No. Please.* At dawn, she finally slept. Hana tiptoed out to practice, and Aviva got up a couple hours later, numb and puffy, in time to catch the very end of breakfast. She approached the communal table, where Theresa was holding court. Everyone fell silent and looked up.

"Morning," ventured a hard-bod. "Are you okay?"

"No," Aviva replied. She lowered herself onto the end of the bench and was overcome with sobbing. The nearest hard-bod spontaneously hugged her, held her. Again with the holding! All you had to do was fall completely the fuck apart! Who knew? Gratitude swept away embarrassment and Aviva cried into the hard-bod's bony shoulder. The hard-bod was undeterred, and held her even closer. Aviva should really learn this hard-bod's name. This hard-bod was all right. Maybe all the hard-bods were all right. Maybe most people were all right.

Everyone sat in silence, waiting for Aviva to calm down.

"A sadistic French bitch 'opened my chakras' last night," Aviva told them. "She beat the living shit out of me. The most traumatic experience of my fucking life. Just brutal. I'm a total mess."

Everyone looked to Theresa for the appropriate response.

Theresa shrugged.

"Well," she said evenly, "I guess you have to ask yourself why you brought this into your life. Why you needed this in your life. And what you have to learn from it. Then: let it go!"

She went to lodge a formal complaint with the director, a soft-spoken naturopath. He was circumspect and noncommittal. He had the detached bearing of a man hoping to keep himself alive and well long enough for someone to figure out immortality. He could have been forty; he could have been seventy.

"I know Pascale is intense," he said. "But a lot of people come here specifically to see her. She's helped a lot of people."

"It was an assault," Aviva said. "She assaulted me. An assault I paid for. It wasn't 'intense'; It was brutality. And she enjoyed it."

"I'm hearing that this was a very traumatic moment for you, and I'm thinking we should do more to warn clients about her style. And I'm happy to waive the fee for your session. I am sorry your experience was so painful. You might still find that it benefits you in unexpected ways. Oftentimes that's how these things work. It may have seemed extreme, but you will likely benefit from it."

"I said 'stop' and she didn't stop," Aviva said.

The director gave her a pitying look. She just wasn't ready for enlightenment. You could lead a seeker to a holistic assault by the ocean, but you couldn't make her appreciate it, wasn't that the expression? He was giving her her money back; what else did she want from him?

"I'm pregnant," she informed him. "Or . . . was."

Mic drop.

He looked at her with surprise. "Did you tell Pascale that?"

"I sure did."

"Well," the director said, ruffled now. "Well, that's a different story, then."

It was a different story, wasn't it. Wasn't it! It was!

"Oh— Well—that's . . . very different, then. That's—that's very serious, then. I see. I am going to have to let her go, in that case. Are you all right? Is there anything we can do for you? That's a very different story, isn't it? Oh dear."

The language of wellness really came up short when shit got real, because of the way it failed to honor darkness. The way they wanted you to get over terrible shit *immediately*. "Let it go"?! Yeah, eventually you were definitely going to attempt to let it go. But guess what? Shit takes time. (*Time!* Which is host to so much ever-changing *weather*.)

Word got around about the brutality and the (possible?) pregnancy, and soon enough everyone was confiding all manner of reproductive trauma and horror. The retired couple had had a stillborn daughter decades ago, and later a son who lived, but still, forever, it hurt so much when people asked how many children they had.

"I always say two," said the wife, whose name turned out to be Louisa.

"I say one," said the husband, whose name turned out to be Daniel.

The hard-bod who had stolen all the seashells was carrying twins fifteen years ago when routine testing revealed they were "incompatible with life" and would be unlikely to live outside the womb. She had been exhorted to terminate, and she had complied. Fifteen years later, she still dreamt of them frequently. Well, not *them*, exactly, per se, but there were often these two puppies who would follow her everywhere in dreams, just wagging their tails and looking up at her and following right on her heels, and she knew *exactly* who they were. And meanwhile—here she got teary, and it was Aviva's turn to do the holding—she was continually hearing stories, these stories kept coming up in her feed, about women who'd been told their babies wouldn't live, and who'd been advised to terminate, and who'd said "no." She kept hearing about these brave, stupid, crazy women who then gave birth to babies who sometimes turned out to be more or less *fine*, or at least not at *all* as fucked up as had been forecast: some lived for minutes and some lived for hours and some lived for days and some lived for months and some lived for years and some lived to adulthood, and the crazy, stupid, brave women said they were just so grateful to have had any and all time with those babies.

"I should have let them live for however long they had to live," said the hard-bod, whose name turned out to be Jessica.

They sat on the beach for a long time: two privileged, grieving women in a tourist-friendly third-world country. There *was* no such thing as letting go. Letting go was an invention of self-help twats who'd never been robbed of jack fucking shit, who'd never had anything truly precious wrested from their frantic, screaming, begging, pleading grasp.

The playboy's prostitute showed up at dinner to confess that she'd had four abortions, starting at age fourteen. She was twenty-four now. It was no big, she said, it was no big, it was totally no big. But she knew, she was a hundred percent certain, that *if* ever she got pregnant again, which she'd better not because she had the most hard-core IUD there was, but *if* it ever happened again, she didn't care who the father was, she didn't care what the fuck else was going on, she didn't care about money, she didn't care if she had to eat shit for the rest of her life, but she was definitely keeping it next time. Her name turned out to be Gorja.

The services of another massage therapist were offered as a corrective. A lady with long waves of white-silver hair who could often be seen wandering the property singing to herself, and tending the garden. She walked on the balls of her feet, almost dancing. She had smiling eyes and the affect of a prepubescent. She came and fetched Aviva from the juice bar, held her hand, and led her to yet another hidden jungle hut overlooking the sea. She hummed while she prepared the essential oils, and she stroked Aviva's shoulders like she was helping a runty kitten get some rest after a big meal, humming all the while. The humming turned to singing at some point, in a language Aviva did not know.

She drifted in and out. When it was over, the woman lightly kissed Aviva's forehead. Kind touch to cancel out the cruel.

* * *

Hana and Aviva lay in their mosquito-netted tree house, looking at their screens, side by side.

Hana was into some guru in New Mexico. She cued up audio: a distant, grainy voice speaking about grief and praise. Grief is the highest form of love expression, he said. To be able to grieve loudly for something is the highest form of praise. A hundred people sang and wailed together under his direction. *Never stop wailing your grief,* he exhorted. *Everything you do is an offering of gratitude for your existence! When you lose something you love, your grief is an expression of gratitude and love for that thing! The more you love something, the more you value it, the louder and harder and longer you wail when it is taken from you.*

In return, Aviva played a bootlegged interview between Amy and a Moldovan journalist in a hotel room.

"I see you've lost a lot of weight," the journalist said. "You've started going to the gym a lot, they say?"

"It's a good way to start the day."

"Ah. Yes. And how are you feeling today?"

"I'm not very well today."

"Have you got a virus?"

"It's an energy thing."

"Well, perhaps we can talk for just a few moments? Will that be okay? You have many fans in Moldova who would like to hear from you."

"Not very confident about myself. Pretty boring talking about yourself."

"Oh, no, I don't think you could be boring! May I ask why you chose this song to cover?"

"It's quite soulful."

"Is there more to the reason?"

"I work on instinct rather than a game plan."

"You got a lot of new tattoos, I notice. How did you choose them? The motifs."

"I just like them."

"Do you learn from your father? He is a musician?"

"He's not a musician. He's a cabdriver."

"But he likes to sing?"

"Yeah, he likes to sing."

"What does he think of your singing?"

"I'm a lucky girl. He's very proud of me."

"I am sure! What else about your family can you tell me?"

"Quite normal. Quite boring."

"I know it is very important to you to have no bullshit."

"Yeah."

"It is not very easy to talk to you, but I try hard. When you go to an interview on the TV or have anything to do with TV, how much are you planning what you do with that?"

"I don't. Of course I don't."

"And if you're drunk or something you don't care about your reputation?"

"I don't care, I really don't. I really don't care about myself."

"So you're not concerned that people are talking about it or making fun of it or something?"

"No, doesn't bother me."

"Okay. I think, ah . . . I don't know. Do you have anything to tell about the songs, anything interesting about how the songs came out of you?"

"Not really."

"I mean, what do you expect from interviews? I would so much love to hear some stories from you."

"There's nothing to say. I'm quite a boring person, really."

"Ha ha, I don't think so."

"I'm quite boring when I have to sit and talk about myself. I haven't got some amazing opinion. I haven't got an overinflated sense of myself."

"What do you think of your career? Is it fun being so famous now?"

"I'm always working."

"Do you feel like you have to do that?"

"Yeah."

"You like this one band very much, yes? The Specials?"

"Reminds me of a time in my life. I can put on the Specials wherever I am, and I feel like I'm home."

"Okay, can you give me a station identification?"

"This is [Blah] talking to [Blah] on [Blah]. Is that okay?"

"Maybe we meet again sometime, and you get into interviews, like it very much."

"Oh, I'll blow my brains out before then."

A trance dance workshop showed up on the yogis' second-to-last day.

Aviva got friendly with one of them over dinner. Super-cute thick-thighed Irish dyke getting over a bad breakup. At the bonfire she showed Aviva what they were up to: Five stages of movement, five stages of life. Birth to death. She demonstrated. The first stage was slow and earthbound. There was giving and receiving, fluid and considered. This was infancy. The second stage, rhythmic, harder movements, bursts of energy, everything beginning to move up and out, no inhibitions. This was childhood. Third: chaotic movement, abandon, total loss of control. Shame and release. Adolescence. Fourth: reining in the chaos with authoritative, clear, deliberate movement. Adulthood. Fifth: starting to slow down, to forgive, both inward and outward, to get softer again, and to—wait for it—"let go." Aging.

"Do it with me," said the Irish dyke, reaching for Aviva. "C'mon."

The bonfire was huge and crackling. How little we dance! What a strange thing, the postindustrial human body having been almost completely cut off from dance. So bizarre that every single body doesn't have its own intuitive dance practice. That only "dancers" dance.

Barb had taken up Israeli folk dance for a time in the eighties, after she'd discarded Chuck. (They failed to discuss their separation with their kids at all. Can you imagine being that far up your own asshole? Rob had a foot out the door to college, Mike was busy locking up his heart and soul and losing the only key, but Aviva was still so small. Seven? Eight? Children know everything. We always hear this, and we nod, but rarely do we treat children accordingly.)

It was harder than Aviva thought to keep pace with the rhythms, to keep moving without pause. How long since she'd danced?!

The dyke smiled. "You're a natural."

Little self-conscious but banish that! Look at the stars, the moonlight on the waves. Right hip and shoulder tight. Don't fight it; get loose around it. Let whatever you're holding there inform your movement. This was why people got drunk and high: so they could move through their pain, so they could loosen up around what was dead and immovable, scarred, or inflamed, or missing altogether.

The empty-nest hard-bod joined in. Her name turned out to be Joanna.

The anorectic watched from the sidelines. Were those tears in her eyes? Her name turned out to be Susannah.

Hana wandered off down the beach with Jesus, whose name turned out to be Jesus.

There was no wrong way to move your body. Didn't matter how stiff and awkward your movements, how repetitive or lame. How much sticky grief you found in your pelvis when you tried to shake it. We should all dance blindfolded. We should all have mandatory blindfolded dance parties at least once a week. Old, young, rich, poor: it should be a civic requirement, like paying taxes or taking out the trash or being licensed to drive. People who refuse should be fined or jailed.

After hours of dancing, the bonfire down to ember, Aviva went off to enjoy the hugest, most cathartic bowel movement of all time. She slept like a baby, and woke with the sun to commune with the birds.

Final day. The big night. Would she or would she not imbibe? Work with Grandmother plant or sit it out? She had achieved quite a lot of "internal scrubbing" on this little adventure already. *Dayenu?*

There was a beater guitar hanging in a nook off the big open kitchen, and after breakfast she asked one of the staff guys if she could borrow it.

"You play?"

"A little."

"Give us something while we clean up."

He switched off top 40 blaring from the crusty CD/radio above the food-prep area. Aviva tuned the beater. What a piece of shit. Still, always nice to have one of these babies in her arms. Such a perfect instrument. The way it fit.

The kitchen staff weren't paying much attention. Ideal conditions. Secret to happiness? Low expectations, according to the Rabbi.

She picked a bit of "Blackbird," then segued into an oldie about Barb's casual cruelty. The Barb of this song served as a sort of stand-in for all the haters. Barb hissing, "That's enough," while adolescent Aviva tried to master rudimentary chords. "Give it a rest! I'm not in the mood! What an inferior instrument!" And when little V *did* cease trying to master those rudimentary chords, when she *did* give her precious guitar a rest, Barb would thank God: "It's like someone stopped hitting me!" Aviva would very much have liked to hit Barb. *Someone* should've hit Barb. Alternatively, Aviva would have been okay to just be hit *by* Barb, in place of the constant, casual shaming. *Just hit me, you cowardly bitch*, went the song. *And I'll hit you, too. And we can hit each other 'til we're no longer blue.* People always thought it was a simple song about female aggression. Everyone loves a fight.

Yeah: she was going to imbibe. She had come all this way; why not take the full trip? Complete the mission. Grandmother was said to *dissolve all emotional and physical blockages*. Maybe it would accomplish what the acupuncture, the rose quartz, the yoga, the demon drug, the shamanic ceremonies, the tarot readings, the fertility goddess food-cycling, the expensive probiotics, the sex witch, the "visualization," the yoni steam, and Pascale had not managed.

Aviva wasn't fucking pregnant. Had never been pregnant. And what if Grandmother plant was the final hurdle, the final test, the final frontier?

What if it *did* clear all the blockages? What if it awakened Aviva into the yin-state receptivity she couldn't achieve on her own?

Present for the ceremony were Hana, Aviva, Juanita, Theresa, Jesus, two hard-bods, Gorja, and the playboy, whose name turned out to be Aden. The silver-haired singing massage crone turned out to be the shaman, and also Juanita's mother. They gathered at dusk in a hidden cove, half-cave, formed from rock. It was womb-like, because clichés really do exist, and often.

The special brew was distributed ceremonially into handmade clay vessels they were instructed to hold in a specific way. Both hands, head bowed. The only light came from a small fire in the middle of the circle. The shaman chanted and hummed.

Aviva accepted her allotment. She cupped her hands around her little vessel, thinking about how she was going to turn herself over to the hardest-core fertility authorities as soon as she got back home, and let them do to her whatever the hell they wanted, go to whatever lengths necessary to get this shit done. She'd had just about enough of the nonexistent baby's bullshit. Enough was enough; she was going to hand herself over to get it done.

"JUST GET 'ER DONE," she once heard a producer holler. "The perfect is the enemy of the good." Or was that Voltaire? Regardless.

She made a private toast to her elusive baby. Aviva was supposedly this irreverent punk; that's what the critics said. *So provocative!* But look: her reverence is actually massive, and immune to logic. Probably some immunity to logic is a prerequisite for reverence.

She put the vessel to her lips and, at the communal go-ahead, she drank.

It was foul, wow. Hello, Grandmother. She could do with some grandmothering. She hoped they showed up, both her grandmothers, and her stepgrandmother, who had been all right, and *their* mothers, too, all four or five of them, and *their* mothers, and *theirs* and *theirs* as well, eight, nine, twelve, sixteen, all those bygone bitches, right back to the original one, the mud from which everything had sprung.

Fuck you, you stupid stubborn nonbaby. You stubborn little fucker, *fine*. Suit yourself. Suit your *lack* of self. Mama's gonna have herself some fun, or an interesting experience, or some fresh catharsis at the very least. There was no going back; only forward. Rites must be had! If not the rite of pregnancy and birth, well. We don't always get to choose our passages. Fuck you, who assume passages are yours to choose. We can only go through doors that are open to us.

7

FUCKERY

Another bleed accomplished. A clean slate in the offing. How fortunate, belonging to the subset of the human race who regularly gets to experience the very essence of fresh start. Hopes and dreams regularly end up as dust and ashes, but so what? From dust and ashes come *new* hopes and dreams, again and again (and again) in perpetuity (or until menopause). What spiritually blessed creatures are the Havers-of-Wombs! Sorry if that makes those without wombs or with malfunctioning or disowned wombs feel angry or sad or envious or disenfranchised or excluded. Surely those of us without wombs or with malfunctioning wombs or with disowned wombs can take a moment here to reflect upon our *own* spiritual blessings in whatever biological and/or intellectual and/or psychic and/or synthetic capacity said blessings most certainly reside, because *all* beings are of blessed and vital importance, rich in metaphorical and literal meaning and potency. But anyway, kindly withhold scoffing at the idea that the cis-female biological body holds its own special/mystical importance. The cis-male body *also* holds special, mystical importance. And the intersex body. And the asexual body. And the transsexual body. And whatever language is on the rise for whatever has yet to be precisely codified/branded/marketed. We are *all* holy vessels of great, mystical importance, are we not? *Are we not?!* Name it, folks. (Except the TERF body—oh fuuuuuck no: those cuntrags should BURN IN THE LOWEST CIRCLE OF HELL.) Meanwhile, of what service might *you* be to the whole of your community, and to humankind? Humankind is in great need of service, as you may have heard. So let's all be respectful of one another and pleased with ourselves while we enjoy the ride for this short window of time during which we are all embodied alongside one another in this realm, under the watchful eye of the very-soon-to-be-fully-self-aware algorithm, *shall we*? Yes! Great! But we are *not* all the same. So don't you *dare* try to perpetuate erasure upon *me* or I will fucking rip you into pieces *with my fucking teeth*, got it?! Awesome. Okay. Where were we?

Ah yes: Blessed are the Havers-of-Wombs. Blessed are the creatures that can bleed for days without dying.

Here is what happened under the influence of Grandmother plant: Aviva became a mother. And not just any mother: Aviva became *the* mother. The one great mystical mother. Founder of a new race. A hundred perfect, raven-haired daughters issued effortlessly forth from the warm glow at her center, baked goods fresh from an oven. Glory be! One after another after another, perfect sweet human buns tumbled out into independent existence, got right up onto a pair of sturdy little legs, and gazed back at Aviva with pairs of dark, unblinking eyes.

These beings steadily proceeded to grow into young women. So many pairs of absorbing eyes stared back at her, and more kept coming, even as their elders grew uniformly past puberty, sweet breasts budding, hips gently widening, asses rounding, pubic mounds growing thickets of dense, luscious hair.

Someone on the perimeter of the cave banged a drum.

Someone puked into a bucket.

Someone else shrieked crazed, unbridled laughter.

Meanwhile, Aviva observed the spectacle of her issue. Her army of daughters crowded around in the firelight, blotting out all the other seekers, the shaman, the drumbeaters, and the drumbeat itself. And new ones just kept on coming! She couldn't stop them any more than she could start them; she had no control over this process. They stared at her as if waiting for something. To be given orders? And as they aged into young adults, her issue began to break gaze and sort of *sour*. They'd reached fruition, the cycle complete. Each in turn rolled her eyes, like so what, who cares, I'm over you. Each rosebud mouth melted into a smirk, one after another. And then each daughter snapped her fingers and instantly dematerialized before she could bear issue of her own. Snap, gone, snap, gone, snap, gone, self-annihilation in quick, continuous succession.

Still, more kept *coming*. They emerged, they stood, they stared, they saw, they grew boobs and pubes, they got cynical, and they got the fuck out: snap, bye. The rhythm was in charge, and it was impossible to embroider any sort of upset about the disappearances, because more and more new ones kept right on coming. Maybe there was even a recycling of sorts going on? It was getting to be enough, already. It couldn't go on forever, could it? How might Aviva cease all this issuing forth from herself? At first it had been exciting, but now it was more than enough. Worse than enough: sickening.

The ever-undiminishing daughter army made a mockery of the reproductive "miracle," which was an invention, a luxury, a joke, a distraction from the fact that the portal—Aviva!—was being *used*. Life was *using* her. It had no "respect" for her. It found her sense of "self" irrelevant at best. *Ooh, you like "nature," do you? Ooh, you think the mysteries of life are "sacred," hmmm? Ooh, You're into the irrefutable laws of biology, are you? How hilarious, you overeducated postmodern twat.* Did she "love" these girls? She did not. Love was a trick, an illusion, a tool. She maybe wished them well, in theory, but that was it.

"What did you learn?" Hana asked at dawn, as they emerged from their trances, the sound of the surf slowly returning to their awareness. Gorja was loudly crying.

"I'm nature's tool," Aviva whispered. "Everything we do, we think we're actors in some great scheme, but the great scheme is really just using us. We're its tools. Nothing we think or feel is even real. We don't matter. In the great scheme. Everything that needs to happen, happens, like, through us. Upon us. In spite of us."

"Daaaaaamn," Hana said.

"What about you??"

"I experienced an ancestor committing a really violent murder, and I think my family is still paying for it. Karmically. But I feel like I released some of it this time."

They were told not to eat anything but plants, nuts, seeds, and fruits for a few days, drink lots of water, spend at least an hour a day sitting alone with whatever had come up, and avoid any other intoxicants indefinitely.

Back in New York City, still pretty dazed from her psychedelic and chakra scrubbing, Aviva scored a coveted appointment with the man, the myth, the legend: Dr. Arnie Michaels. Under normal circumstances, you had to wait six months for an appointment with Arnie Michaels, but it turned out Sarah knew someone who knew someone, so here they were in front of an imposing stone prewar building on Fifth Avenue, a stone's throw from Central Park.

Arnie Michaels had performed the first successful IVF in New York State in the early 1980s. *But I didn't like doing it,* he explained in his memoir. *I felt like I was playing God. It felt dangerous, unwise. And I knew that there were no lengths to which both scientists and the infertile might be willing to go in the quest to control conception. And I found that idea unsettling. What doors might we be opening that couldn't ever be closed again?* (Props to the ghostwriter.) So Arnie had changed gears, shifted course, and now presented himself as the *alternative* fertility doc, the one who would take all of your out-of-pocket cash *not* to pummel your pituitary into submission, but rather, instead, to gently, holistically encourage and enable said gland to do what it "should." He promised to study you very closely and thoroughly before recommending any treatment whatsoever, and *only* then might he prescribe the most subtle, sophisticated, respectful, simple, non-invasive course possible. He had an acupuncturist, a nutritionist, and an herbalist on staff. He spent unheard-of hours playing detective, reading temp charts, looking at the organism from every possible angle. This was no clinic disassembly line. *My job is to help nature take its course*, the ghostwriter wrote. *I am nature's wingman. I don't want to fight nature; I want to help nature do what it—and* only *it—can do.*

Word on the street was that this dude got *everybody* pregnant, a turn of phrase that made Aviva picture him personally fucking each and every desperate elderly, rich, barren bitch on the Eastern Seaboard, as well as a fair number from Europe and Asia and Africa and the Middle East. Which brought to mind the famous case of the douchebag fertility specialist in Indiana who had, for decades, surreptitiously used his own sperm to artificially impregnate many hundreds of his customers—er, patients. An *actual* army of children had issued forth from *that* psychopath's loins, and they were becoming adults now, and collectively trying to sue the state, but, alas, no legal framework had yet remotely caught up to the technologies that had been in prolific, profitable use all this time, so first they had to get to work *creating* some laws. "Fertility fraud," they were calling it. Cart's way up about a mile on ahead of *that* horse, but Godspeed and good luck, o wretched pioneers!

A discreet gold plaque on gray stone bore Michaels's name in delicate cursive. Pure class, baby: the big league. Sarah was along for the ride, insisting she'd love nothing more than some downtime in a waiting room. A slender young woman in a white silk blouse buzzed them in: "Good morning, ladies!"

It was homey, if home was a cartoonish rendition of Jackie Kennedy's boudior circa 1962. Top-notch Louis XIV reproduction furniture, plush dusty rose carpet, labia-colored silk drapes. Everything peachy, plump, pleasing. A timeless space, thoroughly climate-controlled, air-filtered, humidified: utterly exclusive of weather. There were no periodicals.

"*Gorgeous*," Sarah whispered.

The man himself appeared right on the dot, as suntanned and relaxed as though he'd just stepped off a yacht in the Mediterranean. His wife had decorated the office. His wife had decorated the house in the Hamptons, too. His wife loved to decorate. When she was done decorating someplace, it was usually time to redecorate someplace else.

"I hear you came all the way from *Albany*," he said, reaching to shake Aviva's hand. He said "Albany" wrong, with a long first "A." "And I see you brought your sister!" Sarah giggled like a tween. "Please make yourself at home." He was grandfatherly, if your grandfather was an old-world shipping magnate. "Our lovely Miss Harrison will get you anything you'd like. Tea? Coffee? Just let her know."

There was a round of curtsies and bows before he led Aviva down the hall to the exam room, where she took off her pants and got up onto the table. Michaels snapped on some gloves.

"Let's have a look, shall we?"

Aviva had been instructed to serve as Sam's jizz receptacle the night before, so hopefully she would show up here today with a cache of jizz chillaxin' round her cervix. Michaels's first course of action was to see what condition those sperm were in; this would yield crucial info. Them nutty lil' tadpoles should be all cozied up in the equivalent of swank, spongy cervical hotel rooms, hopping themselves up on delicious cervical serum sugars like free room service, gearing up for the long journey to the almighty egg. Upon confirmation of this, Michaels would know that the problem lay *beyond* the cervix. Simple. But it took a renegade like Michaels—who felt "uncomfortable" going immediately for glandular terror—to undertake this basic, information-gathering step. She lay back and stared at the ceiling tiles while Michaels opened her with the speculum and made some light chitchat about how much he despised the current president. Uh, could we give the politics a breather for just a sec? While the mystical doorway to Aviva's core (sorry: cervix) was being exposed and poked at? The central air hummed expensively. Here came the monstrous Q-tip, and that awful, unreachable sensation: the cervix and the throat being energetically and anatomically aligned, is it any wonder that the sense-memory of this is going to make her literally gag for days to come? Michaels was kind enough to remove the speculum when he was done poking and scraping, but he left her there in the stirrups while he fitted a slide into his microscope.

"So," he said, squinting into the microscope. "So." He was quiet for a long moment. "Where are the sperm?"

He seemed to want an actual answer from her. Aviva extracted herself from the stirrups and tried not to gag.

"There are no sperm," Michaels said. "There is nothing here. You had intercourse last night?"

"Yes."

"And you were on the bottom?"

"Yes."

"Not on the top?"

"Not on the top."

"And no shower or bath after?"

"Nothing."

He squinted through the microscope again.

"Very odd. Your husband's numbers looked fine."

Aviva must be incinerating all the sperm. Aviva was a sperm incinerator. Aviva was an acid lagoon, a toxic dump. In place of cervical serum, atomic sludge. Aviva's cervical hotels were the kind from which travelers were never heard again. No sperm influencers were tagging it on vacation posts. Where were the sperm? Her cervix was a ghost motel. Abandoned. Condemned.

"Get dressed and meet me in my office."

The office was all dark paneling and framed degrees and engraved awards.

"Shut the door behind you."

He gestured for her to sit in the deep leather armchair opposite his mahogany desk. She crossed her legs primly at the ankle and waited. On-stage, she'd be a sweating savage, swiveling and stomping and screaming to bring down the house, but here, opposite the great doctor, she sat up straight and lowered her gaze, hands folded in her lap: submission all the way. If only identity politics had anything whatsoever to do with . . . like . . . actual human behavior.

Michaels studied her file, frowning. She was afraid to move or breathe, lest she disrupt the great man's concentration. A twenty-first-century doctor had the power to manipulate and override biology, bend life itself to his will: What kings and queens could ever boast such power? What generals? What politicians, fascists, despots?

"So," he said, looking up and smiling across the massive desk.

"Yes," Aviva said.

All those raven-haired girls, her great assembled issue, were waiting, quivering, holding her in their collective, merciless, unblinking gaze. Don't fuck it up for them. All of them. Any of them. One of them.

Michaels launched into an astonishing hour of questions and note-taking. Did she or Sam ever take hot baths? (Yes, she did, once or twice a month, with Epsom salts and lavender oil, pure heaven.) Did Sam have heated car seats? (No.) Did she douche? (Oh hell to the no.) Did Sam ride a bike? (Occasionally.) Did Sam wear boxers? (Absolutely.) Did she have her temperature charts on her? (No; they all lived in a server's server's server somewhere and might someday be puzzled over by alien archeologists after all the creatures of the current era were long gone and another ice age had passed.) Did she know that if she held a chart sideways it would be easier to read? (Why, no! Cool beans.) What was her longest cycle ever? (Fifty-seven days, though that was maybe actually a skipped cycle?) And her shortest? (Twenty-six days, just that once, when she'd managed to completely abstain from absolutely all forms of processed flour and sugar and dairy for weeks on end, a singular miracle, never accomplished again.)

Women were complex and fascinating, and Arnie Michaels loved a good mystery. In his spare time he devoured Sherlock Holmes and Agatha Christie. Other than the Rabbi, Aviva couldn't recall *ever* having had a physician's undivided attention for a solid hour. Money can't buy happiness, but it *can* buy a top-dog physician's undivided attention for an hour.

"All righty," he said. "What we're gonna do, first off, is run some tests.

Basic stuff. Nutrition levels. Mineral deficiencies. See where your hormones are on specific days throughout your cycle. Make sure your liver and kidneys are happy. Then we'll make a plan."

"Dr. White doesn't think I'm ovulating."

"Well!" Michaels's eyes twinkled. No stage actor ever inhabited a role so joyously. He loved this gig. All these women! The sad, the hopeless, the weary, the wandering. From Westchester, Dubai, Beijing, Italy, the Carolinas. They came to see him day after day, season after season, year after year. They rented top-floor apartments at the Peninsula and the Plaza. They bought pieds-à-terre nearby. There was no end to these huddled masses, yearning to press their lips against soft, fresh, familiar newborn flesh, desperate to sniff and smooch the nubs of their very own baby noses and toeses. Michaels took them in—all who could pay out of pocket, that is. Lately his wife was making noise about wanting a place on Martha's Vineyard.

"We'll just have to prove Dr. White wrong, then, won't we?"

"Okay," Aviva said, thrilled. What the fuck? Was she blushing?! Was this what people were talking about when they said, with their eyes averted, *I really love my doctor*? Patriarchal sex cult god punishment fantasies die hard, epigenetically speaking.

Maybe the goal was simply to find the right *kind* of fertility fuckery. Like: it wasn't so much a matter of *whether* you're willing to get fucked with, but whom you granted *permission* to fuck with you. Not so much *if* you were going to get fucked, but who was going to do the fucking. Acquiesce yourself to the fuckery. Submission had to go without saying, but you *do* still have choice, ladies: Choice! Choice! Yay!

In the waiting room, Sarah was literally on the edge of her seat: "Well?"

"I feel like I just had a consult with the high priest," Aviva said.

"Anything but American Express," the receptionist said, smiling.

Marcus Copeland had taken it upon himself to memorize her festival schedule, and he let her know he was going to be in Miami, too, and hoped they would have the chance to "really hang."

Somewhere softly lit, she replied, because listen: being faithful had gotten her nowhere. Sam was a great guy, Sam was the best, let's hear it for Sam the Man, but Sam's junk was not, for whatever insane/obscure reason, checking into Aviva's cervical motels. Maybe her cervical motels were too high-priced; maybe Sam's junk was broke. In any case, the Copeland dance was *on.* The seduction tango. Dizzying anticipation. Divine. Who did it hurt, really? What happened on the road stayed on the road; everyone knew that. This was not *about* Sam. This couldn't even really be understood as a betrayal of Sam, because it had nothing to do with Sam. Sam was a great guy. Aviva would make Sam dinner and tidy Sam's house and smooch Sam's dick all her livelong days. She would sit faithfully by Sam's deathbed. Meanwhile, please just let her have some stupid wild little sexual adventure. *Please.* Mama needs to have a good *time.*

A rollicking shiva in the East Village. Her good pal Adnan's aged mother, shitload of cancer, but she had at least gotten to meet her grandkids before she shuffled off this mortal coil. Therefore not, as they say, a tragedy.

Adnan had gotten his start bartending at a downtown rat-hole where he and Aviva formed a close bond during many an interminable open mic. Now he owned three of the best performance spaces in New York and was like a brother to her, which is to say nothing whatsoever like her own still-living brother.

Adnan and his Dutch husband had two small children gestated and brought forth by a surrogate who also lived with the family and served as their nanny. Adnan was old-school Sephardi and the Dutchman was classic modern Euro philosemite. Their palatial superloft was made from two combined lofts. This was what's possible if you stayed in the city long enough and played your cards exactly right.

The place was jam-packed with mourners. The mirrors were covered, and everyone's shoes were off. There were impressive piles of smoked fish and specialty babka and the freshest bagels in town. The absence of music was the only thing preventing it from being a perfect party.

The kids had gotten huge. The baby was toddling and talking, the older girl twerking in sunglasses and a tutu. The surrogate/nanny chased, scolded, comforted, fed, and, in due course, bundled them off to bath and bed at a well-coordinated nod from Adnan.

Aviva chatted with the sixty-something obstetrician who had surgically removed both children from the surrogate/nanny, and the obstetrician's eighty-seven-year-old mother, both dripping in gold and diamonds, with extravagant manicures and perfectly coiffed hair. They could have passed for sisters.

"Eighty-two is too young!" declared the elder, speaking of the deceased. "These days, eighty-two is a *tragedy*. She had so much to live for. Life is endless! Endless! I am going to live to a hundred and *twelve*. My financial planner told me to plan for a hundred and *twelve*!"

"That's a . . . long time," Aviva said. "Too much time is as bad as too little, don't you think? Might become a bit of a bummer at some point."

"Easy for you to say, girlie."

"I mean, once you've met your grandchildren, you can't really complain, can you?"

"She can *always* complain," said the OB daughter.

"You know, they say complaining actually does relieve psychic pressure," said Aviva.

"You're so refreshing!" The elder laughed. "I love young people. But I want to ask you a question. I see your tattoos; you really have a lot of them, let me see . . . Oh, you're covered in them! Look at this! I like that one—that's very symbolic, isn't it? But I am concerned for all you young people nowadays with all these tattoos. Aren't you concerned about putting all that ink in your skin?"

"I never really thought about it before, but now that you mention it, that's actually a very good question. I'm going to worry about that a bit more, moving forward. Thank you."

The old lady guffawed, and Aviva was compelled to spontaneously confide.

"I'd like to be pregnant."

Maybe these archetypes—the rich, powerful mother and the rich, powerful OB daughter, who'd hacked into the wombs of thousands of this city's richest, most powerful incubators—could sanction Aviva's desire and intention. Maybe they would *bless* her, in a manner of speaking. If they found her worthy. You had to ask for what you wanted, did you not? You had to risk saying it out loud once in a while. One never knew where the keys were hidden. The two women checked out Aviva's ring finger, and were satisfied.

"All in good time," said the elder, with a pat on the shoulder.

"I can give you a name," said the daughter. "NYU. Does *everyone*."

"I just saw Arnie Michaels."

"Oh *God*, no. Are you *isane*? Anyone but Arnie *Michaels*!"

"What? Why?"

"It's the twenty-first century, sweetheart, that's why. He's stuck in the year *one*," the daughter said. She held up her index finger in Aviva's face. "The year ONE, sweetheart. Why on *earth* would you fart around with that bullshit, pardon my language? Use the tools we have on hand! The clinics, they're factories, sure, but they operate on statistics and they get the job done. Oh my God, Arnie fucking *Michaels*. *Please*."

"But . . . I mean, what about long-term consequences to women and children?"

"Give me a *break*."

"I had a tilted uterus," said the elder. "They told me it would never happen for me. I finally said, 'Okay! It's not meant to be!' Then: BAM. This one."

"Wow," Aviva said.

"Well, actually, they put in a donut."

"A what?"

"A donut, you know: a donut!"

The OB rolled her eyes: "Some medieval device to straighten out the cervix. Completely obsolete. Ancient history. We don't have to mess around with that kind of bullshit anymore."

"But it *worked*," cried the elder, and knocked back what was left of her Chardonnay. "It *worked*! No one can say it didn't *work*!"

"No, Ma, no one can say it didn't work."

"And then: BAM, sixteen months later, her brother. I didn't know what hit me. Be careful what you wish for! Good luck to you, darling. You're so *refreshing*. I love young people."

Aviva wandered the perimeter, ducked down a hallway. In the playroom, classics were lined up on a low bookshelf: *Goodnight Moon*, *Go the Fuck to Sleep*, *Madeline*, *The Snowy Day*. And what was this? A new addition to the canon: *How to Make a Baby*.

She slid it off the shelf.

Some babies come from their parents' bodies, but some babies come from borrowed parts of other people's bodies. Babies just need a soft, warm, safe place to grow while they wait to be born! Sometimes they can live in their parent's belly, but sometimes they have to borrow a belly! Whoever loves you and takes care of you is your parent. All babies are miracles! What kind of miracle are you? The illustrations were shit; a step down from emoji.

"Well, well," said Adnan, appearing in the doorway. "If it isn't the queen of alt-folk-punk-blues, herself."

He was a legendary hugger.

"May your mom's name be for a blessing," Aviva whispered in his ear.

"Don't give me the scripted shit. You of all people."

"Did she suffer?"

"Yes."

"Well, join the club."

He laughed, and pulled her back in for another hug. Thank God for surrogate brothers.

"I didn't realize *Blade Runner* was in the public domain now," Aviva said, holding up the book. "Suuuuuper interesting prequel."

"Don't fucking start with me," he sang.

A photographer Aviva vaguely knew popped in to say hi and bye. "We have to get home to relieve the sitter," said the photographer.

Aviva was polite: "How old are your kids?"

"Almost two."

"Twins?"

The woman nodded, beaming.

"Wow, what are the *odds*?!" Aviva said. "So cool. Twin *magic*, am I *right*?"

Rest in peace, Aviva, a mostly decent woman whose eyes rolled so far back in her head her brain imploded.

"They're *so amazing*," said the photographer in the kind of sickly, high, tight little voice that indicated having been through approximately thirteen years of prep school.

"Oh, I *bet*. Are they . . . identical?"

"V," said Adnan.

"No, a boy and a girl."

"Oh, *perfect*! How *perfect*. A boy and a girl. What more could you want? Got all those boxes checked, huh? *So* great. Do twins . . . run in your family?"

"Um, no," said the photographer, and made her exit.

"What the fuck is wrong with you?" Adnan hissed.

"Barren bitch on the loose. Out of curiosity, do they charge a dollar amount *per* human life or do you get a twofer with twins?"

"Twofer. Everyone knows that. You really need to chill, love."

"I'm *sorry*. I just— Do you ever look at your kids and go, 'WTF'? I'm not trying to be mean. I really want to understand."

"Human beings are adaptable, V. We get used to pretty much whatever. That's what makes us us. Things change. Always have, always will. Change is how things are, V. You are *literally* the only person in the world who has a problem with this."

"The cool new pope has said he's not so sure."

"I'm telling you. Listen to me: it's not a bad thing. It's just new. It only seems weird from the outside."

"That it does, bro! That it does."

"And *for your information*, the woman you just flamed had her twins because she and that loser she married found out they were carriers of a genetic mutation, and if left to chance their baby would likely have had some fatal degenerative thing where they'd have to, like, watch it die before it was out of diapers. How about *that*, cuntrag? Try putting *that* in your pipe and smoke it, why don't you."

"I'm *sorry*. More power to them. Heaven forfend rich people be subject to the cruelties of nature. *Bless* them."

"Sweetie, you gotta evolve. Relax. Get on board."

"I know. I just . . . Adi. I want a few basic tenets of life on earth to stay . . . the same. Is that wrong? I like *trees* and *air* and *water* and *beaches* and *birds* and *fish* and *soil* and wild mammalian *instincts* and the *mysteries of creation* and *mortality* and all that crazy old-school stuff. I think there might be *meaning* in the shit we can't control."

"Go write a song, girl. Please. That ship has *sailed*. You want to not eat genetically modified bananas? Guess what? *There are no more of the original bananas.* A fungus wiped them out fifty years ago. If we didn't have the Frankenstein ones, we wouldn't know what a banana even *was* anymore. You want to not drive a car? Sorry, the whole fucking country's a highway. You want to relinquish texting? You want to bring back polio? What? Don't ever get on an airplane again, have fun. Speaking of which, did I tell you? Me and Rolf bought some land in New Zealand for when the shit hits the fan. You better be nice to me, or I won't give you food and shelter when the time comes."

"Touché. But the indentured servant/uterus–cum–nanny situation, that's never weird for you guys? At all? That doesn't keep you up at night, ever?"

"Babe, she is so fucking happy. We got her a full set of Vuitton luggage, and we send her to Tulum for a week every year for her birthday. She's been to Paris with us four times. She got to meet *Beyoncé*. She is the envy of all her friends. Her life fucking *rules*. You have no idea. It's win-win. She loves those kids *so much more* because she's not ultimately responsible for them. Everybody is happy. *This is evolution*, honey. It's a trip. Come along into the now. The future is now. It's taken *hundreds of thousands* of years to get to a place this ideal with regard to human reproduction."

"Hundreds of thousands of—what's that you say? Dollars?"

"You're on the wrong side of history, love. You're thinking about this all wrong. You'd better get with the program."

"They need to change those dumbass T-shirts from *The Future Is Female* to *The Future Is Female Body Parts for Sale*. But *wait*: that's also the *past*! I'm so *confused*!!"

"That's not a bad idea for your merch, actually. Yo, seriously. Do it."

"*The Future Is Female Complicity. The Future Is Female Robots. The Future Is Female Collusion.* Oooh, how 'bout: *THE FUTURE IS THE PAST.*"

"V, I say this out of love: Your career is going amazing. You have a hot husband who adores you, even if he is a fucking high school gym teacher."

"History and civics."

"Whatever: he's incredibly hot. Life is about getting what you *want*, bae. That's what we all try to do: we all try to get what we *want*. There's no shame in getting what you want. Literally a million people would change places with you in a heartbeat, and you could go sit in poverty and obscurity and contemplate 'meaning.'"

"Yeah. 'Cause you know what I really want? I want to *relinquish* want."

"Deep. But impossible."

"Fine: I want a whole new wardrobe literally every month. I want all new furniture and light fixtures. I want someone else to clean my toilet and cook all my meals and make my garden grow forever. I want to never be questioned on anything I do or say or think or feel. I want to fuck Marcus Copeland in Miami next week."

Adnan looked at her, shocked and impressed.

"Are you for real? Copeland? For real? Damn. With that hot husband of yours, waiting at home. Is this the channel we're watching now?"

"My point is, I don't see how 'want' gets us anywhere."

"Want is the *only* thing that has ever gotten us anywhere."

"Want is *trouble*."

"Want is *life*."

"Like getting a man on the moon to beat out the other massive corrupt hideous governments hoping to be first to get a man on the moon? Aren't we a special species of ape. Few decades later, and space is loaded with our *garbage*. Want is for assholes. Want don't *impress* me."

"Wooo, Aviva Rosner's going up against *NASA*, y'all! Come and get it!"

"It just doesn't sit right, Adi. Nothing human beings have ever congratulated our fine little selves on accomplishing. Tribal warfare. Artificial intelligence. Colonialism. Nuclear power. Biowarfare. I don't know. None of it sits right."

"You know what else doesn't sit right?"

This was an old joke. The correct response was: "Me after I fuck [name of current love interest]."

"Me trying to breastfeed in the NICU after they surgically remove my premature two-pound triplets?"

"Have you had any food? Come and get some food."

"Not hungry."

Hana hadn't been joking about loss of appetite in the wake of Grandmother. (Though it was also possible that Hana had a bit of an eating disorder, herself. Aviva couldn't help but notice, in their shared tree house, how Hana had spent quite a lot of time with the water running in the bathroom after meals.)

"That is rude," Adnan said. " 'Not hungry'? How dare you. This is shiva. Show some respect and overeat in honor of the dead. And let me give you some of the most incredible 'shrooms Jack Dorsey sourced for me. 'Shrooms are the shit for clarifying desire and intention, which it sounds like you need."

"What do you got for *eradicating* desire and intention?"

"Only death, my love. And soon enough. Soon enough."

Austin, El Paso, Miami, Jackson, New Orleans, Birmingham.

Aviva couldn't be doing festival season with armloads of babies, now, could she?

Ten dates in five states. Or maybe it was five dates in ten states? It was a bunch of dates in a bunch of states. The booking agent was pleased. Jerry was pleased. "Real strong numbers, hon. Would a *little* more social media hustle kill you? Some straightforward posting doesn't mean you're selling out. I didn't understand what your last post even *meant*. You have to make it easier for people to get what you're about, darling. Don't you want things to keep *happening* for you?"

"Well, that's confusing, Jer. I mean, 'things' will certainly continue to 'happen' for me for some length of time, however long or short. Could you be more specific about the 'things' and the 'happening'?"

"Simmer down, you little shit. Try to play nice."

"I *do* play nice, Jer: I play my *guitar* real nice. And I write all of these *songs*. And I play my *songs* real nice."

"Hear me out: Would it work better if we just had someone from the team run social for you? The interns do it; a lot of them are great at it. They all go to Harvard."

"Is there an AI that can do it? I want an AI to do it."

"Also," Jerry said. "More good news! They're adding Ireland to your UK tour. Everyone's excited. Your numbers are in a sweet spot, babe, and everyone is really excited. If you don't get in your own way, this is going to be a big step for you. Germany and Italy next year, and maybe even Japan, they're saying."

She wrote to Amy's mum: *It's me! The lovesick addicted American Jew! My UK tour is happening! Here are the dates. Can we meet up?!*

Sure thing, came Mum's swift reply. *I look forward to meeting you. Let's plan for the 3rd or the 4th.*

It almost certainly had to be a joke. The account was a fake. It had to be, right? This was absurd. There was no way. Aviva was going to show up at some meeting spot and be summarily murdered by a rival superfan, right?

* * *

The menopausal wretch next to Aviva in row nine wept silently throughout takeoff. Stretch pants, stick thighs, swollen feet in rhinestone-encrusted flip-flops, iridescent French manicure on fingers and toes. Fitness tracker, thinning blond dye job. She messed with a prescription bottle, washed down a couple pills with gulps from a plastic water bottle, and then hauled out a roast beef sandwich the size of her head, still wiping away tears. When she'd consumed half the sandwich, she commenced spackling: face powder from a compact, then a densely perfumed hand lotion.

Aviva could take no more. She spoke in a sisterly tone: "You know that stuff interferes with your hormones, right?"

"Sorry?"

"I couldn't help but catch a whiff. Strong stuff. Synthetic fragrance. Messes with the endocrine system. Which regulates hormones in women, men, children, and animals. Which is part of why humanity is becoming infertile. Which is playing right into the hands of the American Society for Reproductive Medicine. Which is where a whole lot of people stand to make a whole lot of money if we can sort of moderately sterilize ourselves? Which is basically what's happening as I speak? Looking *real* good for the ol' ASRM, these days."

It was possible that Adnan's 'shrooms hadn't completely worn off from last night.

The lady looked genuinely confused. She froze, holding the lotion aloft. "Would you . . . like to use some?"

"Oh, thank you, no, I'm *already* infertile. But we *are* in an enclosed space with recycled air, so it doesn't much matter whether or not I use it myself. Though probably having it directly *on* your skin is an order of magnitude more toxic than just inhaling the chemicals, skin being the largest organ of the human body. But, of course, when you next wash your hands, some of those chemicals will go into our common water sources, along with everyone else's runoff!"

"So you're saying this stuff is bad? Would you prefer I didn't use it?"

"Well, I don't know how old you are or what your reproductive situation is or was or might be, but women don't metabolize shit as fast as men do. And very few clinical studies are carried out on women, traditionally. So there's reason to believe that a huge majority of the toxins in our environment actually stay much longer in the bodies of women, wreaking havoc on our endocrine systems in a sort of pretty fucking serious way. Our hormones go haywire, basically. It's a pretty sensitive and mysterious system. So, you know, cancer, infertility, menstrual problems, endometriosis, autoimmune shit, all manner of horror you'd probably rather not think about." Aviva leaned over but kept her gaze straight ahead, like a spy trying to pass off information without arousing suspicion. "It's much bigger than you and me and that lotion. And it might not even matter one way or another, at the end of the day, because it's already too late for me and for you and for, you know, humanity as contained in the future worlds we hold within ourselves, but I don't really know! No one does! We fuck with nature at our peril! Oldest story there is."

The thing about microdosing was that you could just do it indefinitely. Aviva stuck out her hand.

"Anyway, hi! I'm being so rude! My name is Arnie. Arnie Michaels."

"Sally."

"What up, Sal? Sally-*sal*! Lovely to make your acquaintance."

"My daughter got her period two years ago," Sally whispered. "But she's only gotten it again *twice* in all the time since. She still gets cramps pretty bad, but no blood. Do you think that's related to all this hormone stuff? The doctor said she should get on the Pill. To regulate things."

"Oh, right, see, you'll want to find a new doctor immediately, 'cause that fucker don't know *shit*. Gynecology as a field of medicine is relatively new within the realm of science, Sal. And it's literally based on the torture of enslaved women. You'll want to find a doctor who wants to help manage your daughter's symptoms in a holistic way and avoid chemical birth control. That'd be doing her a real solid. The warning signs are good to heed early. And you know you don't need pap smears or mammograms every year unless there are extenuating circumstances, right? Women are often massively overtreated and routinely harmed in so being! I mean, except for the ones in poverty, who are often undertreated. It's all pretty fucked up."

"Jeez, I don't even know what to say. Are you a doctor?"

"Indeed I *am*." Aviva dug Arnie Michaels's card out of her pocket. "And how about you? What do you do?"

"Oh God, nothing. My ex is rich."

"That's *awesome*. Very ideal. So you have plenty of time to do a ton of research, then. Educate the fuck out of yourself. You're lucky. That's cool. What was up with the sob sesh? Everything all right?"

"Yeah, no, my ex, he's just a major asshole. He's actually getting remarried this weekend, and my daughter's with them at this resort and everything, and I just, like, really hate being apart from her. She's all I have."

" 'Your children are not your children,' " Aviva said.

"What?"

"Gibran. Kahlil Gibran. Poetry! No point in being rich if you ain't cultured, too."

"You're a riot. What was your name, again?"

"Arnie Michaels. Great to make your acquaintance. Ask me anything. Don't be shy. Anything at all."

An internet first person in praise of baby weight, written by a forty-eight-year-old who was not at *all* eager to lose hers, having so hard-won it: she'd spent seven years and a hundred and ninety thousand dollars on IUI, IVF, egg donation. She'd had four miscarriages, and now, finally, her very own beautiful baby. The only *other* issue was that the kid's *ears* stuck out a bit much, so at ten months of age they had the baby's ears surgically "fixed." And *now* all was well. At the end of the piece, the lady alluded to her hope for another baby, ASAP, by whatever means necessary.

Pregnancy announcement from one of Sam's cousins, and awww, look how cute that fucking indistinguishable sonogram is. Their fourth. A little *girl* would be joining three big brothers next year, hurrah. Everything pink. Mommy's finally getting her girl. They were going to name the child *Madisenne*. How the precise fucking *fuck* had God Almighty—or call it "the universe," whatever—seen fit to bless these particular skanks with the sacred guardianship of *four* blessed human souls encased in their very own flesh and blood?! How! Why! How?!

The paper of record reported *fascinating* new research suggesting that—hold on to your genitals—the singing of *lullabies* is a powerful tool for creating new synapses relating to the attachment and affection between parent and child. WHAT ON EARTH DO YOU THINK THEY'LL FIND OUT NEXT?

And everyone's favorite former First Lady spoke out about her once-upon-a-time miscarriage: "Why doesn't anyone talk about this? It's so important that we talk about these things." Lady, Jesus H. Christ. *Everybody* fucking talks about these things. All the time. For all of history. But once a freaking year, like clockwork, a celebrity announces a miscarriage with a statement about how nobody talks about this. Instead of pretending you're the first person to ever talk about this, how about just say: Why did I never pay any attention to anyone who talked about this? Say: How odd that I never tuned in to all the talk about these things! Say: Gee, whatever was I paying attention to instead?! Say: Golly, I think I've been hanging out with the wrong people! Say: What other bullshit assumptions might I have been laboring under all this time? Say: Holy shit, am I a brainwashed automaton?!

"Safe and sound," she told Sam. "Dunno about sound, actually. But safe. Amazing hotel room."

"Break a leg, baby. Miss you already."

"Yeah, but you know what, Sammy-Sam?"

"What?"

"What if none of this is my fault? What if I'm tip-top? What if I'm dropping fresh eggs every cycle? One after another. Pristine, nutrient-rich, primo, cage-free, organic eggs. And what if *you're* shooting crap up into my tracts?"

"Your tracts."

"My tracts, yes. Maybe your stuff sucks. Maybe your stuff is old. Maybe your stuff is stale. Maybe your stuff's *lame*."

Okay, she was going to need to cut it out with these mushrooms.

"They tested me, babe. My stuff's fine."

"No: I'm talking *metaphysically*. I'm suggesting that maybe your shit is, like, passive-aggressive. Maybe your shit can't *handle* my shit. Maybe your shit is *scared* of me. Maybe your shit is too *timid*. Maybe your shit doesn't have the right moves. Maybe your shit leaves my shit *cold*. Maybe my gloriousness doesn't want your passive-aggressive shit anywhere *near* their silky membranes. Maybe your shit can't even get past the *door*."

"Are you high?"

"Maybe your shit's stinking up my tracts, is what I'm saying."

"Your tracts."

"Maybe your shit can't figure out how to *traverse* my tracts. Maybe your shit has a bad sense of direction. Maybe it's *you*, is what I'm saying."

"My junk tested fine, babe."

"I'm not *talking* about tests, Sam. I'm talking about life. I'm talking about stuff there *is* no test for."

"Okay, babe. Maybe it is me. It could totally be me."

"And that doesn't bother you? That doesn't, like, demolish your worldview?! That your junk might be, like, useless? That your junk might suck? That you lack the basic capacity even the lowliest shit-sniffing mammal takes for *granted*?"

"It's a bummer, babe."

"A *bummer*?"

"It's a *total* bummer, Aviva. What do you want me to say?"

"I gotta go."

"Hope the show goes really great, babe."

And the show did go great, because this was precisely the kind of foul energy they wanted from her, the bloodthirsty mob. They loved her furious. A channel for their own rage. They paid good money. The roar seemed like it might carry her off the stage. This was a new level of feedback. Young crowd. The kids dug her. The eighteen-to-twenty-fours were suspicious about the way shit was going down in the world, woke to their marrow, and desperately searching for ways to insist upon their own humanity, survive late capitalism, overthrow racism, ensure the intersectionality of their environmentalism, and wrench a political education out of the targeted hyperbole in their feeds. They weren't lining up to freeze their eggs just yet, though any minute the marketing was going to adjust itself to them in some ingenious way, as, of course, was marketing's wont. Regardless, they loved Aviva. All the weirdo gender-fuckery influencers had been listening to her since high school or college, and now all the weirdo gender-fuckery influencers were *taking over the world*. The last shall be first and the first shall be last.

She knew the bassist and drummer from a recording session a couple years back, and they kept up like they'd been playing together all along. Fun to play with backup again, after all this time out there alone. She was a high-wire walker, under the lights, all those screaming, elated faces below. The crowd was feeling her. Dancing, singing along, moving to her rhythm. For an encore, she let rip on "You Can't Make Me," and when it seemed like one encore wasn't enough, she nodded to the drummer to let her go directly into "Rich White Twins," which went over almost well enough for a *third* encore, but you had to leave them wanting more.

Copeland turned up like a bad penny at the after party. A sexy motherfucking bad penny.

"Hey there," he said.

Aviva stared at him, said nothing. Make him squirm; this was *her* show.

"You were amazing," he went on. "Crowd ate it *up*. You *always* that good?"

"Yep."

"I swear to God. Your opening riff on 'Bearded Sophomore' had me feeling Ray Charles, dude."

He knew that the way to make a woman of her ilk wet was to pretend to respect her as a person, an equal, an artist, a *dude*. She was in control. She didn't break gaze. The sex witch would approve. She could feel him in her pants. But Aviva didn't need Copeland in her actual pants tonight, because she was already high off her own greatness, the show like an orgasm. After that kind of show you just wanted to ride the high directly into the sleep of the righteous.

She lost him in the crowd and took a car home. Let him wait. Let him squirm indefinitely. Let him seek her out again. He had to want her real bad if she was going to submit to whatever this was. She'd settle for no less than his complete and utter desperation. Let him follow her around on his knees for a mile, then maybe she'd capitulate. And then he could turn the tables and dominate her, just the way she liked it.

"Ms. Rosner? This is Lynn at Dr. Michaels's office. I have some results for you. Is now a good time?"

"Hi. Sure. Great. Yes."

"Dr. Michaels wanted me to let you know that you test positive for ureaplasma; it's a common bacterial infection that can cause infertility and miscarriage."

"Oh. Shit."

"Well . . . yes. But it's very common. It's *extremely* common. Most everyone carries bacteria of this sort. It's not uncommon at all."

"So . . . why isn't everyone infertile?"

"Well, that's a conversation you can have with the doctor. I'm just calling to tell you that you do test positive for the bacteria. It's one of the first things we tend to look for. So the doctor has prescribed a very strong antibiotic. You and your partner both have to take a full course. Be in touch if you have any questions; otherwise the doctor will see you in a few weeks at your scheduled appointment. Which pharmacy would you prefer?"

"So we get rid of this bacterial thing and then let nature take its course?"

"Then you come back in and talk to the doctor again and he decides what course of treatment will suit you best."

"Riiiiiiight, but what is the next step, usually?"

"Well, I would guess that after the ureaplasma is addressed, he'd probably send you for a hysterospalpingogram."

"The blue dye thing where they chemically blow out your tubes and, like, watch it on TV while you're unconscious?"

"It's routine. And then, likely, a consult for IUI."

"Okay," Aviva said. "Thanks."

She tossed her phone as hard and as far as possible without actually endangering it. C'mon, Aviva, don't be daft, technology and God are not distinct entities. God works *through* technology. God makes technology *possible*. God *created* the technicians, and the methodologies they employ. Stop your bellyaching. Quit your hairsplitting. Just admit you're selfish and scared, and do what the good doctor/God tells you. It's all the same in the end, isn't it?

No. No. No.

Scientists at a remote African gaming preserve were hoping to find a way to artificially inseminate the very last female white rhino on earth using the frozen semen of some of her dead ancestral peers. "We'll know she's in estrus by the way she'll display herself and we'll have that canister ready and we'll hold her down and . . . yeah, that's the dream," said the lead expert on the scene.

A forty-five-year-old art-house heroine had just given birth to her first child. She was glad she'd waited, she said, because she was old enough now to not care about looking old. Having kids in your teens or early twenties, you might bounce back, she said, but for some reason having kids in your thirties totally ruined you forever. Forties was the best time to have kids, because you had to reinvent yourself anyway and probably have some cosmetic work done, regardless.

Harmie Shmendrickson was grinning from ear to ear on a whimsically upholstered divan, clutching a favorite board book in one hand and favorite sock monkey in the other.

A plant geneticist was on a decades-long personal/professional quest to figure out how to engineer and reintroduce the extinct, once-mighty American chestnut tree, which had fallen prey in the early twentieth century to thorough blight triggered by fungus from imported Asian trees. People and things had started moving around and wanting too much, and catastrophe resulted over and over again, but the wanderlust and greed power us ever onward.

Oh, and here was Cracker's little one, pictured literally mixing him a cocktail—how adorable—with the caption: *training 'em young.*

Anniversary of Amy's death, and the news aggregates were all over it. "Twenty Times She Changed Fashion Forever" gave way to "Greatest Heartbreak Songs Ever" gave way to "Nine Pairs of Shoes Every Woman Needs to Own."

Aviva tore her eyeballs from the screen and watched, instead, the landscape whizzing past en route to the airport. Then came the strange impulse to somehow click on the landscape itself, the landscape as seen from the car window, and get to some next-level landscape through the portal of the *actual* landscape. Tap, tap, open it! Shop now! Where might it lead? How much did it cost? Could she double-click and own it in five to seven days for a small shipping fee? Weird how you couldn't click on things in the outside world. Someday, surely.

The air in Austin hung thick. There was a massive, opulent party on a roof deck downtown. DJ, pool, writhing bodies, sexy lighting. Same old scouts, execs, models, musicians, patrons, groupies, wannabes, has-beens.

Aviva and Copeland circled around each other half the night, eyes locking and breaking away. He pretended to ignore her for a while; she pretended to ignore him for a while. It was obviously only a matter of time.

Amy, newly remixed yet again, blasted from a network of very small, potent speakers hidden within the landscaping. You wouldn't believe the terrible men Amy loved, or lusted over, not that she could tell the difference. (*Was* there a difference? Not when you were in it, no. Only in hindsight.) You wouldn't believe how shitty, how stupid and deranged, how sadistic and shameful, how destructive and cowardly these men were. What did she see in them? Maybe they made her giggle. Maybe they made her feel tethered to earth. Maybe they made her feel seen. Maybe they made her come. Dirtbags. Assholes. Liars. Quick-witted, profligate, unreliable, amoral, insincere. Absolute *animals* in the sack. There was scientific evidence to suggest that the DNA from semen stayed inside the female reproductive tract for*ever*. Science, folks.

Copeland sauntered over at last. Score one for Aviva. If this was a game. Which it was.

"What are you drinking?"

"Seltzer with lime."

"Sober?"

"Just hate alcohol. Alcohol hates me. We agree to disagree."

"Got any weed?"

"Nope. And I flushed the last of my 'shrooms, 'cause they had a dark side. *Slicha.*"

"*Medaberet Ivrit?*"

"*Ken, ken.*"

"Who *are* you, girl?"

"Yeshiva girl gone wild."

They monopolized a white linen couch under a potted tree. They inched closer by the minute. Amazing how your knee in proximity to a special forbidden someone else's knee could bring you halfway to ecstasy.

"We're being conspicuous," Copeland said.

"Who cares," she said, trying it on for size.

"OMG, I LOVE YOU," a couple passersby stopped to tell Aviva. She smiled and thanked them graciously.

"Industry servants carrying water for the machine," she said when they moved on.

". . . While congratulating themselves for work they themselves haven't accomplished," Copeland added.

"And waiting with bated breath to find out whose ass they should get to work licking next."

As if on cue, here came Bobbi, an up-and-comer who used to fangirl out all over Aviva, and was now, surprise surprise, hitting it big. If a streaming app was asked to play some soothing music, Bobbi's signature weeper was lately top ten. Followers in the low seven digits, last time Aviva checked, which, fine, yeah: she checked. The algorithm *adored* this mediocre bitch. Aviva had a knack for rejecting groupies who later did well for themselves. Aviva enjoyed having her ass kissed—she was only human—but if she was going to mentor anyone she demanded nothing less than pure genius, and none of her groupies so far could hack it. Sue her: she didn't *want* to extend a hand to any old girl with a guitar. She wasn't going to pretend anyone was great if they were *not* great. (Was it better to be nice or to be honest?)

"Well, well, well," Bobbi said. "If it isn't Aviva Rosner. All hail the OG badass. So glad people are finally *noticing*."

"Bobbi."

"Don't get me wrong, *I* think you're awesome. *So* punk rock. That's always been your thing, right? So much more *boss* than everyone else. Not a *sellout* like the rest of us, right? The coolest. *Aviva*."

"Bobbi, you know what's so funny? My phone can somehow tell when I'm getting ready to take a shit. Must be a new operating system. It knows I like chill, not super-challenging music when I take a shit. And here's what's neat: it always suggests *you*! And I have to thank you, honestly, because the shits I have been taking while you're playing on my shitty little phone speaker are the *most* excellent shits. My sphincters just really *chill* when I hear your voice. Your music is really helping people."

"I can't believe I used to look up to you, cunt. Hey, Marcus. Huge fan. Let's get in the studio sometime."

"Call me." Copeland nodded.

They watched Bobbi disappear into the crowd.

"You don't play nice," Copeland said.

"Nah, see, 'cause I got the *goods*. You only gotta play nice if you ain't *got the goods*."

"Is that a Jesus quote?"

"That bitch is unbearable, man, please. How fucking soulless do you have to be to ruin a cover of 'Angel from Montgomery'? People just like her because she's so *vague*. *I miss walking in the hills with you stoned* is basically the only line, but she's young and cute and we *all* miss walking in the hills stoned with *somebody*, don't we?"

"A lot of folks just need music they can get wasted to."

"Well, well. Aren't we practical."

Yet another Amy remix came on. Who the fuck was DJing? Aviva hadn't heard this one before, but moratorium on the remixes, please. Give the girl a rest.

It was late, and the spell was broken. Copeland was looking at her with a world-weary elder vibe. Total yoni-killer.

Aviva glanced at her device. Yoni-killer number two.

And . . . a good-night text from Sam: yoni-killer number three strikes and we're out.

Two familiar groupies were hanging out by the hotel elevator, drunk as skunks, slurring and leering. They got excited when they saw Aviva: "OMG, I love you, Aviva! I fucking *love* you. I'm gonna make it back to my room, aren't I?"

"Yes, sweetheart, you are going to be in your room in just a few minutes."

"Good," said the groupie. "That's good. That's so, so good. I just love you SO so so so SO much! You RULE! I love you."

"I know you do, sweetheart," Aviva said. "And I, you."

See? She could play nice.

The groupies leaned into each other, kissed on the lips, touched tongues, took a selfie, shrieked. How long before one of *these* girls ruled the industry, sharing this very #throwback selfie to her millions of devoted followers, while Aviva was still rotting in some prestigious club somewhere, keeping it "real" at her own stupid, stubborn insistence?

Where was the elevator? And now—please, no—yet *another* Amy remix playing in the hotel lobby. *Please.* Mercy. Aviva ditched the wasted groupies and the promise of an elevator and ran up twelve flights of stairs to her room instead.

Party no fun without you, Copeland texted later, while Aviva was watching a shitty movie about a homely, sloppy, alcoholic slutbag comedienne who falls in love with a straight arrow and is reformed/redeemed.

Hotel room no fun without you, she replied.

Well we really bailed on the fun, then, didn't we?

She called good old Deja, tour manager extraordinaire, who was living with a new lover in Big Sky Country. The new lover had taken the cash from ten years of touring with an internationally huge girl band and bought herself a cabin on some land. The front woman of the internationally huge girl band had been an infamous narcissist from hell who didn't play an instrument. Deja's lover was going back to school to get her nursing degree so she could work as a home hospice aide.

"What am I *doing*, Dej?"

"Pushing boundaries. What you were put here to do."

"If you don't want to hear about this, if you feel like it's gross, I completely understand."

"No," Deja said. "I'm not the smartest, but I know about this. This is something I know about."

"I'm a terrible person."

"Nah, just human. We don't have enough immediate danger in our lives anymore, in this culture. We crave adrenaline. We crave adventure and newness and that sense of danger."

"Right? It's a drug."

Another call was coming in . . . Barb! Aviva hadn't talked to her mother in ages.

"If I had a daughter, I'd call her all the *time*," Aviva once bitched to the Rabbi.

"If you had a daughter, *mein kind*," said the Rabbi, "you would do a lot of things differently."

"So why don't I? Have a daughter."

"Because life isn't fair."

"*She* has a daughter."

"And she's never bothered to do much mothering, has she."

"She does blow a bit of cash on me from time to time. She can be really nice that way."

"Do you think that's what it means to be a mother?"

She dismissed Barb's call and continued with Deja.

"I can't ignore this. I'm, like, depraved. I need this. It's insane."

"Know the feeling."

"It is the single best fucking drug there is. I have been *craving* it. You don't *get* it in a long relationship, you just *don't*. I love my dude. I am happy with my dude. My dude is the best. But that feeling is just *gone*. I haven't had it in *years*."

"The newness only happens when it's new."

"I'm playing with fire."

"The ass is always greener. He's married, right? How many kids?"

"Two, according to Wikipedia. Wife's an actress. Or was."

"Gets real messy with the wives and the kids."

"You know the old movie *Same Time Next Year*? About the married people who have an illicit rendezvous just once a year and don't speak at all in the intervals?"

"Bougie fantasy."

"I know. But still. Why not? Why *not*?! It happens here, it stays here. It doesn't have to be a thing. It doesn't have to spill over. It's the road! It's sealed. No fallout. He goes on with his fucked-up little life, and I go on with mine. Do I sound like a sociopath? *Am* I a sociopath?"

"There are people who don't need it as much, this drug. They just don't care as much. Or they don't allow themselves to feel the need. Or they sort of beat it out of themselves with cake or wine or Facebook or pills. I envy those people so fucking much."

"The common folk? Don't envy them. I just need to roll around with this dude right now. I don't see the harm in, like, making out with him."

"Making out does seem harmless in the grand scheme."

"I need it."

"No spending the night," Deja said.

"Absolutely no spending the night."

"You do *not* want to wake up next to this guy in the light of day. Text me when you're going to sleep in your hotel room, alone."

"I'll say: 'The eagle has landed.'"

"Yeah, or: 'The eagle has flown into a jet engine.'"

"The eagle has been shot and stuffed."

"The eagle was very delicious in garlic and butter sauce."

Miami was Santa Monica on meth.

Day eighteen, and feeling herself *hard*. She opened her set with a surprise cover. Total reinterpretation. Made another Amy song come alive anew, so everyone could hear it again as though for the first time. Wipe all the god-awful remixes from memory.

Jerry was having none of it.

"She's been dead, what, twenty minutes? As if you could afford to approach with even the tip of your tongue the *anus* of the licensing fee on one of those songs. I'm hanging up now. Goodbye."

Well, fine. Maybe she'd pitch it to Mum at their rendezvous. *If* said rendezvous really did take place. If Mum was, by some miracle, actually *Mum*. Pops was the one who made the business decisions, however. And in theory it shouldn't be a problem for Aviva to get to Pops, because Pops was a dog. Just had to get in the same room with him and wear tight jeans, a nice bra. Cross her legs at the knee and then again at the ankle. The right lip color would alert his subconscious to the fact of her ravishing vulva. Dogs are the best: they'll do anything for treats. So freaking easy, at least while she still had the currency of youth. But Pops was proving unreachable. No social media presence, didn't respond to emails or calls to the Amy Foundation office, nothing. Not the most reliable dude in the world, it was true. Immortalized in song as, frankly, quite the piece of crap. Still, he'd been a prince in his daughter's eyes. True-blue daddy's girl, in spite of everything. And he sure did show up when the wind was in her sails, didn't he. Soon as she began to climb the charts, Pops was there faster than you can say ka-ching. Mindfuck, innit?

A journalist backstage complimented Aviva on the Amy cover.

"I thought I couldn't be more sick of that song, but you dusted it off, wow. Revelation."

And what would this journalist's shitty little blog post be titled? "Women Artists Having a Moment"? "Women Artists with Something to Say and It's About Time We Listen"? "Women Whose Music Matters Now"?

"I can see how you guys are in, like, conversation," the journalist went on. "You gonna do more with her?"

"For sure," Aviva said. "I'm in talks to get a bit of her DNA and see what we can do in terms of, you know . . . resurrection. They're doing it with dogs already, you know. And I want to use my womb in the service of music."

"Um-hm," the journalist said, looking over Aviva's shoulder in case someone more important was in the press tent.

"The voice will still be there—presumably it's genetic—but we're curious to see if we can socialize her so the addiction stuff plays out differently. We'll see what we can do to avoid some of the fundamental traumas and associations and body shaming and such. You know what Margaret Sanger said, right?"

The journalist had his eye on Bobbi, who was swanning past with an entourage.

"Pardon?"

"Margaret Sanger! Feminist icon! Birth control pioneer! Eugenics advocate!"

"I'm sorry, what does Margaret Sanger have to do with Amy Winehouse?"

"Oh *man*, what *doesn't* Margaret Sanger have to do with Amy Winehouse? Sanger said: 'When motherhood becomes the fruit of a deep yearning, not the result of ignorance or accident, its children will become the foundation of a new race.'"

"Okay . . . ?"

"Right? Kills me. Because when motherhood is *exclusively* the fruit of deep yearning, massive industries that profit off child-engineering will rise, the rich will abide, the poor will aspire, and the new race will have just as little clue about what it means to live in peace and harmony with their own and one another's bodies as did the old race, hobbled as it once was by the rules of ruthless biology. The law of unintended consequences: it's everywhere."

"Thanks so much for your time! Big fan." He sprinted off after Bobbi.

This time she and Copeland were straightforward. They skipped the party and took a walk through the city, winding their way back, inevitably, to their neighboring hotels. Copeland was in the four-star hotel, and Aviva in the three-star: blatant reflections of their respective industry status.

They sat on a park bench in a deserted square in Little Havana. He reached over and touched her hair so she felt her sex blossom into fourteen different luminescent shades of purple.

"I like your nose," he said, running a finger gently down the length of her significant schnoz.

"Do you."

"You're so beautiful," he said.

"Am I."

Beautiful: fine, great, whatever, sure. And if she happened to *not* be beautiful? What then? Should she throw herself off a goddamned overpass? It was none of Aviva's *business* whether or not she was "beautiful." It was not an *accomplishment* to be beautiful. That shit was *incidental*. And a trap, by the way! It was enough simply to be incarnated. Incarnation was notable and meaningful; beautiful was for dumb materialists. One *existed*; that had to be enough. And within existence, so much of interest to ponder. Such as: what beauty even was. Anyway, fuck taking pride in currency you have absolutely no part in creating.

Jerry had been brutally honest from the get-go: *You're not that cute, but you're sexy as hell. You're not pretty, but you have sex coming off you like smoke. They either have to want to be you or they have to want to fuck you, and if they want to fuck you then they're also kind of freaked out by you, but you can use that. That's how audience works. You've got a complicated appeal. No one wants to be you. You're not for everybody. But everyone will want to fuck you, because you're so fucking talented. So just keep doing your thing and eventually . . . trust me. Girls like you gotta get in through the side door. Slow build. And by the time everybody's listening to you, they'll think you've been there all along. Let people catch up to you, and they'll think they discovered you.*

"You're unlike anyone else," Copeland said.

"Aren't we all?"

A street person appeared, asked for a dollar.

"Your wife is extremely beautiful," he told Copeland while he waited for them to hand over some cash.

"Oh, we're actually both married to other people," Aviva said.

You never knew where you might find grace. The man shrugged, said thanks, and wandered off.

Copeland leaned over and grazed Aviva's collarbone with his lips like it was nothing, then they got up and continued walking in the general direction of the hotels.

They stopped in front of a newfangled donut shop. Tourist magnet, known for kitsch flavors like "NyQuil" and "Bacon Grease Froot Loops."

Aviva took Copeland by the hand and led him inside.

"These donuts look amazing, do they not?"

"They look . . . memorable."

"They smell good. I want some. We could get them and eat them, but we'd probably feel super gross and sick pretty soon thereafter, would we not?"

"We wouldn't feel great."

"Much like we could go back to my hotel room right now, but then regret it."

"Probably, yeah."

"Much smarter to leave the donuts alone. Steer clear."

But the donuts did look obscenely great. And a year from now, if they maintained generally healthy diets, eating those donuts won't have made much difference at all in the scope of their lives.

They walked on.

Two a.m., shoulder to shoulder on a deserted side street, leaning against the concrete wall of the three-star hotel, facing an old church across the street. The old church was out of place, now, with the buildings that had sprung up around it.

"What would you do to me," she whispered.

"I would take my time," he said. "I would just take a lot of time with you."

Her knees just about buckled. What could be more erotic for a bored, barren, almost-middle-aged bitch than the idea of a new man—a powerful man, a talented and vital and creative, brilliant man—taking his sweet *time* with her? She let out an involuntary sigh, high-pitched, the exact opposite of an *Om*. Every cell in her body buzzing. A person could die from an electrical current gone awry, but it had been so long since she had felt this. Dizzying. Delicious. What was life without this? It was nothing. It was death.

"Desire is *crazy*," she said.

"Desire *is* crazy," he agreed.

A producer they both knew, a solid family man, rounded the corner on his way back for the night. "Hey, guys," he said, averting his gaze as he kept on walking.

Aviva felt suddenly sapped. If Copeland pressed her up against the wall right this minute, she'd be helpless to resist, but it was two in the fucking morning and he was just talking, talking.

"Listen," she said. "Get out of here. Go to bed. It's not worth it. We could have an amazing night, but daylight would smack us both in the face and it would be ugly and sad and you'd go home to your crappy little life and I'd go home to my crappy little life and we'd both feel terrible and have to lie and compartmentalize and even if we wanted more there'd be no good way to continue it or end it and we'd be tormented and it's not worth it."

"I'd like to pause for a moment on the amazing night."

She refused to look at him. "Yes. It would be insane. But not worth it. Go home."

"You're right," he said. "You're right."

Just then, a taxi dropped someone at the hotel, and Copeland jogged over to flag it.

Aviva went inside, not looking back. Some boundaries-pushing rock star *she* was.

EAGLE HAS LANDED, she texted Deja. Then she spent the rest of the night writhing in pent up agony, tossing and turning, wanting him desperately, trying in vain to orgasm on her own. She could not come. She was so pent-up, she could not climax. This had never happened before. The sun rose orange through a crack in the blinds. She was so pent-up she couldn't even *pee*. At seven thirty, she caved, and texted him: No sleep.

Same, came his instant reply.

No orgasm.

Same.

Not for lack of trying.

Same.

It was unhealthy, this kind of pent-up energy. Thwarted desire. She could feel it, and understood that it was bad for her, this rejection of a powerful bodily urge. Henry Miller believed that repressed sexual energy caused cancer. The current was too strong. It didn't matter how good a swimmer you were in a current this strong. You had to surrender to it or die trying to go against it. Die either way, but at least don't die struggling.

I want u, she texted.

I'm dying, he said.

Come over.

When?

Now.

She stood against the far wall; he sat on the bed.

"Pants stay on," she said.

"Pants stay on," he agreed.

"In old Hollywood films, if there were two people on a bed, one of them had to have at least one foot on the floor."

In lieu of response, he placed a foot theatrically on the floor.

"This is the Jewiest illicit encounter ever," she said. "We should make a porno: hours of anxious discussion and we never touch. We could call it *Deep Jew*."

They remained on opposite ends of the room.

"You know what Lenny Bruce said about hotel rooms . . . 'It's just a bed.'"

"This is a parallel universe," she said. "Nothing here will have happened outside. None of this is happening."

"No confessions," he said. "No confidantes. No hurt feelings. No 'processing.'"

"No communication whatsoever," she said.

"I have a *very* jealous wife," he said.

"I wonder *why*."

She made her way, finally, to lay herself beside him. He sat up against the headboard. She propped herself up on her forearms and got acquainted with his scent.

"The light is falling so nicely here," he said, running his hand over her ass. She looked up at him. He smiled. She straddled him, took off her bra, and stuck her tits in his face.

"Get off me," he said, grinning, and got on top of her, wedging a thigh way up into her crotch. It had been a long time since her body had felt this . . . much.

Consequences? She didn't care. Impregnate me! Hurry, while there's time!! As simple and primal and unforgivable and retro as that, so very sorry not sorry. The unspeakable desire to be seeded by a great man in a hotel bed in the illicit morning light of a city not her own. (*Several* great men, why limit ourselves.) The desire to use her body in this way, to use it and use it and use it 'til it was all used up, and then onward, onward, to disintegration in the dirt, where her body would feed new life, where the worms and the bugs would consume her and shit her out so that this pile of matter absurdly known as "Aviva" could become nourishment for plants and fruits and fungi galore. One way or another, sooner or later, with or without any will or ego or insistence of her own, she would prove fertile ground, rich and abundant, rife with nutrients, busy with life. Fuck me, great man. Fuck me, universe. Caress me, earth. Fuck me, sun. Caress me, moon. I am yours, I belong to everything, I am the home of everything, the host of everything, the bearer of everything. And even in not-being I am an eternal source of being.

They made good on the pants rule, though after a while she did beg him to put his hand down hers. He knew exactly what he was doing, *damn*.

"More," she said, out of her mind on the drug desire.

He hesitated.

"I don't *care*," she insisted, eyes shut tight. "I don't care! I don't *care*."

He didn't move.

"I don't *care*," she said again. "I don't care I don't care I don't *care*." Firebomb her whole life. She just wanted to use and be used. Act and be acted upon. The body wanted what it wanted. Desire was *crazy*.

He backed up, no longer touching her. She opened her eyes. His were closed now.

"I don't *care*," she whispered.

"You *do*," he said "You do care."

He was right. At heart she was faithful. What a nerd, ultimately. She rolled over to the edge of the bed and covered her face with her hands. *Shit.* How good did *actual* nihilists have it?! What a divine thrill it must be to actually not care. What a breeze life would be. But fine, it was true: she did care. She goddamn cared. Put a quarter in the jukebox, friends, and let's hear it again: her greatest blessing and her greatest curse, one and the same.

She went to the bathroom and peeled off her undies. Took a while to pee, her body so confused and petulant. When she emerged, she tossed the panties at him.

"I'm assuming you'll want my soaking-wet panties for a souvenir."

He caught them one-handed, held them to his face, and inhaled deeply. With his other hand, he tap-tap-tapped at his device.

"I am now erasing the last text you will ever send me," he said.

She nodded. She was cool. No problem. All good.

He turned in the doorway before exiting, and pointed at her, grinning his stupid grin: "Don't you go putting me in no *song*, girlie."

Oh, dude. Oh, honey. Of *course* she's gonna put you in a song.

She climaxed long and hard alone in the airplane bathroom en route to Detroit. Completely out of control. Bingo: that pulsating throbbing electrical explosive vortex. A life of its own. Thank you, Copeland, for reminding her what that was like. Gratitude. Namaste. Desiring, being desired: purest primo intoxicants. How much power did she have over him? Was he thinking of her? What was the exact scope of her power?

She dreaded telling the Rabbi. She wanted him to be proud of her. How could he be proud of her now? She called from the smoothie place near her gate.

"Are you ready for this? This is a doozy."

"I'm ready."

She gave him a broad sketch. He was unflappable.

"The guy groomed you, Aviva. He's done this a hundred times before. Do you think you mean anything to him?"

"Well. I mean . . . We have a . . . sort of . . . special . . . connection."

"Riiiiiight. Sweetheart, he groomed you. And now he's testing you. This guy has a girl in every port. I'd stake my life on it. He's testing you now to see: Will you play it cool?"

This offended her. Yes, of course she would play it cool! She was the coolest! Unless . . . she wasn't capable of playing it cool. Unless she turned out to be one of those dorks who couldn't separate sex from emotion. Oh my God, she was one of those dorks who couldn't separate sex from emotion.

"It's been a very long time since I felt this way," she said to the Rabbi. "And I keep thinking: *This* is what you need to make a baby. This current. This electricity."

"How do you think Sam would feel if he knew?"

"He'd never look me in the eye ever again," she said. "And I'd hate myself forever."

"Maybe not forever, but for a long time."

"It's just—I cannot *tell* you what this felt like. I'm sorry, I don't want to hurt anyone. I love Sam. But this was something *else*. This was . . ."

"I understand."

"My whole body is still *shaking*, dude. This guy is, like, my soul mate."

"Suuuuuure," said the Rabbi. He rattled off a ton of classic TV couples— *Moonlighting, Cheers, Northern Exposure*—two people circle each other, flirting and sparring, sexual tension thick as fog. Then, finally, inevitably, they hook up and a billion people watch and the show is done for. Doesn't work when they get along. No spark. No frisson. No excitement.

"It's just the wanting that's alluring," he explained. "You once had that with Sam. We all have it in the beginning. But it's short-lived. You could chase it forever. Which is what your friend Copeland spends his life doing. And how many times has he been married, did you say?"

"According to Wikipedia . . . three?"

This time the Rabbi could not stifle his laughter.

"Okay," Aviva said. "I get it, I got it. But can I please just have like ten more minutes to enjoy my postorgasmic glow?"

"A man who marries his mistress creates a job opening, my dear. I suspect you'll be very glad you didn't go all the way."

"I don't think I've heard anyone use the expression 'go all the way' since I was about fourteen. You're adorable. Oh, and by the way, turns out there's some common but also sort of rare and harmful bacteria in my reproductive system. Dr. Michaels's office was good enough to let me know."

A woman who'd sold her eggs without informed consent and suffered terrible ongoing health trouble thereafter was testifying before her state legislature in an effort to get the state to better regulate the process.

Harmie Shmendrickson was at the Brooklyn Botanic Garden, and folks, Harmie Shmendrickson was *delighted* by the existence of flowers! Her smile looked like it was going to tear her very face in two.

A newly published memoir by one half of a former couple who had spent ten years trying to conceive only to finally succeed and then immediately break up and fight a horrific, endless custody battle over the two remaining embryos.

A forty-nine-year-old Oscar™ nominee with infant twin girls (gender selected and surgically removed at a precise hour on the cusp of Sagittarius for certain astrological blessings) was bravely speaking out against Botox and facial filler and "all that unnatural junk."

Gender-reveal fireworks gone awry in New Mexico! Twenty million dollars of damage, and one hundred acres of national forest burned to the ground.

Cracker was video trolling his daughter's nap, during which she was talking in her sleep. *Punk rock*, he observed.

The city rags were having a field day with a Brooklyn lady who had a five-year-old son borne of mucho cash and laboratory hijinks. The family had one embryo left, but it was a *female* embryo, and the five-year-old son was insistent on wanting a baby *brother*. So the mother posted to Craigslist in search of potential embryo trade: Did anyone want this top-of-the-line double-X-chromosome cell cluster?

Home to Sam, and they both took the recommended course of antibiotics.

The antibiotics made Aviva nauseous and depressed. Sam fared better, as per usual, because Sam had been breastfed and was metabolically better primed to handle whatever. Aviva lay in bed for days, out of it. She had been fed as an infant with Nestlé corn-syrup glue microwaved in plastic bottles. Her lips felt like they were going to detach. There was a strange sheen to her skin. She felt like she was walking alongside herself. Immediately after finishing the microbiome napalm, she came down with a grotesque virus. Which made her furious, and even more miserable. Better, perhaps, to have simply lived with the offending bacteria, of which she'd had no awareness whatsoever.

Day thirty-five, and the algorithm kept showing her ads for new, improved fertility vitamins; new, improved fertility-tracking systems; new, improved gadgets linked to the new, improved fertility-tracking systems. The walls were closing in.

Day thirty-six. Day thirty-seven. It was Infertility Awareness Day! Wow, a whole day. Cue the confessionals. Something about pineapples?

Harmony Shmendrickson was really into Magna-Tiles and had been gifted a deluxe set by her grandparents. Happy Harm!

The world was on fire, and Bobbi wanted to make sure we knew she knew it. Also! She had a new single streaming! Check it out!

An obituary: Patricia Frustaci, mother of the first septuplets to have been born in the US of A. Poor Patty had suffered barrenness for years, then had some good luck with the then-fashionable drug Pergonal. A son was born! Glory be. Then, less than a year later, more Pergonal and another pregnancy. But this time, the ultrasound showed seven fetuses.

Oopsie-daisy, way too many fetuses! Not an okay number of fetuses! The doctor advised the un/lucky couple to "selectively reduce," meaning abort at least four. The un/lucky couple refused on religious grounds. Interesting how nobody's ever too deeply religious to refuse the fucking drugs in the first place; they're only deeply religious when the fuckery *works*. Anyway, poor Patty. Poor everyone. About twenty-eight weeks into the pregnancy, four boys and three girls were surgically removed. One of the girls was stillborn. A boy died three days later. Another daughter and another son died a few months later. The three surviving babies went home with severe disabilities, in need of extensive care, physical therapy, and medical treatment. The Frustacis proceeded to sue the fertility doctor who oversaw their case. Eventually (more Pergonal!) they had *another* pair of twins. Then they got divorced. Oh, and also, Patty was apparently bipolar?

The obit ended with an update on the three adult surviving septuplets: one married and a mother herself now (yay!), one finally able to "live independently," and the third cared for full-time by his father. What was the moral of this story? What was the moral of any story? Why on earth would any self-respecting storyteller pretend there's any such thing as a moral to a story? How grotesquely condescending would *that* be? The whole world made up of stories, a blaring cacophony of stories, and every single one *subjective*; that's the whole comedy/tragedy of the whole insane race. Beware pyramid schemes, gurus, and morals.

"So," said Sam. "Now what?"

"Now we rebuild our microbiomes, I guess. And hope for the best. And get on with our lives."

"That's it?"

"I mean, or I go back to the suave doctor in the city and get on board with his plan, which, from what I gather, is the thing where they give me local anesthesia and shoot a 'harmless' chemical dye into my reproductive system to watch how things move."

Sam made a horrified face.

"Yeah, that's exactly how I feel."

"So you're not gonna do that."

"No, I am not gonna do that." She watched him closely for a sign that this was disappointing. "Maybe this bacterial thing we had—and let's be honest, we both know that it was probably me who gave it to you, and I apologize: you married a whore—but maybe now that it's gone, the whole thing will . . . resolve itself."

"The 'whole thing.'"

"The whole— Us. Becoming. A family."

"We're a family whether or not we have a kid, V."

"I mean, sure, whatever, yes. That's sweet of you to say. But I mean, you know, an actual family."

"We *are* an actual family, Aviva. You and me."

"I get that you have to say shit like that, and I appreciate it, it's nice of you, but please be real: without chilluns runnin' 'round to tend the farm and love up on us when we get old, there ain't too much point to the farm in the first place, bruh. Be real."

"'Bruh'?"

"Bruh."

"You know, the cult of the child is really only about a hundred and twenty years old, as an idea."

"Yeah, I took undergrad sociology, too, Sammy. Barren women are evil and unlucky; that shit's as old as the sun, but it hides in, like, 'classics' and 'religion.'"

"The idea of children as fulfillment of a sentimental ideal is really recent."

"Not in Judaism. It's all over Judaism. Children are the *future*, man."

"Well, yeah, Judaism is way beyond the rest of us."

"Maybe you might want to think about . . . converting. Only if you want to, though. They don't even let you unless you totally, totally want to. You'd get to dip in the mikvah. Wouldn't *that* be a great story: the pathetic, cursed couple who couldn't conceive, how they despaired, how they suffered, until BAM: the gentile ritually immersed."

"Would be a good story. But I don't think it works that way, babe."

"You don't know how it works. Nobody does. That's the problem. Or the solution."

"Did you have anything to eat today, babe?"

"Can we ease up on the 'babe'? It starts to sound kind of hostile after a while, don't you think? *Babe?*"

"Okay, babe. Okay."

The bleed. A fresh disappointment each and every time. A brand-new dimension of sorrow, *every time*. You'd think it'd flatten out. You'd think it'd get monotonous and boring. The predictability, the repetition. But there's fresh loss, somehow, every time. A whole new dimension of brand-new sorrow each and every time, and no two ever alike. It's like how people talk about loving all their many children equally, if not the same. Your heart *grows* and *expands*, people always beam and crow. *You have an infinite amount of love! Each child only adds more love. I had no idea I could love so much!*

Aviva would have to take their word for it on all that alleged infinite multiplication of love, all those preening fucking parents, but so it went with the downward spiral of yet another barren cycle. Who knew a person could grieve this much? Her grief just kept growing, expanding, multiplying! An army of grief. A multitude of ghostly, sorrowful issue. She carried an infinite expansion of grief within, see, and that's what we call *irony*. Isn't life a gas?! Maybe she should begin to give her absences *names*, draw herself a family tree of nonentities.

Not a crowd-pleaser, this story. How many more cycles left until it was over for good?

Hey, "God"? By which is meant "universe"? By which is meant "storyteller"? How about giving this pitiful bitch a flippin' baby? Just let her have her stupid baby! Then the *real* comedy/tragedy can begin, the one in which she finds out that there are whole new realms of Christlike suffering reserved exclusively for those who truly, deeply love and are selflessly devoted to their all-too-mortal children. Just let her have her baby? Let's go. Please? She's done her time!

The bleed. The end.

(Nope: the beginning.)

8.

FASHION

"Reason for your visit to the UK?"

"Work."

"What kind of work?"

"I'm a singer."

Passport control looked at her like, Sure, who isn't?

"I'm a *musician*," she amended. Six dates at intimate venues in England, four in Ireland, two in Scotland. A girl and her guitar in a country not her own. Oh, and dinner with Barb, who happened to be en route to Israel for an interfaith mission, and was spending a few days in London to ease the jet lag.

"Where will you be staying? What's this address?"

"Camden. A friend's place."

An Airbnb, actually, for a week of indulgent hang time, on her own dime, before the shows.

"And what else will you be doing while you're here?"

"Soaking up the vibe."

Passport control exhibited the faintest shadow of a smile.

Aviva's long-awaited date with honest-to-goodness Mum was scheduled for the day after tomorrow, but that was none of passport control's business. Anyway, in all probability she was being pranked, and the Mum thing would end in disappointment and humiliation. Some dryly cruel

British reality show specializing in luring dumb Americans into fake encounters with public figures and/or their bereaved survivors. Was that too cruel even for British humor? Why on earth would the real Mum (Mum!) agree to meet?

The official waved Aviva through.

Her suitcase didn't turn up at bag claim.

The carousel turned and turned, emptied out, and ground to a halt.

At the office, a teenager gave her a form to fill out. "They'll usually call you within twenty-four hours with an update on its whereabouts. If you bother them they'll give you an allowance to buy yourself necessities in the meanwhile. Squeaky wheel gets the grease."

So Aviva set off into the foreign night with nothing but her guitar, shoulder bag, and the clothes on her back. What was the point of bringing stuff anywhere, anyway? You never knew what the weather was going to feel like until you were in it, and over the time it took to cross any distance whatsoever you became a different person, with different needs and different wants.

She paid a small fortune in advance for a taxi, too beat to deal with public transport. The driver, in his shiny dark suit, looked a lot like Amy's favorite lead backup singer: tall, bald, bright smile. Aviva involuntarily entertained the notion of fucking him. They drove for the better part of an hour before anyone spoke.

"Long drive," Aviva said.

"Talking to me?"

"Yeah. Long drive."

"London's a big town. I like driving, though."

"Good thing!"

"I like meeting people from all over the world."

"Yeah, that must be cool."

"You, where are you from?"

"New York."

"Ah," he said. "New York! I've never been to the US."

"It's very large."

"Yes, very." His eyes darted up at her in the rearview. "And what brings you the UK? Vacation?"

"Work," she said.

"What kind of work you do?"

"I'm a musician."

His eyes were big. "Ah yes, you are traveling with the guitar!"

"Wandering minstrel." Wandering menstrual, more like.

"Wow," he said. "I think it was good that I got to drive you tonight. I have a feeling about you. I am a musician, too!"

"What do you play?"

"I write songs on the computer. The computer plays them for me."

"Cool."

"You don't like computers?"

"No, I mean, I like them . . . sometimes. Not all the time. Or maybe I'm afraid I like computers too much."

The flash of his eyes in the rearview again.

"I like to feel the vibration of the instrument against my body," Aviva said. "And the human voice. I like bodies, vibrations, you know. Machines . . . I don't know. They're okay. I guess. They're fine. I flew here in one, didn't I. We're riding in one. They are useful. I appreciate their utility."

"Human is made in the image of God," he said.

"So they say."

"But machines are made from human mind."

"That's the thing. Can we be trusted?"

"No choice!" He laughed.

The eye spark in the rearview again; was sex maybe so dangerous and wild and serious and powerful that we are maybe even collectively better *off* avoiding its organic physical pull? Better off masturbating in private to visual stimulation provided by armies of the virtual enslaved, reproducing in laboratories, only daring to look into one another's eyes through screens? Maybe these things have evolved to our benefit. Safe-guards.

More silence, until Aviva asked: "What's your favorite part of London?"

"Southeast," he said. "It's full of nightclubs. I club a lot. I love to club. I used to, anyway. I don't so much anymore. I am a changed man."

"What changed?" She expected to hear about a wife, a child.

He shrugged. "Age."

"Time!" She laughed. "Oh yeah. Let's hear it for time."

"Time," he said. "Yes."

Time and weather: it had taken on a life of its own, like flour and yeast and water and egg in her practiced hands. She knew how to work it, what it should feel like, how much more and of what it needed, before leaving it under a damp cloth to rise. Soon she'd put it into the oven and bake until golden. Nothing we can do about time and weather, time and weather, coming for you. Nothing to be done about time and weather, time and weather, nothing to do.

"I like to sing, also," the driver said. "I am just shy, and the computer is not shy."

"No, the computer is mos def not shy. The computer knows no shame. It's hard to sing with a real voice," Aviva said. "Takes practice to find it, even."

"But it heals the soul," he said.

"I hate when people say, 'I can't sing,' or 'I don't have a good voice.' That's such bullshit."

"Nobody has a bad voice! It is how you use it."

"Exactly. Some just refuse to use it. And what can you do about people like that? Or the ones who won't dance because they're afraid of looking stupid. Isn't that the saddest? Bums me out. Such an honor to have a voice and a body in the first place, don't you think? And then to not use it . . ."

Eyes in the rearview again. "Yes," he said.

They drove the rest in silence, and when he pulled up in front of the address, he asked her to autograph his business administration textbook. "Anywhere you like is fine."

Inside, on almost every page, were drawings, beautiful little studies in blue ballpoint. Aviva lingered over them.

"Did you do these?"

"Yes, I draw whenever I can."

"Renaissance man!"

He beamed. "I have a feeling about you." He glanced up at the dilapidated apartment building. "You sure you're okay here?"

"Oh yeah, they left me a key under the mat."

He looked doubtful, but drove off when she waved from inside the vestibule.

Say goodbye to your daddy, she told the nonexistent girl army who lived in merciless purgatory at the margins of consciousness, just for the sour enjoyment of envisioning their dumb faces collectively crumpling.

The Airbnb turned out to be a dumpy studio on the third floor of a water-damaged building. There was wall-to-wall carpeting, on top of which lay a huge shag rug, like sinking your feet into a dirty mop. Air quality like an endocrine disruptor's flatulent asshole. Potpourri and "air fresheners" everywhere. Enough scented candles to permanently disable the ovaries of Gaia herself, but not quite enough to cover the stench of mildew. The pasty young couple who made their home here grinned in a dozen framed photos. They owned four board games, zero books, and a flat-screen. (Unfair. Upon closer inspection there were exactly three books: *You Are a Badass*, *Harry Potter* number four, and *The No-Fuss Housewife Saves the Day*.)

Aviva slept for nine hours and woke with no clue where she was, and diarrhea. Her throat was on fire, her mouth dried out, and a raging headache hammered at her skull. Dehydrated and/or dying.

There was a text from Mum: Could they postpone their date until later in the week, please? She was very sorry, but her MS was flaring up and she needed to rest. Poor Mum! If Mum turned out to be a fiction, so be it. Aviva's expectations were as low as could be. She didn't *want* anything from Mum. (Was that true? Was that possible? *Was* there such a thing as a human interaction that didn't involve want or need or exploitation or violation of some sort?) Hey, family of dead celebrity, I'm aimlessly sniffing around because that's what creative people sometimes do, but don't worry, dinner's on me!

No word from the airline regarding her suitcase. She dialed the hotline and got the runaround en route to a nonmachine.

"How can I help? Hello? I can barely hear you," said the nonmachine. "Can you speak up? What is the claim number? *Nine-oh*, you said? Okay, let's have a look. Yes, well, it seems that your suitcase went to . . . Florida. We believe it's there now, although there has been a delay in confirmation from that office."

"How is that possible? I flew JFK to London direct!"

"It happens, unfortunately. Your voice is quite—I'm having a *very* hard time hearing you. But I can assure you, we're doing our best. We do offer a stipend for necessities. We appreciate your patience. For international inconveniences, we can offer fifty dollars."

Fifty dollars wouldn't go far with Aviva's taste in clothes. She needed her armor! Her comforts! Her impeccably curated stash of sartorial anti-depressants! Her well-honed personas! Defenses, costumes, quirks, communiqués! She needed her stuff. Her aesthetic arguments. She felt naked in some deeper, metaphorical way, stripped of her stuff. Her clothes.

"It's just that I'm *pregnant*," Aviva said, "and I have some . . . special . . . *medication* in there that I, like, really *need*."

"Oh. Oh dear."

"And I'm scared I might lose the baby if I don't get my stuff back as soon as possible."

"Oh— That's— I'm— Please hold."

Just because Aviva couldn't pull off the whole Miraculous Origin and Sustainer of Life thing in reality didn't mean she didn't deserve to be treated like a goddamned queen. Bow down! She was beatific as *hell*. Those self-satisfied bitches with their mediocre artless vanloads of offspring, burning up the planet with new mouths to feed and packaged food and family vacations and wrapping paper and new bikes and social media tripe, all that self-satisfied Wooo-hooo look at meeeee I'm responsible for a whole new generation of emotionally crippled chronically depressed attachment-starved oxytocin-deprived fucking sheep who live inside their screens, aren't I *special* . . . ! Sorry, where were we? Right: on hold with a call-center employee who would no doubt be suddenly willing to move heaven and earth in service of a *pregnant lady*. Fertility may indeed be sacred, but only insofar as it takes place safely within the ruling class.

"Ma'am? We've located your bag. It *is* in Fort Lauderdale—a long story, but there's been some trouble with the baggage handlers at JFK. Utilizing a few connections, we think we can have it in London in about twelve hours. I've marked it highest priority. Our delivery service will drive it directly to your address, no charge, and I'm going to give you a special number you can call to track the whereabouts of the item in transit. We are going to resolve this as quickly as possible, and we sincerely apologize for the inconvenience. And for your trouble we'll be offering you an increased stipend of two hundred dollars."

"Let's just pray the baby hangs on."

Camden was buzzing with tourists, pubs, and young, attractive vagrants. It was like some sort of Amy-themed amusement park. It was ground zero. The girl was *everywhere*. On the side of a building, rendered in psychedelic rainbow, twenty feet high. On rows upon rows of T-shirts for sale. On magnets, curling her lip. Keychains, in silhouette. Huge, laser-cut earrings in the shape of stilettos, with her dates and RIP in script. Posters upon posters upon posters. The girl was everywhere. No, the *persona* was everywhere; the girl was long gone.

Aviva roamed the Stables in search of the recently unveiled Amy statue, the precise location of which Aviva's handheld computer refused to disclose.

Along the way she spent her lost-luggage stipend (and then some) on a tooled leather purse from Morocco, a pair of purple angora harem pants from Nepal, a vintage abstract Hermès scarf in vivid orange and cobalt blue, a pair of wide, thin silver hoop earrings, and a crop top with Amy's cartoon face on it.

And what costume shall the poor girl wear to all tomorrow's parties?

"I like your Diana Ross hair!" a gutter punk hollered.

Aviva curtsied.

The question, as ever: Who did she want to *be*? Rockability princess? Punk goddess? Pretty lady? Basic bitch? Earth-mother yogi? Arty femme? Arty butch? Arty queer? Arty asexual? Liberated whore? Enslaved whore? Tribal chic? ALL OF THE ABOVE. Refuse to choose. Let "nothing to wear" be as dumb and apocryphal as the idea of "writer's block" or "I can't sing" or "I don't dance" or "If so-and-so doesn't love me back I'll *die*." Always, always something new and interesting to wear, lyrics burning to be written, a song demanding to be sung. Swing in her hips a given. Always the promise of getting over some asshole who'd never deserved her in the first place, because the world was full of exciting *new* assholes.

Here was a stall with nouveau-vintage-street-wear-skate-punk-yoga stuff, like what you might wear if you were the empress's right-hand woman in a dystopian future. No garment made any sense on its own, but if you layered them thoughtfully, you might resemble the doomed planet's assistant shaman. Aviva alighted upon an oversized deconstructed sweatshirt, perfect for lounging *or* wearing as a minidress with, oh, say, boots and black lipstick and the huge silver hoops and the vintage scarf as a headwrap. Oh yes. The sweatshirt was emblazoned with a delicate pattern that turned out, when you looked closely, to be made up of a thousand little pills. Fashion as literal medicine. Swipe of plastic and it was hers.

They'd dressed their baby girl beautifully, good old Chuck and Barb Rosner. Like a doll, in tailored little jumpsuits and dresses with whimsical details and patterns. Liberty prints. Eyelets. Corduroy. Smocking. Classic attire, fit for nobility. Hand-stitched embroidery, covered buttons, puff sleeves. Their handsome dark-eyed clever little girl. They dressed her up like a dolly because that's what it must have meant to them to have a little girl. No stained hand-me-downs or dirty naked joy for *their* little love object. Their dolly's job was to reflect nicely back upon *them*, reinforcing *their* superficial values. And what happened when their lovely dolly hit puberty and turned into a literal fucking monster? What did they do when their elaborately outfitted little dolly girl sprouted scary-big lopsided titties and a full goatee and a face full of pimples, her hair turned frizzy and unmanageable, to say nothing of the fact that she suddenly had some opinions and feelings and ideas and interests and observations of her *own*? Why, Chuck took the back exit and was rarely heard from thereafter. And Barb? Barb got to *work*: put that monster on synthetic estrogen and made her eat nothing but grapefruit and cottage cheese, even though the pantry also happened to be stocked with all manner of "low-fat" processed sugar garbage and those very exciting new potato chips containing a chemical that supposedly made fat melt out of your gut, but actually just gave people such life-threatening diarrhea that eventually the FDA got around to banning it. Good *Lord*, in any case: Barb *regulated* that monster. Regulated her *but good*.

And what of the monster? She was supposed to recognize herself as such, accept her lot, be a good girl, and either shut the fuck up or kill herself (which is another way of shutting the fuck up). If your creators don't love you, no one ever will. She was supposed to build herself a house of shame. She was *not* supposed to start cultivating style, giving zero fucks whether you understood or could contextualize her. She was *not* supposed to pick up a guitar and teach herself some chords, and open up her big fat ugly Jew mouth to *sing*. She was not supposed to emerge with grit and humor and grace. Style is what one does when one *has no choice*. Style is never borne of ease or entitlement. Style comes from when they wish you were dead but you refuse to die.

"Hey Little Rich Girl" by the Specials blasted over the sound system as Aviva shook her ass down another row of stalls. What she coveted now was a pair of delicate pink ballet slippers. Real ones, not dumb common "ballet flats." The kind of actual satin slippers Amy had favored when she wasn't torturing herself in those moronic Betty Boop heels.

And where the heck was that Amy statue, anyway?

A pair of policemen came ambling along, both gorgeous and built, practically glowing in a nicely coincidental shaft of sunlight.

The evasive little brat army, dejected in the margins of Aviva's consciousness, perked up, and commenced shrieking: Ooooh, Them! How about them? Them! Themmmmm!!

It occurred to Aviva that she was really going to miss the feverish drive of her sex when it began, at some point in the hopefully still distant future, to fade out.

"Excuse me, officers, but do you know where I might find the Amy statue?"

"This actually isn't our usual beat, madam, so we're just as much tourists here as you."

They wandered on, and the evasive little brat collective sighed theatrically, but she treated them to a delectable vegan hot dog with all the toppings, and then she purchased a boatneck tee depicting Rosie the Riveter as a skeleton. *We Can Do It!* . . . Meaning, what, *die* someday? Indeed: we *can*!

Around another corner, there it was: the statue.

Just the evasive brat Aviva had come to see. Schnoz was a good likeness, but the upper curve of the lip was off, and the angle of chin was wrong. Someone had placed neon orange mirrored sunglasses on her face, and she wore wreaths of cheap bead necklaces.

Face-to-face with the patron saint. Well, face-to-chest, because the monument was life-sized. So petite. Cast in iron. No pedestal. Feet firmly planted on the ground, albeit in those dumb stilettos. This was how short she was?! The tiniest. Aviva towered above her, could look down at the top of the foot-high beehive. Aviva could've placed her tits on either side of Amy's wicked schnoz and orchestrated a proper motorboat if she'd wanted to! (She did kind of want to.) She set down her shopping and made herself at home on a bench to see what this statue's daily life was like.

People put their arms around it, took selfies. People smiled in passing, made lewd jokes, broke into song. Rehab? No. Rehab? No. Rehab? No. Lots of folks wanted a picture with the infamous little lady, who stood there un-ruffled, hand on hip, the set of her mouth not quite right. Two little boys dutifully posed for their father.

"Smile!" said the father. "Say 'Junkie'!"

"Junkie," the boys obeyed.

"It was actually alcohol, sir," Aviva called out. "She had kicked the hard drugs."

"Say 'Alkie,'" the father amended.

"Alkie," the boys chorused.

During a tourist lull, Aviva approached. Without thinking, or she surely would have censored the impulse, she leaned down and softly pressed her lips up against the metal cheek. It was cold. It was not skin. It was not even wood or stone. It was many, many, many human revolutions removed from Genesis. It wasn't even something humans could directly make by hand. It was made by something made by something made by humans. But it was going to last a very long time. Longer than flesh, of course, and longer than wood, and longer, probably, even, than stone.

She eased the sunglasses off and understood why some true-blue apostle had put them there in the first place: the eyes were fixed. Dead. Empty. You don't leave dead eyes staring, startled, into the void of eternal everything-ness. You cover dead eyes. Out of respect. A mercy.

Some fertility doctor in California was liking all of Aviva's bullshit lately. Why on earth?! The doc's feed consisted of: 1. Ultrasound and postsurgi-cal images of uterine fibroids and polyps and compromised fallopian tubes, as a sort of public service announcement/consciousness-raising effort, with hashtags up the ass, 2. Elaborate omakase meals, shot up close, which strangely echoed the ultrasound and postsurgical photos of fucked-up fe-male reproductive organs, 3. The doctor with her #girlsquad, a gang of similarly coiffed and made-up Asian ladies, all in the same identical side-turn, hand-on-hip, shoulders-lifted, elbows-out pose. Was there some kind of aversion therapy behavior modification happening with this pose? Did someone *beat* the women who didn't assume this precise pose the moment there was a camera nearby? Was there some kind of electrical device implanted in these bitches' *brains* to enforce this pose? And 4. Photos of expensive gifts from grateful new parents: Boxes from Tiffany, Cartier, Geary's, Christofle, Gucci, Prada, Hermès. Luxe bouquets of roses, peonies, orchids. Champagne by the case. Lucky me, she hashtagged. I love my patients! Grateful doctor! Medicine! Health! Fertility! IVF! Pineapples! Happiness! Babies! Trying! Cycles! Twins! Twin magic! Multiples! Mamas! Mama love! Blessed!

A highbrow glossy magazine feature about women over forty having babies. "At this age," quoth a chic gallery owner, "I feel like we have a better sense of who we want our children to *be*."

A nine-year-old whose case had been a watershed for the surrogacy industry died yesterday. A hetero couple had paid a surrogate to carry this child. The maternal DNA had come from a fourth-party "donor." All fun and games until, in the second trimester, an ultrasound revealed severe birth defects—several organs in the wrong places, heart malformed, brain malformed. The customers—er, parents—wished to return the item—er, terminate the pregnancy. But the surrogate refused. So they offered her an extra ten grand if she would agree to terminate. Still, she refused. "I just felt really protective," the surrogate recalled. Many lawyers got all sweaty and pissed, but the legalities were, of course, muddy, profitable technology having long since left legal ethics or moral frameworks in the dust. The customer/parents decided that, fine, the surrogate could go ahead and birth this doomed baby, but since they were the legal owners—er, parents—they would then immediately surrender the monster to become a ward of the state, whereupon it would be institutionalized, and then they could simply walk away, unburdened by the imperfect creature of their own design. But the surrogate—wow, what a badass (or, you know, nuts)—crossed state lines to birth the child in a jurisdiction where *she* would be considered the child's legal mother. Then she gave up the child for adoption, and some saintly adopter of severely disabled children adopted the child, who underwent a hell of a lot of surgery in her short life, and who never learned to walk or talk, but who did learn to communicate effectively via sign language and emerged as a spirited "force of nature." "She was the heart and soul of our family," quoth the adoptive mom. "She lived her life to the fullest. She loved cuddles and hugs and music. She was always the first to comfort anyone who was sad or hurting. We will miss her terribly."

The shit-for-brains comedienne wanted everyone to know that we women aren't *alone* and we should all, liiiiiike, *support* one another because being a woman is *hard* and b.t.*dubs* she had just frozen seventeen eggs and was still *super* high on whatever they had used to sedate her but oh-em-geeeee, she's, like, totes *obsessed* with her doctor u guyzzzz!

Sextuplets were born in Alabama! Their names were River, Styx, Stallion, Seahorse, Radar, and Rascal, and they were all in the NICU indefinitely.

Ooh, and what was this? Some geneticists in a Siberian lab seem to have accidentally created a hybrid between a sturgeon and paddlefish! They weren't even aware it was possible! Color them surprised! Isn't science amazing? They assumed this hybrid fish, yet to be named, would be sterile, because offspring from two different species, such as horse and donkey (or, say, Chuck and Barb Rosner), is usually infertile.

Mule can't birth shit.

An Amy exhibit, curated by her loyal brother, up at the Jewish Museum. Big bro had collected a number of his famous dead sister's personal effects, and offered up his own loving narrative. Portrait of a nice Ashkenaz gal gone completely off the fucking rails.

Should Aviva eventually kick the bucket before *her* brother, Mike would no doubt spend the rest of his time on earth telling anyone who'd listen what a mentally ill piece of shit she'd been.

The gallery was empty except for Aviva. The walls were blush pink. Photos and dresses and heels and notes and artifacts were arranged artfully behind glass. A couple guitars. A mannequin in a miniskirt, a microphone stand. Snapshots and press portraits and rejected album cover shoots. A CD mix made for a friend, titled *Human Blues*.

Aviva flagged a docent.

"Excuse me, but is there any way you might be able to show me this object?"

She needed to see the track list. What kind of curator wouldn't have realized the track list was all that mattered about this object?!

The docent said no, unfortunately, there was not an interactive component to this exhibit.

On the way out was a small table with stacks of Post-it notes, a dozen Sharpies, and an invitation to share your thoughts. A ten-foot stretch of wall was already covered: *Too bad she was so self-destructive. Beautiful angel! Idiot killed herself. Best songs ever. Wasted talent. Disturbed Jewish girl. Mental illness is bad. Such heart and soul! Tragic genius. AMYYYYYYY. Drugs are terrible! Thank you for the music. Just say no. Leave the poor girl alone. I love you so much. Beautiful singer. Baby girl.*

Barb at the Tate Modern.

"What's the matter with you? You look terrible. What's happened to your voice?"

"Little under the weather."

Aviva felt, in fact, like the bottom of a shoe, but there was no use being needy or vulnerable around Barb.

"Gonna be hard to do your little shows if you have no voice."

"Oh, wow, I hadn't thought of that."

They went their separate ways in the permanent collection. Barb was only interested in any given museum's café and gift shop, but get her in a gallery and she'd study every last word on every last placard so that she could lecture you on the objective merits and sociological significance and methodology and context of everything on view. In other words, she sucked all the joy and art out of art and joy.

Aviva preferred to drift and absorb. If she didn't learn everything or see everything or know everything, okay. There was an element of faith at play. She'd see what she saw.

When she tired of looking at things, she squatted against the cool brick wall underneath a fifteen-foot-tall Louise Bourgeois *Maman*, taking succor and rest. No one fucked with a fifteen-foot-tall spider. She was debating whether or not she felt crappy enough to justify resting her head against the nice smooth stone floor and just curling up right there for a brief nap when a security guard marched over and told her to get up.

He was mildly cute, compact, young-ish, with kind eyes.

"We ask that patrons use the benches, ma'am."

"Forgive me," Aviva said. "I'm just—pregnant, so I get tired, you know?"

He lit up, as delighted to hear this news as if it were his own seed taking root within her.

"My *wife* is actually expecting right now, as well," he said.

Team procreation! They high-fived in the echoing hall, under Bourgeois's massive eight-limbed matron. His wife was a bit farther along than Aviva, judging by the looks of it. His wife was, in fact, about ready to "pop"! Which was an adorable way to describe the process by which a person with female reproductive capacity safely passes, through the pelvis, cervix, and vulva, ideally without fear or intimidation or misinformation or nonconsent or time constraints or literal constraints, a new human being.

The plan was to get Barb good and soused before depositing her back at her hotel. Not that Barb needed convincing.

"Vodka tonic," she told the waiter even before taking off her jacket.

"Same," Aviva said, though she had no intention of drinking it. Old spy technique: let Barb get shit-faced and loose-lipped, sink some ships. Aviva's drink would stay miraculously full.

The menu looked delicious, they agreed. They discoursed upon each other's outfits, discussed the province of each accessory. They made comment on respective hairdos, including past and possible future cuts. After the server took their food orders, Barb asked for another drink and cut the shit.

"*Here's* something that's going to *really* drive you *nuts*. Are you ready? Remember your friend Jenny?"

"There are such a shitload of Jennys, Mom. Can you be more specific?"

"*Jenny!* From that *theater* thing. You guys were thick as thieves! You wanted me to drive you to Redondo *Beach* that one time, and I said absolutely *not*. Who lives in Redondo *Beach*? *Honestly*. You went your separate ways, but *Jenny* went to UCLA undergrad and dated the oldest *Applebaum* boy, while he was in *law* school! They went out for *years*. His mother was practically planning the *wedding*! She was *very* upset when they broke up, but then he married a gorgeous girl from San *Francisco*, *very* wealthy, and everyone was happy. Meanwhile, *they* have three of the *most* beautiful little boys I have ever laid *eyes* on, frankly."

"I'm sorry, who are we talking about and why am I supposed to give a shit?"

"Your friend *Jenny*. From the—what was it called? That theater club you loved. Well, it turns out, after she broke up with the Applebaum boy *she* married a *very* nice young man whose family has been part of my synagogue for *years*! So who do you think turned up at services last week?"

"Jenny."

"With, are you ready? *Newborn twins!* Do you believe that? What a small world! Anyway, I *knew* you would absolutely *hate* hearing about it. I know how you feel about the twins business. But there was a *lovely* baby naming and the grandparents sponsored a *very nice* Kiddush. What a gorgeous family. Two little baby girl twins, one very fair and one very dark. I mean: one with a full head of black hair and one just totally peachy and pink and bald. They don't even look *related*. *Wow*, does your friend Jenny have her hands full. They have plenty of help, though. Another *very* wealthy family. Anyway, Jenny knew exactly who I was, and came over and asked about *you*. She said she *follows* you. She said I must be *so* proud. I said to be honest I'd be a *lot* prouder if I was sponsoring Kiddush to celebrate the naming of *your* twins!"

Aviva took a fake sip.

"*Joking*, Aviva, *joking*. Don't get upset! I am *very* proud of you. You know that. But, *anyway*, turns out Jenny is still friends with the Applebaum boy she dumped, so he and *his* family were at the Kiddush, too. With those *gorgeous* boys of theirs—I'm not kidding when I tell you I have *never* seen such beautiful children in my *life*. But, you know, the *middle* Applebaum boy, it's really terrible, he married a nice girl from the Valley and they had a *lot* of trouble, tried *everything*. Complete nightmare. It almost bankrupted them, frankly. It's not funny. Why are you laughing? They almost had to sell their *house*. Eventually they gave up and adopted. A toddler. From China. *Terrible* idea, if you ask me. That just *never* works out. They're going to have a *mess* to deal with. That *never* works out."

"I think it works out sometimes."

"Never. It *never* works out. You have no idea what you're talking about. It's a complete disaster."

Aviva followed all the Applebaum boys *and* their boring-ass wives, so she knew most of this bullshit already. Middle Applebaum, the new adoptive father, had actually been her first sexual experience, not counting the Beverly Hills pediatrician who'd fingered her at every checkup from age seven to seventeen.

Middle Applebaum, though, *damn*, what a cutie. She recalled one particular Friday-night dinner at his house. All the adults downstairs doing some spirited, extended Birkat while she and middle Applebaum were upstairs in his room with the dormer window, all silent and giggly, full of electric mutual understanding. She remembered sitting on his lap, fully clothed, feeling his erection up against her ass crack, their arms wrapped lightly around one other. Nothing more. No big thing. Consensual. Sweet. They were in different grades at different schools: she a sixth grader, he an eighth. They never ran into each other in daily life. It didn't go anywhere.

But Barb was now staring at Aviva, eyes full of tears.

"What, Barb."

"I want to say something, Aviva, and I hope you won't get angry with me. You're always getting so *angry* at me. I really think Mike is right and you might have a bit of a *problem* with *anger*. But this is what I would like to say to you; just try to hear me out: I think that you are going to be very, very sorry if you don't have children. You are going to regret it for the rest of your life if you don't have children. It's all fun and games now, I know, I know, all your music and traveling and whatever it is that you do, but it's going to get old. Nobody wants to see an old lady singing. A day is going to come when you're going to be very, very sorry you never had children."

Isn't it funny how the worst people in the world are always the most full of advice? Aviva nodded slowly, like this was something new to consider. She took another fake sip.

"I know what you mean. Without kids, I just don't know what my life *means*. Whomever can I harangue and manipulate? I guess some *animals*, maybe. I'm going to have to figure out a way to eviscerate *some* vulnerable creature's soul."

"You don't have to get *angry*, Aviva, for heaven's *sake*. You have a real problem with *anger*. I just remember how you were as a little girl, with your dolls. Do you remember all your dollies? You were *such* a good mommy to all your dollies. You were a *natural*."

"Cabbage Patch Kids, oh my God. I wanted to visit that factory in the worst way. You could pay to watch them being born! From cabbage!"

"You were meant to be a mommy."

"You even got official adoption papers for those things. You had to fill out *paperwork*. What the fuck is it with little girls and dolls? And big girls and babies. *Christ.*"

"And do you remember *my* doll? Elizabeth Ann?"

"Of course, here we go. What was she made out of? Wood, right? With those real eyelashes and the glass eyes that rolled back in her head. She scared the shit out of me."

"She was a huge deal. She was a very big deal. Grandma and Papa gave her to me for my eighth birthday, but they barely let me touch her. She was *expensive*."

"Didn't you give her to *me*? Isn't she technically *mine*?"

"Why do you think I was so happy to have a daughter?! I wanted someone to give her to!"

"That's lovely."

"I'm actually having her refinished. I found a guy in Chicago who specializes in her, exactly her. There aren't many of her *left*. In the *world*. He even offered to buy her from me, and you would not *believe* how much he was offering. She is *rare*. But I'm having her refinished to give to Jazzy."

"But you already gave her to *me*! She's *mine*!"

Barb shrugged as if to say: you are a dead end, and as such do not count.

"Are you going to let Jazzy actually have her? And, like, touch her?"

"Probably not! She's worth a fortune!"

Dinner was cleared away. Did they want dessert? No, but a third vodka tonic for Barb, please. And another for Aviva, too, why not. The waiter winked, noticing her first was still full.

"Mom, you remember my rag doll Sweetie? In the white dress with pink roses? And sleeping eyes and the little smile and the yellow yarn hair? Is she still around somewhere? Do you know where she is?"

"Oh yes, she was your first baby. You loved her. I still have her."

"Would you send her to me? I want her."

"But you know she isn't the original Sweetie."

"What do you mean?"

"You *loved* that thing, and I mean *loved*. You loved her *so* much. Too much, frankly. It was gross. And she got just really disgustingly *filthy*, Aviva. She got to where she actually stank. I don't know what you were doing with that doll. But you refused to let us wash her. So we had to throw her away."

"You *what*? But you said you still have her."

"We waited 'til you were sleeping. On garbage night. You wouldn't let that thing out of your *sight*, so we had to wait until you were asleep. That thing *stank*, let me *tell* you. Oh, don't look at me like that, you would have done the same thing. We couldn't wash the stink out of her, even if you *had* let us try. I was just happy to get her out of the *house*." Barb shuddered.

A sick wave crested all up into Aviva's stomach and lungs and nipples.

"You took my Sweetie under the cover of night?"

"You made *such* a scene the next morning, oh my *God*. Cried like the world was ending. Wah! Wah! Wah! Like somebody *died*. God, I thought you'd never shut *up*. I guess it's good you don't remember."

"Yeah, I imagine I was inconsolable."

"So Dad had to run out and buy you a *replacement*. It was ridiculous. He could never stand to see you upset for two seconds. He went to the toy store on Barrington, remember that place? And he bought you a new one, the same exact stupid doll. He brought it home and said, 'Look, honey, we found Sweetie!' But you were too smart; you knew it wasn't the same doll. The new one was spotless and didn't stink, and you knew *right* away she wasn't your Sweetie. You took one look and shoved her out of your *sight*. *That's not Sweetie.* What a pain in the ass. Well! Let's not dwell. Have you spoken to your brother lately?"

"Which one? I speak to Rob all the time. The living one, not so much."

"Well, you didn't hear it from me, but there is trouble in paradise."

"Nothing a manicure and a new purse and some medical dermatology can't fix, surely."

"I don't think so," Barb sang. She actually had a decent voice. Too bad she'd never learned to use it. (But what if she *had*?)

"What's the story, Barb."

"I can't say more than that," again in singsong.

"Are they splitting *up*?"

Barb was giggling maniacally from the effort it took to pretend to want to keep a secret. Completely soused. Mission accomplished.

"Are you for *real*, Barb?"

Barb turned instantly serious: "It's just *awful* for the twins. I'm so sad for the *twins*. Don't say *anything* to *anyone*; it's not *public* yet."

"Wow. I did not see this coming. Who'd have thought *Mike* would be the one to recapitulate the precise nightmare of our hideous childhood?

I feel almost absolved of the need to self-destruct now. This is fucking amazing."

"Don't be cruel, Aviva! The poor guy has been sleeping in his *car*."

"Like, in the driveway of his two-million-dollar house?"

"This is all according to Dad. Pretty pathetic, if you ask me. Mike doesn't speak to me these days."

"I cannot imagine why. You're so trustworthy and not at all manipulative. So I take it you're speaking with Dad again?"

Barb shrugged. Chuck and Barb, Barb and Chuck. Of all the people God could strike down with infertility, why not Barb and Chuck?!

"Were you on the Pill when you met Dad?"

"What on earth does that have to do with anything? Maybe. I don't think so. I don't remember. Why? Who cares?"

"Because you know that women who are chemically castrated are, like, sensually *disabled*, right?! You literally cannot sniff out an appropriate pro-creative partner if you are on synthetic hormones."

"Is this one of your crazy theories?"

"Um, no, it's called science, Barb. *Science*. We're all supposed to sit up straight in the church of science."

"Oh, relax. I am the source of all your troubles, *right*, *right*, I know. Blame the mother!"

"It's just, you know, you do happen to have some extremely fucked-up-slash-damaged-slash-dead children, Barb, pardon the reality check. I mean, putting aside the fact that you and Chuck hate each other, if you hadn't been chemically *castrated*, you may have been able to literally smell the physical wrongness before you procreated, is all I'm saying."

"I don't hate your Dad. I can't help how he feels about me, but I only wish him well," Barb said. Then she lowered her voice to a hiss: "And ex-cuse *me*, you little shit, but my children are *not* fucked up."

Aviva drew herself up to full height and brought forth her identical hiss: "Who the fuck are you *kidding*, Barb? One died young of cancer, one is a traumatized depressed fascist bastard from hell, and the baby is a barren malcontent. You can't stand soaked in the rain and swear the sun is *shining*, Barb."

Aviva stood and grabbed her jacket and walked out of the restaurant without looking back.

There was a bench across the street.

Barb was semiconciliatory when she emerged. Barb secretly loved it when Aviva outdid her, hiss for hiss. To mother was to try and mold a person to your very own specifications, for better or for worse.

"To this day," Barb said, sitting down and hooking her arm through Aviva's, "one of my biggest regrets in life is that I didn't have more children. I should have had *ten*. There is *nothing* more important in life."

"Maybe you would have gotten into a groove by kid number five or six or seven. Maybe you would have hit your stride, set your ego aside."

"There is nothing nobler than having children, my darling. I could *throttle* myself for not having more. And it was so *easy* for me."

"I am very sorry that you feel this lack so acutely, Barb."

"Stop calling me 'Barb.' It's not funny."

"Okay, but, like, hold up, *Mom*, how old are you? Seventy-three? Listen, I don't want to pressure you or anything, but: you got plenty of cash, and things are *happening* right now. A seventy-two-year-old in India just had twins. A sixty-one-year-old in Nebraska served as surrogate for her son and son-in-law using her son's sperm and the son-in-law's sister's eggs. A fifty-seven-year-old just served as surrogate for her daughter. The baby was severely underweight and had a mild heart defect, but after a couple weeks in the NICU came out swinging. I have no doubt there's a clinic out there that will *gladly* take your money and try to break some records, Barb. Whatever you have to do will be *worth* it. Motherhood is indeed the noblest occupation; I really could not agree more. It would be a terrible shame to turn your back on the possibility of more kids. Just think about it, will you?"

A begrudging smile on Barb's face. They got up and walked the glittering city.

There was a guy singing his heart out by the Thames, guitar case open at his feet. Both the guitar and the guy had seen better days. His eyes were shut in concentration, his timbre was rich, and his rhythm was arresting. His voice—it came from the right place. Some might call it the soul, but let's not get *too* anticapitalist. Sarah would call it the lowest point of the hammock of the diaphragm. Aviva fished out a ten-pound note and threw it into the guy's case.

"You have *got* to be kidding me," Barb said. "Pretty free with your money, there, aren't you, girlie? Hey, Mister! Don't quit your day job!"

"So," said the Rabbi. "Is the meeting with Amy's mother happening?"

"Tomorrow, hopefully. Seems like we're on. Fingers crossed."

"How do you expect the meeting to go?"

"I don't know. I want to look into her eyes and thank her and, like, pay my respects. Is that weird? But I still don't understand what's in it for her."

"Maybe it's comforting for her to meet people who love her daughter. What will you do if it's disappointing?"

"I have no expectations, so it can't be. I did see Barb tonight, though. Speaking of disappointment."

"And how was that?"

"Fine. Terrible. Mike and What's-Her-Face are breaking up."

"Well, that's not at all surprising."

"It isn't? I find it surprising."

"You thought they were happy?"

"I mean, not *my* idea of happy, but I'm a psycho who insists on being *honest* all the time. How am I supposed to know what counts as happy for other people? I always assume people like Mike and What's-Her-Face are happy."

"They're not."

"Remind me of that more often, would you? I haven't been sleeping so well."

"Dreams?"

"I dreamt Sam's dimwit sister-in-law was watching my precious baby daughter for me while I was doing a show, and when I took my precious beloved baby back into my arms I kissed her *incessantly*. Just kissed and kissed and kissed her. We were a perfect dyad, me and my beautiful baby girl. But then I noticed she had a *huge* burn down the length of her back. And I was *incensed*. I mean, I went *bananas*. I wanted to murder the dimwit sister-in-law. I was about to kill her, straight up."

"It's about your mother."

"*Dude!* Come *on*. In other news, I have surpassed fifty thousand followers."

"That's wonderful, darling!"

"No, dude. It's not wonderful. It's creepy and grotesque, and it's not even enough to matter anyway."

"Well, it seems like that's what an artist wants, right? Fans? Listeners? You have an ambivalent relationship to fame. An internal conflict. We've always known this."

"It's pure politics. And that's why I feel so diminished by it, even though fine, sure, it's what I 'want.' What I worked toward. From way back before my goddamned frontal lobe was fully formed."

"And what's the alternative?"

"The alternative is that I go home and I take on my married name and I learn how to grow vegetables and I don't put pictures of my motherfucking dinner on the internet and I disa-fucking-ppear."

"You wouldn't be happy."

"Why not?!"

"Because you have a gift. And with your kind of gift—"

"What? I owe it to myself to share? Will I regret it, Rav? Not releasing a thousand more songs before I shuffle off this mortal coil? Please, dude. Please. No one needs anything from me."

"You can't help it: the songs will come anyway, whether or not you want them to. You don't have to force the songs. That's what's different about you. With you, the songs just come."

* * *

In the morning, the cunty luteal headache was like Satan trying to murder her from inside her skull. Her throat remained on fire, her voice scratchy. Still no suitcase, and no answer at the special phone number. The imaginary pregnancy was toast. She rested all morning, by which is meant changing clothes several times in between lost hours staring at her device.

T-minus seven hours 'til the date with Mum.

How are you feeling, Mum? I am so looking forward to our dinner!

A smoldering selfie exchange with Sammy-Sam the manny-man.

A long, stilted, emotionally illiterate email from a bewildered Chuck, who had, it seemed, ended things with Charlene.

Nothing from Copeland.

Someone was angry about an injustice in a city not their own.

Someone was angry about an injustice in the government.

Someone was angry about an injustice in history.

Someone was angry about how few people were angry about an injustice.

Someone was on vacation by the ocean.

Someone famous had a milestone birthday.

Someone's twins were dolled up in stripes.

Someone's twins were dolled up in dots.

Someone's support animal was asleep in a patch of sunlight by a window.

Someone's plants were getting repotted.

Someone's grandma had passed.

Harmie, Harmie, what was up with wee Shmendrickson? Aviva had been forced to mute Harm's mom, who had seemingly lost her shit, posting multiple times a day. But it was okay to click on over for a little fix, wasn't it? It was often said that motherhood could be very lonely. There were so many teeth in the mother's huge, desperate smile. What would become of her when the little daughter no longer took delight in posing with and for her?

Another Amy documentary was coming out, and Amy's old friends were fighting amongst themselves about who was authentic and who was a climber.

All the Amy accounts recycled the same photos, the same outtakes. It was like the Princess Di shit: there was only so much. It was not infinite. Once you'd seen it all, you'd seen it all. Aviva's fascination with this particular archetype was petering out. It was almost over. But the thing about archetypes is that they never fully go away.

She watched some clips from *Junior*, a semiforgotten 1994 flop/classic, now streaming. Danny DeVito as a deranged fertility doc and Schwarzenegger as a research scientist, and the FDA refuses to let them test their experimental fertility drug (Expectane) on humans, so they steal a frozen egg and test the drug on Schwarzenegger, who becomes the first pregnant *man*! What a gas! Trans identity politics having not fully occurred to anybody yet! Then the pregnant (and increasingly "emotional," yuk yuk!) Schwarzenegger falls in love with Emma Thompson, the research scientist whose frozen egg is the one the scientists had stolen! HIJINKS ENSUE. Tagline: "Nothing is inconceivable."

Tea-time interview.

"This person has a million followers," Jer said. "Literally, V: A million, okay? I want you to be *nice*. Your *nicest*. She loves you already; just *let* her. *Let* her love you."

"One hour, Jer. I will give her one hour of my time. Time being the only currency, you know. I'm a *person*, Jer, in the *process* of being a person. The fact that I am also a musical genius the world ignores at its peril is . . . incidental."

"Well la-di-da," Jer said.

Aviva showed early and got cozy in the mafia seat, back to the wall, facing the entrance. She ordered a pot of chamomile with honey and set a timer on her phone, because boundaries! Time was worth so much *more* than money. You could never earn more of it. Engineers and inventors and capitalists and programmers of the highest order still couldn't get *near* that shizz. (Ditto weather.)

The influencer arrived in a whoosh of crisp outside air.

"It's *you*! Hello! Welcome to the UK! *So* great you're here. *So* much excitement about you right now! I don't know if you remember me at all; we chatted online some years ago. I've actually been quite a big fan of yours for quite a long time. You're not well known here yet, but I think that's about to change, and I for one could not be happier. Not to be a complete sycophant. Oh, but have you lost your *voice*? You, of all people! Well, you've already got your tea, good, good." She waved down a server. "May I have a pot of your blackest? Thanks." She turned back to Aviva. "Apologies for being late. My kids were a bit of a handful today. To say the least. I'm still a bit flummoxed. One of those days. They're still quite small. I do hope you won't mind that I'm a *mum*. I don't imagine you hate *all* mums! But don't worry: mine came round the old-fashioned way. But don't *you* look fantastic, meanwhile. *Love* those boots. God, you're *fabulous*. Tell me about your style. I notice"—here she paused, proud of the forthcoming observation—"that you sometimes wear quite provocative clothing, while other times I see you in sort of oversized menswear and such, and at still other times in these sort of, well, tent dresses and head coverings, like some sort of 'refugee chic.' Point being, one never knows precisely what to *expect* from you, aesthetically. You con*found*. And we're so used to seeing people in a sort of comprehensive *look*, don't you think? Which brings me to my first question: Who is the *real* Aviva?"

"Depends where I am in my menstrual cycle."

"Ahaaa, yes. Right-o. Course. And judging by your look today . . . may I hazard a guess?"

"I dress how I feel, which changes constantly, which is also the nature of my particular body. Can't step in the same cycle twice. Terrifying, isn't it?"

The influencer switched tacks. "Bit of a crisis for a singer on tour to lose her voice, I imagine."

"You can title your piece: 'Aviva Rosner Has a Cold.' Folk isn't opera. Or pop, for that matter. It's not meant to sound pretty. It's meant to sound however the fuck it sounds. It's the people's music. Sometimes people have colds."

"Okay, so perhaps we'll just dive right into the thorny stuff, then. I've been wondering: What do you think about organ transplants?"

"Why?"

"Human interference in the biological order of things. Breakthroughs in medical science that allow us to override biology and mortality. You know: the kind of thing you seem so riled up about in this album."

"Riiiiiight. Well, I think that if a donor can offer informed consent and a recipient can offer informed consent and surgeons can practice their craft with some intimation of basic humility and servitude within a framework of basic ethics, then that's a pretty cool thing we can sometimes make happen."

"Well, how is it any different?"

"From what."

"Assisted reproductive technology!"

"Clever girl."

The influencer got up and curtsied, then sat down again.

"It's different because a nonexistent person cannot offer consent, to say nothing of 'informed.' Nor, arguably, can a womb-haver who's been heavily socialized to believe that she is only a complete human in fulfillment of her capacity as a vessel for more humans."

"But can't the same be said when conception takes place 'naturally'? Nobody asks the conceived if they'd like to exist."

"Fair enough, but I suppose if one has any inkling of some larger intelligence at play, one might be tempted to ascribe notions of the divine to that process. In that we don't begin to comprehend the driving forces underlying it. And by the way, the almighty egg happens to be very selective about *if* and *when* she welcomes the champion sperm."

"Yes, I've heard that, actually. You're into biology, aren't you?"

"I don't know that I'm 'into' biology, per se, but I do *believe* that it's a *thing*. Like: it *exists*."

"That's a very provocative stance."

"Is it?"

"Well, it has, of late, become the province of some rather bigoted perspectives."

"Thank God I'm not famous enough to get canceled."

"Pretty hard to control how famous you are."

"Seems easy enough . . . to avoid, that is. Harder to force, that's true. Lotta poor souls trying to claw their way toward fame, Lord knows. Simpler to abort, shall we say, but more difficult to make manifest. What the fuck do I know? I guess there are those of us who just, like, emerge, blinking in the bright lights, shocked as to how we got here. But to terminate? No big: just turn down interviews like this one, vanish from the feeds. Easy enough to disappear, I imagine. I'd say I'll let you know, but you'll have forgotten all about me by then."

"Planning on disappearing?"

"It's a thought experiment."

"So—you're saying you *don't* want to be famous?"

"I'm saying I am disgusted by the systems in which fame is a currency. No offense."

"None taken! Then why are you a singer?"

"The songs come. I am their servant. A vessel, if you will. The rest is noise. Fame is dumb. Maybe *not* no offense, after all."

"I happen to agree with you, by the way, that procreation is a destructive convention."

"I don't remember having said that."

"Well, your lyric 'rote procreation is how the devil uses us up in the service of eternal damnation' seems to imply *something* of the sort."

"Creepy the way my shit takes on a life of its own. Comes directly out of my brain and my mouth, but the second it's out, it's some other *thing*. Life of its own. Anyway, the word to focus on in that lyric is 'rote.'"

"You're a bit of a bully, I think. But I quite enjoy you."

"Oh, heavens," Aviva exclaimed in her best British accent. "Not a *bully!*" She switched back to regular speech. "Come to think of it, I had this one friend in school—"

"Just the one?"

"I'm ashamed to admit that as we got older, toward middle school, I started to kind of torture her a little bit. I mean: I turned on her. It wasn't nice of me, and I know it's very common for girls to do this sort of thing as a matter of course, and maybe in future generations it will become verboten, and the human race will truly shed its behavioral tics once and for all, but there it is and I'm sorry."

"Afraid you've lost me."

"At one point I remember torturing this girl at recess or whatever, making her really, really mad. For an appreciative audience, of course. She had no social recourse, which is I guess the point of torturing someone, and eventually she just lost her shit and sputtered, in front of the whole group: 'If you don't have anything to say, don't say anything!' And everyone burst out laughing at her omission of the word 'nice.' It became a sort of catchphrase for a while."

"I don't follow."

"She had *meant* 'If you don't have anything NICE to say, don't say anything,' but she fucked up the colloquial, so we all continued torturing her. *I* continued torturing her. I still feel bad about it. I think it might've, like, altered the trajectory of her life."

"So this story illustrates the fact that you're a bully."

"Also known as . . . a human being. No, that story illustrates the strange ways we come by our ethos. If that poor girl was our Christ figure—and, I mean, she wasn't preaching any particular gospel, and we didn't nail her to anything, but—that line was what she said 'on the cross,' if you will. She said, 'If you don't have anything to say, don't say anything.' And it stuck with me. I believe in it, more and more. It's my ethos. And I have that girl to thank for it. That girl I tortured."

The interviewer sipped her tea, blinking.

"I happened to grow up in that kind of family," Aviva went on. "The psychological torture kind. The kind you only survive if you're lucky or blessed or tough as fucking nails. And survival's a matter of winning some cruel games, really. That's just basic anthropology. And aren't games exclusive to primates? Or do birds and lizards and insects and shit torment one another, too?"

"Exactly what kind of upbringing we talking about?"

"Oh, just your basic self-obsessed toxic assholes," Aviva said. "Regular old manipulative bullshit. Nothing criminal. Not like chain-the-kids-to-the-radiator-and-starve-them or anything. Just, you know, lie-about-everything-all-the-time gaslighting gossiping assholes. Pretty run-of-the-mill. But everyone's parents are assholes, aren't they?"

"Gosh, I hope not! Why on earth would you ever start your own family in that case?! Unless you're some kind of sadist?"

"Obviously! What else could underlie the impulse to procreate in this day and age? Inflict consciousness upon a new person?! Utterly direct that person's emergence into consciousness? Hardwire your own agenda onto a blank slate of a person?! That is unadulterated power! That is straight-up fascist. The sadism goes without saying."

"Back to you being a bully."

"Or maybe I truly *value* human life. Maybe I think human life *is* actually sacred. You know the opposite of truth is the appearance of truth, right?"

"I think we all value human life, don't we?"

"You're joking. *No one* values human life. There's nothing sacred about filial love or maternal love or brotherly love or patriotism or whatever the fuck. It's all a story we tell ourselves to justify whatever we want it to justify. It's a straight-up miracle that people *ever* manage to behave in a decent way toward one another, *ever*. A miracle. It's the *exception* that people ever behave like the higher beings we claim to be. We're animals, hon. Human life is not *sacred*. *Animal* life isn't sacred. Look *around*, hon, maybe a *little* farther than the tip of your nose on Shwitter. *Ecology* isn't sacred. *Children* aren't sacred. *Trees* aren't sacred. *Whales* aren't sacred. Haven't you been paying *attention*?! Do you ever read the *newspaper*? *Nothing* is sacred."

"But *shouldn't* it be?"

Aviva had a good long laugh. The medicinal kind.

The timer went off.

"Thank you sincerely," Aviva said, refreshed from the clarifying laughter. "And with that, I must take my leave. You have a lot of . . . material, I hope? I said some stuff. Shall we take a selfie? Let's get a good angle. I wish you wonderful posting. Tag me! So fun meeting you."

She said you were a prize cunt, Jerry texted. But that's not the worst thing in the world. We can work with that. People don't necessarily want their folk punk heroes to be sweethearts. They don't have to want to marry you, they just have to want to fuck you.

What about kill?

Well, that's okay, too, but only if they fuck you first.

Attaboy, the solid gold perspective I pay you for.

You don't pay me that much, if we're being honest, because you don't make that much.

And whose fault is that?

It was easy enough to find the house at 30 Camden Square. Her final address. The dwelling from which she'd been carried on a stretcher, covered with a white sheet, at twenty-seven years of age. Cursed death, cursed life, cursed girl whose gifts could have saved her, if only she'd valued them. But fuck that, let's not get judgmental about our special archetypal friend. Plenty of not-so-special folx to judge the shit out of.

Across the street was a small park with a big old tree, and a rose garden. The roses were a deep magenta, jauntier than red. The tree was some kind of massive tree. Aviva didn't know what kinds of trees trees were, and always found it jarring in novels when people always knew what kind of trees trees were.

The tree was a shrine. There were objects and communiqués tucked into the branches and propped around the trunk. Sealed envelopes with fat hearts drawn all over them. An assortment of glass empties: wine bottles, top-shelf liquor, bottom-shelf liquor. One devotee had left an unopened red wine with a red bow. Someone had left cut roses, tied with twine. The roses were past their prime, going black at the tips now. Someone had left a full packet of cigarettes. There were several glass votives, all burned down.

Aviva sat on the bench under the tree and breathed the rose-tinged air. So many benches in this country, and so thoughtfully placed! It was quiet, other than the rustling of leaves in the breeze. Aviva had the park to herself. She should have brought an offering. She had no offering.

A black cat approached, sat opposite the bench, and stared at Aviva. The welcoming committee! Aviva felt a need to explain herself to the cat. Why hadn't she ventured out to the grave site instead, to place a rock upon the headstone? Because the grave site had seemed like not the place; this house had seemed like the place. Where spirit remained, that is. If the spirit could be said to remain. In many traditional imaginings, the soul is said to hover near the body after death. For a matter of hours, maybe. Or until burial, or (shudder) cremation. But the soul could also become trapped if death was especially violent or unnatural or out of order or in some way unjust.

Another cat appeared, and wound its way around Aviva's ankles. A little black-and-brown kitty, this one, friendly as can be. Smidge of gray around the face.

Under the bench, someone had tucked a small pair of stilettos, tied together with a white ribbon. Darling, we really have to talk about those stilettoes. We have to talk about evolving your look. Or, better yet, eschewing the whole idea of a look. I see you, babe: spending more and more time on St. Lucia, barefoot, hair free and unmolested, no wigs, no heels, no corsets, no globs of makeup. There's a rumor you were trying to adopt some St. Lucian orphans when you died. And get those fucking liquid plastic blobs out from under the skin on your chest, you ridiculous bitch, what were you *thinking*? Break the chains, babe, go live by the sea, protect your body, because your body is your instrument. Can't make music without a body, sweetie. Not yet, anyway. Soon, maybe. Soon, perhaps. When they get that hologram up and running. How many combinations of notes and sounds could there possibly be, after all? AI should be capable of constructing *something* in the ballpark. Bring you back to "life," rake in the cash.

But what a pity, when you could have lived to be a funny little old lady, could have sung so many more delicious songs. Where did your creative juice go? Your encyclopedic, innate knowledge of soul and jazz and punk and funk and hip-hop: Where did that *go*?! MIA for a while before you died. A person doesn't have to throw herself off an overpass. A person doesn't have to put a gun in her mouth. A person doesn't have to shoot a fatal dose of poison directly into her veins. A person can extinguish herself in commonplace, everyday ways for a long time, walk around like a zombie for a while before her heart stops beating.

So we'll be having suicide on the installment plan. A fine choice, arguably better than a gun or a noose or a razor or a leap. Gradual. Nice and easy. Have another drink. Have some more candy. Get numb, complacent. Never exercise. Exercise too much. Eat pizza, drink coffee, eat wings, drink wine. Stay up too late. Stay up all night. Or take pills every night, tell yourself it's no big. Get high. Subsist on caffeine. Do whatever it takes to make it through the day. Soak up the feed. Read what the robots tell you to read, watch what the robots tell you to watch. Let other people's pretend lives wash your eyes. Offer up your own in return.

Aviva sat there for twenty minutes? Half an hour? She always found it odd in novels when characters knew precisely how long they'd been sitting in organic contemplation.

There were more cats! A tabby, and two more black ones, unless she was counting the same one twice. Who owned this house now, and were they annoyed by the seekers, the shrine, or did they relish their inherited infamy? Had they redecorated? Renovated? Had they left anything exactly as it was, so as to impress dinner party guests?

It was just a house, but maybe the thing that made it special was that it was a place where a lot of people all came to sit and contemplate variations on the same thing. Which made it a temple.

Mum's suggestion was a New-York-style deli in Finchley. But it turned out the deli was closed for renovations, so she told Aviva to pick somewhere else. Aviva knew nothing about North London. She searched and searched and finally, okay, great, how about this Italian place in Barnet. Great, said Mum. And her "Hubby" would be joining them, as well. Aviva made a reservation for three. This was happening.

But what was the point, again? She had no idea what to say to them. Thank you for meeting with me? I too am a musician? A self-destructor? A conscientious objector? A fashion whore? A Jew! A bitch! Barren. Cassandra. Reviled. Addicted. Leaving it all out on the field! Anyone want to share an appetizer?

If this *was* real, they were probably used to it, right? Aviva couldn't be the first. Something about obsession, something about how identification with musicians and artists gives us a way of understanding ourselves and our experiences, shows us who we are, who we're not, who we want to be, and how to enact it, or fake it 'til we make it. In short: save our lives. But not the artist's life, alas.

In preparation, Aviva got a too-hard storefront foot rub. Beat the crap out of me, yes, that's it, pummel this machine into working order, no pity. Bleed, bitch, bleed!

The foot rub left her even more destroyed, and she limped back to her shitty flat, where she collapsed onto the bed, facing the resurgence of the bad, bad headache. Familiar headache. Luteal headache. Angry headache. Early-onset perimenopausal headache. Punishing headache. She nabbed some Tylenol from the medicine cabinet before the wicked ache tipped over into full-blown debilitation, and allowed herself a timed forty-five-minute nap.

It would take an hour to get to Barnet on the Tube.

She was careful not to put on anything too reminiscent of the cartoon silhouette, the caricature—nothing rockabilly or retro, and no stupid eyeliner—lest they assume she was some simple/deranged imitator. But hey, Aviva had been rocking bandanas and massive hoops and tattoos since before she'd known Amy existed.

She settled on the same jeans in which she'd traveled, the hoops, and the vintage Hermès scarf over her hair, which was hideously greasy thanks, again, to luteal phase. The glorified do-rag gave her great confidence, held everything together, and could theoretically even be counted on to keep the headache in check, demons at bay.

(Still no word about her suitcase.)

The Camden Town tube stop was closed, for some reason, and a bunch of agitated folk congregated on the street corner. No time for this, whatever it was. The next stop was a twenty-minute walk. Fuck. She wouldn't dare keep Mum waiting. One wasn't late for this kind of date.

She hailed a cab.

"That's a long way," said the driver. His device predicted thirty-nine minutes. Another small fortune in cab fare, but she had no choice. Her head pounded. She couldn't look at her screen, she was so nauseous. A hot flash, a cold sweat. Breathe, she ordered herself. You look good, and that's as close to feeling good as you're gonna get.

She arrived with just enough time to pee and splash some water on her face, then emerged to see Mum and Hubby standing right out front of the place.

Mum! Unmistakably. She was small and fragile-looking, leaning on a cane.

An overwhelming desire to embrace the woman, a flood of desire. This must be the oxytocin rush of which conscious fornicators and heroin addicts and gamblers and Facebookers and natural birthers and celebrity stalkers were so fond. This was the woman who'd grown Amy. Amy had come from this woman's body.

"Hello!" Mum said. The immediate force of warmth in her eyes: sparkling and clear.

Hubby beamed and stuck out his hand.

"Pleased to meet you," he said with a wink. "*I'm* Mum."

Aviva didn't understand. The actual Mum giggled.

"*I'm* Mum," Hubby said again. "Lovely to meet you. You look about a hundred years old in your profile photo."

"Oh . . . that's a joke. It's Emma Goldman's mug shot. Not a joke, I mean, more of an . . . aspiration."

"Ahhh," he said. "Right. The anarchist! Well, *I'm Mum*."

Huh?! Aviva turned back to the actual Mum, who began to make her way slowly and carefully up the two steps into the restaurant. Aviva held the door with utmost tenderness.

Aviva finally understood: Hubby was her stand-in on Twitter. He represented her, spoke for her. Mum didn't want to spend her time fucking around in that cesspool. Hubby did it for her. So Aviva'd been talking to *him* all these months. Making plans with *him*. Calling *him* "dear."

Once inside and seated at their four-top, Mum dismantled her cane with a few deft motions, wrapping it up with the snap of a rubber band.

"My magic stick," she said.

Aviva sat next to Mum, with Hubby across. Aviva carefully calibrated her distance: close enough to communicate affection, respect, intimacy, and far away enough to communicate boundaries, respect, decency. In physical human relations, in real time and space, it matters most of all what we say with our bodies. And physical human relations in real space and time are, lest we forget, the gold standard.

Mum's eyes darted away and back at Aviva, away and back. She was shy, for heaven's sake! What a darling woman.

Hubby was not shy. Hubby was a flirt, a benign one. He flirted with everyone, flirted in a way that made everyone feel good, lightened the load. There was nothing lurking behind his flirtation; it was pure courtesy. Courtly.

"I can't believe you agreed to meet with me," Aviva said.

"We're people people!" Hubby said.

Aviva was overexcited. Calm down, Aviva! Don't be too solicitous. Relax. Don't aggravate the headache. Take it easy. Thankfully, Hubby dominated the conversation. They'd tied the knot just a few months after Amy died, he said.

In May, a few months *before* she died, they'd gone round her flat to tell her they were going to be getting married in September. "That's nice," she told them. "But you know I won't be there."

"It was in one ear and out the other," said Mum. " 'What? You won't be there??' "

"We assumed she was talking about the paps."

"The paparazzi," said Mum.

"She couldn't leave the house without them haranguing her."

They briefly discussed Pops. They called him by his full name, a sort of mockery.

"He's never responded to me," Aviva said.

"Well, you see, he's a *very* important man," Hubby said. "*Very* busy."

"It's easiest to accommodate him," Mum said. "We don't bother with him. No struggle. No problems. Just let him be."

"You're really a lovely human being," Aviva told her.

Mum looked away, bashful, shrugging, then quickly back again. The light of her eyes when they briefly rested in Aviva's! Amy's eyes. Amy's smile.

Mum and Hubby had been friends since they were teenagers. It was a very small community, up here. The Jews, you know. They had remained friends through their respective first marriages. Hubby's son and Amy grew up together, went to school together. A close-knit community, the North London Jews. Slight alteration in the fabric of time (and weather?) and Aviva could just as well have been born here, to these people. She wished that she had been born here, to these people. They were kinder than her people. More straightforward than her people. Honest, friendly, open.

"Are you all right, dear?"

"I have a bit of a headache. It's actually quite awful. Hormones, you know."

"Oh!" said Mum. "Do I know! Oh!"

"What can you do," Aviva said.

"Bring it on, I always say. Whatever it is, just bring it on. Nothing you can do."

Hubby said something to a passing waitress, made her giggle.

"He can't help it," Mum said, laughing. "We do have fun. We laugh all the time."

Red wine for Hubby, rosé for Mum, club soda for Aviva. She noticed them notice.

"I don't like alcohol," she said.

"You did that already, eh? Did that enough now? All done?"

"Precisely," Aviva smiled.

"Amy was not a nice drunk," Hubby said. "And she knew it, too. She always had to get rip-roaring drunk. She knew she was a mean drunk, a terrible drunk, violent and mean. She always apologized."

"Tell me, will you? I'm curious: Why did I make the grade? How did I rate a meeting with you guys?"

"Oh, we'll meet with anyone—so long as they're a true fan," Hubby said. "And in a public place; that goes without saying. And if we can trust them—"

"So I'm not special?"

"Oh, no, darling, you're *very* special." Hubby winked.

"It's just what we do," Mum said. "Everyone loves our girl. It's lovely."

"They always come to Camden, and we'll go meet them at the Caffè Nero, there, because I can park just out front. There's a Brazilian woman who comes every year."

"So basically it's the longest-running continuous shiva of all time?"

"You got it."

Mum seemed genuinely happy. She spent her time sitting and connecting with people who grieved her loss. People with some idea of exactly what it was she'd lost. People who carried the pain of her daughter's demise in their hearts. Like family.

Aviva was full to bursting, though the awful headache continued to hammer at the edges. What an odd sensation. The thrilling jumble of being alive. This was exactly what she had come for. This was it.

"I'm not interested in what happened to her," Aviva told them. "What became of her. I'm not about all that stuff at the end. I don't care about that part. I mean, I do care, because it sucks, but I'm about the girl. The person. Before. She's it for me."

"You got it," Mum said. "That's right."

"A lot of people only know her as the dresses and the beehive and the eyeliner and the tabloids, but that stuff is like a PS. It's a *perversion*. I only care about the *girl*. And you can see her so clearly if you listen. It's all in the music."

"I listened to some of *your* stuff," Hubby said. "You're quite good. Sort of a ferocious vibe there, innit? You have a unique sound. And you write all your own stuff, I gather. Impressive. Though I've honestly no idea what you're getting on about half the time."

Aviva ignored him, which is how you drive a flirt bananas.

The food came, they ate. What did they talk about? Nothing. Everything. Aviva offered up the facts to Mum: She wanted to have children, but it hadn't happened, and she didn't know what life had in store, but you know, what can you do?

"Nothing at all," Mum said, her eyes holding steady in Aviva's for longer than before. "You take what comes."

"But children are the *best*, I think," Aviva said, moony. She was sitting next to *the* mother. Mum's smiling eyes went away and came back, away and back.

"Children are fantastic," said Hubby.

"But you can't tell them what to do," Mum said. "You've got to let them be who they are."

"She was so lucky to have you for a mum," Aviva said.

"Oh well," said Mum.

"Now she's everyone's mum," said Hubby. "Now everyone calls her 'Mum.' 'How you doin', Mum? I love you, Mum. Are you taking good care of yourself, Mum?" Everyone calls her Mum. She is Mum to them all. Mum to everyone, now."

Aviva couldn't contain herself. She leaned over, put her arm around Mum, and pressed a gentle kiss against her shoulder. "I love you, Mum. How did you learn how to be such a wonderful mum?"

"I learned from *my* mum what *not* to do," Mum said. "Everything I needed to know to be a good mum, I learned from doing the opposite from her."

"I know exactly what you mean. It's like this conscious experiment, doing the opposite of what you were shown. How else does someone get in the habit of making constructive choices? And, like, identify with those choices? Instead of the dark stuff? Because *that* can be creatively valid, *too*, you know? Like maybe even more so!"

"Right you are," Mum said. "Right you are."

"Good things can come from that, right? Staying level and present with how things are? Everything doesn't have to be dark and stormy. Everything doesn't have to be some horrible struggle. I just want to find a way, you know?"

"You will," said Mum. "You got it."

"I went to Camden Square today."

"Oh yes. We were there the day of. The anniversary. It was lovely. So many people."

"A mother and daughter from Argentina, commode-hugging drunk, *weeping* and carrying on like you wouldn't believe," Hubby said.

"They were lovely," Mum said.

"We like to go on the anniversary to see the tributes and such."

"But that was never her home."

"It was just a house."

"Her father bought it; he set it up."

"She wasn't with it by then."

"She thought she was invincible."

"But I don't think she wanted to die," Aviva ventured.

"No. I think if she knew what was going to happen she would have stopped it. She didn't want to die. I think the minute she died she went to heaven and her nan was there waiting for her, scolding her." Mum wagged her finger: "'You see?! What did I tell you?! I told you! What have you done, you stupid girl?!'"

"Nan knew she was an alcoholic," said Hubby.

"Nan did. Nan knew it early. 'She's an alcoholic,' Nan said."

"But you can't help someone unless they want to help themselves," Aviva offered lamely.

"We all tried. Really we did. We wanted to help her very badly indeed. But there was no helping."

"Her father apparently got five grand a week from the tabloids to tell them her whereabouts. That's how they managed to stalk her so effectively. That's the story."

"On the last anniversary, a few of the bodyguards and a few of her friends—her *real* friends, the ones who don't give interviews—met us at the house, and then we went to the nearby KFC for wings and coffee."

"It was Amy's favorite place, KFC. We had the loveliest time. Isn't that strange? All of us celebrating her at KFC? But she loved it there. It was so *her*."

"Then we had the crew back over to our place, and everyone sat in the garden all afternoon and laughed and talked about her." Hubby smiled. "Simple thing, innit?"

"Parties are the best way to remember someone," Aviva said. "It's like, not until you gather that you can feel the presence in outline of the person who's missing."

"You got it. Right you are." Mum's eyes stayed on Aviva longer and longer now.

It was like dying and finding out there really *was* a white light, *and* a beneficent God awaiting you at the end of the tunnel.

They ordered tiramisu and cappuccinos.

They didn't ask Aviva much about herself, but she volunteered; she wanted to be known by them. In a mysterious equation, being known to them meant being known to the dead, and being known to the dead was the same as being known to the unborn. There was some sort of magic here, at any rate, and Mum was its keeper. And what was magic if not belief itself? Some women crawled up mountainsides on their knees to pray to specific rocks or trees. Some women drank bitter herbs and tinctures. Some sacrificed animals; some exiled themselves to silence and solitude and fasting and prayer. Some promised their own souls, or nascent souls, laid down future debts. Stole and lied and demanded and begged. Murdered, mutilated, raged. Wept and wailed. Barren women: their frustration the hidden soundtrack to the forever-spinning world, a world from which something new was always pushing to emerge, be brought into the light, but not by them. Not for them.

"I just really, really want to be a mum," Aviva said.

"Yes," Mum said. "Children are wonderful."

"But it's not happening. It hasn't happened. I've been waiting and waiting. Hoping and hoping."

"You take what comes. That's all you can do."

"I don't want to force it," Aviva said.

"No," Mum said. "You can't force it. No, no."

There was a short struggle between Hubby and Aviva for the bill, but Aviva prevailed, and Hubby shrugged. Mum cheerfully reassembled her cane, and they made their way outside. Aviva was beyond satisfied. She'd never expected this much. She'd eaten a bowl of oily pasta alongside *Mum*, commiserating about the dead and the unborn. She was fine to say goodbye now, to hug them both and call it a night. It had been more than enough.

But Hubby was grinning at her.

"Do you want to hear a very special live recording? There is one copy of it in the whole entire world."

Aviva stared at him, uncomprehending.

"You have to beg me," he said.

"Please."

"*Really* beg," he said.

She got down on her knees, clasped her hands under her chin.

Mum giggled. "He can't help it. We have fun. We do."

"All right," Hubby said. "Let's go."

Aviva got into the back seat of their car, a shiny spotless black Something-or-Other.

"Just a few minutes up the road, here," Hubby said.

The headache was doubling down, however. You're mine, bitch, it said. Stop, Aviva told it. Fuck you.

Sha Na Na came bouncing through the speakers. "If I could be in any band, past or present, it would be Sha Na Na," said Hubby. Mum shimmied in the front seat. They were so fun and easy to be with. Aviva felt like she'd known them forever. Hubby pointed out where he used to live with his wife ("Ex-wife, sorry—you can tell I'm still bitter"), where his son lived now with his own young family, the street where Amy grew up, the pharmacy where Mum had worked all those years.

"She's tough as nails, you know," Hubby said. "Raised those kids all by herself. Always was tough as nails. Wouldn't give me the time of day when we were young."

He smiled over at Mum, who smiled back at him. Aviva could have been *their* little daughter, couldn't she, sitting in the back seat watching familiar affection play out over the same old stories and soundtrack.

At the nondescript little house, Mum reassembled her cane again, and climbed out of the car with some difficulty. Each step was accompanied by a resigned "oof." An accepting and good-natured "oof." What can you do? You take what comes.

Inside was gray wall-to-wall carpet, low ceilings, un-fancy. Hubby went to make tea. The rooms were modest and tidy. Mum sat on one end of a brown vinyl couch, and Aviva sat on the carpet, by her knee, and slipped off her shoes like this was her own home.

"Are you in pain, Mum?"

"I don't let it bother me. I've got this thing. So? So? It doesn't define me."

"When did it start?"

"I noticed some tingling and such after my first was born."

What can we do but acknowledge one another's pain? Why hold back? Aviva rested her forehead against Mum's knee, and Mum immediately reached down to rub Aviva's shoulder.

"Aw," Mum said. "That's nice. Always nice to have a cuddle."

"Did you like having children?"

"Oh yes. Very much. Though it was hard."

"She did it all by herself," Hubby said, returning with tea.

"And I went back to school full-time."

Hubby fiddled with the stereo until a wave of cheers and applause flooded the room.

Live from São Paulo, a medium-sized venue. She opened with "Some Unholy War." "Wait 'til you hear how she does 'Back to Black,'" he said. "She segues it into 'Remember (Walking in the Sand).' She knew her stuff."

Aviva's head hurt so, so much. A cat came sauntering over. Nestled right on in. They had a lengthy love session, Aviva and the cat, with Mum, too, who was now stroking Aviva's troubled head while Amy segued into "Boulevard of Broken Dreams."

Hubby sat in the armchair with his eyes closed, relishing what he'd heard a thousand times before.

"Your tea's gone cold." Mum said when the show was over.

"My head is killing me."

"Let's get you something for that," Hubby said.

"I hate to take painkillers," Aviva said. "I feel like I should *feel* it. Pain being a teacher and all that. I just want to feel everything."

"I understand," Mum nodded.

"That's bollocks," said Hubby. He left the room and came back holding two pills in his palm. "Here you go."

Aviva washed them down with lukewarm tea and rested her temple back against Mum's knee. The soft weight of Mum's hand in her hair felt like the only thing tethering her to this life.

ELISA ALBERT

Hubby beckoned from the doorway.

"Come have a look in here," he said.

The Amy Room, they called it. A small brass chandelier and polished mahogany dining table took up most of the space. The walls were covered with gold records and framed posters. A small display case in the corner held a Grammy and an Ivor Novello. Beside the case stood Amy's red-and-white Fender.

Hubby picked up the guitar and passed it to Aviva, who closed her eyes and took it carefully into her arms, slid the strap over her head. A body: instrument via which vibration could be made manifest. She played a chord progression she'd been messing with, the seed of something, and then God knew what, some thoughtless conversational plucking, the kind of thing you did when you'd exhausted your banter and your head wasn't yet into whatever was next on the set list.

"I wanted that guitar," Hubby said. "The vultures descended upon that house like you wouldn't believe. But I knew: I wanted that guitar."

"I'm so glad you got it," Aviva said. She ducked out of the strap and handed the Fender back to him as if to prove that she wasn't one of the vultures.

"So many things disappeared from that house. The police treated it like a crime scene, but stuff was disappearing the whole time. When they finally let the family in three days later, so much was already gone."

"Who would've thunk it," Mum said, shaking her head. "Our Amy. It's just our Amy!"

"I've got some more stuff you might like to see," said Hubby.

They went back into the den, and he presented Aviva with a pile of spiral-bound notebooks and a shoebox full of photographs. "Have a look at those. I don't know where the VHS tape I want to show you went. Still looking."

Aviva stared at the shoebox and notebooks and at Mum. She didn't want to touch the stuff until she had taken a ceremonial moment to align with it.

"I can't believe . . . this is hers! Her stuff. The girl."

Mum giggled.

Aviva made a sound in the back of her throat, a Yiddish sound, a sound that meant contempt for fame, disgust at the idea that a person—the true essence of a human being—could ever be fully known by or belong to anyone. What a crime it was to think otherwise. She picked up one notebook at a time, and paged reverently through. Poems. Musings. Doodles. Hearts upon hearts upon hearts. She rolled up her sleeve to show Mum the hearts inked up and down both arms. Hearts upon hearts upon hearts. Not the world's most stunning coincidence, admittedly, but Mum nodded proudly.

There was a special obsession with a hot young high school science teacher, Mr. Finch. And birds! So many birds. Aviva yanked her shirt down to show Mum the flock of birds inked on her shoulder. Mum beamed.

Funny little self-portraits, self-effacing, self-adoring. Lists: "My Friends," "My Family," "Boys." "Things I Want For My Room." "Goals This Summer." Pages upon pages of flights of fancy and catharsis and incantation and manifestation, the real kind, not the kind they sell in seminars. Oceans, clouds, trees. A notable absence of moons, however. Darling: Wherever are your moons? That motif hadn't yet hit the culture quite so hard. But if it had? Maybe the potency of *your* moons would have given you different perspective. Maybe you would have guarded and celebrated that perspective, honored it, lived by it, like some people live by the clock of the workaday world. Maybe self-destruction is harder to indulge when you're constantly cycling involuntarily through the great mysteries.

Now the shoebox. The photos.

Obsessed with Minnie Mouse well up through puberty; Minnie Mouse on sweatshirts, T-shirts . . . precursor to Betty Boop, that insane idea of what a woman is, though it's sure a persistent one, isn't it? Unconditional-love-giving, heels-wearing, corset-wearing, ass-twerking tit profferer, at your service.

Here was Nan, doing Amy's hair in the kitchen. Amy's grin! Jews, Jews, Jews. Music was incidental. It could have been paint or clay or fashion. It could have been landscape design or political organizing or graffiti or novels or the stage. Probably not poetry. Probably not journalism. Definitely not criticism.

Big bro always looking resigned: he had no choice but to adore her, and adore her he did, though she was exasperating, and took up more than her share of the oxygen. As if the entire script of their lives were already written. (It was.)

"My *sister*," Aviva said, marveling at the artifacts fanned out around her on the carpet.

"My daughter," Mum said.

"*Our* daughter," Aviva said, and they both surrendered to a giggle fit.

" 'You can't tell me what to do,' I said to my mother," said Mum. "And my baby girl was exactly like me. She was just like I was. We were the same. I could never tell her what to do."

Hubby came back: "Here's that VHS. Found it! Let's pop this in and have a look, shall we? Been a while since we had a look at this one."

Terrible-quality recording, a tiny stage, a chattering audience. The lights go down and the crowd quiets and what do you know: it's a tween production of *Grease*! Lights come up and the scenery chewing begins.

"Let's fast-forward," Hubby said. "Her big number comes later. The rest are shit, obviously."

The show speeds by until, wait, stop, there she is: Rizzo. Tough girl with a perpetually broken heart. Unrepentant slut. Too tough to relish victimhood; too wise to be simply sad. Sadness is not that interesting, but *heartbreak* is a goddamned gold mine, because heartbreak has sadness mixed *up* with joy and anger, and that, friends, is the chemical equation for everything worthwhile in this whole fragmented wasteful joke of a world. *I don't steal and I don't lie, but I can feel and I can cry.* The way you do anything is the way you do everything. The story of anything is the story of everything. The song ended, and the crowd went wild.

"One last little pile," Hubby said, holding out a stack of hand-decorated CD jewel cases. *Human Blues, Human Blues 9, Human Blues 3, Human*

Blues 5. HUMAN BLOOOOOOOOZ. Human Blues #547602. Blues, Human. It was a series.

"She made those for everyone she loved," Mum said. "Everyone she really, truly loved."

They were decorated with stickers and doodles. No track lists after all, however. Perhaps to list the tracks would take something away from the experience. And the discs themselves were missing.

"Where'd all the CDs go?"

"She wasn't the most fastidious girl, you know." Hubby laughed. "I found these in a cupboard in her kitchen. Maybe she hadn't burned the CDs yet. Do you think CDs will be making a comeback anytime soon? I mean, vinyl always sounded bloody amazing, but those things always sounded like shit."

"She used to make a lot for her one friend," said Mum, "the famous hip-hop artist in New York. I always forget his name. What's his name? I always forget."

"Nas," said Hubby.

"I don't think that's his real name. They used to talk all the time, on the computer. They were writing a song together; they were going to do an album together; they were going to have a, a, what's it called, darling?"

"A supergroup."

"A supergroup!"

Then it must have been time to go, because Mum said: "Why don't you take one of those cases with you? For a souvenir."

"Really?!"

Mom smiled, nodded.

Aviva let one of the jewel cases slide out from the pile without paying much attention to which, the way one might slide a card out from a deck at the urging of a magician: no overthinking. Let the card choose itself. No second-guessing. The flow state. Empty, obsolete plastic box, covered in stickers. "Hoomann Blooooooooz" in charming crooked ballpoint bubble letters.

Hubby drove her home in his sleek black Something-or-Other. Very kind of him. Over an hour round trip for him. But he was sanguine.

"Now you get to hear *my* playlist," he said.

Dr. John, Big Daddy, Laura Nyro.

"Death by cancer of the female reproductive system," said Aviva of Nyro.

"Underrated," said Hubby.

"The singer or cancer of the reproductive system?"

Springsteen, more Sha Na Na, Credence Clearwater Revival, and Jerry Lee Lewis ripping the shit out of "Mean Woman Blues" as Hubby pulled up in front of the Airbnb and put the car in park.

"Well," he said. "This is where I leave you."

Aviva unbuckled her seat belt. It was sucked violently back into its compartment. Hubby kept his eyes on the road. Not a dog, this one.

She thanked him effusively.

"Yep," he said.

At six a.m., the lost suitcase was delivered by courier at last. Inside it was nothing of interest to Aviva, nothing she needed or wanted. She put away its contents in her hosts' drawers and closet, where she would leave all of it when she caught her train. She had new things now. She was no longer the person she had been when she'd packed that suitcase, and everything therein was irrelevant to her now. Good riddance.

The bleed. Early, but okay: it was upon her once again. The red tide. Auntie Flo. That Time. Again. Again. Again. Sing it: again, again, again. Aaaaaaand again. The headache dissipated as if by magic at the precise onset of the bleed. She peed and peed and peed and peed, hateful torturous struggle and suffering draining steadily out via the kidneys. C'mon, y'all: bodies are *fucking cool*.

She enjoyed a hot toddy at Amy's favorite pub, which emboldened her to bring her guitar to a great spot under a willow tree by a footbridge over a Camden canal. Lots of passersby, happy hour. A hundred yards away, a mural depicted Amy in classical angel motif, surrounded by cherubs.

Aviva had gone soft. She'd gotten complacent in all those fancy venues, the prestigious clubs and cushy radio sessions, always being filmed and edited and tossed online. She'd atrophied, forgotten what it was like to offer yourself up to absolutely everybody and to absolutely nobody. The nameless minstrel. Nameless menstrual. No mic, no amp, just open guitar case out in front of a little stone bench where she could take a load off. She leaned all the way into her own shit-fucked voice, as though acceptance could heal it. She did the entire first Amy album. And she talked to herself. No one cared.

"I'd like to raise our baby girl from the dead—yeah, you know this bitch, or you *think* you do, at least; she's your fucking *saint*. I'd like to raise her from the dead, tether her to Ani DiFranco as a kind of sponsor, have Lucinda Williams sort of beat the shit out of them both, then let Rickie Lee Jones nurse them all back to health with benign neglect. And what's Joan Armatrading up to these days? Where's Armatrading when you flippin' need her? And Genya Ravan should run the household, you know? Senior-wife-style. So many *brows* need soothing, you know? So much *caretaking* needs to happen. And there's only one way to get all that caretaking done, my friends. Oh yes, you know what I'm talking about: a matriarchy, motherfuckers. A true matriarchy. Don't even get me started on the lost possibilities of matriarchal culture. How is that shit *out* of fashion if it never was *in* fashion?! Tell me, please. It's never too late, though; never too late to have a happy childhood. Anyone else in need of a happy childhood? Anyone else not doing so hot with the childhood they had? Well, join the club. Why does it break some of us but not others? The artist is the child who survived—who said that? Well, I'm the only one who made it outta *my* family alive. I mean, you can be walking around *technically alive* but pretty much dead, know what I mean? *Her* brother just had a baby, folks, a little baby girl, believe it or not. They didn't name her after her auntie, but still, so glad there's a new little baby girl in that family. Do you know what happens to a family when there's loss but no new life? When everything just grinds to a halt and that whole generation-to-generation thing—*L'dor v'dor*, we call it, we Jews, and yeah, lemme know if you've got a problem with the Jews, and I'll fix it for ya, by which I mean I'll punch your fucking face in—but yeah, *L'dor v'dor*. You know what it's like when that just does not *happen*? A curse. A cosmic punishment. Who here believes in God? Anyone for the existence of God? How 'bout just *souls*? Mortality? Can I get a what for mortality?! Thank you, sir! Yes! Yes! Let's make some noise for the finite nature of the body and the infinite nature of the soul! How 'bout it?! Well, I'm a believer. I believe that life is sacred and that it ends in death. And the cause of death is *birth*, folks. So could the cause of birth be *death*?! I don't fucking know. And my advice is to steer clear of anyone who claims they know. 'Cause they fuckin' don't. But here's a song I wrote this morning."

Fun little ditty: "In Which I Get My Period for Literally the Two Hundred and Thirtieth Time," it was called, and the chorus went: *Again and again and again and again and again and again and again.*

A weak undergraduate feminist argument washed up in Aviva's mind like a piece of plastic coming to rest on a beleaguered beach: Back in the day, when women routinely had eight, nine, ten, eleven, twelve babies (before they dropped dead of exhaustion in middle age, of course, or in childbirth if they had the poor luck to be attended by a fucking idiot), a woman wouldn't actually *have* very many periods in her lifetime. Between, say, the ages of seventeen (marriage) and forty-five (merciful death), she would likely be pregnant or breastfeeding for like twenty years in total. So it's really *periods* that are unnatural, some excitable sophomore would conclude, drawing fascinated nods from around the pizzeria booth or seminar table. Never mind whether or not it was *true*; it *sounded* true, and made them all feel powerfully evolved.

All packed up and waiting on the street for the taxi she'd ordered to the train station. Off to Norwich for the first gig. But no taxi. Where was the taxi? There she stood with all her stuff, her guitar and backpack and old suitcase full of new clothes, but the taxi she'd ordered did not come, did not come, continued not to come, and was obviously not coming.

Minutes or an hour passed.

It was also true that Aviva was extremely stoned on a special lollipop someone had thrown into her guitar case yesterday, and time wasn't feeling super linear.

Amy's voice wafted out from somewhere, someone's open window. Unless Aviva was imagining it? Oh God, was she *that* stoned? She felt herself to be in a lot of trouble. She was getting to be very late now. She was getting to be in danger of missing her train. Where was her stupid taxi? She tried calling the dispatch number, but it rang and rang with no answer. She tried looking up another taxi service number, but she couldn't manage to both look it up and dial the number, because she was so devastatingly high.

Fuck! She was going to miss her train. She looked up and down the empty residential street, desperate and stoned, a very bad combo indeed. She couldn't miss her train. She had a show tonight in Norwich. She had her guitar, the body she carried with her body.

As if heaven-sent, an available public cab came rumbling up the road. Aviva waved it down.

Her rescuer was a tiny bleached-blond woman with the leathery skin of many sunbathing-and-cigarette lifetimes.

Oh, thought Aviva, *unbelievably* high: This is an *actual angel*. Pay attention! They are always around us, the messengers! You have to pay attention!

"You saved me," Aviva said, breathless, having loaded her stuff into the boot and herself into the back seat. "I'm so scared I'm gonna miss my train."

"Not to worry, darling," said the driver. German accent, voice sanded down. "I've got you now. No fun to rush, is it. No fun at all."

"My heart is pounding. I need to calm down. Oh God, you *saved* me."

"Take it easy, sweetheart. Take it easy."

The driver lit a cigarette and rested her elbow on the open windowsill.

Flash of her eyes, checking Aviva out in the rearview. "You don't mind the smoke, do you?"

"Not at all."

Aviva was short of breath in a way that freaked her out. *So* stoned. And so out of shape. She needed to get better at cardio. She would either miss her train or she would catch her train, one way or another, but now there was nothing left to do but stretch out in the back seat of this big black British taxicab, bleeding out very heavily into a massive pad, because let's not even begin to get into the metaphysics of tampons.

"I am the source of all my problems," Aviva sighed.

It felt wonderful to be prone, to be a passenger, and to have no purchase, now, on the destiny of whether or not she would not make her train.

"We all are, darling."

"I am way too stoned right now. What the fuck was in that lolly?! And I lost my precious baby," Aviva wailed, remembering her Sweetie doll.

"Oh, poor child. Blessings, my child. Allah sees all. Allah knows all. Allah is with you always."

"That's so *nice*."

"All is as Allah ordains it, my child. Have no fear. There is no death."

"But why has Allah cursed me? Why won't Allah let me have my baby? Why does Allah not want me to have my baby?"

"Oh, come now."

"I guess you just have to take what comes, right? What can you do?"

"Serve Allah! What else! Don't be silly, child. There is much to do!"

"But why would Allah take my baby?"

"In Germany we have in our cemeteries a special place for the children who were never born. Or who were not born alive. '*Sternen Kinder*,' we call them. Star children. My aunt had one. The gravestones have the psalm about eternal hope. It is very important to grieve these children. The grief is the love."

The driver's narrow eyes further assessed her passenger in the rearview.

"You are young," she went on. "If you pray for another chance, another chance will always come. Always! Another will always come. While you are young, there is always hope. The important thing is to relax, and to trust. And once you are old, you don't care so much."

They had arrived. Aviva would maybe make her train, after all. If she wasn't too stoned to figure out which track it was on.

"Blessings upon you," said the driver, flicking her cigarette into the gutter and turning to give Aviva a joyful, indulgent, adoring grin. "Blessings of every sort, child. I like your style. You have great style. Travel in peace."

9

SONG

Is there anything worse than creative frustration? The inability to create: it drives people bonkers. Where does creative energy go, denied an outlet? It stagnates, turns on itself, consumes, destroys. Which is why there is such a thing as war. But Aviva did not have this problem! Aviva's infertility had reached full term. Her blessed barrenness was due any day. Turns out, gestation *is* universal, including the much-heralded nesting impulse. She claimed the attic, the would-be nursery, as her very own studio. No frills, but functional and beautiful. Its very existence and intention: beautiful.

She scrubbed the windowsills, baseboards, wide-plank floors, painted the walls purple, let in a crisp late autumn breeze, and felt, truly, for the first time in—what had it been, now, two years? Three years. Closer to four, now, since the terrible wanting had begun, since every pregnancy anywhere near her orbit had started to feel like a low branch to the eye—that maybe the whole thing, the horror of want that had taken up residence inside her, had been nothing but a passing sickness. A hallucinatory fever of want.

Not everyone could make people. Not everyone could make music. Not everyone could grow food. Not everyone could tell fascinating stories. Not everyone could build machines. But everyone could do *something*, couldn't they? And probably one's energy was best put to use in the service of whatever needed zero coaxing to come.

The fever had broken.

Aviva sat like a proud hen on thirteen fine new songs. A wonderful cycle of songs. How fertile she was! The soil of her self a veritable Eden of song.

I was born like this, sang ol' deadpan uncle Leonard Cohen, *I had no choice.* He may well have been sarcastic, but still.

The attic was a nursery after all, a dedicated space to raise up her bevy of beautiful babes.

"Is it possible that what you have been struggling with all this time is actually the *absence* of desire to have a child?"

"*Jesus*, man."

"I don't mean to question the fact of your grief," the Rabbi said. "I just wonder if not actually wanting to have a baby was too big a taboo for your psyche to confront, so you constructed a different quandary, instead."

"That's a really fucked-up thing to say."

"I apologize," he said. "But sometimes we construct alternative problematic dilemmas we can't ever solve, as a way of sparing ourselves the really shattering ones."

"No."

"I apologize," he repeated. "Because I've also seen people, when they've had to face infertility, cope by sort of turning on kids and the whole idea of kids, because it's just too painful to remain open and loving toward that idea. They begin to act like they despise children and 'breeders' because it's just easier that way."

"I despise the word 'infertile,' by the way. I do not identify as that. I don't want any part of that word. Hate how it looks, hate how it feels, hate how it sounds. I'm not that."

"Do you have an alternative word you prefer?"

" 'Blighted.' 'Bereft.' 'Denied.' 'Free.' 'Future crone nobody visits in the nursing home before she dies alone and no one grieves her.' Lemme figure out the acronym."

"I know of *plenty* of people with children who've languished in institutional care and died alone, my dear. *Plenty.*"

"Look, this is how shit is. I'm not interested in grieving it forever. It's boring. I'm bored of it now. I want to move on. I do not enjoy feeling pathetic. I don't get off on the victim thing. I've cried my share. I'm outta tears."

"I don't blame you. But you aren't pathetic at all. Which reminds me: Did you know that the cure for every single unhappiness known to humankind has long been known?"

"Do tell!"

"It's very simple, but no one can profit off of it, so it has remained a bit of a secret. Which may be for the best, because it really is one *hundred* percent effective. Bordering on transcendence, but my data is unpublished."

"What, pray tell, *is* this miracle cure?"

"Waiting," the Rabbi said. "All you ever have to do is wait. Things never stay the same, for better or worse. No feeling is final, as Rilke said. Cure for every unhappiness. Just wait."

"But you don't mean that in the sense of, like, staying in abusive relationships or sitting out local elections, right? You just mean the sun always rises. You mean it's always darkest just before the dawn."

"Correct."

Aviva had volunteered, but been turned away. She had idealized service, she had shown up at the recruitment office, she had been examined, cosmically speaking, and she had been found wanting. Existential flat feet, maybe. Asthma of the soul. Well, okay. She wasn't going to get the glory of enlisting. Whatever! Maybe all that stuff about the meaning inherent in service was just a story the survivors had to tell themselves if there was any hope of getting a good night's sleep ever, ever, ever again.

Aviva had been called to service of a different sort. Aviva was being asked to tend to the void. Which wasn't actually a void, because from it came songs.

Close the door, putter about, delete the apps, settle in.

Turn down these voices inside my head, sang Bonnie Raitt—and she sounded gorgeous, yes, what timbre!—but bitch didn't write that song.

How many smug but frustrated mommies were out there right this very moment, losing their fucking minds because they couldn't do anything other than "just" the cooking and the laundry and the shopping and the cleaning and the caretaking and the social media terrorizing? Sobbing in the shower because their parasitic beloveds were sucking them dry? Too resentful and exhausted to take joy in the work they'd been called—or had volunteered, or been conscripted!—to do. How many knew how to take care of even *themselves*, let alone their children? Leaving aside, for the moment, all those who paid others to do the laundry and the cooking and the nursing and the dishes and the birthing and the caretaking *for* them. Because, lest we forget: *someone* has to do the cooking and the birthing and the nursing and the caretaking and the dishes. Someone! (Who?!)

Those frustrated mommies DMed Aviva continuously to tell her they wished they could do what *she* did. What irony.

Her songs clung to her skirts. They clamored for attention, and she worked to cultivate the patience and forbearance they deserved, her good, funny, serious, heartfelt, weird, singular little songs. She was deeply engaged with how they were turning out. Their manners, their habits: it was her *job* to make sure they were turning out well. She tended to them carefully and observed with pride how they blossomed into ever-more-mature versions of themselves. They were good little songs. They didn't lie or cheat or steal. They surprised her, taught her, led the way, made her smile. Occasionally they exhausted and infuriated her, but that was to be expected; sometimes everyone just needed a rest. They had been conceived effortlessly, they had sprung spontaneously from the source, but that didn't mean there wasn't hard work involved in giving them form and substance. It was a shit ton of work. And the stakes were *high*, because the world did not need any more crappy, half-baked, maladjusted, manipulative, mindless, derivative, microwaved fucking songs.

Vessel of the Void: Too on the nose for the album title? Would a massive, fresh, bloody placenta in a big glass bowl sprinkled with blossoms be too on the nose for the cover image? What about cycles, spirals, a collection of cycles or spirals or circles, but no moons, fuck no to the moons, more than enough with the moons already. A Fibonacci sequence. Cycles within cycles. How about: *Menstrual Blood on the Tracks*.

She was going to release these songs herself, on some obscure new platform that didn't gouge artists. No executives, producers, production teams, studio time, sound engineers, photo shoots, airplanes, vans, videos, festivals, interviews, overproduced sessions. It would be like free birthing, where they don't even have a midwife, just trust the process and eat the placenta on livestream when it's over.

"For fuck's sake, Aviva. No one wants to hear that shit. I hate to break it to you, but that record-an-album-all-by-yourself-in-a-closet concept, it's gonna A) sound awful, and B) sound awful. No one wants to listen to that."

"That's okay. They don't have to listen. It's gonna pay off in other ways. Long haul. I promise. The rogue thing's a good look, Jer. The metrics are changing. Money is no longer money. Cred is the only real money. Maybe always was."

"No, babe: money is, was, and will always be money. And don't say 'metrics' to me, please. Jesus Christ."

"Jer, I swear. Hey, how do you like that for a chorus: 'Jer, I swear; I swear, Jer.' Cute little hook. I got songs coming out my titty-holes, Jer. The flow, you have no *idea*. It's very strong. I could wet-nurse."

"What the fuck are you talking about? It's really not a great idea to get stoned every day, Aviva. Everyone has to learn that sooner or later. The sooner the better."

"I love you, Jer. I *appreciate* you. You are my dude. Since the start, and I'll never forget that. But, Jer, I'm sorry, I actually don't fucking care what you think. I'm just not gonna do anything I don't feel like doing, like, ever again. Until I die, more or less. And I think that might be the secret. I'm disengaging from worldly matters."

"How nice for you."

"It's gonna work out in the long term, Jer. For you, too. For all of us."

"How long?"

"Either long or *really* long. Or really, really, *really* long; I can't say for sure. But don't worry. Don't worry."

"Some of us have to worry so that people like you can not worry."

"Well, thanks. Thank you. Thanks."

Harmie Shmendrickson was lagging way behind the average percentiles for height and weight, and there was some concern over the fact of her not having gotten teeth yet. She was like a year late on teeth. But her smile remained glorious, and in her eyes there was the unmistakable joy of being alive. She beamed at whoever held up the camera at her. She didn't seem to have any regrets about being alive. She was alive! With her whole exciting life ahead of her. What could be better than that?! She was shadowed only by an anonymous virtual stranger (Aviva), at great physical and psychic remove.

"I thought you took the internet off your phone," Sam said.

"I did."

"So?"

"I put it back on."

A doctor in Australia was discussing his plan to eradicate gene markers for breast cancer in female embryos. "Assisted evolution," he was calling it. "The technology is here," he said. "It's time for the government to step up."

Nothing from Copeland, but she hoped he was happy and well, and that he jerked off to her on the daily. She still sometimes perused his ex-wives' feeds, but less often than she used to.

Scientists were announcing that stress was a problem. This was inarguable now, like gravity. The data was in. And here was an exciting new finding: singing could relieve stress. Researchers believed that the vibrational power of singing could be beneficial for the human body/mind! Thank you so much for your dedication and perseverance, scientists. There's an exquisite velvet floral Miu Miu fall minidress with the most stunning lace piping Aviva would love to acquire for a fraction of the grant money spent on that most recent study.

A clip of Amy's notorious ex on a tabloid news show, complaining about the "lack of human element" in the hologram plan. Dude looked like a shit stain from hell. Still, that deep, sexy voice; that gritty, delicious, satanic pitch. But he looked seventy-five years old, when he was all of— what, thirty-six? Thirty-seven? It *matters* what you do to your body. What you put in and on it, who or what you give it to, how you *use* it, how you let other people use it. There are consequences. Even newborn *babies* aren't blank slates, turns out. (*Scientists Now Believe . . .* !)

Text from Chuck: Hello, my girl.

I'm not your fucking girl.

How's it going, Dad?

Great! Saw great press on your tour in the UK!

Cool. What's up with u?

Flew to Vega$$$ for long wknd. Two single guys on the prowl.

A selfie appeared in which he was spray-tanned and grinning alongside none other than Mike. Behind them was a rainbow cascade of LED lights in what looked to be a VIP bar/lounge with some sort of aquarium.

Party-hat emoji.

Aviva suddenly understood that she was actually hard-core Team What's-Her-Face. She was going to buddy on up to What's-Her-Face. She was going to start calling What's-Her-Face by her given name, whatever it was. She was going to learn What's-Her-Face's name. She regretted having disdained What's-Her-Face. Victim of the system, victim of the system. Aren't we all? Including the architects of said system. Alas.

Hoomann Bloooooooooz! She didn't tell anyone about the artifact from Mum. Not a soul. Not even Sam. They weren't one of those share-a-brain, cultish-devotion couples. Aviva could maintain her own little intimacies with the dead, and with the never born.

She tucked the empty jewel case into the altar she'd made on the deep attic windowsill, alongside pictures of her grandparents, Ma Rainey, the Rabbi, a Charlotte Salomon postcard, assorted fan gifts and talismanic objects, and whatever, none of your goddamn business.

Sarah came to stay for the weekend. Aviva picked her up at the train. They made a simple Friday-night dinner, lit the candles, sang the blessings. God (or, sorry: the universe) had given Aviva Barb for a mother, but it ("it"?!) had also given her Sarah for a voice teacher in that confounding first year of music school. "It" worked in mysterious ways.

"You've made such a beautiful home," Sarah said. "It shines with goodness."

"You can come live with us," Aviva said. "In your dotage. We'll take care of you."

"Be careful what you wish for! I might show up someday with a suitcase."

"Great, it's settled."

"I don't know how your husband will feel about *that*."

"Happy wife, happy life." Sam shrugged.

"Sing it," said Aviva.

"The two of you have much better things to be doing than hanging out with an old lady."

Aviva and Sam made the same face at each other. "Not really," they said in unison.

"Well. That might change. Someday."

The implication being that a child could still find its way to them, by hook or by crook.

Aviva stared into the candlelight until her eyes burned, then she squeezed them shut and saw the flames.

"I should keep my mouth shut," Sarah said, by way of apology.

"You're one of the foremost experts on how *not* to keep your mouth shut, Madame. You taught me to stretch my jaw. You taught me about the vagus nerve. Can I ask you? I've never really asked: Why no kids for you?"

This was received like an obvious, silly joke.

"It wasn't . . . what needed to be," Sarah said. "For me."

She didn't seem bitter. She didn't seem angry. She didn't even seem sad. The matter was settled. How did *that* work? And how long did you have to hang around it in order to absorb and embody it?

"You just . . . never felt the desire? Like, the feeling that wanting it could kill you? Or drive you to murder?"

"No."

Sam moved his salmon around his plate, politely staying the fuck out of it.

"Because what surprises me," Aviva said, "is how the drive to kill and the drive to birth turn out to be close kin. Like, I think it might actually be the same feeling. I have wanted a fucking baby so fucking bad I could really and truly murder someone. *Easily*. Like, murder makes *sense* to me in the light of it." She had her fist clenched around her knife. She held it up as though to stab somebody, knuckles white.

"Well," said Sarah. "You're very maternal."

Aviva put the knife down.

"You know the theory about primordial man resorting to violence because they're jealous of birth and they want to do something that extreme and cathartic?"

"You're so young, sweetheart. You really—"

"Did no one in your family give you shit about it? I mean, society on the whole is pretty heavy into pronatalism, but the Jews are off the fucking charts about it. You might as well throw yourself off a fucking bridge if you're a Jew who doesn't make more Jews."

The look in Sarah's eyes changed.

"I should keep my mouth shut," she repeated.

Sam cleared his throat, stood up, and took some dishes to the kitchen.

"No, darling," Aviva said. "Everyone *else* should keep their mouth shut. In general. You in particular should say *more*."

"Have you considered the mikvah? I hesitate even to mention it, but. These things are very individual. There is a lot of power in the ritual. You might find something useful in it."

"Something useful in just about anything, I guess. Pick a ritual, any ritual! Someone made up a bracha for having your eggs harvested. And there's one for when your surrogate is getting inseminated. Don't you love people? No one who should *actually* shut the fuck up ever *thinks* they should shut the fuck up, ever notice that?"

Sam popped his head back in: "Tea?"

"Women's Blend, please," Aviva told him, then turned back to Sarah: "A delightful herbal mix to support women throughout the reproductive years."

"None of that for me, then." Sarah laughed.

Sam disappeared back into the kitchen.

Sarah waited a beat, then leaned in and lowered her voice: "I'm going to tell you something terrible now—are you ready?"

Aviva nodded.

Sarah reported it without emotion. Maybe she had done some EMDR or some shit. Whatever the case, she certainly wasn't reliving the trauma.

"I got pregnant when I was sixteen years old. Friend of my father's. Highly respected man in the community. No one could know. My mother found a doctor. We kept it very quiet. You had to, in those days. The doctor turned out not to be a real doctor. It went very badly, and by the time they got me to a hospital, it was too late to save my . . ." She waved her hand around in front of her pelvis. "And there you have it. I do recommend mikvah. It's given me a lot over the years."

Aviva woke, sweaty, with a start, from a dream.

Sam turned over, eyes still closed, and felt around to pull Aviva into a spoon.

"You okay?"

"I dreamt my mother peed on my ovulation monitor and I woke myself up screaming, 'YOU RUINED EVERYTHING.' I don't think I even need to tell the Rabbi about this one. I think I get this one."

"It's about your mother, right?"

Aviva had been watching producers and sound engineers at work for years, having to pick and choose what she fought for, deliberate and modulated about how she expressed her preferences, not in control of her own sessions. You don't want to be thought "difficult." You don't want to make enemies from friends.

She had always sort of taken their word for it that she couldn't possibly understand how they did what they did with the buttons and knobs, the monitors and wiring. But she had been learning, watching, listening, asking questions. She knew how to work her modest equipment, how to circumnavigate what she didn't know, and how to make shit sound how she wanted it. Rough-hewn. Lo-fi. No frills.

They spent the Sabbath in the studio. She wanted Sarah to lay down some backing vocals on a little ditty called "The More Things Change, the More . . . Shit Women Have to Do."

"This song is a riot. You have such a gift."

If mothers were ideally so trustworthy and protective and benevolent, weren't said mothers, like, *oppressed* by having to be so trustworthy and protective and benevolent all the damn time? Wasn't that, like, *unfair* to want from a woman-mother-person?

"What was your dream life like?" Aviva asked. "After. What happened."

"I never remember my dreams," Sarah said.

"You must remember *one*."

"You believe in all that stuff?"

"It's not a matter of *belief*. People have dreams. Some dog you repeatedly. You can run, but you can't hide. What was yours?"

"I gave birth to objects."

"Yeah?"

"A book. A landscape photograph. A very nice sandwich, once."

"Yeah."

"It bothered me. I never told anyone. I thought there was something wrong with me. I was never unhappy in the dream, but often when I'd go to show someone in the dream what I'd done, what I'd produced, they would be upset or unimpressed or disapproving, so I stopped showing them after a while. I would just look at the thing and be happy and satisfied, and tuck it away somewhere, for safekeeping."

"When did you stop having that dream?"

"I don't remember."

"You've been holding out on me!"

"I don't believe in dreams."

" 'Believe'?!"

"You know what I mean."

Everyone suffered. It was what you *did* with the suffering that mattered. How you responded to it, engaged it.

The sun set orange through the attic windows, earlier today than yesterday. The days got shorter, and then they got longer, and then they got shorter again. And again.

"Want to lay down one more?"

"I could do this forever with you," Sarah said. "What a space you've made!"

Aviva started in with a remnant of Copeland's mother's ubiquitous Havdalah tune. She wanted to layer it underneath her new song, which was becoming slightly trip-hoppy. This tune was in her marrow. A melody so potent, so ripe, you knew it had been divinely gifted. You let something sit dormant for a decade or two or three, and maybe you thought it was vanished from memory, but it was right where you left it. Didn't Glen Campbell still know how to play and sing all his songs even after his Alzheimer's got so severe he couldn't find the bathroom in his own house?

Annual well-woman midwife visit.

"I do not want a pelvic exam," Aviva said.

"Okay," said the midwife. "I'll just mark that down. 'Declined pelvic exam.'"

"And I don't want a breast exam, either."

"Okay, no problem. Are you familiar with how to do one on yourself?"

"I am."

"And is that something you feel comfortable doing at least once a week?"

"I do."

"And if you notice any changes, you'll give me a call?"

"I will."

"So," said the midwife. "What *can* I do for you today?"

"It was time for my annual, so I'm here. This is as much as I'm willing to do right now: just keep this appointment today. Maybe next year I'll be willing to let you touch me, maybe not. But this is my annual checkup, and I have shown up for it today."

"May I take a blood sample, at least?"

"Sure. Needle in my arm, not an issue."

Deja caught sight of Copeland in deep discourse with a cute brunette at a hotel bar in Nashville.

"Taking it upon myself to let you know that your ugly-ass boyfriend is seeing other people."

"Is she hot?"

"Lesser version of you. Dark eyes, sweet tits, luscious mouth . . ."

"I miss you. Come visit. I need my tits worshipped."

"Maybe in the spring."

"We all look alike. Copeland's love objects. The first two wives, the current wife, me . . . and, wait—hold on . . ."

Aviva dialed up a photo of Copeland's mother. She screenshot and texted it to to Deja.

"We all look like *her*. His dead mother."

"Gross."

"He's working through some stuff," Aviva said.

"Who isn't?"

"Some people aren't."

"Even those people. Especially those people."

"It must feel so powerful for the mothers, don't you think? I want someone to be that obsessed with *me*!"

"Gross, dude."

The leaves had already turned, many were fallen, but wow, November heat wave. Four days of mild and golden glory. Gosh, people said. If this is climate change, I'll take it!

Sam and Aviva leaned against each other in the park, watching the world go by. Sam's arm around her, her head on his shoulder. One of them would die first, and it would probably be him, though not necessarily, and she would hopefully be pretty elderly by then, but still have to go on alone, making life livable for herself until it was her time to go.

But here they both were now.

"I just think it's weird that we have no responsibilities," Aviva said.

"Speak for yourself."

"I mean we have nowhere to *be*."

"I have to be at school tomorrow morning."

"I mean no one is *dependent* upon us."

"We could get a dog."

"Then we'd just be a childless couple with a dog."

"That's true."

"When do you think people will stop asking if we're trying for a baby?"

"When we're really old."

"Are you trying? Are you trying? No. Yes. *You're* quite trying. These conversations are really *very* trying!"

"People are dumb."

A couple of dogs ran to greet each other in the field. One was big and fluffy and brown, and the other was smaller, scrappy, black with white paws. Their people kept distance. The dogs chased and leapt and twirled and baited, wrestling in good fun. But then the scrappy one started to try and mount the fluffy one, and although Fluffy didn't seem to mind too much, the owners sprang into action like the world was ending in fire and brimstone: "No! Luna! Stop that! Dixie! Nooooo!!!!" They pulled the dogs apart and everyone apologized profusely.

"What's weird is that Luna's a *girl*," said Scrappy's person.

"Oh, yeah, no, it's just a power thing," said Fluffy's person.

No harm, no foul. The dogs eagerly reapproached one another on leash to resniff each other's assholes.

"Dixie! That's *so rude*!" Fluffy's owner rolled their eyes at the animals' nasty animal behavior. "So *sorry* about that."

Everyone leashed up their dogs and went their separate ways.

"How dare dogs act like dogs," Sam said.

The last of the dead leaves rustled in the trees.

"The whole awesome idea is to mix up your junk with the junk of someone you like in a bodily sense," Aviva said. "Somebody you like sniffing. Somebody into whose cracks and crevices you feel like *burrowing*."

"I'm with you."

"People can't even be trusted with *dogs*. How do so many of them get to have *children*?! It's like: Come into existence when I say! Be conceived! Because I said so! Fuck that. She doesn't deserve that. We can't tell her what to *do*."

"Her?"

"Microplastics are making all organisms estrogen-dominant. It's all going to be very utopian eventually, they say."

Along came the phalanx of neighborhood moms. Was there some sort of law that they travel in packs?

"I'll create a diversion," she whispered. "You grab the smallest child and walk briskly back toward home. Don't run or they'll get alarmed. I'll meet you at the house. They'll think it was the Rapture."

The gang came to a stop a few feet from Sam and Aviva.

"Cute couple alert!!"

"Hey there, *Mama*!"

"They really are the *cutest* couple."

"Oh-em-gee, what is it *like* not having kids, 'cause it seems pretty darn awesome. Look at you two, just hanging out in the park! Can you guys do this whenever you want? Do you, like, go out to dinner all the time? Your house must be so *clean*."

"It'll be the twenty-second fucking century 'fore *I* can relax."

"MOM SAID 'FUCK,'" screamed a kid.

"Harpoon went to sleepaway camp for the first time this summer," said the freak with the singleton, "and it was weird having her gone. But also pretty fun, to be honest, because we looked at each other and realized: We can do whatever we want! Sleep in, go to the movies on a whim, wow! But that's *your* life, isn't it? Ha ha, we're describing *your* life."

The strange gang of women and children trudged onward. Aviva and Sam watched them shuffle down the promenade.

"Babies don't last forever," Sam said. "Babies grow up."

"Then you need another identity," Aviva said. "Then you need something else to *be*. Way I see it, there are two paths."

"Just two?"

"The first is, you subvert your desires and sacrifice the ego to exactly what *is*—in yourself, in the world around you. No challenging or fighting anything, ever. No attachment to anything. Just, like, put your head down, renounce everything, devote yourself to the simplest daily existence, no complaining, no asking anything in return, accepting all with peace and equanimity. Psychic vow of silence. The stoic route. Entitled to nothing but *maybe* your next breath. *Maybe.*"

"And the other path?"

"Do absolutely *everything*, use yourself up to the fullest, in the most perverse, destructive ways imaginable. Do anything you want. Ignore consequences. Touch bottom. Treat your body like a lame suggestion, or an experiment. Hand yourself over to any and all uses, alterations, machinations, projections, manipulations, whatever. However it occurs to you or your culture or your experts or your relations to use up your *literal* body, which is inarguably the house of the soul, but whatever: ride it 'til the wheels fall off. Just use it the fuck *up*. See what you can make it *do*. Die a husk. No stone left unturned."

"Both ways sound pretty unappealing. Might there be a *middle* way?"

"Oh, sure, Mr. Middle Path. No! No middle path. Only extremes. And the end result is the same either way: 'You' are irrelevant. 'You' are destroyed. 'You' are blotted out. Subvert the ego and be reconciled with mortality. Powerlessness."

"Extremes are lame," he singsonged.

It was easier to challenge someone in song. Speak vociferously into someone's face and they might have you arrested for assault; sing at the top of your lungs as they stroll past on the boardwalk and they might toss you a dollar.

"By all accounts," Sam said, "there are many paths to enlightenment."

"So how come enlightenment is so hard to come by? There can't be *that* many paths, or a fuckload more people would be enlightened, don't you think? Is *having* a baby enlightenment? Is being *refused* a baby enlightenment? Is *forcing* a baby enlightenment? Is *refusing to force* a baby enlightenment?"

"All of the above, none of the above, depending on the individual and the context."

"What does God *want* from me?" Aaaaaand: she was crying.

"You really need to let this whole 'God' thing go," said Sam.

Aaaaaand: she was laughing.

"There is truth in extremes," he went on. "I'll give you that. But never the whole truth. It only matters what makes sense to *you*. You don't need to *worry* about how other people deal with their shit. Your shit is your shit; other people's shit is other people's shit."

"Thus spoke the wisest man in all of Albany."

"Well, *that's* not the biggest compliment I ever heard."

She thought about it for a second.

"The wisest man in all of the *Capital Region*?"

He wrinkled his nose.

"Okay, okay, sorry: wisest man *in upstate New York.*"

"That I can live with."

Another breeze sent the dead leaves into a symphony of crackle.

"What if," Sam said, "we pretend we had kids already, and our kids are all grown-up now? We raised them well. They're happy, functional people in the world. We miss them, but we'll see them next week or next month or whatever."

"Yeah . . . ! We have full lives. We're proud of our grown kids, and we love them, but they don't live with us anymore. We're empty nesters!"

"Feels great that they're independent people, doesn't it? We're so proud of them."

"But they do love us, right? They don't avoid us like we do our parents, right?"

"Right."

"Anyway, just so you know, I'm planning on having an orgasm every single day for the rest of my life. For basic hygiene. You're welcome to be involved, if you'd like."

"I'd love to be involved."

"Okay, then. It's a plan."

Adopt, people say. Fill out reams of paperwork and pay piles of fees and go to China, Ukraine, Africa, Colombia, Venezuela, wherever they've got those extra-special poverty/war babies, and grab one for yourself. Maybe it's a noble thing to do, maybe it's exploitative, who's to say. Even maybe take one of those mildly damaged ones—you can do it! Find out where there are damaged ones available now. The damaged ones are usually free! The *severely* damaged ones they'll sometimes *pay you* to take. Still reams of paperwork, probably, but . . .

Somewhere in the world right now systemic forces are at play leading desperate women to bear children they must then relinquish, and YOU can reap the benefits! You will seem so wonderfully open-minded! People will say how *good* you are for making one of those your own. The photographs will read beautifully in terms of politics, the value signaling unassailable. Make sure you give her an especially ethnic name, but *middle name*, okay, because you don't want her life to be *miserable*, do you? You can win absolutely any argument thereafter, oh yes, simply by adding, "As the mother of a [fill in the blank] child, I . . ." to the beginning of absolutely any opinion.

Or decline, and become, instead, a crone with a doll, or a dog, or a cat, or plants, or piles of rags, special objects you nurse, and sing to, and scold. Maybe go for one of the insanely realistic, expensive weighted silicone baby dolls, or two. Or three. Or four, why not, oh yes, a fourth! The grandeur of four! Five starts to seem like a bit of a problem or compulsion, but four, four is serious and dignified.

Why don't you just adopt?

Yes, one can mother in many ways, one can give love and devotion and time and care to any number of orphaned and/or abandoned and/or abused souls, and what better work could there possibly be on our mysterious and troubled oxygenated rock?

Okay, well, maybe Aviva and Sam *will* eventually adopt: rise to a new ideal, a different challenging manifestation of family. But that possibility had nothing to do with her barrenness coming to fruition. The end of her physical desire/need/*demand* . . . to create someone new from herself. And please, *please*, spare us the anecdotes about your aunt's sister-in-law's best friend's cousin who "gave up" and adopted, only to—surprise!—then immediately conceive a child. Yes, we know. Now shut the fuck up and go away.

Because listen: Adoption is not a flipping panacea. An orphan is not a thing to be used for stanching a wound.

She often saw the booker for the local rock club at the coffee shop, but only just today mustered up the courage to say "hey."

Guy was hot shit around here. Small-town swagger, big fish in a little pond. You wanted to play or hear cutting-edge rock or punk or folk or hip-hop in this shithole town? This was the guy to know. Empty, gaping four-inch gauge holes in his earlobes, big scraggly beard, both arms sleeved in faded-to-blue tattoos, always in a black T-shirt and black jeans and crumbling sneakers no matter the weather.

"I hear you book for Sweethearts," she said.

"You heard right." He stuck out his hand. "Joey."

"I play guitar. And write. And sing."

He smiled politely, like Yeah, who doesn't?

"I'm good."

"Come to open-mic night. Second Thursday of the month."

"Why do we practice our instrument?"

This question had been posed by a sadistic, hateful teacher Aviva had elected to quit after a few punishing months, because he threatened to cast a permanent shadow over her relationship with the instrument.

"WHY DO WE PRACTICE OUR INSTRUMENT?" he repeated.

Aviva shrugged. "To get better at it?"

"NO!"

His face contorted with rage. There had been nothing helpful about him or the way he believed she should relate to her guitar. She had all but erased him from memory, but memory don't play that way.

"NO! We do not practice 'to get better at it,' you weak-minded little girl. Don't you know why you practice your own goddamn instrument?"

"I guess I don't," she said, daring him to get any further into her face. "So why don't you tell me."

"We practice to make playing EASIER," he said.

Fuck you, she had thought at the time, but now she understood how right he was.

When you practice something, you make doing it easier. And when something is easy to do, you are good at it. And when you are good at something, it is easy to practice it. And when you are very good at practicing something, you do so with fluency and grace. The *doing* of it. The *it* of it.

"Ridiculously good news, V. A monster ad campaign for some new laundry detergent saw the 'Time and Weather' demo you slapped up on YouTube, and they want to use it. The detergent's supposed to be good for the environment."

Aviva said nothing.

"Aviva?!"

"What, Jer?"

"They're offering a nice amount, V. For a *demo you put on your You-Tube.*"

"How nice?"

"Very healthy number."

"What's the number?"

It was a very good number.

"Now's the part where you're supposed to say, '*Thank* you, Jerry, my amazing manager! You are truly making all my dreams come true! I get to live out my creative fantasies while having food on my table.' This is money raining down from the sky, my dear. You're welcome."

"Laundry detergent, Jer?"

"It's the eco-friendly kind! I can't believe you. Donate the fucking money to charity, if it hurts so much to sell out, okay? It's *eco-friendly* laundry detergent. I can't believe we're even having this conversation. I'm telling them yes. Goodbye."

"*Mein kind!*" said the Rabbi. "How's things?"

"Confusing. Fine. Chuck is single again."

"Are we surprised?"

"No, but tomcatting it up with Mike in Vegas is a new twist."

The Rabbi sighed.

"In better news, I am a pig in shit about my studio. It's heaven. I love it. And I'm apparently set to make a small mint off a commercial for eco-friendly laundry."

"That's wonderful!"

"Is it?"

"I think a lot of artists would be thrilled to make a living off of their music."

"How do we reconcile the spirit of the troubadour with advertising? Do we just compartmentalize? Meanwhile, there is the *most* insane pair of one-of-a-kind cowboy boots from the finest purveyor in Texas . . . navy blue with white floral inlay. Those boots are mine, the minute I get that check."

"You have no respect for money. Which is admirable, but impractical."

"C'mon, man. Haven't you ever heard 'Real Good for Free'?"

"What is that?"

"Joni. It's about not commodifying things that belong everywhere, in the possession of everyone. It's about how corrupt and sad it is that human beings stratify ourselves so that some people in certain spaces have access to certain music and some do not. Sub in clean air and water and food: same dynamic. Sub in safe touch and bonding with other humans and it's the same. You can't try to profit off things that should belong to everyone, and the best way to dismantle the system is to give away everything you have."

"Does that mean you aren't going to get the boots?"

"No, I'm definitely still getting the boots."

"Who is happy? the Talmud asks."

"She who is happy with what she has, I *know*. And the Talmud *also* tells us to be wary of the chatter of women and avoid talking too much with women. We pick and we choose, Rav. We pick and we choose. Meanwhile, there's this tiny hole-in-the-wall club on Central. Been there for decades. I played there once on tour a hundred years ago. It's where Sam and I met, actually. I'm gonna blow their minds at open mic and see if I can wrangle myself a monthly gig."

"I don't want to see you waste your time, Aviva."

"I'm a bitch with a guitar. I process shit in song. If the club doesn't want me, I'll just be sitting on my front stoop, singing my sorry little heart out for loose change."

"While you cash checks from the laundry commercials. Okay. I think it's great to cultivate a presence in your local community. I think it's wonderful. It's very noble. And it's up to you how you want to share your gifts. You get to design your own mask, be whoever you want to be. And you can change your face. The face you share with the world. Metaphorically speaking."

"How?"

"You wear the mask until your face conforms to it."

"Then what happens when you take off the mask?"

"You have a different face."

Weather turned again, fully to the cold.

It was Aviva's birthday. She was no longer in the hopeful part of her thirties. She was now in the not-so-hopeful part of her thirties. They spent the night at an epic retro-modern wooded Catskills inn with a wood-fired pizza oven.

She'd eaten a little Delta-8; it was nice and mild. She loved her Sammy-Sam. She didn't need anything but him. How many couples feel this way about each other? Grateful and connected and safe. What a feeling. The curve of his mouth. The nicest mouth.

They sat by a huge stone fireplace. Every time the swinging door to the kitchen opened, they could hear strains of the second Amy album. There she was, whenever a server entered or exited, with her haunting lullabies. When the swinging door came to rest, the music couldn't be heard. The door swung open, and there was the voice again.

"This album's overplayed," Aviva said.

"Imagine how good the third album would have been."

"And the fourth."

"Greedy, greedy."

The next time the door swung open, Amy was doing the dirge.

Aviva had done this dirge at Queer Night Karaoke when she'd first started hanging out in Albany. Some of Sam's coworkers had a standing monthly date at this bar.

"You probably hate karaoke," Sam had said. "Coals to Newcastle, and all."

"Are you kidding? Karaoke is the best!"

She played it cool most of the night. Just a basic Lauryn Hill to make clear that she was not to be underestimated, not afraid of the chick blowing her wad on an Alanis, not afraid of the show tunes hacks, not afraid of the hip-hop dorks.

She'd had her hair in a topknot that night, and in spite of being there *with Sam*, she had been flirting with one of the bartenders (old habit, because seriously: Was Aviva really dating a high school teacher in *Albany*?).

On his break, the bartender summoned her to the alley, where he whipped out a little wood one-hitter resembling a miniature coffin. She was prepared to turn the bartender down if he tried to kiss her, probably. But the bartender didn't touch her. Which made Aviva feel dejected, even though *her date was waiting for her inside*.

"Where'd you go?" Sam asked when she came back, stinking of weed.

"Air," she said as she filled out a request form for the famous dirge. You're not supposed to do that kind of true dirge at karaoke; it rattles people. It's impolite. Everyone's trying to have a good *time*.

Some free regional arts rag wanted to profile Aviva for its "New Voices" issue. There was always a nice supply of up-and-comers. Then a huge stockpile of there-they-wents. How are Judee Sill's streaming numbers? How about Vashti Bunyan's? Melanie Safka's? Buffy Saint Marie's? Odette's?! Big ol' pantry stocked with almost-weres, has-beens, weres-for-a-minute. But always such strong, fresh currents of up-and-comers, washing the waters clean. And every so often a supernova, lighting up the sky, burning bright way up high, look at that, so everyone could use them for navigational purposes. The key word being "use." Used.

On the phone, the interviewer sounded about fourteen.

"Congrats on all your success this year!"

"Um-hmm."

"Must be exciting, huh?"

"Mmm."

"What's your songwriting process like?"

"Instinctive. Laborious. Fun."

"Like, how do you come up with your ideas?"

"They come up with themselves. I tune in."

"But, like, how do you write melodies and stuff?"

"Have you ever listened to music?"

"What are your favorite songs you've ever written?"

"I don't play favorites."

"What made you want to write songs?"

"I was a lost, fucked-up, abandoned, ugly-ass beast, and music was the only way I could spare myself from the slaughter."

Silence. Giggle.

"Intense!"

"Tell me about it."

"Um, I really love your whole *look*. Can you tell me about your style?"

"No."

"You've put out four albums already! That's impressive."

"Just getting started."

"What's next for you?"

"Recording and releasing new music on my own."

"Wow! What made you want to do that?!"

"Sick to death of other people's bullshit but still kind of interested in my own."

"What do you mean by that?"

"I want to see what happens when I only please myself."

"Well, I'm sure your fans will be excited to hear what you've been up to! How do you like living in Albany?"

"It sucks. I love it. I'm playing the open mic at Sweethearts next week."

"Oh my God, are you *serious*?! Sweethearts?! Ha ha ha ha, ohmigod, *why*?"

"*Well* . . . ! I just had a baby. So I'm sticking close to home."

"Omigod! That puts your last album into such different *perspective*. Is that something you haven't wanted to discuss publicly?"

"Hell of a ride."

"Went well, though?"

"Totally orgasmic. And she is *such* an angel. Doesn't give us a moment's trouble."

"Congrats! I had no idea! Very cool."

"Thanks. Yep."

"Mine's two, and everyone's up my ass to have another."

"People are jerks."

"Ha ha ha ha, I know, right?"

"Ha ha ha ha, totally."

Still, though, some days were just plain difficult. Some days were just really hard. Some days, she fully understood people who hate kids.

Children had nothing to do with her. They were not her problem. She was not responsible for them. Apart from—ha ha, oh yeah, sure, right, okay—the *collective universal* responsibility, but what kind of sappy wannabe-socialist moron actually believes in *that*? Doesn't look particularly adorable on a fucking *Christmas* card, now, does it? Can't put "collective responsibility for planetary good" on your *feed* or in a frame on your freaking *mantel*, now can you? You need your *own little humans* to style and manipulate and shape and influence and post as you see fit, and in the absence of that, well, piss off and die, loser.

On days like this, people with children struck Aviva as sour and self-absorbed and bored and one-note and obnoxious and materialistic and insanely up their own buttholes. Ye olde cult of motherhood: grotesque, and a sham. Maybe she was kind of *glad* not to get to be one of them. Yes! She was *glad* to have escaped the prison of that particular "brand." Now she was free! . . . To weep for the future without having any part of her own interest *implicated* in said future. (Aside from the whole collective good for the whole collective—YAWN.)

The news seemed like farce on those days, an elaborate bad joke, and the self-aggrandizement of those who "cared" like total satire.

Everyone's full of shit, aren't they? Everything's a lie. Everything you were sold. Everything you expected to get or do or be. Everything you bent over backward to hold tight in your grubby little hands. Those who bought it, and who now had to work overtime to justify it, *they* were the unlucky ones. You, you might actually be the lucky one. You're free! Everything you thought was one way: it's the opposite. The last shall be first and the first shall be last! You have been rejected by nature, by biology, by "the universe," such as it is. You are a dead end. You are only yourself, and no more.

Hats off to those who can sustain, through barren years upon years, through twenty miscarriages and burst ovaries and shyster surrogate schemes, the determination to get pregnant at any cost. Hats way the fuck off. Made of tougher stuff than Aviva. Or maybe just numb. Or maybe possessed. Or maybe dumb.

Aviva, Aviva was different. Aviva was special. Aviva had been chosen . . . to be denied! And Aviva was choosing her chosenness. To exist on the margins, blatantly unfulfilled. This suffering made her *holy*, make no mistake. You can keep your smug fucking broods. Aviva had a higher calling. She could almost hear it, just when her outlook got the absolute darkest. All she had to do was wait, and keep listening. Listen, and keep waiting.

Sweethearts was a stalwart, a legend in its own mind. Filthy, dark, sticky hole on a noisy, disastrous block, crouched between an historic tavern and a makeshift madrassa above an LED-festooned deli. That universal dark, sticky club smell: liquor and beer and cigarettes and piss and puke and sweat and love. Freak refuge, hangout, home.

She'd long since paid her dues on the boardwalk, in the godforsaken/ hallowed halls of music school, in the subway, and in a thousand tiny clubs, including and identical to this one. She'd done her playing for loose change, then a fraction of the passed hat, then the entire passed hat, then a percentage of the door, then a modest living wage, and now enough for bespoke one-of-a-kind cowboy boots with floral inlays. Ever onward and upward, kicking ass, taking names, the pride and envy of her music school cohort, fools who insisted art be a popularity contest.

The big-fish booker from the coffee shop doubled as the bartender and was glad to see her. Maybe a little *too* glad to see her, like maybe he'd found out "who" she "was."

The room was long and narrow from the door to the stage, with the bar taking up most of one side wall, and a couple of high two-top tables along the opposite wall. There were maybe a dozen people there, half of whom were nursing something at the bar, chatting, not interested in the music. The other half were there to get up and play. Nobody was just there to listen.

Aviva was up fourth, after a guy with an unnerving falsetto, a gal with lovely shoulder blades but nothing melodies and lyrics, and a trembling middle-aged man whose two songs were fucking excellent.

"Hey," she said to the room when she was under the single bright light of the stage. "My name's Aviva."

No one cared.

She started with her sad old song off *Dying to Meet You*, the one of some television renown. Why not give people what they want, or what they think they want, or what they'd want if you alerted them to the fact of it? "Hey," said a drunk at the bar, "I know this song! Where have I heard this song?"

"Well, *she* can sing," said another. The gal with the lovely shoulder blades took her leave, as did another of the barflies.

"Thanks for the music," he yelled as he put on his jacket. "Now I gotta face the music at home!"

Aviva put a capo on the Epiphone. A girl and her guitar. Oh, what's that, lil' baby? You hungry, lil' baby? Here, lil' baby, let me feed you. She offered it a titty.

"I'd like to try out a new one, if you'll bear with me."

Yes, they would "bear" with her. They didn't have much choice, did they.

"This one's called 'Can't Step in the Same Cycle Twice.'"

You can keep yer fuckin' litters; no one's more mother than me, went the chorus.

"Wooooooooo," said a drunk.

"O-*kay*," said the trembling older man with the excellent songs.

Aviva checked the booker/bartender's face and enjoyed the shining intensity she saw there. He was impressed.

Two songs were supposed to be it, but the night was slow, and the girl who was supposed to go on next had had a change of heart, freaked out, and was being hectored by her friend about how she needed to get over herself or she'd never know "who" she "really" "was."

"Go ahead and do a couple more, if you want," the booker told Aviva.

"Yes," screamed one of the drunks.

"Okay, I'm gonna do some covers," she said.

First, the refusal to get sober, the "No, no, no." Don't tell me what to do. A song so iconic it was practically in the public domain. Doom with a healthy serving of defiance. Her bloated, dissected, pinned, and labeled broken heart. But the beat is a kick in the pants, a joke. Dancing on her own grave.

"You sang the *shit* out of that," someone said.

"LOVE HER *FOREVER*," shouted a drunk girl.

"Who *are* you?" said a barfly to nobody in particular.

Next, the dirge. Sounded like a love song when Amy sang it on some beautifully lit little stage festooned with roses, hair and the makeup and liquid plastic tits and flawless little dress. Lovesick Betty Boop is going to be just fine, folks. Sounded like something else entirely when she was onstage in Belgrade, doing what turned out to be her final show, disheveled and harshly lit, blotto, a mess. She'd been a reliable punch line for such a long time by then, the lowest-hanging fruit. No one felt sorry for her; everyone just rolled their eyes at the wild, crazy, hell-bent animal spectacle. She wore yet another traditional, old-fashioned dress in Belgrade, a dress you could shake your ass in, a dress to bare those emaciated thighs. But as usual, the belt was in the wrong place, inches off the waist seam. Slovenly. A comment on formality. A failure at formality. She was way off the straight and narrow. She couldn't find the straight and narrow with a compass and a map. She was not going to be okay. Say what you will. Say she is lazy, unsupportable, self-destructive, a bore. Feel better about yourself because she's so much more fucked up than you are. Good for you. Say she is difficult. Say she is *mentally ill.*

"This is a song about what happens when . . . Oh, fuck it." Stone-cold serious just before she opens her mouth to sing, then the coy smile to deploy brutal lyrics.

Her voice was shot in Belgrade but no less beautiful. Raw. Like Billie Holiday when *her* voice was shot. Same spectacle, different era. With talent that big you could usually phone it in and still more than satisfy your audience. Not in Belgrade, though. In Belgrade they wanted their money back.

She's out of it. Unfocused. Riveting in the way of all wrecks. The backup singers doing their best to hold it all together, but she can barely remember the lyrics. Look at her, stumbling around that stage, floating, gliding, stumbling again. This is what it looks like at the end. This is the end. She was dead two weeks later.

Oh, but let us not focus on the death! Let us focus on the life. The work. Which is inextricable from the death. At twenty-seven. Alone, in her bed. Of heart failure. I thought it was heroin, someone always says. I thought it was withdrawal, says someone else. I thought it was suicide, says another. I thought it was an eating disorder, says another.

The fans don't care. The fans keep screaming. The fans are watching their own creation. The singer need not be there at all. And she knows this! She knows that she herself doesn't matter at all, the inconvenient person. A hologram would do. A projection. A figment.

Here's an offering, she says. I know it's flawed, but I tried. Here's the effort I made. Believe me when I tell you that it was the *most* I could possibly do.

The word "offering," in its archaic definition, means *to get close*. Colloquially, it means to present something as an act of worship or devotion.

Could there be dignity in sadness? In repose? In rest? How about in mortality? There had to be. No fighting it. You are a passenger. A blip of a gazillion bacteria animated by some mysterious electrical cascade, and isn't that *enough*? Good God, it *is*. *It has to be.*

How could she waste so much talent, power, privilege, fame, money, status, potential? She could have anything she wants (except for babies!), but *she doesn't want anything* (except for babies).

Sweet baby girl. Let me nurse you back from the dead. I'll gather you up in my arms, my darling.

Or no: Leave the imploded girl to the silence of her grave. Leave the nonexistent to their nonexistence. Some girls refused to live, and some girls refused to be born. And any half-decent mum knows you cannot tell a girl what to do.

Behold the Holy Trinity: the Nonmother, the Nondaughter, and the Holy Ghost.

Listen, you may not love her voice, you may not like her style, you may not want her in rotation, you may not vibe with what she's got to say or how she's saying it or how it makes you feel, you may not relate to all the reasons why she feels the way she does, but you have to admit: the girl can fucking *sing*.

Thanksgiving at yet another townie cousin-in-laws' brand-new McMansion out on the edge of the edge of a suburb. Everyone was there, all the usual talk about cruises and car dealerships and trips to Atlantic City and Ancestry.com and how Uncle Bob's dementia was going. Kids, kids, kids. Babies, toddlers, school-agers, tweens texting like mad. Mackayla was, alas, at her boyfriend's. Mackayla's mother was *not pleased* about this, but you had to pick your battles with teenagers, apparently. Aviva loitered in the kitchen, smiling her serene, blind smile: She had forgone vision correction, no glasses or contacts, and was mercifully unable to focus on exactly who was who or what was what. She smiled vaguely in the direction of whoever seemed to be speaking. How pleasant it was, comparatively. Things were simply better when she was functionally blind. Corrected vision was necessary, sure, yes—thank you, science; thank you, optometry; thank you truly and deeply. Gratitude. But uncorrected vision remained a straight-up mercy, at least for tonight.

There was a special cousin in attendance this evening, a rare guest of honor from out of town. Hotshot cousin. He had excelled in school and gotten the fuck out of town, become a surgeon, made a name for himself at a big hospital in Boston. He blew through town every several years to let the working-class relatives sniff the hem of his garment.

Hotshot's wife was dazed, elsewhere, out to lunch. You didn't need twenty-twenty vision to spot a zombie. They had a raging three-year-old and a disturbed seven-year-old whose obsession with Aviva started out adorable but progressed very quickly to terrifying. The seven-year-old would not leave Aviva alone. She was completely without boundaries, desperate for attention and affection and physical intimacy.

"I wish *you* were my mom," she kept saying, clutching Aviva's hand and gazing up at her. It was flattering for a minute: See how intensely maternal Aviva was?! She squeezed the girl's hand and winked at her and made a face like Shut up, cutie, or the normies are going to start getting weirded out.

"You're my mom," the kid declared.

"She just *adores* you," said the vacant mom from across an expanse of granite, and then she had to go chase the raging three-year-old, who had escaped out the front door and was sprinting, screaming and crying, out into the cul-de-sac.

Aviva couldn't be sure (see also: –6.43 vision in her better eye!) but as the night wore on she thought Hotshot was staring at her, a demonic little smirk on his face. Resting rapist face.

The little girl yanked Aviva toward a love seat, and sat on Aviva's lap. The girl did not seem like she had bathed recently.

"Where's *your* baby?"

Aviva looked at the kid for a long moment.

"My baby's not here."

"Oh," said the kid, as though this saddened her greatly. And then: "*I'm* your baby!"

"Okay, sweetheart: you're my baby." Aviva wrapped an arm around the delighted child and drew her close. The child squeezed her cheek to Aviva's and hung off Aviva's neck, then tried to straddle her.

"Whoa, there, cowgirl," said Hotshot. "Let's give the nice lady some space, shall we? Remember what we talked about in Miss Nancy's office?"

He plucked the kid off Aviva and set her down a few feet away.

The child screamed, "I hate you," and threw a punch, which Hotshot held off without much effort, smirking for Aviva's benefit.

"Go find Mommy and tell her it's time for your medicine," he said calmly.

"I hate you," the child whispered, stone-faced.

"Go," he said, less calmly.

The child stormed off sobbing, whispering, "I hate you I hate you I hate you."

"Kids are such dicks," Hotshot said to Aviva. "You're Sam's wife. The singer. Seems like you're doing pretty well for yourself. How does that work, exactly? In the music industry."

Money, he meant. He meant money.

"Yeah, I'm a pretty big deal," she told him, giving him her heavy-lidded, one-sided, dimpled smile. It was cool how this dude was finding new ways of ripping people's bodies apart and putting them back together again in the hopes of cheating death or whatever, unless you entertained the idea that death wasn't the end of the world, that the disappearance of your lil' ego wasn't a tragedy, and that it could be okay to die, just as it could be okay not to be born. But who wants to entertain that depressing shit? No one's gonna paste *those* lyrics over some fucking TV credits. Or a detergent commercial. Unless you Trojan horse that shit, make it sound like a love song.

Hotshot switched tacks: "You and Sam seem like a great couple."

"We are."

"Seems like you have a good thing going on."

"We do."

"That's great," Hotshot said.

"It is."

Hotshot narrowed his eyes: "But don't you think there's something kind of off about people who don't have kids? It's against nature. Reproduction is the most basic function of all beings."

She felt sewn to the love seat. She looked in the direction of his face and inhaled thoroughly, head high. Exhale.

"We would have *loved* to have kids," she said. "We thought about it a lot. But we actually decided not to when we saw how fucked up yours are."

Belated birthday box from Barb in the mail.

Cutie Pie, said the note. *I hope these things give you a GIGGLE! They certainly made me think of you. I know how you like to stay cozy. I'm very happy you were born and have loved every second of being your mom. (Well, maybe not EVERY second!! LOL!) I am taking a VERY interesting class on antisemitism in medieval Iberia. Look it up! Our people will forever persevere in spite of endless attempts to DESTROY us! Love you, cutie. 'Til 120. Xoxoxoxoxox, Mom.*

Nestled in bubble wrap was a silver-framed photo of Aviva's grandmother, Barb's mother, as a little girl. And four pairs of socks, each with a different witty design and catchphrase. *Proud Plant Mom*, said one pair. *Shhhh, I'm Overthinking*, said another. A third was printed all over with the word "no": *No No No No No No No*. The fourth depicted a flag that said *Your Team Sucks*.

Lastly, there was a paperback with a splashy pink cover: *Are YOU the Reason You're Not Getting Pregnant?*

Aviva put the framed photo on the mantel, the socks in a tote bag, to be donated to the homeless shelter, and the book in recycling.

She was on her way to get a new tattoo when she walked by a young vagrant on Lark Street, sitting on the sidewalk by the Trinity Church parking lot.

Filthy nomad punk with a beautiful friendly black mutt wearing a bandana. Written on his guitar: *BLM* and *Fuck the Police* and *This Machine Kills Fascists*.

"I like your style," he called to Aviva.

His eyes were bright, his smile genuine. His hat was upturned on the sidewalk in front of him, with a nickel and a few pennies inside. He wasn't playing his guitar, though. He was resting his arms on it while he drank a forty.

"Little cold to be out here," Aviva said.

"I'm used to it."

"Play me something."

The guy looked bashful. Was he blushing under all the grime on his face?

"Really?"

"Yeah, really! Isn't that what you're here to do? No one's gonna throw money into your hat if you're not playing."

Put down that stupid fucking forty, dumbass, and get busy doing what the good Lord put you here to do.

"Okay," he said, jazzed someone wanted to hear him play. "Okay! Let's see . . ."

Aviva knelt and involved herself with the beautiful dog, cutest babe that ever there was, soulful, suffering, dear eyes, fat and old with nipples all distended by what had presumably been a whole lot of ethically questionable litters.

"All right," said the guy. "This here is a Robert Johnson song."

Aviva braced herself for painful caterwauling. She'd give him some money regardless. But what emerged from the kid was a gorgeous, perfect, changeable, heartfelt howl. He had impeccable timing. The song was an extension of his essence. All she wanted in a singer and then some. Keep your auto-tune, your polished teenage fuck-dolls stating the obvious, your breathy blow-job bullshit. Keep your feel-good anthems. This was soul. This was the blues.

She had been ready to give him the five in her wallet anyway, because of the bashful blush, the twinkle in his eyes, the dog, the Woody Guthrie shout-out on the guitar. Because itinerancy was the soul of the blues, and even if he'd sucked, she was still grateful he existed.

But he didn't suck. He was gorgeous. He held nothing back. He could play, and he could sing. The stretch of sidewalk was transformed by the sounds he made. Time stopped, and the weather became irrelevant. Robert Johnson! Met the devil at a crossroads and sold his soul so he'd be able to play the blues. Dead at twenty-seven (*that* again!) by the side of a farm road in Mississippi. When the kid was finished, Aviva hooted at the top of her lungs, clapped long and hard.

"That was . . . *beyond*," she told him.

"Awww," he said, looking away. He reached for the forty as she put the five in his hat. "I thank you, ma'am," he said. Their eyes met for a second. It was enough. More than enough. Almost too much. A hell of an actual lot.

"You, friend," she said, pointing at him, "are *good*. You are fucking *good*. Don't you dare ever stop. We need you, dude. We are going to need you for a very, very long while. You better take real good care of yourself, dude." (Do not throw your life away, motherfucker. Do not waste yourself on those stupid forties. Do not get lost on these streets. Do not wind up dead by the side of a road somewhere. Please?)

"Awwww," he said, hanging his head and blushing some more. "I really appreciate that, ma'am."

"All right," she said, and waited until he glanced up and met her eyes one more time. She gave the sweet dog a last scratch behind its floppy left ear, and took her leave: "You made my day, dude. Don't forget it."

Then she continued on to the tattoo parlor, the kind of establishment where you don't need an appointment.

Aviva described what she wanted, and the grizzled OG tat bitch did it: an empty Moses basket, to remind her of all the time she'd spent keeping an eye out for any lost or discarded babies, relinquished or otherwise abandoned babes, floating up the river, or nestled in the reeds, or whatever, maybe tucked up alongside the guardrail on the highway, who knew? One never knew. Remember the Epiphone? *TAKE ME.*

They watched a comic-book action movie (Sam's choice) about a girl with an amazing ass who could beat the shit out of like thirty heavily armed people at once. The fight noises were like exaggerated porno sound effects, all that flesh sucking and wetness and grunting and groaning.

"People realize they're just watching secular porno, right?"

"I know," Sam said, mesmerized. "It's really dumb."

Aviva aped the rhythmic grunting of the fight scenes.

"Do you not want to watch? We don't have to watch this."

"No, I don't care. I can see how it's sort of beautiful, in its way. Like, the choreography and whatnot. And it's nice, the little story line about family and loyalty. It's deep."

"We can stop. We can watch something else."

"Nah, it's fine. And her ass, Lord almighty."

"It's not yours, but it's pretty good."

"Such an ass man, you are."

"*Your* ass man."

"I think I just wanted a baby for the unmitigated titty worship, you know?"

"I can learn."

The next morning, getting out of the shower, she heard the strains of the howling blues, floating up and across the parking lot all the way in through her bathroom window. It was him, the Robert Johnson kid, with his anti-fascist instrument and his canine companion and his bashful smile and his naked song. He was singing for Aviva. He was singing *loud*, just for her, hoping that his voice would somehow find its way. And it did! She heard him real clear. He was singing in solidarity with her, even though he knew nothing about her. He was singing in her honor. He knew enough, and he sang out their shared grief. The particulars were unimportant. In his voice was loss, hopelessness, exaltation, and communion, plain as day.

The world belongs to the bereft, his voice said. The world belongs to *us*. To you and me, lady: *our* kind. The losers. The broken. Pity the fools who get what they want—or what they think they want—because they will never, ever understand. All that stuff about the meek inheriting the earth? You better believe it. Cling to your heartache, mama. Hold your grief close to the breast. No one can take it from you, no way, no how. We know the truth, which is that power and domination are for the weak. And we don't gotta bother with any more profane, useless, bullshit, clamorous words about any of this crap, because we have *song*. Talk is cheap. We can sing, instead, way high above (or below?) the din.

Note from a fan:
I'm sorry if this is stalkerish, but I am obsessed with Womb Service *and I love you and I just wanted to share a photo of my new baby girl. I hope this isn't weird. Her name is Aviva, and I sing her your songs all the time. I hope she's as badass as you.*

AUTHOR'S NOTE

This book is a work of fiction and a product of the author's dream life. All news-feed stories and celebrity quotes are real. The meeting with Amy's mum and stepdad in chapter 8 is based on real events, but the ensuing conversations are invented. "Aviva Rosner" is a figment of the author's imagination, blissfully unaware that she is the protagonist of a novel, and not intended to portray any real person in word or deed. Any resemblance to actual persons, living or dead, is either obsessively honorific, purely coincidental, or a tool for exorcising massive resentment.

ACKNOWLEDGMENTS

Wild, boundless gratitude to and for my superlative husband and our beautiful son: love you guys beyond. Thank you, Virginia Center for the Creative Arts, Nederlands Letterenfonds, and the Hanse-Wissenschaftskolleg, for precious time and space to think and work. Thank you, Jen Beagin, Nalini Jones, Cassie Kennedy, Rebecca Schiff, and Ed Schwarzschild, for vital early reads, perspective, and much-needed encouragement. Thank you to my parents. Thank you to my coworkers, neighbors, students, teachers, elders, and friends; you know exactly who you are. Thank you to the dream team: Sarah Bowlin, Amy Guay, and Lauren Wein.

ABOUT THE AUTHOR

ELISA ALBERT is the author of *After Birth*, *The Book of Dahlia*, *How This Night Is Different*, and editor of the anthology *Freud's Blind Spot*. Her fiction and essays have appeared in *n+1*, the *New York Times*, the *Guardian*, *Time*, the *Literary Review*, *Bennington Review*, *Tin House*, *Los Angeles Review of Books*, *Michigan Quarterly Review*, the *Cut*, and in many anthologies.

HUMAN BLUES

ELISA ALBERT

This reading group guide for Human Blues *includes an introduction, discussion questions, ideas for enhancing your book club, and a Q&A with author* Elisa Albert, *intended to help your reading group find new and interesting angles and topics for discussion. We hope that these ideas will enrich your conversation and increase your enjoyment of the book.*

INTRODUCTION

What should we do when we don't get what we want? Scorn the universe? Use everything in our power to push back against our lot? Or accept what we're given—and not given? Singer-songwriter Aviva Rosner is settled in a sweet marriage, but she can't get pregnant. Like any good artist, she mines her frustration and ambivalence, goosing the status quo and raising plenty of uncomfortable questions about fertility, culture, money, and power. This is the internal-turned-external conflict that drives Elisa Albert's blistering and virtuosic *Human Blues*. Capacious, profane, searching, messy, and electrically funny, *Human Blues* takes on the subject of the ego as it relates to creation and procreation, life force and death drive, resistance and surrender, all while asking: Which is the right path for Aviva? Aviva's singular voice carries readers across the sometimes-brutal waves of nine fruitless menstrual cycles, while an unexpected obsession with the iconic Amy Winehouse comes to anchor her ambivalence. Notwithstanding any preconceived notions about the costs, risks, and benefits of the fertility industrial complex, it's a riveting, daring tale.

TOPICS & QUESTIONS FOR DISCUSSION

1. There are nine chapters in *Human Blues*, with titles like "Fame," "Breath," "Fashion," and "Song." Think about these titles as a whole: What do you make of their progression? What are they suggesting or encapsulating? Think about each chapter/cycle in the context of its title: Why do you think Albert chose that particular word?

2. Brainstorm some adjectives you would use to describe Aviva, Sam, Jerry, Barb, Chuck, the Rabbi, the unconceived child, Amy Winehouse, and other characters that interest you. Do they share any traits in common? What aspects of their personalities resonate with you?

3. From Mike's wife, "What's-Her-Face," to Holly and Barb and Mum, Albert gives us many distinct examples of femaleness and motherhood in *Human Blues*. Is there a depiction of a "type" of woman or mother that you find most compelling or relatable? Is there one that makes you feel uncomfortable? Why?

4. How does Aviva wield profanity and humor to deal with grief and heartache and rage and frustration? What are some quips that shocked you, or that made you laugh?

5. Out of all the conversations that Aviva has in *Human Blues*, those with her therapist, the Rabbi, engage most directly with her quandary. Do you think the Rabbi does a good job of guiding Aviva? If you were Aviva's therapist, what advice would *you* give her?

6. Consider Aviva's past and present romantic and sexual partners, like Jeff, the Cracker, the Love Fiend, and Marcus Copeland. What attracts her to each of them? Why do you think Aviva and Sam are ultimately together, and how do you feel about their relationship by the end of the novel?

7. Why does Aviva become so obsessed with Amy Winehouse? What does the novel gain from mining this obsession in conversation with Aviva's fertility struggles? What does Winehouse represent to Aviva, and what does her story have to do with the baby Aviva so badly wants? How would you describe the clarity Aviva gains from her time with Winehouse's Mum?

8. Whether or not you've navigated your own fertility issues, in what ways do you identify or empathize with Aviva's struggles and questions? Was there anything she experienced or expressed in her quest that you hadn't considered before? Did reading *Human Blues* give you any new perspectives?

9. By the last page of the book, do you think Aviva arrives at a place of peace and fulfillment? Did you as the reader experience catharsis or resolution? Did the ending conform to your expectations?

ENHANCE YOUR BOOK CLUB

1. Think about other books that deal with motherhood, music, desire, trauma, family, feminism, infidelity, drugs, and religion (not necessarily all at once). How is *Human Blues* different? What do you especially appreciate about Albert's approach? What challenged you?

2. Albert made a Spotify playlist for *Human Blues* featuring "Bad Blood" by Taylor Swift, "Binary" by Ani DiFranco, "Phone Down" by Erykah Badu, "Life's a Bitch" by Nas, and "Foolish Little Girl" by The Shirelles. (You can listen to the playlist at https://tinyurl.com/3fhnaxc4.) What songs would you choose if you were to make a sequel? Come up with three to five each, discuss your selections, and make a new playlist for other readers to enjoy.

3. In what ways are you satisfied or dissatisfied with mainstream cultural conversations around menstruation, fertility, and the intersection of medical technologies with the reproductive body? Are you comfortable sharing your own experiences as a person in a menstruating body? In what ways have you felt empowered or disempowered in this context? Have you ever felt mistreated, confused, ignored, or condescended to as a person with a menstrual cycle? What kinds of legacies do you think you inherited around discussing or not discussing your reproductive health and life?

A CONVERSATION WITH ELISA ALBERT

How and when did the idea of menstrual cycles as a framework for the novel strike you? What was it like working within that structure?

Very early on I knew that Aviva's story would have to center her menstrual cycle, because it just seemed super obvious: A person trying to conceive experiences time through the lens of their cycle. I was delighted with this idea right up until I hit the second chapter, at which point it dawned on me that I had bit off quite a ridiculous lot to chew!

Is there an Amy Winehouse tidbit that didn't make it into the book?

A friend who once worked as an assistant fashion stylist in London told me a story about some special designer bra-top that she delivered to Amy for a photo shoot, but then the thing went missing and my friend got into some mild trouble over it. Not terrifically illuminating, but there you have it.

And I do always want to reiterate the fact that when Amy was alive, at the peak of her fame, she was *so* reviled and mocked and baited in the press. Dying young conferred her angel/martyr status, but the poor girl was harangued and put down and insulted a *lot* during her life. It's important to remember that women who don't "play nice" are often roundly punished. Easy to forget once they're safely dead and sainted.

Is there a minor character in *Human Blues* that is of special interest to you, one that you might have explored further if you'd had the time or space within the world of the novel? If so, why?

Any minor character within any narrative has the potential to be at the heart of a different narrative. I can imagine a scathing novel illuminating Mike and how and why he lives his life in such opposition to how his sister lives hers. But truly, for any character of any size, there's a whole complex story there, for sure. It would be a relief, frankly, after building this huge Aviva tale, to relegate her to the margins of someone else's story!

How do control and release interact in the context of Aviva's world-view?

Knowing what to hold on to and what to let go of, and when, and how—these are the big questions of life. Aviva wants to live authentically, be awake, outwit shame. What she finds is that there is no prefab road map. No easy answers. Only more questions! We all have to puzzle through the hard stuff for ourselves, while we're on our own journey.

Is there a moment, sentence, or section in *Human Blues* that you found especially fun to write?

So many, I couldn't begin to count. Once I locked in on Aviva's voice and the larger structure, I found a lot of freedom and vitality in following where she led me. I wanted nothing to be off limits. The more dangerous the territory, the more fun to explore (at least in the relatively "safe" realm of narrative).

Do you think Aviva handles her celebrity well? Would you ever like to be her level of famous?

Aviva loathes fame. She finds it false and shallow and just a bizarre garbage dynamic of projection and power imbalance. Artists are "supposed" to respect and admire and covet fame. It's purportedly the "goal" of any creative pursuit. Aviva calls bullshit.

She paraphrases Rilke's idea that fame is just the accumulation of misunderstandings surrounding a name. This is part of what fascinates her about Winehouse, whose icon status doesn't do her humanity any favors.

I like musician Kristin Hersh's take on the matter: "Fame's for dorks."

As you were developing and writing *Human Blues*, did you turn to any other books or media for inspiration? If so, what are they and how did they influence you?

I'm a voracious reader and consumer of high and low and in-between culture. It all goes into the stew. Philip Roth's novel *Sabbath's Theater*, which features one of his thorniest, most unrepentant narrators to maximum effect, was definitely a source of "permission" and a lot of joy. And I fully ascribe to what Adrienne Rich said about art: that it "means nothing if it simply decorates the dinner table of power which holds it hostage." Literature is a gorgeous way to explode the political/cultural/social status quo.

If readers could think more deeply about one idea or concept in your book, what would it be and why?

In what ways is the female reproductive body powerful? What does that power look like? Feel like? What diminishes or invalidates that power? Who or what does that power threaten? How are we complicit in our own degradation, and why? What roles do shame and ignorance play in how we form and access ideas about these things? Who do we trust when it comes to understanding our bodies? How can we become more embodied, more honest, and less fearful? What does that look and feel like?

I guess that's more than one idea . . . sorry not sorry.